D1329300

C

London-reared of Irish parents, Kate Kerrigan worked in London before moving to Ireland in 1990. Her books have been widely acclaimed – *Recipes for a Perfect Marriage* was shortlisted for the Romantic Novelist of the Year Award and *Ellis Island* was a TV Book Club Summer Read. She is now a full-time writer and lives in County Mayo with her husband and sons.

### Praise for Kate Kerrigan

'With echoes of *Angela's Ashes* and even *The Notebook* . . . *Ellis Island* is a feel-good story about love, freedom, belonging and the meaning of home'                    *Stylist*

'An enjoyable romantic tale that you'll want to devour in one sitting'                                        *SHE*

'A moving portrait of love and marriage through the eyes of two women . . . the author looks closely at love as a romantic ideal and poses the question: Can a woman learn true love?'                    *Sunday Express S Magazine*

'This book is one to keep. Anyone who reads it will return to it, time and again, either for the story or to seek out one of the many old recipes'                    *Ireland on Sunday*

'An intelligent, droll and heart-warming read . . . Kerrigan is a lovely writer and her book breaks from the traditional mould of chick-lit'                    *Sunday Tribune* (Ireland)

Also by Kate Kerrigan

*Recipes for a Perfect Marriage*
*The Miracle of Grace*
*Ellis Island*

# CITY OF HOPE

## KATE KERRIGAN

MACMILLAN

First published 2011 by Macmillan
an imprint of Pan Macmillan, a division of Macmillan Publishers Limited
Pan Macmillan, 20 New Wharf Road, London N1 9RR
Basingstoke and Oxford
Associated companies throughout the world
www.panmacmillan.com

ISBN 978-0-230-74771-5

1 3 5 7 9 8 6 4 2

A CIP catalogue record for this book is available from
the British Library.

Typeset by CPI Typesetting
Printed and bound by CPI Group (UK) Ltd, Croydon CR0 4YY

Visit www.panmacmillan.com to read more about all our books
and to buy them. You will also find features, author interviews and
news of any author events, and you can sign up for e-newsletters
so that you're always first to hear about our new releases.

*To Tommo – for all the hope.*

Thanks to the human heart by which we live,
Thanks to its tenderness, its joys, and fears,
To me the meanest flower that blows can give
Thoughts that do often lie too deep for tears.

*William Wordsworth, extract from*
*'Intimations of Immortality from*
*Recollections of Early Childhood'*

# PROLOGUE
## IRELAND, 1930

The church was packed.

Usually if we were late we sneaked in the back door and sat in the side pews, which were neutral ground. The front pews were where the big shots sat – the doctors, teachers, dignitaries and the wealthier local businesspeople. As successful shopkeepers, my husband John and I fell into the latter category, but we rarely took up our seats of privilege, opting instead to bury ourselves in the middle aisles among our country neighbours.

This Sunday, with the distraction of my recent pregnancy, we went straight in the front door without thinking.

The working men stood at the back, starched and sniffing in their Sunday suits. Their backs pressed against the wall so that the cream paint bore the shadow of their hair grease and their nicotine-stained fingers. John, a farmer, crossed himself at the holy-water font, his shoulders hunching with humility as he joined the line with his peers. I prickled with irritation as I realized I would either have to stand at the back or walk through the church alone to find a seat.

My suit was a mauve two-piece I had collected just the day before from Fitzpatrick, the tailor, and I was wearing a fresh pair of stockings, straight from the packet, posted to me from Saks Fifth Avenue. My blouse and hat were a matching shade

1

of navy, the hat a small trilby – the latest shape – and my hair beneath it curled into tidy waves.

In such a get-up I would normally have strutted unbothered up the aisle to find a seat. I might even have rested myself, defiantly, at the front, next to the doctor's wife, just to make a point. But that Sunday was different – the excitement and anxiety of being pregnant had unnerved me.

I scanned the pews to find somebody I could sit with and spotted the red curls of Veronica, my shop assistant, at the end of a pew in the middle of the church. I squeezed in next to her, and as she made room she smiled at me. Her teeth were still terrible, I noted. Broken and yellow, and she was barely in her twenties. I promised myself I would talk to her about it during the week. Maybe arrange for her to see my dentist in Galway before Christmas and see if he couldn't fix them up a bit. I hated it when the girls who worked for me had the look of poverty about them. I paid them well, but in Veronica's case, working in the country shop, it didn't follow through in her appearance. She was wearing the same drab old hand-me-down coat of her mother's that I had seen a thousand Sundays before.

I reached into my pocket book for my rosary beads and, with a small shock of panic, realized that I had left them at home, so I closed my gloved hands into fists so that I could substitute my fingers for them. It had become my habit over the past eight weeks that I would arrive at Mass early and say a decade to the Blessed Virgin for the health of the life inside me. The routine had become ruined by our lateness, and now aged Father Geraghty was already droning on in his monotone voice, distracting me. Veronica's wet coat was pressed against my side and I became uncomfortable and agitated. Why was the stupid girl still wearing that old coat to Mass? As I tried to concentrate on praying, each Hail Mary became overshadowed by a list of clothes I had given to Veronica over the years: a primrose-coloured cotton dress, a red cardigan with black ribbon trimming, the green tweed coat I had worn on my trip home from America.

The priest led the confessional and the crowd began to chant, but as I tried to stand up and join them, I became dizzy. I sat down again and, as I did, felt a terrible pain lift me up out of the pew. As my body doubled over, Veronica put her arm around me and helped me up the aisle.

The blood poured down my stockings as I left the red trail of our newest child behind me on the church tiles.

After a week the weeping stopped and gave way to an empty bleakness. It was the third baby I had lost. None of them big enough to bury. This last one had released itself in the bathroom of Father Geraghty's house, the nearest place to the church, and then been discreetly disposed of by his housekeeper. There was no trace, no evidence that the small life had ever existed; no prayers said. The thread of life had been there, and now it was gone. Like a spent rose discarded from a vase – its beauty had been too brief, too transient to grieve for.

I sat in bed and looked out on another dull day. The sky was grey and flat like a dirty sheet, making the green of the land seem to glow. Even in the driest summer, the green never faltered. In the winter, patches of life broke through the snow. John's fields were rich and fertile; his wife a barren failure.

Outside the window a dozen birds busied themselves among the branches of the laburnum tree, pecking frantically at the small bags of nuts I had hung for them. Among them was a bullying goldfinch, its elegant gold-and-black wings and painted face a signal to the ordinary brown tits that they were lesser creatures. Perhaps that was why God wouldn't let me have a child. I was too proud, too grand for Him.

John carried me in a breakfast tray. I had barely eaten since it happened. Even Maidy's delicious brown bread crumbled into tasteless dust in my mouth and made me retch. I felt as if nothing belonged inside me except a child.

I took a sip of coffee. It was bitter and I grimaced.

'It's burnt,' I said ungratefully, pushing the tray back at him.

I wanted John to leave me alone again. I could not bear to look at him. I had known this man all my life and I sensed the mourning behind his capable demeanour. His disappointment and grief were as clear to me as they were invisible to everybody else.

'You have to eat something,' he said, sitting down.

I picked up a piece of bread and shoved it into my mouth, glaring at him angrily, hoping it would silence him. Like most countrymen, John was not given to revealing his emotions. I realized that was one of the rare occasions when he wanted to put his natural reserve aside. I tried to move out of the bed, but he was sitting in my way.

'I wanted to say, Ellie . . .'

He was looking at the floor, his feet square on the ground, his elbows resting on his knees, with his large hands dangling between them. The soft cotton of his collarless work-shirt stretched across his broad back as he hunched forward in an effort to get the words out.

'I wanted to say, Ellie – that I don't mind . . .'

It was excruciating to watch him try to get the words out, so I helped him.

'Don't mind what, John?'

'. . . that I don't mind if we don't have a baby.'

I didn't know what to make of it. John was longing for a child, I knew that.

4

He lifted his head, turned to face me and took my hands in his, wrapping his warm, rough palms around my fingers until they were all but enveloped.

'I love you, Ellie,' he said, 'and that's enough for me.'

IRELAND, APRIL 1934

# CHAPTER ONE

It was spring. Wispy puffs of smoke released themselves from our chimney and hung in the still air. As I stood outside our cottage door I could smell the sharp tang of winter being smothered by a softer season. Half a dozen swallows swooped and swerved around the small apple trees I had planted eight years ago, and the daffodils with their sure stems and gaudy bonnets stood firm and glaring against the struggling sun, willing it to show itself.

The sun had passed over the lake beyond our bottom field and turned it into a circle of dazzling light. It flickered as the blurred shadow of my husband, John, walked in front of it. He was on his way back to the house and, as he had been up half the night delivering lambs, was doubtless starving with the hunger. He was a good twenty minutes' walk away, having to negotiate the rocky bog that separated our farm from the grazing land beyond. John was not yet forty, but he had the gait of a much older man. He was carrying something in his arms. I could not see what it was from that distance.

I went back into the house and placed my recently acquired heavy iron pan on the range. The oven had been heating for an hour and, as I threw the sausages in, they started to sizzle right away. I got a warm feeling of gratitude at the ease and simplicity of my new contraption.

I was thirty-four, back living in a house on my husband John's family farm near the town where I grew up. Although electricity had come to Mayo, it had not stretched as far as our home, some seven miles from the nearest town. However, in the past few years John and I had modified the small cottage that he had inherited from his parents, adding three rooms to its original two and attaching every other modern convenience. We had a tank for collecting rainwater on our roof, and as a result enjoyed the luxury of running water. There was a Tilley lamp in every room, and two battery-operated radios that I had brought back from one of my regular trips to Dublin.

I left the butter dish down on the bare wood of the table, with two mugs, knives and forks and the teapot. John liked to drink his tea from a tin mug, which he kept hot by the fire. The coarse skin of his hands worked as a protective leather from the hot metal, and I had picked up the habit from him and, dispensing with many of my fancy ideas about how one should sit at table, now joined him in his casual breakfast routine.

We breakfasted like farmers, on bacon from our own pigs, which John still salted and cured himself in a small shed out the back of the house. We had sold all our own meat in our shop at the bottom of our lane – but since the electrification of Kilmoy it made more sense to sell the animals live to the local butcher, who kept the meat in fridges and sold it weeks after it had been slaughtered. He provided us with what we needed, but John still preferred to slaughter and butcher a pig himself for our table.

'I'm afraid I'll get soft,' he said. 'Farming isn't what it used to be.'

Marriage wasn't what it used to be, either. When we first married I baked my own bread in a cast-iron stove on the fire. Now we bought white bread wholesale from a bakery that delivered every second day to our shop. Veronica, our shop-girl, sliced it on a machine I had shipped in from England.

'I don't know what's wrong with a knife,' John had said when I proudly served him his first slice from the delicate loaf. 'It's more like a communion wafer than bread,' he complained.

That was John – he liked things to stay the same, where I was all for mod cons to make life easier. He would have preferred to have less money and just farm himself for our table, and have me at home keeping the house tidy, baking and preparing the food he grew – as his parents Maidy and Paud, and their parents before them, had lived. I liked things to change all the time. He sometimes became frustrated with me always starting up new business ventures, adding modern features and building extensions to the house – but my husband understood my nature. He complained about me working so hard to build the business, and I complained about him being old-fashioned, but we were soft on each other nonetheless. The unspoken shadows of the children we didn't have moved silently between us, their spirits floating through the unused nursery I had decorated during my last failed pregnancy, privately reminding us both that their presence would have changed everything.

For all that, John and I were happy together. We had married for love, not land or money, like many of our neighbours. The feelings we had for each other as teenagers had deepened and grown in adulthood, and although the early years of our marriage had been blighted by poverty and war, and although the years since then had not seen us blessed with the child we longed for, our love for each other had held true.

The sausages browned neatly in the pan and, as I had risen early, I had taken the extra hour to bake John a soda cake. I cut it into rough chunks, buttered it and arranged it on a plate, then filled a saucepan with water to heat on the stove for his shave. I had a freshly ironed shirt and corduroy trousers laid out for him on the bed, with a good Foxford wool jacket. As a working woman, I enjoyed the domestic routine of these early Sunday mornings: getting the house shipshape before dressing up for the day. Our neighbour Mary, Veronica's mother, did all of the heavy housework for me, washing the floors, dusting and polishing the ornaments and trinkets in our drawing room, so that baking the occasional cake and tidying around the place was an indulgence for me, and not the dull hardship I had once found it to be. Today we had arranged to collect John's recently widowed adoptive mother, Maidy, on our way back from Mass. His adoptive father Paud had died not six months earlier, and Maidy, a woman in her eighties, was now bereft. While she occasionally came to stay overnight, cooking for us and fussing over us as she did when we were children, she was still too fit a woman and too proud to move in with us.

I heard John lift the latch on the front door and called out, 'Take your boots off – the floor is freshly washed!'

Why must he *always* come in through the front door of the house, I thought, on top of the good linoleum flooring, when there is a perfectly good door to the kitchen!

'I've something for you,' he shouted back.

'We'll miss the midday Mass, if you don't get a move on.'

'Hang on . . . hang on.'

John stood in the doorway holding to his broad chest a bundle inside his jacket. His face was reddened with the exertion of the long walk home, the few grey hairs at his temples coarse against the black curls that were stuck with soft rain and sweat to his face. John had seemed tired lately, rising late and without his usual zest. He had taken to bathing in the house with water that had been heated on the stove, rather than outdoors in the yard from a bucket of fresh well-water – as had always been his way.

The lambing season had been busy, with many late nights, and he clearly needed more help on the farm. Some of the local boys that he used to help him had taken seasonal jobs in England, potato picking in Yorkshire most of them. When they returned the young men were put straight to work by their mothers on their own farms, building houses, fixing sheds – they had neither the time nor the need to work on another man's land, even that of a popular figure like John Hogan, but it was too much for him, managing it all on his own.

'There's no need for you to work like this, John – we have enough money coming in, without you killing yourself.'

When I spoke like that, he would rise even earlier the next day and come home looking more worn-out and tired than before, so I said nothing. John was a man of the land, and there was no arguing with him over it. Also, he was proud, like all men, and it didn't do for me to be always reminding him that I was earning such a good keep.

However, this morning his blue eyes shone wild with delight. He looked the same as he had done when I had first fallen in love with him at sixteen. Fresh and full of the heart of life, like the outdoors – a man made of earth and air.

He held out the bundle for me to look inside. I peeled back the collars of his worn farming jacket, and inside was the face of a newborn lamb.

'He wouldn't stand like the others to suckle. I think he's sick and I don't know if he'll last. He needs minding.'

My first instinct was irritation. Bringing a farm animal into the house! Would John never grow up and get some sense? But I put away my annoyance and indulged him. It was too early in the day for a fight.

The newborn's eyes were still closed. I put my finger to its protruded mouth, and I was startled when it took the finger and started to suck.

I let out a laugh, 'He's alive then!'

'Will you mind him, Ellie?'

John was smiling as if he knew I would. I looked back at him, arching my eyebrows inwards to let him know I knew what he was at. Playing the game of a cross wife to his laddish charms.

'Give him here to me – and go and get me some milk. You've no sense, John Hogan – not one ounce.'

I took the animal from him and sat with it on my lap, then peeled back the coarse fabric to look at it properly. Tiny and helpless, its skin was soft and pink, still hairless. I blew on its face and the newborn lazily opened its eyes – two black beads blinked up at me blindly. Its lips pouted for my finger again, 'Hurry with that milk, John,' and at the sound of my coarse voice its long legs started to buckle against me, then kicked at my thighs with its sharp hooves.

I put the lamb down just as it started to stand.

'Well now, there's a miracle,' John said as he came back in with the milk.

As the lamb found his feet, it started to cry and staggered around the kitchen like a drunken man.

I laughed as John chased around trying to catch it, eventually picking it up and taking its ankles together in a firm grip.

'I'll carry it back down to its mammy,' he said. 'Stick a couple of those sausages and a bit of that bread in my back pocket, like a good woman.'

'Be back in time,' I shouted after him, 'or there'll be murder!'

He waved his free hand at me briefly, but even as I said them the stern words crumbled in my mouth.

As I watched my husband and the rescued lamb disappear into the circle of sunshine that blistered off the lake, I felt the hollow darkness of my own womb calling.

# Chapter Two

It was Monday, the day after John had rescued the lamb. I rose at eight and was surprised to see him still in the bed beside me. The soft white sheets thrown back from his naked torso, the dark skin of his weathered face stopped in a low V above the whiteness of his broad chest, which rose and fell in long, slow breaths. Usually he was already on his way back from the far fields by the time I woke, and we would breakfast together before he drove me into Kilmoy. This morning he was in a deep sleep.

As well as being tired of late, John had been slightly terse with me over small household matters, which was not his way. Usually I brushed such moods aside. John had encouraged me in all of my ventures, and put up with my unconventional outlook in a way that most men would not, or indeed could not, have tolerated. He hated me being away from him, but he was stoic and forgiving, so the odd outburst over sliced white bread or a repetitive meal neither surprised nor frightened me. Marriage had taught me that love was more substantial than the mere continuing of the yearnings of youth. Our ongoing passion was fuelled by everyday tolerance: the challenging dullness of knowing each other too well passed with fortitude and faith, so that when the brightness of first love renewed itself, in the comfort of tears after a loss, the warmth of a hand held at a graveside, the curve of a naked shoulder revealed with the breeze catching a summer dress, it burned brighter and with more arched desire than the innocent voracity of youth could allow.

However, today I was irritated by his laziness. John transported me to and from our business premises in town every day, most of the time in our new Ford car, but sometimes he insisted on taking the old horse and cart so as not to draw attention to our wealth. We were rich by our neighbours' standards, but we remained modest in our outlook – preferring not to take our places in the front pew at Mass, or show ourselves off with flashy trinkets and attitudes like other successful businesspeople in town. Our humility had paid off, as the ordinary people continued to see us as one of them, and supported us with their goodwill and custom. John said that wasn't the point – we were ordinary people ourselves, he reminded me; country people.

This morning I decided to take this change in our routine as an opportunity to do something different. I was more than capable of driving the car myself, although John insisted that it was not safe for me to be behind the wheel of a motorized vehicle on our small country roads.

'It's not you I'm worried about – the farmers around here aren't used to cars. You could run into cattle on the road, or steer yourself easily into a ditch . . .' His objections to me driving myself were, I suspected, more to do with his fear of my independence than fear for my safety. In any case, he didn't like driving much himself. Aside from taking me to work and back, most of the time the dusty black Ford lay idle in the drive while John preferred to take the horse and cart on errands.

So I dressed quickly and left him a note saying 'Taken the car' on the kitchen table, grabbing my moment of independence before he woke up.

The car jerked, pushing me forward so that my head almost

bashed off the thin steering wheel, my hands sliding off the tan leather. I got a firmer grip on it and wrenched it into first gear, then twisted the key, put my foot on the accelerator and sped out of the yard, barely scraping through the narrow gap in our drive, spitting up a cloud of dry mud and stones behind me.

At the end of the lane I saw Veronica, strolling towards our shop.

The one-storey building was built by John with the help of our neighbours on my return from America. For the first few years it was a real hit, with people coming from miles around for the unusual luxuries I provided them with – tinned fruits and spices, as well as fresh vegetables and meat from our own farm. Since electrification, however, business had dropped off and people were choosing to shop in Kilmoy. There were now one or two hackney cars operating in the area, so those people with money to spend on the more expensive imported items I had been offering were able to shop in the auspicious surroundings of the nearest town, especially as the competition had widened the pitiful selection of goods on offer when I first returned from New York. Now our country shop largely provided the poorer rural community with basics such as sugar and tea, and drew only a small, but respectable profit. I spent very little time there myself now, leaving it in the hands of my shop assistant, Veronica.

Poor Veronica was not the brightest of girls, but the locals knew her and she was as much a part of the furniture there as the old oak counter and the stone flagging on the cold-room floor. Her unmarried mother Mary was my housekeeper, and the two women's lives had improved immeasurably with my own support and John's. As long as the shop paid their wages, I would keep the small business ticking over for them alone.

Veronica looked so startled when she saw the car speeding

towards her with me behind the wheel that she fell against a hedgerow. I steered it to a halt too close beside her, almost sweeping her skirts under the wheels.

'Holy God!' she cried out. 'Sorry, Ma'am – you gave me a fright.'

I had long since given up trying to get Veronica to call me Ellie, any more than I could persuade her into my smart hand-me-down clothes, or get her to learn to read. She could do as much counting as the shop needed, given that most of our customers were honest neighbours and left the price of everything in the tin box themselves.

'Oh, here comes John.'

A big smile spread across her face as I looked behind and saw my husband haring down the hill. Veronica loved John. Everybody did. He had a natural, easy way about him; acquiring from Maidy and Paud the gift for knowing how to be with people, it had carried him from childhood to adulthood, gathering a fond reputation that only increased with time. My parents had been reserved outsiders, and while I had rejected their rules and snobbery at a young age, some of their forced propriety was in my blood. I was sharper by nature, and friendships were formed slowly and with a degree of caution. Any ease I had with others came from having known John all my life and learning to emulate him somewhat. Although I worked hard, and tried to be as friendly and accommodating as I could be in business, I knew that my success in Kilmoy was nonetheless largely due to the fact that I was John Hogan's wife.

John gripped his trousers at the waist, his braces flapping at the hips, his shirt tails caught under his arms flying out behind him like wings. He hopped as he gathered speed, accommodating his bad leg.

I got such a fright when I saw him coming towards me that I automatically turned the car key again and, as if I were making a 'getaway' in an American gangster film, stupidly put my foot on the accelerator, causing the car to jump forward again, hitting my head off the low roof and pushing the front of the car into the hedgerow, so that Veronica had to jump to one side to avoid me.

'Where are you going, Ellie?' he asked through the open window.

'To Paris,' I said. I had frightened myself, and was annoyed that he had thrown me with his sudden appearance. 'To work – you fool. Where do you think I was going?'

He opened the door.

'Come on, Ellie, you can't drive.'

I had never liked being told what I could or could not do. Not by my parents, when they had refused to let me play with John as a child and I had been caught climbing a tree in his breeches; not by the rich socialite who had employed me as her lady's maid in New York; or by the leering men in the Manhattan typing pool where I had worked subsequent to that; or by the bossy aul' bitches who judged and jeered at me when I returned to my 'poor lame husband' after the war.

Most of all, I disliked being told what to do by John. Which is why, in his wisdom, he either bowed to my wishes or, at the very least, prefaced his requests of me with a polite pleading for my own welfare. That I didn't prettify my own demands of him with the same please-and-thank-yous did not occur to me, certainly not in that moment. I was hotheaded, spoiled perhaps, but that was my entitlement as a modern woman. I didn't smoke in public, or wear a feathered hat to Mass (as I would have liked to have done sometimes) for his benefit – but I was not going to be told by anyone to get out of a car that I had bought with my own money and had shipped by my own arrangement from England.

'I can so drive.'

'No,' he said firmly, 'you can't. Look at Veronica, you nearly ran her over.'

'Yes,' the silly girl said brightly, pulling at the front of her dress coquettishly, as if I wasn't there. 'She nearly killed me.'

I resisted reprimanding her. The child got away with saying the worst possible things on account of being somewhat simple, although in her dealings with my handsome husband John I sometimes suspected she was putting it on.

'I am perfectly capable of driving, John.' I nestled down into the driver's seat to make my point. 'I lived in New York, remember?'

My assertion that I had picked up knowledge about driving through my sheer proximity to cars and traffic for a time in my twenties always amused John, which irritated me. But instead of fobbing me off, as he usually did, he opened the door of the car and got in beside me.

'You can't persuade me, John, I am determined to . . .'

'Don't go into town today, Ellie,' he said.

Although his voice was gentle, in the tone of a pleading request, I answered it as a demand.

'Don't be ridiculous. It's a Monday.'

'I know,' he said. John looked worried and tired. There were the beginnings of dark circles under his eyes. It was the first time I had truly noticed how drawn he looked. 'Just take the day off. We could go for a walk . . .'

'A *walk*?'

My voice sounded cruel to my own ear and I realized I felt not irritated, but angry. John was trying to lure me away from who I had become – a successful businesswoman who spent her days away from the home. I needed to work, he knew that. I needed the distraction of other people, of being too busy. It was our unspoken agreement that I would not spend my days in the company of the ghosts of our unborn children. If that meant not spending my days with him, either, well then, that's the way it had to be. The time for dwelling and wishing and grieving was behind us – behind me. I would not go back. I would not go for walks across the fields we had walked as children, and be reminded of what we did not have. I would not pick armfuls of bluebells from the woods, or search for rabbit holes, or cross streams in a single adult stride and search their dim banks for wild garlic, or sit with him quietly on top of a purple bog hill and look across his land and imagine. The small girl in the yellow pinafore for whom I had fancifully sewed four years ago, sitting by my fire ripe with joy and expectation, with a daisy chain trapped in her long, tangled curls; our baby son chasing after John, a stick for searching rabbits scraping his stout legs as he ran; John with an infant wrapped around his shoulders, pointing to the stars on a soft summer evening, with another clutching at my milky breast – those dreams had taken me over and had almost destroyed me. I could look at my husband and love him, and I could live in our house – I could even close the door of the nursery and forget what was behind it. But the land itself, the playground John and I had explored and enjoyed as children, was saturated in memories of what had been, and was a constant reminder of what would never be again. Nature itself reminded me of the unnatural lack in our coupling, renewing itself with every season – rebirth, growth, the seemingly eternal sturdiness of the trees we climbed. The trees I had hoped our own children would climb. I needed to work so that I could forget.

'I'll go for a walk with you, John,' Veronica said, appearing at the window.

'Go and open the shop up,' I said crossly, 'it's near nine.' As she stood gaping, waiting to be asked again, I shouted, 'Go, girl!' And she hurried down towards the low building in front of our lane. 'I can't take the day off, John – I have things to do.'

'I know,' he replied, but he didn't move, just said again, 'I'd like us to spend the day together today.'

Whatever silly notion he had in his head, he could forget it.

'Either drive me in, or I'll drive myself, John – but it's nine already and I've got to go.'

He looked at me, and when he saw I wasn't going to change my mind, his features hardened and he got out of the car, closing the door behind him.

'Drive yourself into town so,' he said.

'I'll be back early.'

I kept my voice cheery and light, but I knew I had upset him. More than that, my refusal to take the day off had unsettled something in him. That's the nature of love that I found hardest to fathom. The way it can endure the heat and fury of a big fight, and yet the small details – a sideways glance, an untimely comment – can throw it off balance and strike dread into the heart. I thought about changing my mind. He had never made that request so directly before. Perhaps he had something important to say? Whatever it was, I decided it could wait.

'See you later?'

John was already gone, his back to me, walking slowly up the lane towards the house. I turned the key in the ignition and lurched the car awkwardly into first gear.

# CHAPTER THREE

On the drive in I felt badly at the way I had left things. My husband and I fell out with each other rarely, and almost always on the subject of my putting work before home. The day was bright and dry, an important detail, as I had no idea how to operate the windscreen wiper. It had been wrong of me to leave John alone, and in bad form, and the beauty of the sun filtering through the hedgerows and heavy trees, dappling the road in front of me with golden spots, was spoiled by guilt over my rejection of him.

I brushed the thought aside, deciding that I would come home early and perhaps call in on Maidy and bring her back with me to stay with us for a few days. A few of Maidy's big dinners would put him back in good form, surely, and the rhubarb patch at the back of the house was already bearing huge pink sticks of fruit. I didn't have the time to harvest it myself, but my mother-in-law would surely pot up some of her delicious jam. I'd bring her up some crystallized ginger and a few bags of sugar from the shop and leave her to it.

The fine weather and plans to restore bliss at home put me in a better mood. I had been right to put my foot down. John would soon come around to the way of me driving myself. It would leave his mornings freer, and it wasn't the first time I had got my own way and been proven right. I had gone to America against his wishes soon after we got married, to earn the money to pay for his hip operation after he was shot in the war, and without which he might never have walked again. When he refused to join me there, I had come home. Eventually. Albeit cutting short a new life of adventure and freedom – but our love had been born again, and I had held the skills and attitudes of my time away to build us a wonderful, affluent life in Ireland. I had always believed that money was freedom, and the grinding poverty of our early years of marriage had taught me that. John disagreed with me, but we rarely argued the point, and although it had been almost ten years since I had come home, we never discussed my time away from him. The three years in New York had passed quickly, for me at least. Young as I was, I could have come home earlier, but became caught up in myself with the fashions of the time and dancing, and some small romance that had long since faded into insignificance against the comfortable mix of fire and home that John inspired in me. John didn't ask about any indiscretions I might have committed during my time away from him, and I didn't offer any. But sometimes I got the urge to 'confess' to him how I had almost got swept away by another man. John knew everything about me, had shared every memory of my childhood, every small detail of our lives together, except for those missing three years in America. I knew that any revelation would only disrupt the steady flow of our marriage, but there were times when I felt like clearing out the litter of my memories – sharing the attentions of other men with him, so that I could truly let them go; but also, and perhaps more darkly, let him realize all I had given up for him. All I could have been, if I had stayed in America; all he had lost, in refusing to leave his precious farm and join me there. In a cruel corner of my heart I still wanted him to see all that I was without him, so that he might love me even more, knowing that he almost lost me.

I was fully satisfied in our love, but I always yearned for more. Ambition fuelled my success in business, but it was a failing in my marriage.

I drove cautiously as I neared the town, heeding John's warning about other cars; I concentrated on keeping the wheel firmly pointed at the centre of the road. By the time I got to the steep hill at the top of Kilmoy town, it was just after half-past nine and I was feeling rather pleased with myself. Although the weather was furiously changeable in this part of the country, it had stayed dry and the sun gave complement to the gentle thrum of our town coming to life.

When I had returned from America ten years previously, Kilmoy had been recovering from the ravages of our Civil War and 600 years of oppressive British rule. It was a dead, grim, grey shell of a place compared with the excitement and glamour of the life I had briefly lived in New York. I had settled back into the town, revising my fashionable wardrobe and my new modern ideas, still holding on to enough of them to build a successful business and establish myself as a respected shopkeeper. My expectations had adjusted to fit back into the humbler lifestyle of an Irish countrywoman. In the last few years, it seemed, life in Kilmoy had raised itself up to meet me. Although we were still far behind England and America in terms of money, and our people were still emigrating in their droves, life was not as miserable as it had been when I left.

Since the treaty had been signed, and the ensuing Civil War had burned itself out, our new leader Éamon de Valera had restored a pull-together order in the country of my birth, and everyone was making a special effort to recover. The houses and shops on the main street of Kilmoy had been painted and the streets paved. The grimy shop windows of our down-at-heel drapery and grocery shops were revamped and, on market day, the farmers who traded their livestock had even organized a rota of washing down the newly tarred road with buckets of soapy water, to clean them for the townspeople in the coming week. A new spirit of hope prevailed. The World War was over, and Ireland was free – our neighbours in the six counties of the North that were still under the control of the British were soon forgotten. Even John had left his politically passionate youth behind him to join in building de Valera's respectable, peaceable new Ireland. The only reminder was his slight gait, the results of shot hips during his service in the Irish Republican Brotherhood.

I drove down the steep hill (my hand cautiously holding the handbrake), past the low cottages on its edges and the grander two-storey homes closer to the town centre, finally parking the car in one sharp sweep on the paving in front of my premises.

At the first signs that our town was on the brink of thriving, I had cashed in the dollars I had saved just before the Wall Street Crash and used them to buy this tall, narrow building. It had been rented to an old solicitor who had since died. The English landlords had left the building to turn derelict and were anxious to offload it, so I bought it for just a few pounds. John, a trained carpenter and handyman, renovated it in a matter of months (anxious as he always was not to be distracted from the business of his farm, he could be relied upon to complete my commissioned biddings quickly, if not without complaint!)

I loved our country-cottage home, and the small building with the corrugated roof that still housed our first shop, but this smart building in town was a source of tremendous pride for me.

The glossy navy door to the side of the shop-front had a brass plaque to its left on the smart grey plaster advertising 'Hogan Ladies' Secretarial Services and College'. The stairs were immediately inside the door, carpeted in a striking swirling red pattern – kind on the feet of the dozens of typists, students and customers who trooped up them every day.

Secretarial skills were something I had brought back with me from America, and although the machines were relatively scarce when I had first returned, they had grown in popularity almost overnight when the Civil War had ended – and the typewritten letter was fast becoming an essential part of Irish business. I was almost instantly overwhelmed with requests of work, not just from local solicitors, but from all the businesspeople round about. Many of the poorer small farmers had missed out on their schooling, and our service offered them the opportunity to write letters without the embarrassment of highlighting that they could neither read nor write. Within weeks of opening the school good families from all over the county, and neighbouring ones, were signing up their daughters to learn these essential new modern skills, without having to go to the bother or expense of sending them to Dublin. Many families in the town were taking my students as paid boarders, and this, in turn, had turned me into something of a heroine amongst the local women, who had once disliked me for the ambitions I had brought back with me from America.

As I opened the door, I could hear the clacking of typewriter keys that always caused a tingle of nostalgic joy in my fingertips. The sound of a busy office brought me to New York, much as the smell of freshly burning turf reminded me I was in Ireland; to experience the two of them together always gave me a stab of pure happiness. Katherine Murphy came bounding down the stairs to greet me, her ear tuned to the subtle sound of the opening door beyond the clamour of the typing pool. Katherine was my right-hand woman, an exceptionally bright and capable person in her mid-thirties, who managed and tutored the students. She was wearing her usual ensemble: a long dirndl skirt in Foxford tweed, sensible cream cotton blouse, heavy stockings and a pair of flat, manly brogues.

'Morning, Ellie – all under control here.'

They were her first words to me every morning, a brightly conveyed invitation to go away and let her continue her work in peace. I paid Katherine well, and she was worth every darn penny, not only for her reliable work practice and skills in managing flighty young girls, but for her loyalty to the job. Despite the fact that she had natural attributes, glossy hair and a broad, friendly smile, Katherine kept her appearance dowdy and her manner abrupt so as not to attract attention from the opposite sex. She was not even within a whiff of finding a husband, but I recognized that it was best to leave a woman like that well alone, and resisted the urge to offend her with offers to glamorize her.

I liked Katherine as she was and, my mind having been opened in New York, readily accepted her somewhat masculine manners for what I believed they represented. In any case, romance and marriage were the death-knell of my business, especially with de Valera's law that women give up work and keep house after they get married. The country needed the women to keep the home-fires burning, for the country to get back on its feet, he claimed. Yet who was going to do the typing, and run the shops and hair salons, I frequently argued with John? My husband would look at me sideways and say nothing. The Taoiseach's manifesto of an old-fashioned Ireland with comely maidens baking bread in whitewashed cottages was John's dream for us. He would not fight me over it, particularly as it was understood between us that my love of work was only a poor replacement for our not having a child. There were times when I was guiltily glad to have my sorry condition to excuse my hunger for business, my greed for success.

Directly above the typing school the top floor of the house

was a one-bedroomed apartment where I sometimes worked late and caught up on our paperwork. On the rare occasion that we stayed in town, John would meet his farming friends in the pub and join me later, when we would eat a meal together, then fall into bed exhausted and make love to the sounds of the townspeople bustling outside. The apartment was indulgently decorated, the walls covered with the finest damask paper, with good mahogany furniture, delicate china and embroidered linens I had inherited from my mother. I had made us a cosy nest there, trying to lure my husband into town life. Move him to where the action was. Distract him with the luxury of light switches and hot running water. He indulged me by staying there for perhaps two, sometimes three nights a month, but tonight would not be one of those nights, I thought wistfully.

'Are you coming up?' Katherine asked.

'No, just popping my head in to see if you're okay? I'm gonna check out the salon.'

'Rightio. See ya later.'

Katherine had trained in England and I in America, and we often spoke in colloquialisms to remind ourselves that there was more to us than the parochial constricts of our small surroundings. Kilmoy was officially a town, although it was, in truth, no more than a village by English or American standards. Placed in the heart of sprawling County Mayo, it was too far from the sea to be truly scenic, and too far from anywhere else to be of much interest to anyone living outside it. With little experience of life outside its one trading street and the farming townlands around about it, its inhabitants looked to studying each other's lives for entertainment.

On the ground floor of my building was an old shop-front where I had started the hair-salon business just a few months beforehand. We had already taken delivery of the first permanent-wave machine in our county, and within days there had been women queuing up for the wooden chairs against the green tiled wall. News travelled fast in Kilmoy, and from the first day we opened our doors I knew this risky venture was going to be a success.

'Morning, Ellie. Good night?'

Pauline had opened up the shop and was setting up the perm machine – a metal Medusa, with twenty coiled springs protruding from a wide head-height centre, lobster-like claws clenched treacherously at the end of each one. These opened onto the curlers, which were then doused in a foul egg-smelling liquid, the claws gripping them then setting the curls into place by means of the miraculous feat of electricity. It was as dangerous as any medical operation that I knew, but Pauline moved around the metal beast with deft confidence, her chubby fingers with the pointed red nails pulling the silver snakes into neat curves.

Pauline was a rather plump, vivacious English girl who had a broad north-of-England accent and wore far too much rouge. She had come to Ireland chasing after a handsome local lad whom she had met and fallen in love with while he was working over in Yorkshire. After four days' travelling, hitching lifts to the boat in Holyhead, then down from Dublin, engaging in God knows what kind of adventures en route, she arrived in Kilmoy, only to discover that young Rory Gallagher was already married with a child on the way. I found her crying on the street, her gaudy appearance disintegrating in the rain.

Having been an outsider myself, both in my own town and then in New York, I took the waif home and fed her, giving her a bed for the night. A trained hairdresser, Pauline repaid me by refreshing the fashionable bobbed haircut that I had been maintaining myself (rather badly) for years. The idea of the hair salon came to me then, and as she did not want to return to

England (having stolen the money from her hard-working parents' savings to pay for her boat passage), I opened the salon in her name – and had the local signwriter boldly paint 'Pauline's English Hair Salon' above the door. My shocking rebellion in marketing Pauline as a daughter of our former oppressors worked in so far as – whatever else one said about the English – they knew how to beautify themselves better than us poor Irish.

'Not bad, Pauline, thanks. Quiet.'

My wildest night could not, I suspect, compete with Pauline's soberest midweek flings. She was out on the town with a different local lad every evening, and had quickly gained a reputation as quite the popular party girl, determined to show Rory what he was missing, while the poor lad was still trying to appease and reassure his young wife. I was lucky that the hunger for a neat hairstyle in most of the local women outran their horror at her promiscuous behaviour. I wished she would cool herself down, but there was little point trying to explain the presiding Catholic outlook in rural Ireland to this young, godless Englishwoman.

The perming process took some time – up to two hours – and we only had one machine, so I had a small chaise of my mother's by the door, and a pile of fashion magazines for customers to flick through. I picked up the latest copy of *Vanity Fair* magazine and rifled through it. I had been so busy with the salon that I had not got around to reading it. I still wrote to my old school friend Sheila, with whom I had been in service. She had married a wealthy businessman of good stock, and in every letter pleaded with me to come over and visit her: *'Alex has become so boring, Ellie – tediously bourgeois in his attitudes. I long for your company and the fun we used to have.'* Sheila always sent me a copy of the American magazine, and I loved to keep up to date with the comings and goings of New York society, indulging in the fantasy that I might see news of some of the people I knew from my time over there. *Vanity Fair* sometimes promoted the *Ocean Liner* in the small advertisements near the back. I vaguely noted them every time, and had kept my passport and papers up to date, out of a kind of wilful sentimentality. I knew I would never travel to America again. John would not entertain the idea of travelling abroad, and the subject of my going alone would have been too fraught with the memory of how I had left him before. I could live without America, but I couldn't live without John. That was the choice I had made ten years ago when I returned to my husband in Kilmoy. I had known then that it was an irreversible decision, so I just nursed my occasional dream and made sure it never grew large enough to make me bitter or to fill me with longing.

The real truth of my return from New York was that I had left someone behind there, too. I had fallen in love in America. John didn't know that, although I sometimes thought he must have suspected as much, but he was sensible enough never to ask me directly. I had been so young, so impressionable, and it was no surprise that my head had been turned. Charles was young and handsome, like John, but as the son of a shipping magnate he was wealthy, too. He had asked me to marry him, but before I had the chance to make up my mind, the decision to return to Ireland had been made for me by my father's death. When I arrived back in Ireland, that old love – for home, for John – took hold, and America, Charles and all they had both meant to me became as vague as a photograph.

Although sometimes – on mulchy rainy days when I was feeding the hens, or cleaning the cow dung off the front step, or John came in looking for his dinner and my hands were sore from peeling spuds – when my spirit deflated with the ordinary drudgery of everyday, married life, I would call to mind my old lover and allow myself to remember Charles and me standing in the porch of that rose-covered cottage on his brother's grand estate and him giving me a bottle of Chanel No. 5.

The perfume was long since gone and, as time went on, the image faded and seemed more remote and my dreams of girlish romance became a distant memory. Other desires took over – motherhood, success in business – and I gradually let go of my New York past and built up my life in Kilmoy, making sure that I had all the glamour and excitement I needed on my own doorstep.

I pottered over to the cosmetics counter and started to apply make-up at a large, bevelled mirror that sat on the wide counter built for that purpose. I had originally created this scented corner in the salon to mask the chemical smell of the permanent-wave machine. Clients were invited to sample scents and cosmetics from the fashionable companies Max Factor and Helena Rubinstein, a small range of which we had on sale. However, the goods on offer in the local chemist shop were so meagre that I found within weeks I had to replenish our stocks and we were making almost as much money from the cosmetics as from the hairdressing services.

I looked in the mirror and groaned with frustration. I had tried to keep my skin fashionably pale, but there was already a scattering of freckles across my nose where I had been out tackling our overgrown vegetable patch the week before. The rustic nature of my country life with John and the relative sophistication of my working life in town were incompatible, I had long since decided.

Beads of sweat were already forming on my temples and fuzzing my hair out of the newly straightened bob I had painstakingly fashioned the night before. I had to heat the irons in the solid-fuel stove, instead of using the perfectly good electrical ones in the salon. I was shot through with frustration at John's stubbornness.

The day had not even begun and the salon was too hot already, with the sun shining in the front window and bouncing off the mirrors. Once the machine went on, it would be unbearable. I had yet to get a proper blind for the window, and wondered if there was any such thing as an air-conditioning unit over here, that I could purchase to cool the air? I had seen one advertised in an American magazine, but it would be impossibly expensive to ship to Ireland from there. Did my suppliers in England have them, I wondered? Oh, there was still so much to be done. My head was buzzing and the day not even begun.

As I opened the door, old Mrs Fitzpatrick, the draper's wife, came in. She had long, greying hair that had been tied up in a bun for as far back as I could remember.

'Hello, Madam,' Pauline marched over to her. 'You after a perm?'

Mrs Fitzpatrick ignored her, pointedly. In all probability Pauline had led one of her grandsons astray the night before, and I had missed out on the news. I'd surely catch up as the day went on.

I gave the English strap a firm look, to let the old lady know I did not wholly approve of my charge, and said, 'Pauline, go and give those mirrors a good polish through, would you? The sun is showing them up.'

Mrs Fitzpatrick followed her with a poisoned look, until I thought perhaps she had come in exclusively to reprimand the girl.

'I do not want my hair done, Mrs Hogan. I have come to speak with you on another matter entirely.'

She looked across at Pauline, whose substantial form was squeezed into a tight flapper dress. Her plump arms strained against the short sleeves, almost at tearing point, and the white, puckered flesh wobbled as she polished, pretending not to listen.

'Alone, if you please.'

Oh God – what had the child done last night?

'Pauline, run over to the shop and get some more tea.' Then, to buy more time, I added, 'And see if you can get some scones from Mary – they might not be out of the oven yet, so there'll be a bit of a wait. I'll deal with things here until you get back.'

'Yes, Ma'am,' she said.

'And put your apron on, for goodness' sake, girl.'

I felt bad being stern with her, but I was only trying to protect her somewhat against the tight-lipped old biddy's onslaught.

Pauline tiptoed out the door, all but curtsying to us on her way out. I took a deep breath to launch my defence.

'Mrs Fitzpatrick,' I started.

But the old woman held her hand up to stop me and said, 'I am here with a business proposition.'

The Fitzpatricks owned the only draper's shop in town. It was an outdated, scruffy-looking shop, and although they had made some efforts to smarten it up a year or two ago, dressing a single draper's torso in a red jacket, that jacket was now faded with age and, with obviously dusty shoulders and curling lapels, was more a source of annoyance to their customers than a temptation. I knew, by the erratic opening hours of late, that the couple were struggling to manage the business on their own.

The old lady rubbed the protruding knuckles on her gnarled hands as she talked. Arthritis, by all accounts – her sewing days were surely coming to an end.

My mind began to race as I suspected what was coming.

'Mr Fitzpatrick and I are not getting any younger and, as you might know, despite our efforts to persuade Thomas to come home and take over the . . .'

35

*I'll buy it!* I wanted to blurt it out immediately, but had to wait for the old woman to go through the whole rigmarole of explaining the whys and wherefores.

'. . . the business, he is doing well – very well – over in England, working as . . .'

She went through all of her five sons, recalling how exceptionally well they were doing in England, their acquisition of wives and children and money, describing their grand houses and their many achievements to me in detail. She then gave me a history of her business (*not* potted), dating back to her grandparents-in-law insisting on every generation's impeccable reputation as the finest tailors and draper's shop in the Western hemisphere, before – having almost talked herself out of it – she finally, reluctantly, said, '. . . so we have decided to sell the business.'

# CHAPTER FOUR

John was furious.

'What do you *mean* you've agreed to buy the Fitzpatricks' shop!'

'They offered it to me, John. The old lady came to see me in the salon, and all but pleaded with me. I couldn't refuse her.'

I shouldn't have blurted my news out the moment I came in the door, especially not after having left things the way they were that morning. I should have kept it to myself for a few days, been more discreet, more wily in my presentation. Passed it through Maidy first perhaps, and got things back onto a pleasant footing with John – baked him a cake.

But that wasn't my way: why should I alter my manner of doing things to please my husband? In any case, it wasn't *our* way to tiptoe around each other, either. I couldn't understand why he was getting so het up.

'I thought you'd be pleased for me. For *us*?'

'Us, Ellie? *Us*? Do we not have enough already? Enough money, enough shops, enough to be doing already, without you running about opening another bloody business? Well, I've had enough, Ellie – *ENOUGH!*'

He banged his hand on the table, his fist clenched, his eyes red and shot through with anger – and something else . . . ?

I jumped with shock as a cup on the table clattered to the floor and smashed on the tiles. I had never seen him this angry before.

'This is our future, John. I am working to secure *our* future. This shop will bring in everything we ever dreamed of . . .'

'All *you* ever dreamed of, Ellie. All I ever dreamed of I already have – you and the farm and—'

'The *farm*! Sure, we'd live on potatoes and air alone, if it was left to you.'

'That's right – I've never been enough for you, always wanting more, more, more. What is it now – a bigger car? To be driving around Kilmoy in a Rolls-Royce? Is that what you want?'

'Oh, don't be so stupid, John.'

'That's it. Stupid John – good for nothing, only driving his wife about here and there . . .'

My fire was up now. If he wanted a fight, I'd give him one all right.

'Well, I can drive myself now surely, John Hogan – sure, I hardly need you at all.'

'For Christ's sake, Ellie, why can't you just leave it alone and be grateful and happy with what we've got?'

'Because, John,' I wanted to wind things up now, for that was enough fighting and it was time to put my foot down, 'I am always right – and you know it. The offer is in, the deposit is being transferred tomorrow to secure the sale, and in two months we will be the owners of Fitzpatricks' Drapery, and that is the end of it.'

'No, Ellie, NO!'

Again, the fist on the table – and the legs of it all but bounced off the floor. He looked at me, his face ruddy with rage, his eyes slanted through with something that I did not recognize – something strangely inappropriate. Tiredness? What was wrong with him? He seemed to gather himself slightly and sat down in the chair, as if exhausted by the fight.

'I am going outside to feed the hens,' I said haughtily (although I had not fed them myself in weeks), 'and when I come back, we can talk about this properly.'

The air outside was spring-fresh. It was early yet, the sun had held since morning, but a small scatter of rain was interfering with the leaves of the tall sycamore trees over the hen-house at the back of our yard. It needed sweeping. That was my job – one of the many household chores I had willingly performed, and with pleasure and gratitude for our soft, simple life in the early days. Now the ground was littered with leaves, and the crisp top ones flittered across with a small breeze, revealing the carpet of mulch beneath them. I had perhaps been careless with our home, especially since the salon had opened – but John had always picked up where I slacked off. It was unlike him to let the yard around our house grow so unkempt – and now losing his temper? Perhaps there was something more wrong than was apparent. Perhaps he was tiring of me? Yet we had made love the night before, although thinking back, his ardour had cooled somewhat in the past few months. He had taken to retiring early to bed, and was more often than not asleep when I got in beside him. Could my marriage be falling apart? The very rock on which my life was built, the one thing in which I held all confidence, the person who had given me grace all my life – could I be losing him?

No. It was too ridiculous a notion. Yet I had been working too hard lately. And John was right, I worried about the businesses and yet never about us. Had he taken that as an invitation to stray? He was, after all, alone in the house all day – and my mind wandered to what options he might take for himself. The scattering of widows and half-witted girls to whom he might have access, and the mere idea of John making good on poor Veronica's crush, amused me so greatly that my spirits lifted.

I walked to the shed and picked up the bucket of hen corn. It was right next to the door and damp, again – it was unlike John to not bother placing it on the high shelf where it was kept dry.

I grabbed a handful of the damp grain and on the way over to the pen I tore up a few sticks of rhubarb from the patch behind the shed. They came too easily at their creamy roots, and I resolved to come back for more later and spend the evening creating a scene of domestic warmth, if not for the benefit of John, then at least for my own pride in front of him. I still had the crystallized ginger in my bag that I had picked up in town for Maidy's jam – although, in my excitement, I had forgotten the woman herself.

In the pen I scattered the damp grain through my fingers and across to the scrappy, hungry birds. I was still wearing my good shoes, but decided I would chance checking for eggs anyway. If my marriage was in jeopardy, it was no use worrying about mud on my buckles. They had been laying very badly lately, according to the number of eggs in the house. John collected them each evening before I came in from work, but we had had none for the past few weeks.

I picked my way across the filthy pen and opened the door of their house. The smell hit me first. There was a dead hen decomposing on the hen-house floor. Rotten eggs were broken all around her – and a good dozen or so were piled up on the seats so that the poor animals would barely have had room to sit down.

Suddenly the sight of this small disarray sent a feeling of panic rushing through me. John had not been attending to his animals.

This was not like him at all. He was not himself. There was something badly wrong.

I threw down the bucket and left all as it was, running back to the house in six long strides.

John was slumped on the kitchen table. His arms hung motionless by his sides.

# CHAPTER FIVE

I lifted his head – his eyes were glassy, his mouth half-open as if waiting for a kiss. I shook him: 'John, John, JOHN!'

He let out a long gasp and his eyes turned to me with a look of pure terror.

I didn't want to leave him, but my gut clenched with the certainty that I had to act quickly. Before I had the chance to think anything through, I ran to the car and cursed as my hands shook in the ignition.

'*He's breathing. I can't have been gone five minutes . . .*' I talked to myself aloud in the car. '*Doctor Bourke will be at home, get to Doctor Bourke's house – ten minutes – five. Five minutes to the town. Five minutes to get him, and five back again. Fifteen minutes. Nothing much can happen in fifteen minutes. He'll be fine. Put your foot down.*'

I kept my eyes on the road ahead and sped as fast as the car would carry me. Blind to the world, hedgerows scraped, the mirrors bashed off on trees, my heart banged against my chest with a kind of elation.

'*I can do this.*' I said it over and over again. John had been shot in these very bogs out on manoeuvres with his IRA unit. I had thought he was going to die then, and he didn't. This would be the same. I had thought he wouldn't walk again, and he had.

I had made that happen. I had brought him back to life. I would do it again. *'Eyes on the road, Ellie, faster, faster.'*

I left the engine running, pulling the car clumsily up to the pavement outside Doctor Bourke's house, and banged and banged on the door until his lazy maid answered it, then pushed past the girl and grabbed Doctor Bourke from his tea. The genteel domestic scene of crockery and fresh linens left behind in a flitter of panic, his charming, elegant elderly wife left open-mouthed in the wake of my unseemly shout: 'It's John! I think he's dying!'

Even as I said the words, I didn't believe them. It was a ruse to make the old man move faster.

He barely spoke in the car, but I babbled against the doctor's natural reserve. He was being the professional, staying silent until he got the lie of the land.

'I was only gone out of the house five minutes and when I got back he was . . .'

I stalled at describing his condition. When we got home he'd be all right and I'd look like some fool. John was a strong man, he survived the shooting and nothing could be worse than that. I had probably just been unnerved by our fight. I was stressed with the day, that was it – overreacting.

'He was breathing, maybe he just choked on something. I just got a fright, see what you think. I was only gone five minutes.'

When we got back into the house, John was still in the chair as I had left him.

Doctor Bourke went over and put his hands to his neck and shook his head.

'I'm sorry, Ellie.'

What did that mean – he was sorry.

I ran over to John, and took his shoulders and shook them. Why wouldn't he wake up?

'John, John,' I said, 'Doctor Bourke is here. JOHN!'

I pulled the chair away from the table, struggling against the weight of him. 'For God's sake, help me move him,' I said to the old doctor, 'help him to stand up. Do something!' Why wasn't he *doing* something?

I put my face against John's and kissed him and whispered into the bristle of his warm face, 'Wake up, John, please wake up now . . .'

Doctor Bourke came up behind me and put his hands gently on my shoulders, coaxing me away.

'He's gone, Ellie.'

'No,' I said, 'no!' I shook him off and ripped at John's clothes. I pawed at his strong body beneath his clothes, the sinew and muscle – moving, always moving. He wasn't stiff, he was still warm. I put my head to his chest, to the heart that beat against my back every night as I slept, to see if I could hear his heart. I crept my hand up to it and beat out the rhythm, one-two-three, one-two-three – I could make it start again, I knew I could.

Doctor Bourke put his hands on my shoulder, his long bony fingers gripping me more firmly this time.

'Come away now, Ellie, come away.'

The confident touch of the old man was real as he dragged me back. John did not rise to stop him. Could it be true?

I looked at the figure in the chair. Back arched, arms hanging rigid against his side, his naked chest unresponsive to my touch, his mouth hung open, his eyes were staring emptily at the same corner of the ceiling. It was a stranger – just some lifeless doll.

'No!' I said again. 'No, no, no,' and I ran from the house.

That was not John in the house, it couldn't be. He was outside. He was down in the bottom field tending the sheep. The body in the chair was some trick, a dream, a confusion.

I ran from the house to find my husband, my shoes sliding

across the damp grass. I tripped across potholes until I threw the shoes off, my stockings ripped on sharp stones, my skirt tearing against the brambles as I ran.

'John,' I called, 'John, John, John.' I shouted out his name, repeating it over and over again until my voice became nothing but a hollow howl, absorbed into the vast emptiness of the bogs and fields all around.

I knew he wasn't there, but equally I knew that it wasn't him back at the house. That lifeless, rejecting corpse was not my husband. It was an aberration. The knowledge of that calmed me somewhat as I gathered myself and walked slowly back towards the house. I could not go back in, so I went and sat in the hollow of the large oak tree at the edge of our first field. This was John's smoking stool. I tossed back a pile of brown mulch with the toe of my stockinged foot and the ground beneath was littered with small white stubs of paper. John's leather tobacco pouch was hidden away, tucked into the mossy pit of two low branches. John did not like to smoke in the house, preferring to come out here after breakfast and have the smoke snatched away by the wind. The cleansing air of nature diminished every human endeavour – smoke rings disappeared with the merest flick of wind, on a still day they floated to the edge of the large oak's canopy of leaves and John felt he had won. He loved to battle with nature; keeping the nettles at bay around the house, pulling them with his rough, bare hands. My husband bathed from a tin bucket outside in our yard on the coldest of days. While others lay cowed in their beds by wind and rain, John faced the worst weather to tend his livestock, comforting and caring for them. When he was done, he came home to my fire and my food, and I comforted and cared for him. That was how it had always been, until I'd lost hope in the possibility of our increasing our family, and disappeared myself into the world of avarice and achievement. I couldn't think about that now. I picked up the worn leather pouch that Paud had given him for his fourteenth birthday and put it into the pocket of my apron. (I had put my apron on when I went to feed the hens. I had remembered to do that, even though we had been fighting, remembered to protect my smart work clothes.)

Doctor Bourke came and found me.

'We should go and tell Maidy,' he said.

'Yes,' I agreed.

I didn't go back into the house. Doctor Bourke looked down at my bare feet, but passed no comment.

In the car he spoke, cautiously and briefly, about the details. He was doing his duty. Trying to ground me, to try and help me take it in. John had suffered a massive heart attack. It might have been coming on for months, years maybe. Men didn't like to visit doctors – it was a common enough problem, he assured me. John was one of those stoic people who kept their ailments to themselves. The change in temperament, the early nights, the loss of appetite, these were all symptoms, signs that something was amiss. Signs I had missed.

I half-listened, nodding my assent with irritated nods of the head until he stopped, awkwardly. We drove in silence then for the seven miles to Maidy's cottage, the place where John had grown up. The old couple had adopted their nephew, John, when he was nine. His mother had died first of some unnamed illness, and his father (Paud's youngest brother) shortly afterwards – of a heart attack, I now remembered. Maidy and Paud had no children of their own and, to all intents and purposes, John was their son. I drove more carefully on this journey, concentrating my thoughts on Maidy, on how she would react to this news. It was terrible news – just some terrible fact that we had to relay.

*'John is dead.'*

Three words, that's all it was, the saying of three small words. They were in my head, but I would not – could not – let them pass into my heart. I kept telling myself that it was a bad dream. I made myself believe that if I just kept putting one foot in front of the other, it would go away.

The light was fading and, as I drove, the road ahead evened to a grey line, blurring into the heavy blanket of foliage at its edges, drawing down the curtain of night, further softening my grasp on this terrifying reality. The journey to tell Maidy 'John is dead' was happening, but it didn't feel real.

Doctor Bourke went in first. I stood outside the front door of the cottage while he told her. There was the heavy scent of lilac around the door, and a basket of freshly picked potatoes on the stoop, an early spring crop, the earth on them already dried in the sun. Maidy would barely brush off the dust before boiling them briefly, then leave them in the pan covered in a clean cloth to steam themselves soft. We ate them as children with our hands, straight from the table, the warm, salted butter that she made herself sliding down our chins. Some things never changed.

I heard a scream from inside the house. The three words were said, and I could comfort her now. She was standing in her working apron, stained with the mud and flour from her day's work, her homely bosom shaking with instant tears, her hands outstretched as she reached for me. I fell against her, my jaw tight as I held onto her, clenched her fleshy back and guarded myself against her raw, unavoidable grief.

I held Maidy and comforted her, but I did not cry, or let myself fall into a wife's natural keening.

I held myself together like a rock. I would not look into the void.

# CHAPTER SIX

I drove us all back into town, calling in to Heffernan, the undertaker, on the way, before dropping Doctor Bourke off at the priest's house. They would both follow us down in Father Geraghty's car.

'Drive slowly,' the doctor whispered to me as we arrived. 'Let Heffernan get there before you, and deal with things first.'

I nodded as if I was a character in some film that he was giving his commission to. This task was nothing to do with me somehow, it was about protecting Maidy. The old woman sat shocked into silence in the back of the car, her large frame covered in her Sunday coat and hat, which I had gently dressed her in before manoeuvring her into the back seat.

'I want to be with him,' she insisted as I drove off alone with her. 'I need to see John. He's in the house alone. You shouldn't have left him,' she cried from the back, a thread of accusation pleading through her grief, 'for the banshee to get him, Ellie. The banshee will get him.'

'Shhh now, Maidy. We'll be there soon. Settle yourself, we'll be there in a minute. Take out your beads and say a decade – they're in your pocket.'

The platitudes of comfort fell out of me naturally, as if this were her drama, not mine. Repeating the motions I had gone through with her in the hours after Paud's death. Except that I had felt a sickness then in the pit of my stomach and wept alongside her. I did not weep now. I couldn't. If I wept, I would not be able to drive, or look after Maidy. If I wept, it would mean it was true. I would not weep and let the sadness pass into my heart. It was too huge. I would explode with the pain of it.

'Hail Mary, full of grace, the Lord is with thee; blessed are thou amongst women, and blessed is the fruit of they womb, Jesus . . .'

*'Holy Mary, Mother of God, pray for us sinners, now and at the hour of our death. Amen.'*

I picked up the second half of the chant and we prayed out loud, backwards and forwards, she gleaning comfort from the mercy of God in her hour of need, while the familiar mantra only succeeded in clearing my mind of all else but the road – strengthening my resolve to detach myself from what was happening. Maidy giving herself up to the truth, me saving myself from it.

When we got to the house I saw Heffernan's funeral hearse in the yard. The horse was munching on a hedgerow at the top of the lane, and started when I caught him in my lights. He opened his lazy eyes wide, as if embarrassed to be caught in the act of eating at an inappropriate time.

I took Maidy out of the car and led her towards the open door of my cottage. *John's cottage. Our cottage.* I could not go in. I called Doctor Bourke out, and he came and took her arm. He looked at me quizzically as he led her inside, and I shook my head.

'I can't believe it, I just cannot believe it, John, my John . . .' I heard Maidy wailing from inside, and the low mumblings of the priest offering her comfort.

I was alone again. I began to pace up and down the yard. It was pitch-dark, save for the glimmering light that came from the small windows of our house. I concentrated my mind on the ground beneath my feet, the cold creeping up my bare legs where the stockings had torn. I needed to feel things from the outside in, to quell the panic rising up in me, to push it back down. I stopped at the door of the barn, where a hardy old rose bush pushed proudly up from an otherwise dead patch of earth. I grabbed at it blindly and pressed, until I felt the thorns pierce my hand, then shook it off and sucked the blood from the plump skin at the base of my palm.

'Are you not coming into the house, Ellie?'

It was Doctor Bourke.

He appeared suddenly in the darkness. I could just see his profile against the light of our open door.

How long had passed since I had called into his house to collect him? How long since he had been here, tending to John's hips after the shooting? Hours, days, years – it seemed to me to be one and the same time.

'No.' And in a sudden urge for familiarity, to be heard by another human being, I said, 'I can't – not while . . .'

'Would you like me to ask Heffernan to take him back into town? Now that Maidy has seen him.'

'Yes,' I said, 'I would.'

He put his hand on my shoulder and held it there for a moment without saying anything, sliding it gently away as he walked off.

I reached into my apron pocket for warmth and my hands fell on John's tobacco pouch. I went over to the oak and, feeling my way in the dark, placed it back where I had found it a few hours ago.

He might want to come back and smoke.

I waited until I saw Heffernan's man lead the horse over to the door of the house, then turned my back as they loaded the funeral carriage, and until I could no longer hear the loud clopping of its hooves on the lane.

Father Geraghty was still in the house. He would stay there all night until the neighbours came at first light.

The two of them sat by the fire and prayed. Maidy's face was pleading with me to join them, but I couldn't.

I could not sit still. Instead I busied myself frying us up a simple meal of potato cakes, eggs and bacon. Father Geraghty ate heartily (as priests always did, even under the most appalling of circumstances), and although Maidy and I barely touched the food, the making of it and clearing up afterwards kept me distracted. I cleaned out the fire and set a new one, baked a loaf for the morning and made more tea. Their prayers halted, Maidy and the priest's eyes followed me anxiously around the room, but I refused to sit and allow myself to lapse into the awkward waiting silence of the bereaved. I longed to put on the radio and break through the wretched atmosphere, to fill the room with music, a joyful noise to help me mask the truth. I wanted to bring life back into the room, to interrupt the slow mortification of silence, the growing emptiness. The truth.

At a little after midnight Maidy sent Father Geraghty home. It was a break in protocol, but he was old and I could see that Maidy was exhausted from having to deal with him by herself.

'Ellie and I need some time alone,' she said. My heart raced at what I knew was coming.

'Would you like me to stay and talk about the arrangements?' he asked.

'No, thank you, Father,' she said. 'Ellie and I can arrange that business between ourselves. You'll call again in the morning?'

'Of course.'

There was such calm, such normality in their exchange, that I told myself I could do this after all. 'Business,' Maidy had said. Yes, this was just business after all.

I saw him out of the house and, taking the Tilley lamp from the table, I lit a path to his car.

'Thank you, Father,' I said.

He looked paternal in this soft light. They had been friends, this old priest and my own staunchly religious father. They both had pointed grey features and an impenetrable dedication to the Catholic faith, sometimes at the cost of other things – in my father's case, affection for his wife and only child. John was the man in my life who had taught me how to love.

When I went back to where Maidy was I said, 'I don't want him laid out at home, I want him kept in a closed casket by Heffernan until the funeral.'

The words were out before I knew it. I was surprised by how voraciously this opinion had seized me. I had never thought of John dying before, and yet I was certain what I wanted. Or, rather, what I didn't want. Over the coming days there would be weeping and wailing, people calling to the house with platters of food, neighbours prodding and poking at my conscience, talking about how, why, when John died, discussing things in every minute detail. They would dig for my grief, as surely and as deeply as the grave we would bury him in. I knew that I would not be able to endure it.

'I don't want any fuss,' I said.

Maidy was shocked.

'Well, I've never heard of such a thing, Ellie. Where on earth did you get an idea like that? No, John will be laid out in his own house. It's bad enough he was taken away by Heffernan to-night, but I know you needed a night's grace. However, he'll be back in the morning, then I told Heffernan I'll arrange the body myself. As his wife, you will help me. It's the way.'

I shuddered at the mere thought of seeing John's dead body again, never mind touching it. In America, people were cared for by funeral homes with dignity and propriety. Caskets were opened or closed, as the family wished. It wasn't the way here. Bodies were laid out in the house by their families, if they were able (and Maidy was versed in the practice, having laid out half the townland in her time, as well as her husband Paud not a year before), then left as a centrepiece in their kitchens for partygoers to drink and dance and weep over – the older, more polite ones admiring their remains with ghoulish curiosity. I would not have John, or me, subjected to such a savage practice.

'I don't want his body back in this house, Maidy. I don't want everybody in, looking at him.'

'You can't do that, Ellie,' she said firmly, 'it's not how these things are arranged.'

'I'm his wife,' I said, 'and I shall do as I like.'

'And I'm his mother,' she answered, 'and I know about these things.'

For a moment we stood on the edge of our respective anger. My decorum was informed by blind terror, I knew that, and fury rose up in me that this old woman, with her broad, hardy grief, was going to grab my heart and tear it open.

Maidy's face was hammered with age. The benign, chubby woman I had fallen in love with as a child was slimmer and starting to sag. Her skin was looser, her lively, laughing eyes jaded with the passing of time, for she had been considerably weakened by her husband Paud's death. She needed to see John and carry out the ritual of his passing in the way that was familiar to her. She was ready to fight me for that privilege. I was weakened by my love for her, but my love for John was stronger. I would not see him dead. I could not.

'For John,' she said, 'think what he would have wanted.'

'*Would have.*' The past tense again. Why did everyone have to keep saying it? Catching me off guard. I was angry – with her for pushing me into sadness, and with John for leaving me alone at the time when I needed him most.

'I can't,' I said, as close to tears as I had been since I had found him. My petulance eased as I spoke the truth, and as it left me my knees buckled. 'I can't look on him.'

Maidy caught me, put her arms around my waist and guided me to sit by the stove with her. She smelt of bread and carbolic soap, the smell of home – of a love so old I feared it was lost to me forever.

She settled me into Paud's old armchair, the one he had given to John when we had first moved into his parents' cottage some fifteen years before. The bright flowered fabric was darkened where both of our men's heads had slept against it, full of the food and comfort their wives had created for them after all those hard days working on the land. I leaned back into it, and behind my eyes conjured the shadow of John's face.

'I can't believe it, Maidy. I can't believe he's gone, I won't.'

Maidy stayed silent as I wept out my words, tears pouring down my face.

'I can feel him here, Maidy. He's still here, in this house, in this chair. He's not gone. He's not left me.'

I caught my breath as I spoke, and licked the salty water from my lips, and pushed the spilling tears away from my cheeks with a careful swipe of my palms. I could only allow myself a small leak from the vast well that was building inside me, mopping at the surface as if it were only spilt milk from the glass of a clumsy child.

Maidy would need to see his body and cry and keen with the women. The routine and ritual of death in a small Irish town would take their course, and Maidy was right – it was what John would have wanted. It wasn't what I wanted, although in truth I could not say what I wanted, except for that fact that I did not want my husband to be dead.

# CHAPTER SEVEN

I woke suddenly from a deep, velvety sleep and lay in the bed. The light was barely filtering through the curtains. Where was John? Gone to the sheep already? The lamb – was he checking on the newborn lamb he had brought in the day before?

The first neighbour arrived soon after dawn. Brid Donnelly was an old matriarch and Maidy's oldest friend.

'Maidy, Maidy, Maidy,' she cried from outside the door, 'your boy is dead – your darling John is dead. He's DEAD!'

Oh God! I heard the latch open, then Maidy howling, and in my mind's eye I saw Brid, wiry and dressed in her widow's black, putting down a tray of freshly baked scones on the stove, then taking her oldest friend's hands in hers and shaking them vigorously, whipping her up into a frenzy of emotion, holding and comforting her as she keened. 'Whist now, Maidy, he's in the arms of the Good Lord,' she said. 'His Mother Mary herself is holding him now to her sweet bosom, welcoming him into the land of eternal light.' As Maidy calmed, Brid sat her down and started the business of the Irish wake. 'God bless you, Maidy, and all belonging to you, but how did it happen?' A chair scraped the floor and I knew Brid had settled herself by the hearth, where she would stay for three full days and nights, until my husband was covered over with earth and the women were all cried out. It was barely 6 a.m.

I stayed in my room and listened as they all arrived – the stage was being set for the theatre of death – from the privacy of our small, familiar bedroom, with the worn blue candlewick bedspread, the faded flowery cushion that Maidy had fashioned from a discarded dress of mine, the long bolster pillow filled with the feathers from the bellies of the ducks John reared as a child.

I recognized the voices of each mourner as they arrived and imagined the scene in the kitchen playing out. Padraig Phelan, a pleasant school teacher and John's closest friend – they had served together during the War of Independence. He spoke too quietly for me to hear his words, but I knew the timbre of his low voice from the background of men's secretive war-talk during my early years of marriage. He would have a bottle of whisky in his pocket and place it discreetly on the sideboard in the parlour. He would have arrived in Father Geraghty's car from the town, and the priest would probably have drunk the whisky before anybody knew it was there. And Mary Murphy, her son Cahill beaten to death by the Black and Tans when he was just fifteen; the boy's murder had precipitated John's full commitment as an IRA captain, fronting the unit in conflicts that would lead to his injury. Always a fierce, substantial woman, her strong character had been diminished by her son's death. Carrying the unsolved death of her son, she would walk the seven-mile pilgrimage from her home in Kilmoy to pay her respects, leave a basket of bread or biscuits behind her, but would barely sit down before leaving again.

Liam, John's farm boy (although he was in his thirties now), came in without introduction, but I knew the thud of his boots as he cleaned them off on the stoop. He would be empty-handed and, as the afternoon wore on, Liam would fall into a drunken stupor of grief until the loss of my husband, his beloved mentor,

gave way to his maudlin mumblings at not being able to secure
a wife. Behind him came our neighbours the Morans, Vincent
and Carmel, with their various small children, who ran around
outside, disturbing the hens and crashing through the muted
atmosphere with their energetic squabbling and delighted cries.
They loaded up their cart and left again soon afterwards, with
promises to return later that evening.

With the arrival of each guest I became less and less inclined
to leave my bedroom. By nine the house was humming with
people, their footsteps and loud chatter reverberating off the
cast-iron frame of the bed. The house seemed, quite literally, to
be coming alive. I didn't want to see any of them – even the dear
ones. The only person I wanted to be with in that moment, the
person who could reassure and comfort me in my hour of need,
wasn't there. They were kind people and meant well, but their
mission was truth and resolution – to confirm the black and
white of life and death. So I stayed there, in the grey cloud of
my bed. I rolled into John's pillow and smelt the earthy tang of
his sweat, pulling the coverlet up over my head. He was in the
next room entertaining the visitors with Maidy. He was down
in the field tending the newborn lambs. I hummed and tried not
to listen, but their voices crept through the gaps in the wooden
door, the cracks of the walls.

'Can I see him, Maidy?' somebody finally asked. 'Is he in the
parlour?'

The scraping of a chair on the floor.

'No,' Maidy said.

'Sit down, woman,' Brid asserted, 'he's not arrived yet.
Heffernan will bring him over later.'

'Later?'

'He was moved from the house?'

'Ellie needed some time – to settle herself.'

The room went silent. I clenched the pillow.

This was so hard for Maidy, but they all knew it was my choice, not hers. John should have spent last night in his own house. It was the way. Nobody would speak ill of me outright – not there and then – but I would be the talk of the county. If I had had the closed coffin, I might have made the national news! I felt a flood of love for Maidy's generosity, her loyalty – and my spirits lifted briefly from feeling something other than this cloying, building dread.

However, the dread soon returned with the squawking arrival of Kathleen Condon.

'Oh, oh, such tragic, tragic news. How is Ellie? She must be distraught.'

Kathleen was my envious classmate from national school. She had been a nasty, outspoken child, and adulthood had taught her not much more than to couch her barbed comments with fake concern.

'Imagine losing a wonderful man like John – a war hero!'

'Kathleen,' I heard Maidy greet her, 'what a beautiful cake. Thank you.'

'Sure, what else could I do, Maidy – for my *oldest friend*. Where is she? I expect she's getting all dressed up for the visitors. Ellie *always* likes to look her best.'

'She's still sleeping,' Maidy said. 'She's taken it very badly.'

The room went quiet as the dozen or so bodies contemplated my grief.

'She found him,' Brid Donnelly broke the silence, 'sitting at the table, drawing his last breath.'

'She was out feeding the hens.'

'It was a massive heart attack – she drove into town to get Doctor Bourke.'

*'Drove? A woman?'*

'Interrupted his tea . . .'

'He wouldn't have liked that.'

'A heart attack, you said?

'Just like his father.'

I could endure it no longer.

I pulled on my clothes, sneaked out into the back passageway, lifted the latch on the back door and quickly, without looking back, made my escape.

I drove fast, looking neither left nor right, but keeping my eye on the grey line of the road, carefully avoiding the early mourners who passed me on their way up to my house to offer condolences.

Heads turned as I left clusters of well-wishers staring in indignation after me along the hedgerows. I didn't care. I wasn't ready for them, for their platitudes and their apple tarts. I wasn't ready to see anyone. I could not imagine I ever would be.

In Kilmoy I drove straight onto the paving outside my building and ran directly upstairs to my small apartment.

As soon as I got inside I thanked God for the comfort of this small second home. This was a place with which John had no real affinity, my own private sanctuary. For a short while I would be able to forget. I pulled over the heavy velvet curtains, and the noise from the world outside receded. Then I turned on the large radio, and as it warmed up the crackling baritone of John McCormack singing 'The Mountains of Mourne' filled the air. I stood for a moment and thought about tinkering through to find a more cheerful tune, then decided it wasn't worth the bother. Mr McCormack would do while I made myself tea. I plugged in the electric kettle and took out a china cup and saucer of my mother's. As a child I had studied the Willow Pattern and had dreamed of foreign places, blue pagodas, strange-looking people in long, squared-off robes. I took down the tin of imported Earl Grey tea from the cupboard above the sink, and the small silver teapot that held just enough for one cup. Then I sat on the chaise, against the embroidered cushions, and settled myself into genteel cosiness. For a moment I felt I might stay there forever, hidden, keeping the world at bay. I tried to concentrate on some fashion magazines, then a book, then fiddled with the radio, but it was no use. Kilmoy would come knocking. John would be buried this day or the next. I'd have to get myself ready. It was pointless running away. I would have to face it.

I went to the bedroom and opened the door of the old mahogany wardrobe. It was where I kept my best clothes, for there was always the danger of them getting damp out in the house, with the exposed cottage walls. I searched through it, baulking at the black woollen dress and matching coat that I always wore for funerals. I should like to wear navy, I thought petulantly. No, I should like to wear forest-green, John's favourite colour on me – or red! Damn them all! I pulled out the black suit nonetheless and laid it on the bed. I had a hat and a veil somewhere. I stood on a chair to look on top of the vast, deep wardrobe. The hat toppled from the large, green leather trunk I had travelled back from America with. It was covered in a thick layer of dust and I spluttered as a cloud of grey flew in my face. It needed dusting. I would dust. That would keep me occupied! Reaching up, I tugged at the handle and the huge, heavy case toppled to the ground with an almighty crash, almost knocking me from the chair.

Within seconds there was a loud knock on the apartment door.

'Ellie?' It was Katherine's voice. 'Ellie, are you in there?'

I had to let her in, or she would think I was an intruder and call the guards. I opened the door.

'Ellie,' she said, 'are you all right? I heard about John.'

There was no false pity, no dramatic pronouncements – my protégée just stood and looked me squarely in the face. Dear, reliable Katherine.

'Do you need me to do anything?' she asked.

The question was so genuine that it begged consideration.

'Come in,' I said.

I commissioned her to take a hackney car to my cottage, calling in to Heffernan's on the way, giving him a brief note confirming the funeral arrangements. She was to take Maidy aside and let her know that I would be staying in town, and not coming back to the house to wake my husband. I would see her the following day for the formalities.

'The house will be filled with people,' I said, justifying myself. 'She won't be alone for one single moment – she'll understand.'

Katherine nodded and took my request on board without question.

As she was leaving I saw her eyes pass over the trunk that was sitting just inside the bedroom door.

# CHAPTER EIGHT

The coffin was removed from Heffernan's funeral home at 6 p.m. the following evening.

I had sent a request to Maidy to have John's coffin closed and taken up to Heffernan's a few hours before the church service, so that his funeral procession could take place directly from there. They had never, to my knowledge, seen anybody's removal from the funeral home before. Bodies were always taken straight from the home to the church, and usually left there overnight with the keening widow and her family watching over the closed coffin. There was usually a removal service the night before and a funeral Mass before the burial. The official mourning period was one month. This ended with a Month's Mind Mass, to signal that it was time for the family to return to 'normal' life. These rituals were, I knew, important landmarks for the bereaved, but God and Church held no comfort for me and I had lost what little sense I had of holding with convention. I wanted the whole thing to be over and done with as quickly as possible. I had let Maidy wake John in our home, and now she had to respect my small break with protocol.

At half-past five I was sitting on the edge of the bed in the apartment, dressed and ready. Fully made up, I wore a moss-green silk scarf and gloves as a tribute to John, the black trilby hat pinned neatly to my bun, the veil pulled down fully and tied at the back of my neck.

I could not move.

I knew I had to go, but the thought of it had filled me with such an unnameable fear that I was paralysed.

I sat looking over at the clock at my bedside. One minute passed, two, three minutes. I had to get across to Heffernan's and take my place alongside Maidy in the funeral home, while people came to pay their respects and look at the coffin. Not at John. Not at my dear John, but a box. A wooden box. I tried to persuade myself that's all it was, but still, I could not move.

Five minutes. It was twenty-five minutes until the funeral, and I should have been there twenty minutes ago. The curtains throughout the apartment were closed, but I could hear people gathering in the street outside. Waiting. The longer I sat here, the more of an 'entrance' I would have to make. The grieving widow in black, with her fancy get-up and her airs and graces, keeping everyone waiting. Still I could not move.

There was a knock on the door. I started, then heard the gentle turn of a key.

'Ellie?' I heard Katherine call through from the hall. 'I have Maidy here.'

Maidy stood in the bedroom door. Her face was bloated from the tears of the past twenty-four hours, and she looked tired, but stoic.

'Come on, Ellie dear,' she said, 'it's time.'

We walked out of the building, and the main street of Kilmoy was lined with people as far as my eye could see. Everybody knew John. Everybody loved him. I kept my head down and gripped Maidy's arm. A path cleared for us into Heffernan's. Everyone fell silent; a cloud of solemn respect hung in the air.

The funeral home had cleared its small back room to accommodate my unusual request. The little window was open and there was incense burning in a pot by the door, but it barely masked the acrid smell of dead bodies and the chemicals they used to preserve and prepare them.

I retched and swallowed. Soon this would be over. An hour at most, I told myself. The coffin sat on a makeshift table and there were two large church candles, on stands borrowed from the church, burning at either end. A slim spray of prepared flowers sat on the lid. I had filled our house with flowers all through our married life. In the early days in jars and bottles, latterly in cut-glass vases. I felt a stab of regret that, despite Heffernan's efforts, the place looked shabby and makeshift. What a chapel I might have prepared here, with my good lace tablecloth and arrangements of wild flowers from our own garden. It was spring after all, and the world was coming to life.

Heffernan, with his grim, apologetic face, sat us on two wooden chairs facing the coffin.

'Are you ready?' he asked.

I nodded, although I did not feel ready. I did not feel ready at all.

I don't know how long we sat there and took condolences, but it was certainly hours. People shook our hands and embraced us and offered their sympathy: 'I am sorry for your trouble,' in an interminable line that went on, and on, and on. Most I recognized, some I did not. Every one of them stopped and spoke to us in turn. 'John was a wonderful neighbour,' 'I fought with him in the GPO – a hero,' 'How shall you live without him?', 'We'll miss him.'

I shut down. I did not have room to absorb all their grief, when I could not even accommodate my own. Maidy was strengthened by their friendship, their goodwill. I could see her all but swell with gratitude at their kind words. I felt diminished by them. As the line went on, I felt such an exhaustion wash over me that I thought I might fall asleep in the hard chair. The room was hot, and by the time the last mourners came, it was all I could do to hold out my limp hand and nod politely.

The crowd moved on to the church, but there were enough besides to line the streets four deep as Maidy and I, the most meagre funeral party Kilmoy had ever seen, walked behind the coffin up the road. Padraig Phelan and five other uniformed men from John's old IRA unit carried it. They were all big men, but had grunted as they lifted the ornate mahogany box from its stand up onto their wide shoulders. John was in there. John was in the box. I swallowed hard. How much longer would this take? An hour, two? I thought of my black shoes pinching the corners of my feet, of the gravel on the road beneath their thin leather soles, of the fresh air, breathing in deeply – at last! – and each breath glued my spirit together, tightening the screws on my dignity and decorum, girding me against the pity and the curiosity of the crowd. All eyes were on us.

'No children,' I heard somebody say.

'A double tragedy.'

The men struggled up the steep hill towards the church. People, more people. I had become used to them now. Talk rustled through them gently, like wind through foliage. They were as inescapable as the hedgerows that lined our fields keeping the cattle in, delineating what belonged to whom. John belonged to Maidy and me alone, they were meaningless to me. I gripped Maidy's arm and felt her weight against me as she struggled up the hill. The crowds outside the church moved aside for us, and inside it was packed to capacity. One empty pew at the front was clear, for 'the family', our privileged sanctuary from the jostling elbows of the shuffling, coughing congregation, an empty stage on which to display our howling grief or maintain our stoic dignity. How could I do anything other than act, with so many people watching me? How could I believe that this drama and pomp were really happening – that John was really dead?

The service was short. Padraig spoke briefly about John's great bravery during the war, and Maidy and I followed the coffin again out of the church to the graveyard. Maidy sobbed and I held her firmly, as I had after Paud's funeral. I imagined that it was Paud in the box and that John was walking solemnly behind us.

The crowds receded again as we stood by the grave and said the Sorrowful Mysteries, Hail Marys rising up from the crowd towards heaven as the men balanced the coffin on its rope hoist. I looked into the hole beneath it. Dry earth. Mud.

Liam, the smallest, youngest man among them, struggled to hold the rope steady. There were beads of sweat breaking out on his forehead. He had called me out to the scene of John's shooting when he was no more than a boy. With a flash of clarity, it hit me. It was John in the box. He was locked in the coffin and they were going to bury him in the ground. John was alive! I had seen him breathing! As they lowered the box, I let out an almighty howl.

'Ashes to ashes, dust to dust.' The priest threw a handful of earth down on the coffin. With its dull thump, I threw myself forward and shouted, 'No, no – you can't do this! He's alive – John's still alive!'

I ran to the very edge of the grave and would have climbed in, except that Padraig and Liam held me back.

'Come on now, Ellie.'

I screamed. Rage and fear consumed me.

'Open the coffin. I want to see him! Open it, now. He's still alive, I know it. John's not dead – not John, not my John!'

Padraig put my arms around me and held me together. The broad chest of a man, the scratch of his wool coat against my face – John, but not John. John was gone. He was dead. It was the truth. At last, it was out.

Maidy stood behind him, and held her hands up to her face in shock.

'Oh, Ellie,' she said, 'oh, Ellie, Ellie, Ellie.'

She held her arms out to me, but I did not want to go to her. I did not want to give in to this truth. I would not look at John going into the ground. I would not look on him.

I broke away from Padraig and ran through the crowd. Out of the graveyard, past the church, beyond the foliage of faces – their judgements, their shock, their pity.

I scrabbled in my good clothes down the hill of the main street, past the shops – closed in my dead husband's honour – and I ran and ran until I was at the door of my building, and then I ran up the stairs. Once inside the apartment, I ran straight to the bedroom and, without thinking, flung open the dusty trunk. I emptied all the drawers of dresses, skirts, undergarments, a hairbrush, mirror, cosmetics, throwing everything into it, then I banged the lid shut.

I would run, and leave John behind. As I had done before. Then he would be here waiting for me, and I would be away, making things right. Making things better for both of us.

All of my papers were kept in a bureau upstairs. I praised my luck in having an organized mind as I pulled out my passport and all my American papers. There was a small lead safe under the desk, where I kept an amount of cash, away from the prying eyes of the local bank and Irish taxman. I opened it hurriedly and counted out almost two thousand pounds, which I crammed into the purse-belt that I used to keep my money safe on my travels to Dublin, placing it under the waistband of my skirt.

I took the pen from its holder and a sheet of writing paper from the bureau and hesitated as I began to compose a note to Maidy.

In the end I forced the words onto the page in a hurried scrawl: *'Sorry, Maidy, I have to go away. I will be in touch soon. With love, Ellie.'*

It was disgracefully brief, but all I could manage. I folded the paper in two and put it into my coat pocket.

I dragged the trunk as far as the top of the stairs, and met Katherine coming up.

'Jesus, Ellie – are you all right?'

I didn't stop to talk. If I stopped, she might persuade me to stay. Or rather I might realize I was being foolish and want to stay myself.

'Help me with this,' I said, all but throwing it at her.

The two of us manoeuvred the heavy trunk down the narrow stairs and lifted it into the back seat of the car.

'Where are you going? How long will you be gone?'

I answered her quickly, before she asked me all the other questions I didn't dare ask myself: *'What will I say to people? What will I tell Maidy? Why won't you stay for a few days and sort things out?'*

'I don't know, Katherine, but I shall write to you directly I get there and give you instructions.'

It was a lie, for I knew exactly where I was going, but as for how long? Time was meaningless now. Death had made a cursed trick of it. It seemed an age since I had left the apartment that afternoon, and yet, in that moment, it was as if the past twenty-four hours hadn't happened at all and John was still waiting for me back at the cottage.

As I turned the key in the engine I said, 'Look after things for me here, Katherine.'

She nodded. 'Of course.'

I handed her the note for Maidy, my fingers clutching it, reluctant somehow to let it go. I was frightened by the speed and ferocity with which I was running, guilty at leaving Maidy behind, yet knowing that I had to go, and knowing that I could not take her with me.

I looked into Katherine's face, filled with sensible concern. If she had pleaded with me to stay, I might have been persuaded in that moment, but it wasn't her place to interfere with my plans. In any case she understood how wilful I could be.

'I'll leave the car keys with the stationmaster in Ballyhaunis,' I said. Then, letting go of the note, I continued, 'Look after Maidy,' and sped off before I had the chance to change my mind.

From Ballyhaunis I would take the next train to Cobh in County Cork, where I would purchase myself a first-class passage to New York. Leaving John and all else behind me, once again.

NEW YORK, MAY 1934

# CHAPTER NINE

I was woken from a fitful night's sleep by the gentle tap of room service at the door. I must have ordered breakfast the night before. I remembered now.

I had checked into The Plaza in the early afternoon. The first-class porter assigned to me on the boat had telegrammed through my room booking and had then ordered a car to drive me from the quayside straight here. I had alighted from the stark sunshine of New York City into the marbled, mirrored luxury of The Plaza lobby and come straight up to this room.

I grabbed my robe from the end of the bed and answered the door. A tall Negro man stood behind a silver-service trolley: 'Breakfast, Ma'am.'

I started slightly. I had not seen a black face since leaving America almost ten years ago.

'What time is it?' I asked, as he smoothly wheeled the trolley in over the deep, salmon-pink carpet.

'Nearly eleven, Ma'am – I called earlier, but there was no reply, so I figured you were still sleeping. I brought the tray back down, and had them do it up again for you.'

Wealthy and all that I was, by Irish standards, I was not used to such sublime service.

'Thank you,' I said and wrapped the robe around me. It was

plain blue cotton, not at all grand enough for my luxurious surroundings. I would have to buy another, a silk one, if I was to stay here.

He lifted the huge warming silver lid, revealing a small toast rack with the same grandeur as if it hid a suckling pig, then poured my coffee with a flamboyant flick of his pristine cuffs, bowing slightly to incur my approval as he swept his hand over the tray to indicate the cream and sugar.

I was in a different world, far from the chill of our cottage, or even the apartment, with its modest electric stove. I had nothing to attend to. All my thoughts could be occupied entirely with the rarefied decorum of a hotel breakfast and my own beautification.

The waiter hesitated at the door, and I rushed apologetically to my purse and took out a dollar.

He bowed again with a 'Thank you, Ma'am' and was turning to leave when I quickly asked, 'What is your name?'

'Jerome,' he said, the thread of a smile playing on his long, stern face.

I reached out my hand and he shook it formally. His long, slim fingers felt cool and dry, like freshly ironed linen.

'Thank you, Jerome,' I said, and he bowed again briefly.

I was truly back in New York. Except that, this time, it was not as a lady's maid, but as a lady myself. I knew, from my years in service to the rich socialite Isobel Adams, how the politeness and gratitude of a guest were noted by those who ministered to them. I understood how things were here. I belonged, after all.

On my journey out from Ireland I had been driven by my need to escape. I knew from a new *Vanity Fair* magazine that I had been flicking through, only a few days before John's death, that the RMS *Majestic* was stopping the following day at Cobh from Southampton, on its way to New York. On my escape from John's graveside, this pointless, passing fact had pressed itself to the front of my mind and become my certain fate.

Once in Ballyhaunis, I managed to convince myself that it was a prudent, if somewhat hurried decision, and as the train carried me out of Mayo I was only aware that I was moving – away, away, through the flat fields, past the houses of people I didn't know, and nobody was looking at me, nobody knew or cared about the details of my life. It was a relief. Once in Cobh, I hurried to the ticket office, showed them my passport and previous American papers, paid for my passage and was afforded the luxury of boarding the RMS *Majestic* immediately. The ship was vast, seemingly bigger than Cobh itself, and I could comfortably hide there. I wandered around, exploring my surroundings, the shops, restaurants, hair salon and beauty parlours. As a porter carried the shabby trunk – my only piece of luggage – into my first-class cabin, a well-dressed couple passed by on the way to their quarters.

'Good evening,' the man said, tipping his homburg hat.

'Looks like we're neighbours,' said his wife as she held out her hand and introduced herself. 'Penelope Hunt – and this is my husband, Giles.' English. I had no desire for company, but I smiled politely and did the same.

'Ellie Hogan.'

The woman opened her eyes slightly, and I saw them flick down my plain black coat. She was surprised, no doubt, at a woman travelling alone first-class – and an Irish 'peasant' at that. I was not in the humour for any company, let alone theirs, but I did experience strange comfort from the fact that they were strangers. They did not know about John, or that I was still wearing my funeral suit – and in their not knowing it, I felt safe, and for a moment was able to not believe it myself.

In my cabin I studied the fine wooden panelling and felt the comfort of the rich carpets, lay down on the cool sheets that smelt of starch and lavender and fell into a sleep so deep that I did not dream. The next morning as I woke the ship was pulling out of Cobh harbour. I had forgotten where I was, and instinctively felt for John in the bed next to me. The pain of remembering peeled back my feeling of peace, and altered it to panic as I heard the distant thunder of the engines and looked out of the cabin window to see the expanse of water that had already separated us from the land. It was only then that it truly hit me what I had done. I was running away. I had left Maidy, and my home, and John behind. Not John himself, but his graveside, his farm, our cottage – everything I held dear was over there, in the increasing distance, the disappearing toytown of Ireland. What had I done? The panic grew stronger and I wanted to run again. Back, back, back to Kilmoy, to settle things. Perhaps it wasn't too late? Perhaps they would commission a small boat to take me back before we moved too far from land?

I rushed out of the cabin and into the narrow corridor, but there was nobody around. Everybody was on deck – watching Ireland disappear into the distance, relishing the great adventure of this transatlantic crossing.

I stood there and willed myself to calm down. I could not get off the boat. I was here now, and I would just have to go along with it. I persuaded myself that I was doing the right thing. Maidy was strong, she would cope and, in any case, she had the support of wiser women than me. I would send her a telegram from the ship – that very day I would do it, and tell her that I would be back home to her in a couple of weeks. As for the welfare of my business, it was more than safe in Katherine's capable hands. In any case I did not want to think about it, as I felt that my distraction with work might have been the cause of John's death. John is dead, he's dead – he died of a heart attack a few days ago. How many days? A week? Four days. Three, three days ago. He was buried, in a box in the ground in Kilmoy. Yammering facts, insufferable truths – urging me to fall headlong into their swirling pit of pain, snatching at my heart with their sharp claws. I would not go under. I would step aside adeptly as they swiped at me. I wouldn't – couldn't – accept that John was dead. Not now, not yet. There had to be a way to make these terrible feelings go away. I could not endure them. I did not have the wherewithal to mourn. I was too hurt, too shocked, too angry.

So I buried John for the second time that week. I took the pain of his death and locked it in a box in my mind, and resolved not to open it again until such time as I felt able. I could put things out of my mind when I had to. I had done it before, when I came to America as a young woman. I would telegram Sheila and tell her to meet me in New York – at The Plaza. It would be wonderful to see my old friend. I would enjoy this holiday and return to Ireland soon, refreshed and strengthened by this break. Then, perhaps, I might be able to grieve for my husband. I was doing the right thing in coming away as I had. Surely I was.

Over the coming days of the journey I lost myself in the routine of first-class travel. I bought myself a bathing costume in the shop, and started the day with a swim in the vast blue indoor pool on the lower deck, then went back up to my quarters, dressed and ordered breakfast in my room. I bought myself two simple day-dresses in the boutique, and a pearl hairslide for my hair. I had my bob tinted and waved, and my nails painted in the beauty salon. In the afternoons I read in the smoking lounge, taking great interest in the papers, and in the evenings I retired to my cabin again, where I took my meals, listened to the radio and read from the large selection of novels in the ship's library. I lived within the walls of the ship and did not go up on deck once during the journey. The sight of the sea seemed to compound my fear, with its never-ending grey expanse of nothing, glimmering prettily at the surface of its murky, murderous depths.

Sitting on the edge of my unmade bed in The Plaza, I plopped a perfect square of white sugar into my coffee cup and smiled as the sweet, brown liquid jumped over the sides of the china cup. For the first time since leaving Kilmoy I felt – happiness was too strong a word for it – but somewhat settled.

I closed my eyes to savour the coffee and tried to imagine that my grief was being washed to one side, with the foreignness of that first sip. As the fresh, sweet, silky liquid slid down my throat, I thought how coffee was the drink of a New Yorker. John never took to it. I grabbed onto the familiarity of the bitter taste, and rolled my mind back to my heady New York past: before John's death had plunged me into terror; the days before I had lost everything; the days before I had acquired everything to lose – the days of freedom. This trip would not bring me back my youth, or make me forget all that had happened. However, it would, I decided, offer me some distraction; a shady place where I might take shelter before the sharp, searing truth of John's death burned me from the inside out.

I knew he was dead, but I still could not look. This trip would offer me something else to capture my attention. As I placed the coffee cup back down in its saucer, I gently closed the door on my pain.

# CHAPTER TEN

I gave my key to the concierge in the lobby of The Plaza.

'How long will you be staying with us, Ma'am?' he asked.

'Some time, I think,' I said, playing the part of the confident, wealthy, independent woman. It felt good to be somebody else. I smiled at him and, in smiling, my spirits lifted. Could running away be that simple?

It was raining as I stepped outside, to the clatter of the carriages and men selling apples alongside the gates of Central Park – the streets seemed busier, more populated than I remembered. I planned to walk, but then recalled that spring showers in New York could be ferocious, so I asked the doorman to hail me a taxi to Saks Fifth Avenue. I thought it was only just around the corner, but did not want to take a chance on my memory.

I knew, from what I had read in the papers, that New York had changed. The events of 'Black Thursday', heralding the start of the 1929 stock-market crash, had made world news, although we Irish had been so poor for so long that we hardly believed it could be as bad as it was. Men throwing themselves off high bridges, because their businesses had gone bust, was not something the average Irish person could fathom. I had cashed in my American savings in 1928, four years after my return, and finally accepted that I would probably never return. A year later

I was reading about how people in New York were struggling to pay their utility bills. In the meantime, we in Ireland still had no utilities to speak of. No electricity in rural areas, and to many the telephone was still a contraption they barely believed existed. I could not dwell with any seriousness on things being 'bad' in America. However bad things were, in my own mind at least, New York would still have to fall one helluva long way to be as backward as Kilmoy!

The taxi snarled along the wide avenues. New York looked more or less the same as I remembered, but it felt unfamiliar. The shine had gone off it somehow; the swagger and celebration and excitement I had been hoping for were not here. I recognized the big stores, the same ornate architecture, but Manhattan was not as I had expected it to be; there was something missing that I could not quite put my finger on. In my memories the sun bounced off the windows of the tall skyscrapers, sending out glimmering shards of light. But now the gold on the buildings did not seem to glitter, and many of the doorways were dark, as if there were people or secrets hiding behind them, waiting in the shadows. Fashionable ladies still walked up and down Fifth Avenue, but they did not make the same stylish parade I remembered from my time here in the 1920s. Instead they walked fast, their eyes fixed on the pavement ahead of them, as though there was some unnamed menace following them.

The air inside the taxi was heavy, syrupy with the stench of warm leather and sweat and bad perfume. The driver asked me where I was from, and I told him.

'Ireland?' he said. 'Hope it ain't as tough over there as it is here. I got six kids,' he said, pointing to a faded photographic portrait on his dashboard. A family sitting stiffly in a studio, all dressed up like a bunch of Victorian gentry, except with wide American smiles. 'Wife's brother was a photographer. Lost his job last year, driving a taxi now, like me. It's not mine, you understand — working twelve hours a day and barely covering the rental.'

As he dropped me off, I tipped him generously after his tale of woe. It irritated me to do so, but I had no desire for an angry cab driver to be calling out after me in the street. As I handed the money over, he held my fingers for a moment and said, 'Well, thank you, Ma'am,' with such soft gratitude that I realized I had misjudged him and felt both guilty and pleased.

Once inside the golden doors of my favourite department store, with the bright lights glittering over an unending universe of beautiful things, I allowed myself to be transported back to the breathless wonder of my early twenties, standing in Isobel Adams' wardrobe as her new maid for the first time – the fairytale of being in a place where the real world of work, and hunger and hardship, that I had known in Ireland became almost instantly replaced by brightly coloured feathers, sparkling beads and sequins. My head had been turned by the greed for glamour, and John had never embraced this side of life as I had. To John, beauty was solely what God put before us in nature: my eyes matched in the colour of spring bluebells; the dark autumn bog reflected in the colour of my hair. I could see beauty in what he saw, but it never worked the other way around. John refused to appreciate my love of good design and modernity. There was a prick of prideful defiance as I realized that I was here on my own terms now, in the heartland of distraction and the foolishness of 'female frivolity' – as he saw it. This was, I decided, where I belonged on this day, bathed in the beautiful golden lights of money and style. I had found my antidote, and for the next few hours gave myself over entirely to the distraction of shopping.

I stopped at every cosmetic stand, sampling rouge and lipstick and creamy pansticks to cover my freckled Irish complexion. I allowed myself to be sprayed with perfume samples at every turn, then went to the lingerie department and bought a foundation garment to smooth out my figure. The choice of outfits was vast: I fingered fur stoles, and patent bags, and scarves of a silk so light and soft they were all but indiscernible to the touch. As I had been unpacking that morning I had realized that all the costumes and clothes I so valued in Ireland either seemed to me too plain or reminded me of times when I had dressed for John. My husband had no interest in fashionable clothes; dressed hair and make-up did not impress him, but rather served only as a reminder of the time I had been away in New York, leading my life without him. I had kept myself smart nonetheless. Perhaps, I realized with a stab of guilt, to cruelly remind him of that very fact, but more often to keep hold of that part of myself that I believed was chic and discerning.

In the end I purchased two outfits, one for day – a green polka-dot dress, with a large cream bow that sat flat across my breast – and, for the evening, a cerise-pink gown that fell to just above my calves, with handkerchief sleeves and a chiffon underskirt that was just visible below the hem. A deep-navy belted coat with a wide skirt, and matching navy shoes and bag, would do for both outfits.

As I swung out of the doors back onto Fifth Avenue I felt curiously tired. The experience of shopping had consumed me so utterly that it had left me feeling drained and ill at ease. The rain had cleared and the air smelt so fresh, after the heavily perfumed atmosphere of the store, that I decided to walk back to the hotel. I swung my two bags at my sides, as if deliberately trying to fuel my limbs into a feeling of light-heartedness to suit the sunny day and my carefree girl-about-town demeanour. I needed something else, some other task to distract me. As I reached Grand

Army Plaza at 59th Street I decided to call up to the apartment building of my old employer, and see if cross old Mr Flannery was still on the door. What an excellent idea! What would he make of me now? Little Ellie Hogan, the green edge gone off her, a proper lady, surely!

I walked right past the big gold general on horseback, straight through to the park, and turned right. Past the zoo and down the tree-lined mall, on to the glorious bandstand, where Sheila and I, two young girls, picnicked on summer days. The memories hopped alongside me like a talkative child, but as I tried to scoop them up, the specifics slipped away and left me with only the broad idea that back then I was happy; that it took little more than a clement day and a new dress to make everything bad melt away. I needed Sheila here to make the past real, to bring it back properly.

I had telegrammed my old friend from the boat telling her when I was arriving, and expected there might even be a reply from her when I returned to The Plaza. She would travel up from her home in Boston and stay for perhaps a week, or maybe more, with me there. Her husband was wealthy and she had no children, so she would be at leisure to entertain me, as she had always promised in her letters. We would walk in the park and things would be as they were before. There would be afternoon tea dances, and nights out in jazz clubs; we would shop and talk, and my oldest friend – silly, vivacious Sheila – would help me forget. Her jokes would swipe away the gnawing ache that kept creeping up on me, troubling me, making me feel ill at ease. She would soothe the pain and complete my denial.

I walked and walked, past the lake and the boathouse (where we had taken out small rowing boats in the company of some nameless young men who had fawned over us both), and on towards the old reservoir. But the grand tree-lined lake I had been expecting to see was gone. In its place was a field of flat, grey earth – scattered with men and machinery digging in the distance. It was such an ugly sight among the beauty that I was pulled out of my private thoughts and stopped to look and see what was going on. I tried to get my bearings and couldn't. Three shabbily dressed men were sitting on a makeshift bench of rocks and wooden planks.

'Hey, lady,' one of them said, 'looking good today.'

They weren't drinking and they didn't quite have the ravaged faces of street bums, but they weren't workers, either. One of them wore a dusty suit, a grubby white shirt and a tie poking up from beneath the upturned collar.

'Got a cigarette?' he asked.

I ignored him and, gripping tightly onto my Saks bags, kept walking. The atmosphere of the park had changed. There was an air of, not menace exactly, but something else – something I recognized? *An unpleasantly familiar reminder of something I had forgotten.*

Further along I noticed a small grouping of makeshift shacks in a corner behind a huge, grand building that I guessed must be the Metropolitan Museum. A gang of young boys stood at its edges, and one of them pushed forward and stood in front of me, brazenly asking once again, 'Got a cigarette, lady?'

A woman's voice called out from one of the shacks, 'Hey – Jake! Stop bothering people. I've told you before!' Her accent was Irish, although tainted with the tempting American twang I had gone home with. Kerry, perhaps?

The boy looked at me, annoyed to have his begging interrupted, before getting out of my path and going back to the shack to his mother.

A young girl, no more than twelve, sat on a park bench nearby, listlessly watching the drama. She was wearing dirty clothes and a broken, hopeless expression.

*Poverty. That was the thing I remembered.* I had read in a paper over breakfast on the boat how the Hooverville homeless settlement in the dried-out Central Park Reservoir had been cleared some years before, to make way for the new Great Lawn. That must have been the expanse of earth I had just seen being planted. This suburb of four or five shacks had surely sprung up in its wake, to house the most desperate of families. Trying to survive the Great Depression, hungry, their children cadging cigarettes from strangers. Uprooted by city officials so that they could plant flowers and shrubs in their place. A few of them were hiding away in this dark corner, tolerated perhaps by guilty authorities who knew they had nowhere else to go.

For all that I pitied these unfortunates, I was upset to have had my fantasies crudely interrupted by their plight. Without looking back, I quickened my step until I reached the next gate and walked back out onto the street. The day was still dry and bright, but as I turned left, the Saks bags felt suddenly heavy in my hands and my spirits were tainted with the memory of hunger.

# CHAPTER ELEVEN

820 Fifth Avenue had not changed so much. The red carpet and awning outside were faded, but the grand entrance with its filigree doors did not seem as intimidating as it had done when I had first arrived here as a young girl of twenty in my torn coat and with my small cardboard case to join my school friend Sheila in service to the spoilt socialite Isobel Adams.

I suppose it was foolish of me to expect old Mr Flannery to still be on the door after all these years.

A much younger man, thirty perhaps and handsome in a dark Italian way, headed me off as I reached the entrance.

'Can I help you?' he asked, but his attempt at officious authority was loosened considerably as he looked me up and down. He was not appraising my wealth, but my feminine form. Irish men never looked at women like that, at least not in such an obvious way.

'I used to work here,' I said, 'for Isobel Adams?'

His stiff doorman's demeanour relaxed and he leaned against the awning post and crossed his arms. I was a mere servant like him, and he could expose me to all his laddish charms after all.

'Is that so?' he smiled, and shook his head. 'Well, I've never heard of her.'

Isobel's respectable husband must have given her the flick,

or perhaps he had finally persuaded her to move to the family home in Boston.

'What about Mr and Mrs Flannery? Old couple, Irish?'

He took out a packet of cigarettes from inside his coat pocket.

'You from Ireland? You got a cute accent. Cigarette?'

He held out the pack and I shook my head. As if I would stand smoking in the street, like a lounge-girl. I was sorry now that I had dropped my act of being a grand lady.

'Mr Flannery used to be the doorman here.'

'You staying around for long, Pretty? I could show you around.'

He drew on the cigarette and blew smoke in showy rings. This cheeky lizard was so sure of himself, so different from the respectful, formal demeanour of Mr Flannery.

'They were an older couple – well, I suppose they've moved on.' I turned to leave. 'Thank you for your time.'

'Wait,' he said, and threw his cigarette on the floor and stubbed it out right there on the carpet (small wonder it was looking so shabby). 'The old guy that was here before me was a Paddy, he was here for twenty years or more – fierce old bastard?'

'A respectable gentleman,' I said haughtily, 'that was him.'

'Yeah, that,' he said, cowed somewhat. 'Anyway, he died – that's how come I got to be here.'

I must have looked shocked, because his voice softened and he said, 'Hang on, Pretty, I'll go inside and see if I can find out what happened to his old lady.'

I stood for a moment and waited. It was lunchtime and the road along the park had quietened down. From the upstairs window of Isobel's apartment I remembered seeing right into Central Park – the world from up there was green and lush, the sky close and, in the spring and summer at least, relentlessly blue. In calling on the Flannerys in this way I was seeking reassurance that things had not changed. It seemed that everything had changed. Except for the fact that I felt as helpless and as far away from home as I had done the first time I stood on Fifth Avenue as a budding domestic servant. There was no beautiful view from down here, just railings and pavements and cars. People were going about their business, and I had no other business to attend to except grieving for my dead husband or waiting for the boy to come back and give me news of the Flannerys. So I waited.

'You're in luck, Pretty,' he said, 'old Sam in the basement says Paddy's old lady is living just around the corner – working in a laundry or something? Anyways – I wrote it down . . .'

I thanked him and quickly took the piece of paper from his lingering, outstretched hand, walking away before he started up his flirting again.

Time was, I thought, when I might have swung my hips for him, just for the sake of it. However, the years that had passed since I last walked on this street made it seem like a lifetime ago, and the girl I once was like a stranger.

The mystifying nature of New York building numbers had not changed. The street was easily found and was, indeed, only just around the corner from plush Fifth Avenue, but it was lined with down-at-heel brownstones, each with their crossing fire-escapes and multiple ground-floor, first-floor and basement entrances as confusing as the next. After several fruitless attempts at finding the address, a harried-looking woman at an anonymous apartment door, rollers in her hair and with a worn, angry face, nodded to the left and said, 'Basement – next door,' when I showed her the piece of paper in the doorman's scrawled hand.

Ming's Chinese Laundry was not marked on the street. As I walked down the narrow steps I could feel the heat of the steam, and the smell of bleach and blue rising up from the open door.

Behind the counter sat a small Chinese man, almost invisible behind shelves of piled-up sheets.

'Help you, lady?' he said, barely looking up.

'Does Mrs Flannery work here? Mrs Bridie Flannery?'

Behind him was the crush of a sweatshop. Dozens of small Asian men and women worked in a toiling assembly line of machinery. Among the hiss of steam irons, the one open door to the front greedily grabbed the heat and sent it out into the alley in a boiling cloud. It felt as if I was at the gates of hell and I half-prayed he would say he had never heard of her.

'What you want her for?' he asked.

Oh dear God! I strained to look and see if I could see her.

'I'm her daughter,' I said firmly. 'I am in town unexpectedly and I . . .'

'She not got daughter,' he said, eyeing me with deep suspicion.

'Her niece, then,' I said. I stood and stared him out. Could Mrs Flannery, the fierce old Cork housekeeper who had taken me in and minded me in those early years, really be working here in this terrible place? 'Listen, I have come all the way from Ireland to see her. Just five minutes. Ellie Hogan. Tell her Ellie Hogan is here to see her.'

I put my bags down on the floor to indicate I was going no-where.

'Come back at three o'cloh,' he said. 'She on break then.'

I checked my watch – it was ten to three – then snatched a pen and cleaning ticket from his desk, before he could object, and wrote my name on it.

'I'll wait outside,' I said, 'and give her this before she comes up.'

I sat on the top step of the basement and waited, smoking cigarettes like a hooker. To hell with decorum, I thought, to hell with everything. I was angry. Mr Flannery was dead and Bridie was working in a laundry. This was not what I had hoped for,

for them or for me. It was depressing, and part of me wished I had never bothered on this stupid quest. I had been looking to escape from misery, not find more! Although, I was irritated to realize, I felt more of a sense of relaxed freedom sitting smoking on those laundry steps than I had swanning around Saks. For those ten minutes I hoped it was a different Mrs Flannery who would come up the steps to meet me, and I could go back to The Plaza and resume my luxuries.

And it was a different Mrs Flannery.

The plump, capable woman – the mother figure who had reminded me in her substantial build (if not her cross nature) of Maidy – was much reduced. I felt a pang of pity as I saw her walk towards me, recognizing the same brown Sunday coat and hat, which she was now barely able to fill. The clothing aside, I would not have recognized the hearty woman I had left just over ten years ago.

'Well?' she said.

As soon as she spoke, my heart warmed and I was glad I had waited. She was as gruff as ever. The fight might not yet have gone out of her entirely.

'Bridie – I am so sorry to hear about Mr Flannery.'

Such was my respect for her late husband that I realized I did not even know his Christian name. As young servants, Sheila and I had called him 'Grumpy'. Mrs Flannery had called him much, much worse.

'I only have half an hour,' she said, 'so you can put that cigarette out and come upstairs for your lunch. It's only soup, but you're not starved, by the cut of you.'

I smiled, following her in the front door of the building and to a tiny room on the third floor. I was thrilled to be in familiar company, and I clung to that fact so as not to let her see how appalled I was by the conditions in which I had found her.

The room was small, with a bed at one end, a table, a chair and a makeshift stove at the other. She had to go out to the hall way to a shared toilet to get water to fill the kettle. Aside from the small size and lack of facilities, I was relieved to note that the room was spotless and that she had not lost her house-proud ways. While she was gone, I put the stove on under the pot of soup, buttered two slices from a packet loaf, and found bowls and side plates from one of only two cupboards. My stomach shrank with the meagreness of the contents. All the things they had acquired over their years together, gone. It was one thing to be young and poor, as I had been, but quite another when you were old.

'I see you've made yourself at home,' she said when she came back in with the kettle. She was pleased about the company. We sat – I on the edge of the bed, and she on the one chair against the table – and I coaxed the story out of her.

Mr Flannery had died unexpectedly after a bout of pneumonia only three years beforehand. Shortly after that, Isobel Adams had, indeed, returned to Boston and, after thirty years of service to the family, Mrs Flannery had been let go. There was no pension for those in service, but it was understood that – with their living expenses having been catered for over a long period of time – both she and her husband had been well paid over the years and had made ready for a comfortable retirement. After her husband passed away, Bridie had even harboured some dream of returning to her native Cork. Mr Flannery had always managed the money side of things, but when Bridie had gone to the bank and made enquiries, she discovered that the money he had securely put aside for their pension was, in fact, in risky stock, and they had lost the lot. Even the rent on the apartment they had lived in for the past twelve years was in arrears. Too proud to approach Mr Adams for help, Bridie had sold all their belongings to clear the rent, then secured herself a job in the local laundry.

'I'm lucky,' she said. 'I could have been out on the streets, like those poor devils over in the park.'

There was no time left for my news before she had to rush back to work.

She allowed me to help her down the basement steps. It was easier coming up than going down, she said.

I could hardly bear to part with her there. I wanted to do something for her, give her some money, but I knew enough that my charity would only offend her.

'I'm meeting Sheila in the next few days,' I said brightly. 'Perhaps we could come and take you for tea?'

'That wretched flibbertigibbet,' she said. 'I've no desire to see that girl!'

I smiled at the memory of Sheila's cheek and old Bridie trying to keep her in her place.

'Well, perhaps I'll come again and take you out? Do you have a day off when I can call for you? Sunday perhaps?'

She did not ask where I was staying, or why I was here, just shook her head slowly, her voice hard and careful.

'I think it's best not. You've seen me now, girl, be content with that.'

I would call again, although in truth I did not want to. I had come to New York to be made content, to feel free and happy again.

My feet and bags felt heavy and I took a taxi back down to The Plaza, even though it was a short walk away, then went back up to my room and lay down on the soft, silk coverlet. I couldn't sleep and I was too afraid to cry. Paralysed, I read my crime novel and waited for Sheila's telegram.

# Chapter Twelve

Sheila arrived on a lunchtime train from Boston. She insisted I did not come and meet her at Grand Central, but waited instead in the Palm Court of The Plaza.

I spent the morning getting ready, meticulously applying my make-up, and curling and recurling my hair until it was lacquered into set curls around my face. I tried on everything in my limited wardrobe, and settled on the green dress I had bought in Saks. Sheila was even more passionate about her appearance than I was, and it was she who had ignited my interest in fashion, cutting my long, dark hair into a bob when I had first arrived here, borrowing clothes from Isobel's wardrobe and dragging me off to dances and jazz clubs in feathers and froth – partners on the glorious adventure of girlish glamour and romance.

Sheila had fallen in love with and married a wealthy man, Alex Ward, a decent, kind person. The Wards were Irish and had a large company manufacturing and fitting windows in the building boom of the 1920s, and Sheila and I had worked in their typing pool for a while. Alex doted on Sheila, and while she undoubtedly loved him, I often worried that her feelings for him were rooted in him constantly indulging her whims for finery and excitement. I had wondered how long it would be after they got married before he expected her to settle. In one of her letters Sheila had hinted that she had managed to avoid getting pregnant through her own design: *'There are all kinds of ways available here, Ellie, you can't imagine, and the doctors act with complete discretion. Alex says he wants a child, but I am certain he would despise my getting fat and going through all that hardship as much as I would!'*

By midday I was dressed and fidgety with excitement. I decided to go downstairs early and wait for my friend.

I checked my appearance in the mirrored panels of the elevator. My lips were plump and red, my skin white and my eyes darkened with grey kohl. I tried to admire what I saw, step into the armour of style and beauty that I had created, but I was unconvinced by my attempts. I looked like an elegant version of myself, but it was an artifice. Sheila would make it feel real. She would bring me back to who I was, who I used to be.

I gave my name to the concierge and he seated me in a quiet corner of the Palm Court. There was a small scattering of people taking tea in discreet couples, and the murmur of low conversation and tinkling china drifted across the vast ballroom. Pale light shone through the glass-domed ceiling, making the white linen tablecloths almost glow.

I had finished my book the night before and asked the waiter to bring me the newspaper. Adolf Hitler had become Führer of Germany; a prisoner had drowned trying to escape from a newly opened prison, Alcatraz; and New York's Public Works Administration was pushing forward plans to build new apartments for slum-dwellers on a site in Williamsburg. A few months ago I had devoured the *Reader's Digest* through my regular subscription, entering the worlds of other people, other places – the hysterics of politics and disasters from the comfort of my small, rural life. Now I just had the dull sense that the world kept turning:

men in uniforms were starting political movements; cops were chasing Bonnie & Clyde across America; somebody saw the Loch Ness Monster in Scotland; dock-workers were on strike in San Francisco; yet here I sat, apart from it all – a painted, paper flower, too delicate to move, knowing that events were unfolding, but remaining utterly detached from it all.

Only one thing in the paper caught my interest – an advertisement for the film *Cleopatra* by Cecil B. de Mille, showing at the Paramount Theatre in Times Square. We could go there tonight, Sheila and me, then find the small Italian bistro we used to frequent – the one with wine bottles as candle-holders and gingham tablecloths and a shebeen out the back where the dock-boys drank during Prohibition. What a plan!

'Ellie!'

I heard her shout from across the room. Sheila looked just as she had when I had left her. Slim, her short red hair smoothed into sharp points at her cheekbones, a tight houndstooth coat screaming across the room.

I stood up and we ran towards each other. Our embrace was warm and effusive, and we kissed and hugged and squealed until our voices clattering across the discreet company made everyone turn to look.

Eventually she dragged me over to the table and said, 'Tell me everything. *Everything!* Why are you here? How long are you here for? I don't care – you're here and I am *beyond* thrilled. Oh, I am so, so excited to see you, Ellie. No, wait: tell me nothing yet until I light a cigarette. I want to hear *every* word. I am *enthralled* to hear your news!'

She rooted in her bag and took out a cigarette while I signalled a waiter for more coffee. Then she lit the cigarette with a large gold lighter, holding it expertly between her puckered red lips, narrowing her eyes as the smoke drifted across them, and put her elbows on the table, her gloved hands under her chin and said, 'Now you have my fullest attention – shoot!'

I had not told her in my telegram that John was dead. I did not want to tell her now.

My oldest, closest, dearest friend – I did not want to say it out loud and spoil our reunion.

'John died.'

'Oh,' she said, and for a moment I thought I had offended her. She put the cigarette in the ashtray and reached her gloved hands across to mine. 'Oh, Ellie, my dearest, dearest Ellie. Are you terribly upset?'

How could I begin to describe it? The two words as I had said them had reached down into the depths of my gut and clutched at me like claws, pinching pain out of me. I wasn't ready. Not ready to drag it all up and spread it out on the table in front of us. Not here. Not now.

'I can see you are,' she said, holding my hands tighter.

I slid them away from her grasp and reached across to her packet of cigarettes, taking one and lighting it. I dragged on it deeply, and allowed the smoke to camouflage my pain in its pretty white cloud.

'So I came over here on a holiday – to see you and to try to . . .'

'Forget?' She finished my sentence.

I couldn't confess to it, but she was right. I worked hard to hold her concerned eyes, filled as they were with kind pity. Briefly I saw us locked into my hotel room, with me weeping and screaming and letting out all the poison and the pain I had been storing up, while Sheila ministered to me with kind words and her unique brand of plucky strength.

'I . . .'

I was at a crossroads, and I knew Sheila would follow me down any path I chose to take.

'You look *wonderful*, Sheila. Really, it is so good to see you – the coat?'

Sheila closed her eyes, smiled briefly to herself and when she opened them said, 'Schiaparelli, darling – it cost Alex a bloody fortune and, frankly, I think the cut rather ordinary – I am beginning to suspect the boutique I bought it from was passing shoddy clothes off to fools like me, who want to dress like a European! Boston is really so parochial. And here we both are, back in New York. Oh, Ellie – let's have some *fun*!'

That night we eschewed the film, but easily found Tullio's, the Italian restaurant we had eaten in every week while we were working in Ward Windows' office. The office building itself was gone, Sheila told me, when I suggested that we call in.

'The building business in New York collapsed – no money in windows any more, it seems.' She hurriedly lit a cigarette in the back of the taxi. 'I don't want to talk about all that end of things – I leave it to Alex. Money, money, wretched money: it's all anybody ever talks about these days. Such a bore!'

She didn't offer any more information on the subject, and I didn't ask. I quietly hoped her husband's business affairs hadn't suffered too much in recent times. Especially not while he had Sheila to look after.

We found that Tullio's was still run by the same family, and we sat at the same red banquette with the same gingham table-cloths, and it seemed to me that it was the same bottle with the same red candle dripping clumps of wax down the sides that had always been there. The fat old Italian mama in the family-run kitchen brought us out two huge plates of spaghetti and meat-balls, carrying us back entirely to our past as two unmarried young women working in downtown Manhattan.

We reminisced eagerly about those days: her clever nabbing of a wealthy husband, my brief indiscretion with Charles Irvington, the shipping magnate's son. 'He was *mad* about you, Ellie: remember how we met him that night in this very spot – your millionaire admirer, drinking out the back with dockers! Thank God Prohibition is over . . .' she added, pouring us both another glass from our second bottle of deep red wine, 'although, I must confess drinking *was* more fun when it was illegal.'

We talked about our schooldays in the Jesus and Mary Convent in Mayo – one or two of the nuns had died, I told her – and then she regaled me with a much more interesting anecdote of what had become of our first employer, Isobel Adams.

'She was quite a different kettle of fish towards me when I turned up one night to a party in her house.'

'*No!*' I said, disbelieving.

'Oh yes,' she said, sliding the cigarette out of her mouth with great aplomb, 'you can't imagine how thrilled I was to be introduced to her formally by a mutual friend. Her face!' Sheila looked around as if afraid she would be overheard, and then whispered, 'It *seems* we shared a lover.'

Her eyes narrowed as she slyly studied my face for shock. I was shocked, but not so surprised, and in any case I hid it well. We were having such a lovely time, and the wine was warming me, and I felt happy for the first time since . . . so I simply said, 'I don't believe you.'

'Oh – he chose me over her, it seems. She's aged badly, Ellie . . .'

'But she can't have been that much older than us?'

'Too thin, and quite dowdy, since moving back from New York and in with that ghastly old husband of hers. Turns out he's a real boring old toad – very rich, of course, but fat and so *dull*. I felt rather sorry for her actually.'

I had met Mr Adams only once during my time working for

his wife in their Fifth Avenue apartment. Bridie Flannery had always described her male employer in hushed tones. '*A real gentleman, Mr Adams is. Old money, but no airs – the only stupid thing he ever did in his life was marry that idiot upstairs.*'

'Oh, guess who I went to see yesterday?' I said.

I told her about old Mrs Flannery and her predicament, and while Sheila pretended to listen, I could tell she was disinterested in news of the old lady.

'I told her we might call up and take her for tea one day? It would be such a treat for her.'

'That aul' bitch – no, thank you,' she said. 'She was perfectly *horrible* to me when I worked for Isobel.' Then she added as a courtesy, 'Of course, I am sorry for her trouble.'

We talked only about the past from then on, and touched rarely on what had happened to us both in the years in between. My success in business, her success in social circles, news of our families, the health and wealth of our marriages we left for another day. She planned to stay with me at The Plaza for two full weeks. There was plenty of time to fill in all the details in the coming days. For the time being our fond remembering helped me to forget – and I was content with that.

# Chapter Thirteen

With Sheila there to amuse me, my efforts to distract myself were cemented. For the next few days we shopped, took lunch in various hotels and restaurants, and in the evenings after dinner we retired to my room in The Plaza, where we talked and sat easily in each other's company. We read magazines and gossiped about the film stars of the day. We tried on each other's clothes, and played with our hair and make-up as we had done as girls. In those first few evenings I was comforted by the familiarity of Sheila's voice, the smell of her perfumed skin in the bed beside me. The intimacy of our friendship mimicked the intimacy of my marriage. We were so happy to see each other again, it was a type of falling in love.

As the week went on, however, Sheila's mood towards me changed.

On the fourth day she had seemed somewhat unsettled in herself. She had snapped at a young shop assistant who was trying to fit her with a hat, and had barely touched any food all day, only puffed on cigarettes constantly. In the afternoon she stopped at a pharmacy and bought a bottle of decongestant medicine that she sprayed up her nose (in a most unladylike fashion) immediately we got out onto the street. She staggered backwards slightly, laughing, then seemed to think about offering some to me before putting it in her bag. She had no symptoms of a cold and, when I pressed her about it, she said sharply, 'My ailment is boredom, Ellie.'

I didn't know what she meant, except that I must be boring her. Sheila immediately pushed the cruelty aside, saying, 'Darling Ellie – let's go and annoy the girls on the perfume counter at Saks again.' She was markedly jolly for the rest of the afternoon, although it was a while before I noticed her furtive sniffs from the medicine and realized she was getting high. I felt such a fool for assuming she was ill that I said nothing. This was some new fashionable behaviour, no doubt, that her hick Irish friend was unaware of.

As I collected my key, the girl behind the desk handed me a card. For a moment I became excited, imagining it was a letter from Katherine, or Maidy. But there was no envelope, only a square of expensive card with elongated black lettering. Beneath today's date it read: '*Solomon R. Guggenheim Collection of Non-Objective Paintings*. Solomon Guggenheim invites you to view six new works by the artist Wassily Kandinsky in his private suite.'

Sheila was craning to read it and, as I handed it to her, she exploded with excitement.

'Oh my goodness, Ellie – Solomon Guggenheim!'

'There must be some mistake,' I said to the concierge. 'I don't know this man.'

'It's a public viewing, Madam,' he said pointedly, looking at Sheila, who was hopping about with pure pleasure, 'although this is a rather exclusive preview for Plaza guests only.'

'Will Solomon himself be there?' Sheila asked, trying and failing to attain some measure of decorum in her voice.

'I have no idea, Ma'am,' he replied. He looked from me to Sheila, taking in the measure of us both. Much as I was embarrassed by my friend's sudden burst of energetic keenness, I did not like his snobbish attitude, especially not towards a paying customer. I took my key from the desk and walked away without thanking him.

We took the lift to Guggenheim's private suite, presenting our invitation to the uniformed boy as we entered. I had dressed plainly in an expensive navy dress, while Sheila was wearing a trouser suit.

'It will be an "arty" crowd,' she had exclaimed as we were preparing for our outing. 'We must looked elegant, but under-stated, Ellie – on *no* account are you to wear the green polka dots!' Her frothiness had begun to grate on me, and I tried to push back my growing reservation that spending so much time in her company had been a mistake.

'I wonder who will *be* there? Oh, come on, Ellie – you look as glum as a nun!'

Sheila would not stop talking, and far from cheering me up as I had hoped, her incessant babbling and all her nervous energy was having the opposite effect on me. As she was fixing my hair I felt suddenly tired and craved the release of sleep: the escape, the solitude of it.

'There,' she said, clipping the pearl hairslide to one side of my bob, 'all done.'

The navy dress seemed black in the muted lamplight of the hotel room and, decorated only with a simple set of beads, I looked dressed in mourning. With the sight of my features set in, I forced a smile and said, 'Let's go.'

The lift opened straight into the foyer of the Guggenheim apartment. It was large, but not nearly as ornate as I had been expecting. Sparsely decorated with white panelled walls and occasional tables and chairs, all squared off in black and glass lines, its symmetry was reinforced here and there with mirrored panels.

The paintings themselves stood out in colourful contrast, which, I supposed, was the idea. It was just eight o'clock and there were perhaps a dozen people milling around, taking wine glasses from uniformed waiters.

'I don't see Solomon here,' said Sheila, looking about her for fellow social butterflies, her eyes flicking over my shoulder to see what fresh blood might be coming out of the lift.

I stood and looked at the nearest painting. It was a series of triangles and lines, mathematical forms thrown together in mashed shapes. It made no sense to me, but I found the bright colours – blues, reds, yellows – and the clean black lines that joined them, strangely hypnotic.

'Oooh, look,' Sheila said, '*men!*'

She walked off, but I didn't follow her. I wondered what the painting meant and took a step back, almost colliding with another observer – a woman of about my age. She wore a large black dress-coat with a wide purple shawl collar.

'It's hypnotic, isn't it?'

Her accent was foreign, German perhaps, but with the tinge of American that everyone seemed to pick up, after even the shortest time living in New York.

'Yes,' I said, 'what is it, do you suppose?'

'With Kandinsky one can never be quite certain; he is as much of a prophet as an artist, but the colour – the shapes – the perfect, exciting geometry of it – that is enough in itself to enjoy, I think, without learning what is behind it. Hilla Reband,' she said and held out her hand. 'I'm the curator.'

'Ellie Hogan,' I said.

'Do you like art?'

We stood for a few moments and had a most interesting

conversation. She was Mr Guggenheim's art advisor, she said – and an artist herself. She had hopes that the philanthropist would open a gallery at some point in New York, so that the wider public could share the collection that she was helping him build. As she talked I became enthralled by her, not so much by what she was saying, her academic style of speaking, but by her confidence, her sense of purpose. As she was excusing herself to move on and mingle, she passed by Sheila, who, unaware of her importance, gave the artist a blunt and disinterested look.

'Come on, Ellie – we're going,' she said, taking my arm.

'But we've just got here.'

'This is Eric and . . .'

Two men had joined us.

'Geoff,' the older one said, holding out his hand and grinning.

I didn't like the look of them. Although they were impeccably dressed in smart evening suits and silk scarves, I knew by the cut of them they were typical Good-Time-Charlies, and Sheila's eyes were glittering with excitement and adventure.

'Eric and Geoff are taking us to El Morocco!'

'The nightclub,' Eric chortled, 'not the country.'

I was not in the mood for exploring New York nightlife.

'Excuse me,' I said, taking Sheila aside. 'I'd really just rather stay here for an hour, then go to bed,' I said. 'I'm tired – and we don't know them.'

'Oh, for God's sake, Ellie – you are such a *bore*. Fine, I'll go by myself.'

I couldn't let Sheila walk off into the night with two strange men, and was irritated that she still had the same shallow de-sires, the same irresponsible urges that had got us into so much trouble in our twenties.

'Come on, Ellie.' She squeezed my arm, seducing me as she always could. 'It's the most exclusive club in Manhattan – all the stars will be there. We'll dance and have fun – never mind those two, we'll drop them as soon as we're there.'

I looked over at Geoff and Eric, loitering and confiding like schoolboys. Waiting for the fun-loving girl's sensible friend to give the green light to their lascivious intentions.

'I've checked them out – Geoff has an apartment here, and they are both *very rich*,' she whispered in my ear, 'and so they'll surely behave like gentlemen. Come on, Ellie, what harm can it do?'

She was right. We were in New York, the night was young and it had been so long since I had danced or listened to jazz. I wasn't an innocent child any more, and this was, after all, why I was here: to enjoy myself and forget.

'Come on then,' I said.

Geoff was the older man, in his mid-forties perhaps and not as dashing or handsome as his younger friend, Eric. He had his own car and driver waiting outside, but made a point of opening the car door for me himself, then guided Eric to sit opposite us in the back of the luxurious, leather-seated limousine. The car pulled up outside and our host thanked the doorman by name, then ushered us straight past the awning and inside. At the door Geoff made a show of having booked his 'usual booth', then stepped aside to let us ladies walk before him into the club. It was a small act of courtesy to impress on us his gentlemanly status, but for all that it was contrived, I found his good manners nonetheless somewhat comforting.

The older man sat next to me in the booth, keeping a respectable distance and offering me a cigarette from his gold case, before taking one himself. He asked me questions about myself, but I revealed very little, as did he. I didn't mind. I wasn't remotely interested in him, beyond the fact that I had been dragged along by Sheila, who was already flirting with Eric, whispering in his ear and giggling. Both men were undoubtedly married (although neither of them wore rings), but I did not feel we were in depraved company. This was 1934 after all – modern times – and we were just four people enjoying a night out.

The place was lively, with a buzzing crowd listening to fast jazz, and the walls were covered in the distinctive black-and-white zebra print that was familiar to me from society photographs in *Vanity Fair* magazine. I decided to relax thoroughly and allow myself the pleasure of feeling as if I had 'arrived'. I was back in the place I had always loved – the world of society and fashion that I had tried to re-create in the elegance of my small apartment – I was here again at its epicentre. Dancing, exotic foods, bubbling champagne, jazz music, elegant people in beautiful clothes swirling around me; sucking my shaken, uncertain centre up into a whirlpool of life.

Geoff ordered us food and champagne with great aplomb, and as it was the first time I had eaten lobster, he charmingly helped me negotiate the small silver hooks to dig out the sweet meat from the strange pink claws.

As the champagne took hold, I got the urge to dance. Geoff was an ungainly dancer, but he made me laugh. He was quite sweet, I thought, as he threw his arms up in the air in an old-fashioned Charleston, trying to impress me. We had fun. Sheila and Eric had gone from the booth when we got back. They had been canoodling in full public view while we were dancing, and although my tolerance towards Sheila's undignified behaviour was muted by the fun I was having myself, I still feared the worst. Geoff kindly demurred and went to find them. I sat on my own, picked at the tray of sweets that had been left for us, and poured myself another glass of champagne. I felt utterly happy, giddy and laughing slightly to myself at the memory of poor Geoff's dancing. Sheila had been right after all. This was what I had needed. To forget. To feel alive again.

Geoff was only gone for a few minutes, but when the three of them came back, something in the atmosphere had changed. Nothing I could quite put my finger on, but it seemed to me that they were sharing a secret. I thought perhaps that Geoff had found something out about Eric and Sheila, but they were all smiling and the younger man took my friend straight up onto the dance-floor, where they threw themselves about with almost comical speed and abandon. I felt suddenly uncomfortable at how drunk I was, and asked Geoff if he could order me some coffee. He shoved himself in closer to me on the banquette and smiled at me, rather stupidly, before clicking his finger at the hostess and calling, 'Over here! More champagne!'

I did not like the way his thigh was pressing up against mine, but I didn't want to be rude. He was just drunk, but he seemed to have changed since disappearing. 'I think it's probably time I was getting back to the hotel,' I said.

'Are you tired?' he asked, leaning in closer.

'Yes,' I said. His hand reached down beneath the table and squeezed my thigh. I felt a leap of horror, then he removed it and fumbled in his trouser pocket.

'I've got something for that.'

He took out a small box, not his cigarette case, and laid it on his lap where it couldn't be seen. He flicked it open and it was filled with white powder.

'This will liven you up, Ellie – let's keep the party going.'

It took a few seconds for it to sink in. Cocaine! I wasn't stupid. I knew about drugs, how the scourge of low society had become the recreation of high society. It had only recently been outlawed with the same vigour as had been shown during Prohibition in the 1920s.

He closed the box and put it on the table in front of him, and his hands went down again. I was frozen with fear as I felt his fat fingers move down my thighs, seeking out the hem of my skirt, sliding it up, up my legs.

'Come on, little Irish girl,' he whispered, 'relax. Look at your friend – she's having a good time.'

I tried to stand up, but his hand was pressed against my groin, searching me out. I wanted to cry. Stupid, stupid! How could I have been so reckless? I looked about me – all pretence at decorum or style seemed to have fled from the room. Everyone was drunk; people flung themselves around the dance-floor with abandon, with the Negro band blowing harder, plucking faster – egging on the rich white fools to exhibit their lust, their deranged desires. I had to get out of there. I set aside my sense of endangerment and found anger was close to hand. I pushed him away using all my strength and called out, 'NO!'

I shoved him hard, and he banged his head against the sharp edge of the banquette. People at the next table turned to see what all the fuss was about, but I didn't care. I grabbed my bag and pushed through the crowd of revellers, shoving them aside in my sober march. 'Sheila,' I shouted, heading straight across to her on the dance-floor, 'we're going!'

I grabbed her arm, but she just laughed at me. Hysterically, throwing her head back, she shook herself easily out of my grip.

'I'm not going anywhere,' she slurred, smiling. Eric grabbed her hand and pulled her, in one stoned stumble, back into their wild dance.

'Bye, Ellie – bye-di-bye . . .' she called back at me, waving and laughing, oblivious.

I was furious, everyone was looking at me and I stormed off, but as I was collecting my coat from the check-booth I realized I had to go back for Sheila. She was my friend, and I could not in all conscience leave her in that drunken state in the company of two strange men. I checked out her coat, marched onto the dance-floor and threw it over her shoulders.

'We're going back to The Plaza,' I said.

Eric was furious, but she held up her hand and whispered something to him that made him smile.

'Come on then, Ellie,' she said, 'I'll walk you out.'

As we hit the fresh air she stopped by the awning and took out a cigarette. Her coat was perched over her shoulders and she secured it with a small shrug. She seemed suddenly to have sobered up.

'I'm not coming back with you, Ellie,' she said. She showed me her profile and her eyes squinted against the black sky as she lit the cigarette. She took a deep drag, her lips tightening around it in a hard pucker.

'To tell you the truth, I've left Alex.'

'When?' I asked.

She looked at me directly. Her expression was hard, and any shred of sweetness was gone.

'When do you *think*? Just before I came to see you.'

'Why?'

'He caught me, with another man. There, I've said it. I suppose you're shocked: Miss Goody Two Shoes – I knew you wouldn't approve, that's why I kept my mouth shut.'

'You could have told me.'

'It doesn't matter, Alex is broke anyway. The marriage was dead long ago. Hence the affair.'

'Let's go back to the hotel and talk.'

Sheila stubbed out her cigarette and pulled the coat back around her shoulders again.

'I'm sorry, Ellie, but I'm going back in.' She turned on her heels.

'Sheila!'

Her name came out in a disapproving squall that made me sound like a school mistress. I hadn't meant it to sound like that. The truth was that I was frightened – for her or for myself, I wasn't sure.

'Ellie, look.' She came over and put her hand on my arm. 'You've got enough on your plate, what with John dying and . . . I know it's sad and everything, but I . . .' her eyes fell at the ground as if she was ashamed, then she lifted her chin in defiance, '. . . well, I can't be miserable, Ellie. I need to have fun, I need to feel alive. Eric and Geoff—'

'But you don't even know them!' I protested.

'How well do we know anyone really, Ellie? I know their type – they have money, and they are generous with it and just want to enjoy themselves. I'm pretty sure they're harmless, and anyway, Ellie, I can handle myself well enough. Really, you are such a square. I am going back in.'

She turned on her heels and left me there. I felt as if I had been slapped in the face. Despite that, part of me still wanted to follow her and warn her about Geoff's behaviour towards me, but even as I thought it, I realized how prim it would sound. *'He put his hand on my leg.'*

*'You are such a square, Ellie!'*

Sheila could look after herself, and although I had hoped she would look after me too, it seemed I had been wrong.

A crowd had gathered around me at the edge of the awning in their shimmering evening coats and tuxedos, waiting to go in. I stood to one side to let them pass, alone, shaken, prim and shockingly sober. For a moment I envied Sheila's wilful abandon, but I had no desire to go back in and join her.

# CHAPTER FOURTEEN

There were taxis pulling up along the road, but I needed to clear my head, so I decided to walk back to the hotel. The night air was fresh and the streets were well lit, so I started up East 54th Street towards the park.

I was wide awake with anger and confusion. I didn't know when Sheila would come back to the hotel, and had made no arrangements about keys. Or if, indeed, she would come back at all. I had come looking to her for comfort, and she had betrayed me in her selfish, self-centred way. But then, I knew what Sheila was like, so why had I travelled all the way across the world to follow a stupid dream?

More annoying was the fact that I was still worried about her and what fate might befall her at the hands of those two men. Then I remembered having been in a constant state of fear for her propriety when we were younger, and what a pointless, thankless exercise that had turned out to be!

Sheila would be fine. I, on the other hand, was a widow, wandering alone around the streets of New York City in the middle of the night. It was Sheila who had abandoned me, and not the other way around.

Anger quickened my pace.

I had no idea what time it was. The sky was blue-grey, with

pencils of peach light framing the tall buildings. I thought perhaps it was nearly dawn. The shops were closed, but street sellers were already wheeling their carts. In Dublin the women in the city centre sold fruit out of children's prams, but it was the first time I had seen it here. On every street corner there were men selling apples and oranges, out of bags set on makeshift stalls of cardboard boxes, prams and wheelbarrows. Many of them seemed to be burly Irish men, the size of navvies, their faces broken with the shame of selling oranges at a dime a time to pitying passers-by – one step away from begging.

As I passed one such stall, the tang of the fresh fruit tempted me to stop. I rummaged in my bag for change, while the man minding the stall looked away, tapping his feet nervously. I assumed he was embarrassed at my making him wait for his money and cursed myself for not having the change in my pocket. I would buy two, three oranges – but as I was handing my change over, a well-dressed man stopped and, leaning across me, took an orange off the stand and walked off without paying, as easily if he were taking food from his own larder.

'Sir? You forgot to pay . . .' I called after him.

He turned to me, laughing, and waved the orange at me. He had stolen it! From a poor man, trying to make ends meet! It was an outrageous act of ignorance and cruelty – from a well-to-do! I opened my mouth to call out again and shame him, but the orange-seller put his hand on my arm to stop me.

'Leave him, lady,' he said, 'we all have to pay protection in this town, one way or another.'

Protection? I knew about the gangsters operating in this city – they had run booze through this place like water during the days of Prohibition. They came from all places, they were Irish, Italian, Polish, and I had drunk and danced with them in the speakeasies – and had known they were running on the wrong side of the law. Protection was the money they took from the bar owners to keep the police at bay. It was part of doing business in those days. Everyone drank, so everyone broke the law during Prohibition, even – especially – the police. So many of them were Irish, and who could expect an Irishman not to drink! There had always been the nasty side of crime, of course, but the gangsters were the top end of it and generally kept themselves to themselves. They made their money bootlegging and running nightclubs; they had their battles – I read about brutal shootings – but generally it was with rival gangs. You minded your business, and they minded theirs.

With Prohibition gone, clearly things had changed and they were resorting to stealing oranges from poor men.

The seller took my money and I thought about asking him where he was from and passing the time of day, but he handed me an orange and continued loading his stall. He didn't want to talk. He was just surviving – so I moved along.

The streets were not as bustling as they were during the day and for the first time I noticed that many of the shop-fronts were boarded up. Outside one of them I passed a small mountain of blankets and boxes and stopped, briefly, to investigate. As I looked down, an infant blinked up at me from among the woollen debris, its tiny face peering out from the cloister of its mother's bed. I got such a shock that I kept walking and, with each step I took, had the guilty feeling that perhaps I should go back. But to do what, exactly? Wake the woman up? Give her money? Take the child? Such a gesture seemed so vast and yet so pointless. There were clearly thousands of such unfortunates all over New York City. It wasn't my place to interfere. I had enough troubles myself, but the incident jolted me out of my anger towards Sheila and the pity I was starting to feel for myself.

We were poor in Ireland, but I had never seen a woman and child sleeping on the streets. In Dublin perhaps, but certainly never in Kilmoy; the vagrant tramps who walked the land were accommodated in family homes when the winter came. Even those in the filthiest condition were found a bed, or a barn to sleep in, once they knew what doors to knock on. I had come to New York to escape my own problems and I had not been expecting to be confronted with the problems of others. First, the terrible outcome for my old matron, Bridie, and now this human suffering – people living in shacks on the edge of the park, families sleeping in doorways; while I could not, nor did I want to, blinker myself like Sheila, I was nonetheless disappointed that the vibrant city where I had come to live as a young woman now held the same dull ache of depression and desperation that I had come to escape – then and now.

In a moment of clarity I realized that I wanted to go home.

I would return to The Plaza and ask the concierge to book me on the next passage back to Ireland. I would put this trip down to a moment of madness, a mistake. I chose not to remember what had compelled me to leave in the first place.

Lost in my thoughts, the practical details, the certainty of my decision, I did not notice that I was heading up the side of the park and onto Fifth Avenue, automatically taking the familiar route back to the place where I used to work.

I was stopped in my tracks as a small man stepped out from the railings of Central Park right in front of me. I almost jumped out of my skin. Instinctively I pulled my purse to my chest. What had I been thinking, walking along the side of the park at this time of night, when New York was surely rife with vagrant criminals, just as the taxi driver had said.

'Got a cigarette?'

It wasn't a man after all, only a young boy. I recognized him as the same one who had stood in my path the week beforehand. He was alone, and without the cheeky bravado of his gang.

'Sorry if I frightened you, lady. It's not for me – it's for my mom.'

Under the burn of the street lamp I could see he was no more than fourteen or fifteen. His face was brown with sun and dirt and his hands hung limply by his side, his shoulders slumped in the expectation of rejection. I felt suddenly furious, although I wasn't sure why. Perhaps it was the glow of expensive champagne still fizzing inside me; or my rage at Sheila for her wretched, covetous adventures; or rage at myself for following her.

'Where is your mammy?' I asked.

He turned to walk away, but I couldn't let him pass.

'Take me to your mam,' I said, grabbing his arm.

'I don't want no trouble, lady, I just want to get Mom a smoke to calm her nerves. We've had a bad day.'

'I want to help,' I said, 'take me to your mother.'

He looked me in the eye with suspicion and his face turned cold with defensiveness.

'She don't want no-one to see her down at heel. She's a lady – good as you!'

I took my cigarettes out of my bag and gave him the pack. He took one out and handed them back to me. I nodded for him to keep them, then he took a box of matches out of his pocket and lit it, dragging the first pull gratefully into his lungs.

'Thanks,' he said, stopping to study it. 'I'm sorry for what I said.'

'No problem.' I smiled at myself for falling into New York slang. 'Your mam's surely more of a lady than I am.'

He stayed silent.

'I saw you the other day in the park,' I said. 'You were living at the back of the museum.'

'They kicked us out,' he said, 'waited till dark, so they wouldn't be seen. Bastards!' His voice rose in anger. 'There was only three families in there, and we kept the place tidy – we weren't bothering nobody.'

This very boy and his little gang had bothered me and, I imagined, many other smart Sunday strollers.

'They got us out of our beds, and stood over us while we packed up. I'd have decked one of them easy, but Mom didn't want no fuss.'

He had the cigarette nearly smoked down to the butt.

'Like I said,' he took two fast drags and threw it reluctantly on the floor, 'she's a lady.'

'I'd sure like to meet her,' I said.

He looked at me again, softer this time; 'I dunno . . .'

'Hell, I'll follow you anyway.'

'Suit yourself,' he said, shrugging, but he held his step steady beside me.

All along the road I noticed that the gates to the 'people's park' were padlocked.

Roosevelt had been elected; 'The Great Depression Is Over!' the headline in the paper had read. They were gentrifying Central Park, taking it back to the haven it was before the Hooverville homeless took it over. They had promised to rehouse as many as they could in new developments on the outskirts of the city, out of view. It was business as usual, and nobody wanted to accommodate the raw despair of bodies in doorways and families in makeshift shacks. They wanted to put the bad times behind them. De Valera had promised to deliver Ireland from the jaws of our war. To put us all into whitewashed cottages and bring us back to the days when women churned butter and bred babies, and the men worked the land. I had refused to conform to this vision, despite it being my husband's fantasy. I had worked hard – not for the money alone and for the independence it brought, but also to rebel against the idea that we could return to an old-fashioned Ireland. I would not be complicit in the lie that women were mere home-makers, when my time in America had made it clear to me that we could be so much more. This situation – the stark contrast in social circumstance that I had experienced that evening – was part of the same fiction. Walking towards the steps of the museum, I felt the truth of this family's plight coursing through me, alongside an inexplicable, but none-theless urgent desire to do something about it.

The boy's mother was sitting on the steps of the museum with her head in her hands. A young girl, no more than ten, sat with her arm around her mother's shoulders comforting her; they were surrounded by bags and boxes. Daylight had not quite hit, and the dawn sky I had suspected earlier had been an illusion created by the city lights. She stood up as we reached her and I sensed she was summoning up the energy to berate her son, although the distressed expression on her face suggested that she did not have the wherewithal to do so.

In that moment I did not think about Sheila, or going home; I did not feel the dull ache of John's death, or the urgent need to avoid it. I was free from all thought or feeling other than rescu-ing this woman from the situation she had found herself in.

I held out my hands and took one of hers with unwavering kindness and said firmly, 'My name is Ellie Hogan, and I have come to help you.'

# CHAPTER FIFTEEN

The woman was Irish, like me. 'There but for the Grace of God . . .' Perhaps that was what had motivated me, or perhaps it was just another distraction. She did not take as much persuasion as her son had believed she would, but I knew that would be the case. Desperation and pride are not comfortable bedfellows. I knew what it was to be hungry and cold; to weep for the want of a meal; to linger at a kind neighbour's fire, hoping to carry home some of the heat to your own empty grate. For all that, I had never been without a roof over my head. I could not imagine the hardship of it until I saw that small family sitting with their goods and chattels on the steps of the Metropolitan Museum.

As soon as I said the words, 'I have come to help you,' I immediately began to panic about how I would follow them through. The woman must have thought I was some class of professional do-gooder; that I had a plan, or somewhere to take them. I had neither. I thought briefly about taking them back to The Plaza, but knew that it wasn't an option. I might sneak them into my room, but if the staff saw me arrive with all their goods, they would certainly know they were a vagrant family and dismiss us at the door. I was so angry at the injustice of their plight, I would certainly have fought it out, but I didn't want to put the woman through that humiliation.

I had only one other option.

'Gather up your bags,' I said, leaning down to pick up the heaviest of them, 'and follow me.'

We were not five minutes by foot from old Bridie's bedsit.

The family followed me up the steps of the brownstone and stood behind me nervously, as I rang and rang the bell on the peeling front door. Eventually the Chinese man who ran the laundry answered it, furious and cursing in his native tongue. I swept him aside, apologizing, and assertively signalled the family to follow me up the steep stairs, despite his angry protestations.

Bridie was already at the door, in her nightgown, looking out to see what all the commotion was about.

'I need your help,' I said. She was confused and still half-asleep, but stepped aside to let us in.

We crowded into the tiny room, bags and all, and stood there awkwardly. The woman looked about her, clearly thinking that if this was the best I could do, she would have been just as well off staying where she was. Her lips were tight with pride, but she said nothing. Bridie's face had a similar expression, as she had clearly only just come to and was furious at my landing in on her and exposing her unmade bed, her small private world, to strangers.

'This lady and her children need somewhere to stay,' I said, and before Bridie had the words out to object, I added, 'Do you know of a place they can rent?'

'There are rooms in the building next door,' she said. Then, looking them up and down she added, 'If they have money.'

'They have money.' I looked at the woman and nodded. She looked back at me and a hint of anger flashed in her eyes, so I winked at her and it was replaced by instant relief and gratitude.

'Well, you just got the landlord up out of his bed, and he'll not be best pleased. I'd give him an hour or so to cool down. I start work at six, so I'll talk to him then.'

'Thank you, Bridie,' I said.

'We'd better feed these children then so,' she said. 'For good-ness' sake, Ellie, pull that cover over the bed and give them somewhere to sit down. You have names, I suppose?'

I had become so caught up in my mission I had forgotten to ask.

'Maureen Sweeney,' the woman said, 'and this is Jake and Flora.'

'Maureen, eh? One of our own so,' Bridie said, then handed the kettle to the boy, saying, 'Here, lad, make yourself useful and go and fill this. The bathroom is on the next floor down.'

The old lady made porridge with tinned milk and used the last of her sugar to sweeten it, and we ate from her two bowls in rotation. She fed the mother and daughter first. Jake refused when she offered it to him, but she said, 'You'll eat it, boy, and be grateful. You need all the strength a full stomach will give you, to look after your mother.'

'Thank you, Bridie,' I said, taking the last bowl. 'I'll replace it.'

'Damn sure you will,' she said, 'and more besides, for getting me up at this ungodly hour.'

With our stomachs full and our hands warmed with the con-viviality of tea, we sat and Maureen shared her story with us, as best she could in front of the children.

Her husband was an American of Irish parentage, a profes-sional man who worked as an accounts clerk in a bank. She herself had come here as a young woman and trained as a nurse. When the children came along, they rented a fine big house in Yonkers, outside the city, and she gave up her job and they lived in great comfort. 'We were so happy,' she said. 'Patrick was a hard worker . . .'

She trailed off, girding herself against the bad news that was to come.

'As it was, I asked him to buy us a house, but we were so happy in the one we were renting, and he said our money was safer in stock. We lived frugally and went without luxuries, so we could put all but our basic living expenses into shares. "We're getting such good rates, Maureen, you'll see. Another couple of careful years and it will all be worth it," he said. Our money was growing, and Patrick would get so excited reading the papers. He'd show me the stocks-and-shares lists and tried to explain, but I didn't really understand. I trusted him. He was securing our future. When I pressed him for a washing machine or a new dress, he'd say, "Soon, Maureen – soon we'll have all the money you could ever dream of. A few months longer," he'd say, "it would be foolish to cash it in now, we'll wait."'

On Black Thursday they lost everything.

'Patrick tried to shield me from the worst of it, said his job was secure and that he would get us back on our feet.'

She spoke quietly. She didn't sound as bitter as she had a right to. She obviously loved her husband, for his motives, if not his foolishness.

'I discovered that he had lost his job in the bank, when I went to buy fish one day and found him queuing for work at the docks. He hadn't paid the rent for months, and we lost the house shortly after that. He moved into the Hooverville in the park to look for work in the city, and I took the children to California, where I was promised work as a nurse.'

Her face betrayed there was no happy ending.

'The job fell through, so I borrowed the money from a cousin to get us back to New York. When we got to where he had been living, Patrick was gone . . .'

'He'll be back, Mom.' Jake's face was burning with shame, but he stood up and looked me square in the eyes. 'Pop went off to find work and he'll be back. He'll be back with money in his pocket, and now he won't know where we are – he won't be able to find us!'

Bridie handed him a few cents from her purse.

'Whist now, boy, you're upsetting your mother. The two of you run down to the shop, it'll be open now, and bring us back a loaf. No dithering, mind!'

His mother nodded at him to do as he was told and they left. Bridie and I were enthralled by her story and were anxious for her to finish.

'There's not much else to tell. Patrick just disappeared one day, about a week before we had got back. His buddy said they had been unable to find work. Patrick had left all of his belongings behind him and just – disappeared.' Her voice cracked slightly and she paused. She closed her eyes, rallied and continued. 'Patrick's friend Joe moved us into where he had been staying, and when they cleared the reservoir, he helped set us up in the . . .' she halted over the word 'house', '. . . the place where you found us.'

Bridie and I exchanged a glance, both thinking that the worst must have happened to her husband, and we both noted that our own troubles had been dwarfed by her terrible tale.

'Mother of God! I'm late!'

Bridie leapt up from her chair, gathered herself for work and left. She came back up a few moments later, accompanied by the landlord, who said he was prepared to let us have a room.

When the children returned we followed him to the house next door and up one flight of stairs. He showed us into a filthy room: windows you could barely see out of for soot, two narrow beds, a table and two chairs and a broken cupboard. I opened it and found a dead mouse and no crockery.

'Two dollars a night,' he said. It was an astronomical rate to charge for a hovel. However, we had little choice, and he knew it.

'We'll take it,' I said and took two dollar bills out of my pocket.

'One week in advance,' he said, looking over at the mother and her waifs and holding out his hand for more.

'One night,' I said, looking at him with as much loathing as I could muster without having him turn us away, although I knew that was unlikely to happen, once he saw the weight of my purse. 'We'll pay again tomorrow.'

He snatched the dollar bills and went.

'I'm sorry, Maureen,' I said, 'it's awful.'

'It's fine,' she said. 'We'll have it fixed up in no time – won't we, children?'

Jake was already testing the bed and Flora was digging around in a bag, from where she pulled out a cleaning rag and started to wipe around the place.

'They're good children,' I said.

'I've done the best I could for them, under the circumstances.'

We stood for a moment in awkward silence. I felt she wanted to thank me, but didn't know how.

'I'll go now,' I said, 'and let you settle yourselves in. I'll be back in a few hours with some supplies.'

Maureen followed me out the door.

There was no suspicion, only curiosity and soft gratitude in her voice as she said, 'Ellie – why are you doing this for us?'

I stopped to think about it and answered her, 'Honestly, Maureen? I don't know.'

# CHAPTER SIXTEEN

I had no idea what impulse had driven me to help the Sweeneys, but it had left me feeling elated, and as I walked back to The Plaza I felt a true sense of achievement. The trees overhanging the park railings seemed greener to me than they had done before, and such was my feeling of goodwill that I found myself smiling at passers-by.

However, when I got up to my hotel room I felt suddenly exhausted. The first thing I did was check if Sheila had been back, and I found that she had. All of her belongings were gone from the room, and there was a note on the bed scrawled quickly on Plaza notepaper: '*You missed a great night! Geoff invited me up to the Hamptons for a "holiday" – here's the address, if you want to join us.*' The address was illegible. Whether she had fled my company through embarrassment or chagrin did not interest me. Certainly the other events of the night before had put her to the back of my mind. I was relieved that she was safe, but also relieved she had gone.

The bed was turned down from the evening before, the chocolates still on the pillow. I lay down on the firm mattress with its tapestry coverlet and closed my eyes, but found I could not sleep.

I had been awake for twenty-four hours, yet I felt anxious to get back to my mission.

This was ridiculous. What mission? What was I doing? What madness had overtaken me, pledging responsibility for the welfare of a whole family, getting involved in somebody else's hardship, when I had myself to look after? I had my own family back in Ireland. Maidy, would she forgive me for having abandoned her, as I had?

Sitting up in frustration with myself, I looked about the room. The luxurious curtains, the ornate black-lacquered lamps, the deep, velvety carpet – I felt my heart heave with a sadness that this was not where I wanted to be. However much good sense told me that this was where I belonged, that this was what I had earned, that the luxury and privilege of The Plaza were my rightful reward for years of work and due comfort for the terrible thing that had happened to me, it felt wrong.

I changed out of my evening clothes and put on some slacks and a light sweater. As I took them fresh from the bag I had purchased them in, I realized that they had cost me as much as a month's rent for the Sweeneys in a decent apartment. The hairslide had fallen from my hair somewhere on my travels, but I felt nothing at its loss except for the hope that somebody deserving had found it.

I packed a few of my new clothes into a bag, with the thought of giving them to Maureen, and left the hotel again.

I shopped for food in a small grocery store, then stopped at a drugstore and considered buying a few bits of inexpensive crockery. I decided against it. In all likelihood Maureen would have some already, which she had used in her ramshackle home, and I did not want to insult her pride further by suggesting that she had less than she had. As I placed the dime-store plates back on the shelf, I had a peculiar feeling that I needed Maureen's friendship more than she needed mine.

On my way into the brownstone I saw Flora playing nicely

on the steps with another girl of around her own age, and Jake standing nearby smoking the last of my cigarettes. Flora greeted me cheerfully, but the lad merely nodded at me briefly, defensive at the lack of a gang of followers, and doubtless looking to acquire new ones. He was a good kid who loved his mother, but would surely not be for much longer, if their lives did not change.

Maureen answered the door and, as I entered, I saw that while the room was far from transformed, it was clean and orderly and I was relieved to see that I had been right about Maureen salvaging things from her past life. The table was set with decent, Willow Pattern crockery, and stretched across it was a linen tablecloth – in want of a good iron, but nonetheless with pretty, hand-sewn embroidery at its hem.

'I have some tea,' she said.

I took a fruitcake out of my bag and laid it on a plate.

'Tell me about yourself, Ellie,' she said, pouring tea from a simple brown earthenware teapot into one of the Willow Pattern cups. 'I know nothing about you, only your name.'

Maureen had lost the fraught stare of the victim I had rescued, and I saw at once that she was an ordinary woman like me. She had tidied herself, her long brown hair was up in a neat bun, her face was kind and relaxed, on the pretty side of plain, although still too thin for her bone structure. Her eyes were warm and interested.

I gave her a potted history of my life. How my well-to-do parents had disowned me when I refused to enter the convent, and about running away at eighteen to marry my childhood sweetheart John. His injury in the War of Independence had plunged us into terrible poverty, and that was how I had ended up in New York, working as a maid to help pay for his operation.

'You're not a maid now, I take it?' she asked.

'No,' I said, 'I trained as a typist, then went back to Ireland when my father died and started up a business in my home town.'

'So what brought you back here?'

I girded myself against telling a lie, but found I did not want to.

'My husband died.'

She leaned towards me and put both her hands over mine.

'I'm sorry,' she said. For the first time since it had happened it felt right to say it out loud. I did not feel the pain rising. Perhaps it was gone.

'So I came here for a holiday.'

'And you chose to spend your holiday rescuing poor creatures like me from the street?'

I smiled. I could not explain myself further, nor did I want to give her details of my stay in The Plaza, or of my old friend Sheila giving me the run-around.

I stood up and walked to the window. Tenements crowded in on each other, grimy windows with scraggy net curtains barely hiding one family from another. Treacherous metal steps butted up against each other, with children sitting out on them, five floors up, smoking, and flimsy rags of washing flapping around in the filthy air. There was no room to breathe; this place was one step up from a slum, the whole area a prison of sorts.

'Where was your house?' I asked her. Maureen politely took my cue to talk about her life again, although she doubtless would have preferred to explore my troubles further.

'Yonkers,' she said, 'in the Bronx, but a respectable area nonetheless. We had a fine garden and the children were happy in school. We've been gone from there five years now.'

'I wonder if it is still available for rent?'

She saw where the conversation was going.

'Really, Ellie, you have done enough . . .'

'No,' I was adamant, 'this place is not suitable for you and the children, and the rent is outrageous. I am almost certain that for a few dollars more we could get your house back.'

'Really, I can't let you do any more for us, you've already been so kind.'

I sat down and looked her straight in the eye.

'Maureen, please,' and the words came from nowhere, 'I need some purpose, something to do. Let me help you, for my sake, if not yours.'

'The house will surely be gone,' she objected.

'Well, let's go and see – do you remember where the landlord works?'

She nodded.

'Then it's settled.'

We left the children with neighbours, and a message at the laundry instructing Bridie to feed them during her lunch break, then took a taxi to Grand Central, and the train from there out to Yonkers.

We walked up a short, steep hill from Ludlow station, then left down Fairfield Road towards Yonkers village. There was green space between the large, airy, clapboard houses and pink blossom scattered on the ground. The air smelt of lilac – it was so much lighter and fresher that it was hard to believe that the stodgy, crowded atmosphere of the city was less than an hour away. It felt as if we were in the country. My walk was purposeful and brisk, but as the houses gave way to the shops and bars at the heart of Yonkers village, Maureen's step slowed and her demeanour became slumped and sullen.

'I don't think this is a good idea, Ellie, really.'

Shame – the humiliation of a life lived and lost. I became even more determined to restore her pride. Kind words or condolences would only diminish her further and, in any case, I was full of action.

'Just show me where the landlord's office is,' I said, firmly taking her arm.

She stopped outside an office in whose windows there were drawings and some photographs of houses. Maureen baulked at the door.

'I can't go in,' she said.

I slipped a dollar into her hand and left her sitting in the cafe next door while I went about her business.

Her landlord, a Mr Williams, was in, and I found him to be an amenable man. In any case I was all business, with money in my pocket; and I understood, more than most, that a transaction was a transaction, whatever its past history or cause – money in the present was always welcomed. I encountered no suspicion or doubt, which told me that the Sweeneys had perhaps been more decent tenants than Maureen had feared. Their plight was the plight of many, and as the circumstances of the Depression had revealed themselves, doubtless men like Mr Williams were more sympathetic than their harsh roles of landlords had formerly allowed them to be. Evicting families was an unsavoury business, and I guessed that this mellow-faced man had his own family to feed and was simply doing his job. I explained that I was a friend of the Sweeneys and had come to restore them back to their family home. He explained, regretfully, that the house had recently been sold. Despite, or rather because of, the slump in property prices, the area had become popular with prospectors as a place for good, cheap investments.

Were there any other houses in or near that particular street, I asked?

'There is one,' he said. 'It is for sale, but it has been on the market for some time and there is little interest being shown in it. I could certainly let you have it for a reasonable rent, until such time as we find a buyer.'

'Can we go and see it now?' I asked.

'I should warn you it is in a state of disrepair.'

'There is no harm in looking,' I said.

And he nodded. 'My car is just outside.'

I stuck my head into the cafe and called Maureen out, giving her no room to object. Whatever had passed between her family and this landlord, I would insist that she faced the demons of her past. It seemed to me that the level of her shame was greater than it had a right to be, and the landlord's attitude to her confirmed that.

'Good afternoon, Mrs Sweeney,' and he held out his hand as if at a church fete, 'how nice to see you again.'

She took it and said, 'Mr Williams.'

'I trust your husband is well?'

She looked at me nervously and replied, 'He's very well, thank you.'

He opened the door for us and we both climbed into the back seat, then he drove us up and down nameless hilly streets lined with mostly empty houses, many of which were derelict. Countless windows gaped emptily, like sad eyes behind overgrown shrubs, their clapboard sidings peeling and torn, with broken pots and prams in the porches, the debris left behind by the thousands of ordinary families whose lives had taken an extraordinary, shocking turn for the worse. There was no reason for Maureen to feel ashamed at what had happened to her. It seemed that her plight was that of many families in this area – the genteel stature of the buildings decimated by the poverty of neglect; the hope for the good life they promised now dashed.

I pointed out to Mr Williams that there seemed to be a lot of empty properties in the area.

'Prospectors are only interested in investment, not development. They buy the houses cheap and just leave them empty, hanging onto them until the market picks up,' he explained, 'which they believe it will.'

'And what will happen then?' I asked.

'Then they'll sell them off again, or rent them out for a great profit.'

'It seems a shame to leave them like this, when so many people in the city are homeless,' I said.

'Sure does,' he replied, looking at me briefly in the driver's mirror.

Maureen stared pointedly out the window, her lips set, and I felt a stab of guilt for my insensitive remark.

He pulled up alongside a large clapboard house. 'Here we are,' he said.

The house was huge and, I could see at once, in as bad a state of disrepair as the landlord had warned us. Several of the windows were gone, and the garden was a jungle of high thistles and weeds. But the boarding looked sound, and there was a large porch wrapping the whole way round it. He took the keys out of his pocket and walked us around the vast inside. There were cobwebs everywhere, and in the dining room my heel went through a rotten floorboard and almost snapped off. The few sparse furnishings left by the last tenants were broken, and damp wallpaper peeled from the walls. But there was a large kitchen, which, while filthy, still had a small stove and a large refrigerator that would have been too heavy for even the most determined of looter to carry, so it was possibly still in working order. There were seven bedrooms, and at least four of them had functioning beds, even if the mattresses were musty – they would soon be aired. There were no fewer than two indoor bathrooms, with baths and toilets intact. An idea formed itself inside me.

'We'll take it,' I said.

'I can let you have it for five dollars a month,' he said, sheepish to be asking for any money at all.

'Not to rent,' I said, 'to buy.'

He raised his eyebrows in surprise, and Maureen looked at me as if I had lost my mind. For a moment I thought that perhaps I had. But if I bought this house and restored some order to it, it would rise in value. I had enough cash on me to make a good deal there and then and, in any case, I disliked giving money to landlords – especially the class of landlords here who were throwing families out of their homes, only for the buildings to stand empty and rot. This way Maureen and her family would have the security they deserved. And as for me? Well, I had my sense of purpose back.

Aside from my love for John, that had always been the thing that had kept me going.

# CHAPTER SEVENTEEN

I did not stop to consider anything beyond the setting up of the house in Yonkers. I had a sense of elation and excitement that dwarfed all thoughts of returning home. In deciding to purchase the house, I was certain I had found a solution of sorts. I now had a reason to be here. This was a fresh start, a new beginning.

That very afternoon we returned to Manhattan and Maureen packed up. We waited for Bridie to finish work, and when she came back I informed her that I had acquired a house in Yonkers and was enlisting her as my housekeeper, and she was to start work the next day. The old woman objected huffily, but had begun packing her things before she had finished pretending she had better things to do.

'We need to establish now, Ellie,' she insisted, as she wrapped her crockery in kitchen linen and placed it carefully into her small leather bag, 'I'll not do heavy lifting, and I don't clean ovens, or windows . . .'

I wondered if I should tell her what I was leading her into, but decided it was just her pride talking. Whatever dirty jobs might face us all when we got there, it was surely better than the long hours and endless exploitation she was currently experiencing at the hands of her ruthless employer.

Maureen, who had quietly remained in a state I took to be

speechless shock – not just at my purchasing the enormous run-down house, but at the determined vigour with which I was moving – looked at me pleadingly as if to say, *'If only she knew.'*

Doubtless she was nervous of what must have seemed like a kind of mania that had overtaken me. I was nervous about the feeling myself, but kept moving nonetheless. With each new task I gave myself, I became more and more convinced that I was on the right path. I was running again, away, away – as I had been on my journey from Ireland. Except this time I was moving to-wards the right place. Not merely escaping, but going to a place of my own determination.

Early the following morning I checked myself out of The Plaza, then collected the others, stuffed the five of us into a taxi with all of our belongings and headed for Yonkers.

I asked the driver to stop along East 54th at the dime-store where I had seen the homeless mother and infant.

There was no trace of them. The doorway where I had re-membered them sleeping had been swept clean. Perhaps I had imagined it, but a sign in the window saying 'NO VAGRANTS' reminded me that I hadn't. I determined at that moment that I would never walk past such a sorry sight again.

I made one more stop on the way, to Mr Williams' office to settle our business.

I had negotiated hard, and the owners had agreed a price quickly. With so many properties lying empty, and theirs one of the worst of them, they could not believe their luck. I gave Mr Williams a cash deposit and, as promised, he allowed us to move in straight away. The process was fast, and as I finished sign-ing the documents he expressed to me how impressed he was to meet a woman who did business with such confidence and expediency.

'In my experience,' I told him, 'men are equally likely to dither about as women.'

It put him in his place, but I was flattered nonetheless to have been singled out.

As we were leaving I turned to him and asked, 'One more thing, Mr Williams. Do you know any honest men who might be willing to do some work on the house? Help us fix the place up a bit.'

He let out a sort of dry laugh, but not unkindly. 'Any number of men available all the time. Come back after lunch and I'll bring you down to the Labour Exchange.'

We arrived up at the house on Fairfield Road and the taxi man deposited us and our dozens of bags in the front yard. As he drove off, heavy globules of rain began to drop onto the bags, and I was grateful for the excuse to move us all quickly inside, before the awful magnitude of my task had hit home.

The house looked grimmer than I remembered it. The electricity had been switched off, and we were hit at once with the sweet, acrid smell of rotting flesh – dead mice under the floorboards, I hoped.

As we stood in the half-light I saw Maureen look over at Bridie. I didn't dare look at her myself.

'Now,' I said, 'here we are,' and moved purposefully towards the kitchen.

'Well . . .' Bridie said, in a thunderous whisper.

Maureen scuttled ahead of me into the kitchen, terrified that the old broad was going to give vent ungraciously to her own trepidation.

'Jake, Flora,' I said, taking a deep breath, 'go outside and gather all the rubbish from the yard and put it into a pile at the back of the house.'

'. . . this is a *fine* house for you to take a woman of my age into.'

'I'm sorry, Bridie,' I started. She lifted her small bag, indicating to me that she planned to walk out there and then.

'I shouldn't have taken you here, I just had this idea that . . .'

She put her bag up onto a chair and opened it. Then she took out a starched white apron, pulled it over her head and tied it around her shabby coat.

'No time for any more of your silly ideas, girl,' she said. 'Let's see what has to be done and get on with it.'

All three of us went to work and tried to fix the place up as best we could. Maureen found an old sweeping brush, and Bridie huffed and puffed, opening and closing kitchen cupboards and exclaiming in horror at how anyone could leave anywhere in a state like that.

The children barely followed my instructions to tidy the yard, for they were so excited running in and out of the house telling their mother about various finds: a broken doll, the guts of a swing 'with a real seat', which needed only new rope to make it work again.

Jake found an old, rusting bicycle hidden in the back shed.

'It's working, Mom,' he said, red-faced with excitement, pulling it up onto the back porch, 'and a pump right here.'

His surly demeanour had disappeared and he was like a young child.

'Can I keep it, Miss?' he asked me. I looked at Maureen, uncomfortable at him deferring to me.

'Ask your mother,' I said, 'and please, Jake, if we are to live under the same roof, you can call me Ellie.'

'Are you going to live here with us?' Flora asked.

'For a while anyway,' I said, 'if that's all right with your mother?'

'And her?' Jake asked, looking at Bridie doubtfully.

'I have a name,' she glowered at him with a teasing, grumpy face. 'It is *Mrs Flannery* – and as I have no place else to go, we'll have to put up with each other for a time yet, young man, so you had better get used to it.'

We had passed a grocery shop on the way up the hill, so I sent the children off with Jake's 'new bicycle' to get us some supplies: Ajax, matches, a new sweeping brush, soap, polish, white vinegar for cleaning the windows, bread, milk and tea – anything I could think of that we were in immediate need of. I paused slightly when giving Jake my dollars, and he looked so sweetly ashamed at handling my money that I immediately felt guilty.

'Would you like some cigarettes?' he asked.

'No,' I said, 'but perhaps some candy would be nice.'

They returned quickly, and we women scrubbed and wiped and swept and polished, barely making a dent on the place, until it was time for me to keep my appointment with Mr Williams.

I declined Jake's offer to use the bicycle and walked down the hill to the village. In my head I listed all of the jobs that needed to be done to the house, in order of importance. A number of windows needed replacing, plus several of the worst floorboards; the kitchen table needed to be sanded and brought back to a habitable standard; mattresses carried to the garden and aired – we could do that ourselves, once we had a fine day. The list of jobs immediately reminded me of John, a trained carpenter. I was in the habit of instructing him in building shelves and cupboards – he had built our shop from the ground up, with the help of our neighbours. I was well versed in describing what I wanted done in the way of building work, and assessing how long it might take! The value of it I had never had to worry about, because my husband had been my most willing employee. I missed him. As I walked I breathed in the wet, muggy air and remembered where I was: New York. Not Ireland, where the air was fresh and sharp, and filled with the waft of turf fires and wet grass and mint. I brought myself back to my previous time here, full of purpose and determination. This time was the same. As before, I missed John and wished him there by my side to share this new life. As before, he was somewhere else, a long way away, and I would have to make do without him and carry on. I held onto the angry betrayal of John in not joining me here, convincing myself it was his choice and not God's design that kept us apart. I used anger to steady my brisk walk, and did not allow myself to long for him.

Mr Williams suggested that, as it was dry, we walk to the recently opened Labour Exchange in Yonkers.

I followed his lead. A block from his office, we came upon a line of men queuing in the street. Barely speaking, they exchanged nods and cursory male mumblings, and smoke curled up from the cupped palms of their hands as they hid the luxury of their cigarettes from each other. I looked ahead and saw the line stretch for almost two blocks: gangs of men, tall, short, young and old, in a uniform of jackets and caps and with resigned, bored faces. They moved quietly aside as we passed them, and it gradually dawned on me that this was the line for the Labour Exchange.

As the line began to thicken to three, four, five men deep, Mr Williams leaned in to me and said, 'It's best to come up the front – these men have been queuing the longest and are the keenest for work.'

Cars and trucks were parked carelessly around the street, and the men gathered in rowdy bunches around affluent-looking employers looking for casual labourers, raising their arms and shouting out, 'Mr Joyce!', 'Hey, Bill!', trying to get their attention like keen schoolchildren with a teacher. The employers pointed out faces in the crowd, calling out names when they could, and the men rushed forward, piling into the back of pickups, where they sat, their feet tapping, bristling with relief.

I felt a rush of gratitude that I had Mr Williams with me. I would not have known where to start in approaching these men, and was terrified of getting caught up in their hungry mash. Already overwhelmed with the scale of their joint desperation, I considered walking away, simply buying a hammer and some nails and doing the job myself.

'Wait here,' he said into my ear, steering me aside from the heaving crowd at the door and closer to the road. 'I've a man in mind.'

As he turned I called after him, 'I want a carpenter,' afraid that he might return with a pitiful weakling who wouldn't be qualified for the job. Mr Williams smiled knowingly, and I realized that he had the measure of me. 'And a good one at that, who can glaze a window – and somebody strong!'

The landlord deftly negotiated himself into the centre of the crowd, disappearing among the mass of flat caps and raised arms, and emerged a few moments later with a man of around his own age, in his mid-forties, whom he brought over to me.

'Ellie,' he said, 'this is Matt Murphy. He's as good a handyman as you'll find anywhere in New York.'

# Chapter Eighteen

Matt had the look of an Irish navvy. His square head was topped with thick, short brown hair that he struggled to comb to one side; his broad shoulders and wide chest seemed vaguely uncomfortable in a brown suit that hung badly and looked as if it had seen better days. But his face was open and warm, his eyes sparkled with intelligence and although he had the stodgy, awkward demeanour of a country Irishman, it was something that I was familiar with, so I hired him on the spot. He had a faded canvas knapsack secured to his back, which indicated to me that he was homeless, and a heavy-looking bag of tools that he lifted with one broad fist as if it were filled with feathers.

We walked back to the house, with him towering above me and slowing his stride so that I could keep up. As we crossed the main roadway he shuffled awkwardly, clearly uncertain as to whether he should offer me his free arm or not, anxious to do the gentlemanly thing, but not wishing to offend me. Although I had no need to, I slipped my hand in between his torso and upper arm, hooking myself onto his big frame. I felt him freeze with embarrassment and immediately regretted it, but it would have been worse to pull away, so I linked with him all the way home.

On the ten-minute walk I dragged his story out of him. He

was from Leitrim, a quiet, unpopulated place. The only child of a widow, Matt had been thirty before he found himself a wife, and his mother (having expected him to stay at home looking after her, as was the way with the last son left at home) was so disgusted that she threw him out of the house. A wealthy cousin living in England gave him a small cottage and some land, but the land was poor and they had no stock, so he came to America to earn some money. He sent his young wife home every penny that he earned in the building trade during the boom years – a small fortune. She sent him back letters with descriptions of a new house, cattle and a tractor. There was no need to come home just yet, she said, for she was managing the farm herself with the help of his brother and some local men. When times turned hard in America, he asked her to send him the price of his boat ticket back. It was then that she finally confessed that she had hooked up with one of the local men helping on the farm and had married him. He delivered all of this is a matter-of-fact tone that was surprising, given his quiet manner.

'How did she do that,' I asked, 'when she was already married to you?'

'She told them all I was dead.'

I gasped.

'Even your mother?'

'I was dead to my mother the day I got married,' he said, 'she made that very clear.'

'That's awful,' I replied. My parents had disowned me when I married John, but I had become reconciled with my mother after my father died. Such cruelty, to be cut off from them like that. I could scarcely believe what he was telling me, but while Matt's tone suggested he was making little of it, I surmised that it was more due to pride than a carefree attitude.

'I don't mind,' he said, and there was, I noted, no hint of regret or cynicism in his voice as he added, 'America is my home now.'

I paid Matt a few dollars each week and made up a bed for him in the drawing room on the ground floor. Living in a house with three women, he wanted for nothing in the way of food and comfort and within a few days he had relaxed in our company. It seemed that Matt was a warm and funny man, and I was touched by his constant expressions of gratitude and appreciation for all we did for him. Here was a man in his late thirties, only a few years older than me, who had been treated badly at the hands of the two most important women in his life – the people from whom he had the right to expect loyalty and love – yet he afforded the women in our house the greatest of respect. He was not afraid to lift a cup, bring his own plate to the sink or make his own bed. After a hard day's work, Bridie would chide him for offering to help and insist that he sit still while she fussed about him. Matt would blush with pleasure at being treated like a king, and sometimes, leaning back in his chair, full of meat and potatoes, he would pat his stomach and light a cigarette and I would get a glimpse of the self-satisfied Irish farmer he was born to be.

With Matt's help, and my smart accounting and careful shopping, the house was transformed on less than a hundred dollars.

Matt fixed up what meagre furnishings had been left to us with a sturdy, deft hand and a craftsman's finish. He was a quiet soul, personable, but cautious – he followed every instruction I gave him, but also took the initiative as if it were his own house, mending the roof and restoring the tiles on the walls of the porch. In those two months I incurred my greatest expenses through the materials he bought, doing justice to his craftsmanship by replacing rotten mahogany panels on the walls of the old dining room, cracked tiles in the hallway. He worked from early in the morning and often, in those early days, late into the night after dinner – sanding and hammering and French polishing everything in the house. When he was stripped to the waist, I noticed that his torso was softer and broader than John's had been, his muscled arms marbled with the veins and sinews of an older man. I was comforted by Matt's age. Perhaps he reminded me somewhat of dear Paud, or perhaps it was just that he was so different from John, in both appearance and manner, that I felt safe sharing my home with him.

We added to Matt's restored furnishings entirely with second-hand goods from the many house clearances and charity shops in our area. Mr Williams tipped me off about upcoming house evictions, and I purchased the finest curtains, sheets, blankets and a generous stock of crockery and accoutrements for the kitchen, for little more than the price of a month's grocery shopping. I was saddened to know that I was playing even a small part in profiting from people's misery, but justified the fact that I was helping others in the process. While not entirely inured to it, as time passed I came to adopt a practical attitude to the poverty that was all around.

We worked hard, all six of us. As agreed, Bridie took on the role of housekeeper, preparing all of our meals with a commitment to both comfort and frugality. Despite my protestations she insisted on running the kitchen on a shoestring: 'Simple food is better for the digestion in any case, and as long as I have my flour and potatoes, we'll none of us be wanting.' When I offered to bring more luxury ingredients in, I would get the sharp end of her tongue: 'It was far from coffee and chocolate that *you* were reared!' Like the others, it hurt her pride to be living off my charity. She was anxious to do her part, and if she was charmless in its execution, I could see past it to the kind heart underneath.

So we bought large sacks of flour, rice, pasta, sugar and potatoes, and crates of unmarked tins from the dime-store. Bridie made her own delicious bread every day, and created miracles out of canned sausages and peas.

Maureen kept the house clean, working assiduously each day from room to room, week to week, wiping and polishing every surface, sweeping and mopping every floor, ironing and starching every sheet, until the grime of the old house gave way to the glowing spotlessness of the new. Flora, whom we had enrolled back into the local school, helped her mother with the cleaning and set fires for the evening when she came home. Jake, who – much to his mother's despair – had refused to return to his schooling, set about proving his worth to the new elder man in the house, and turned out to be a diligent and willing worker.

At first Jake regarded Matt with suspicion, having cast himself as his mother's (and to a lesser extent my own) keeper. However, it was clear that with his quiet, professional manner, Matt was not a personal threat to any of us. He gained Jake's trust through guiding him in his work, and soon despite (or perhaps because of) Jake's fondness for his lost father, Matt was rarely seen without the surly teenager hovering close behind him, waiting for his next instruction. Matt had farming in his blood, as did I, so between us we dug and planted a vegetable patch in the back garden and commissioned Jake to care for it, and before long the two of them were conspiring to build a chicken pen in the garden.

'No!' Bridie exclaimed, when the subject of keeping hens was mooted. 'I'll not have those filthy creatures near the house. We'll buy eggs from the shop, like normal people. I draw the line, Ellie – I draw the line at saving money on eggs!'

I promised Bridie that I would spare her the hardship of ever having to pluck and gut a chicken – her parents had farmed poultry in Ireland, and she had been killing and plucking hens as soon as she could walk, which explained her reluctance to get involved with them again. So Matt and Jake bought four fine Rhode Island Whites from the Saturday market, with plans – once Bridie was calmed – to invest in a cockerel to breed out of them for meat.

Before the summer was rounded, the house was running with happy efficiency, and there were no problems to speak of. I still had some of the money I had brought with me from Ireland, and everybody was contributing and playing their part. There were curtains on every window, to keep out the blistering August sun, and the garden was bearing sweet tomatoes and plump, crisp lettuces – with the onions already picked and hanging in the porch to dry. We bathed in baths freshly enamelled by Matt, using water from the tank that he had welded back into working order. We ate the best of Bridie's food, slept each night in crisp, starched sheets, and each morning put our bare feet down on soft, clean rugs.

On one such morning I woke and realized that the house, and therefore the mission that had been driving me for the past few months, was complete.

With that knowledge, the buried dread made its return.

I drew back the curtains and the searing light of New York ganged in on me. Outside my window white apple blossom branches, weighed down with burgeoning fruit, wilted in the sun, and three fat cats sat shading themselves in a neighbour's porch. The house opposite was still empty, bleak and wasteful as this one had been. Now it was filled with people and life, but they weren't my people and this wasn't my life.

I had lost my life with John's death. I had a graw for home, but I didn't want to go back to Ireland. I wanted to see Maidy, but I wasn't ready to face what I had done in leaving her alone, as I had. My escape was not complete, as I had hoped it might be. I was still running, but I had not been watching where I was going; my feet had got caught in the rushes of an invisible bog and I was stuck.

I had to get them moving again. I needed something else to do.

I dressed myself, then went downstairs, made myself coffee and sat in the shade of the dining room, smoking.

Matt had restored and polished the mahogany panels on the wall, and I had picked up a rather old-fashioned and ugly dining set of Victorian furniture in a garage sale. The floor was bare wood, with no rugs or side tables or ornaments to create the illusion of home, and the room had something of the sparse, institutional atmosphere of a convent.

Sitting there alone in the dense, smoke-filled air, with the daily sounds of Bridie and Maureen going about their chores muffled by the heavy wood, it seemed to me as if I were in a waiting room of some kind. Even though this house, this situation of living with strangers, was of my own making, I felt estranged from it; estranged from myself.

In the bareness of the room and its silence I heard God tapping at an empty corner of my mind; the ancient, white-bearded patriarch of my childhood whispering, offering me his comfort. I had not spoken to God or paid Him any heed since John died. He was, for all the years I had placed my trust in Him, a cold, cruel being who had taken my husband to his icy heart and caused the misery and hardship I saw all around me. I tried to ignore Him, as if He didn't exist, but I could feel Him there despite myself. My faith that He existed was too strong to ignore, but I felt angry that He had let me down, and I would fight Him nonetheless – if not with the justified rage that had chased me to America, then with my indifference towards Him from here on in.

I extinguished my cigarette, and resigned myself to busying myself for the day, when there was a knock on the door.

Mr Williams had a letter in his hand.

'The postman gave me this as I was coming in,' he said, handing it over.

It was from Katherine. A large, heavy package – accounts from the business in Ireland. I set it aside.

He stood in the hallway, shuffling awkwardly until I offered him coffee.

'You've made a fine job of the house, Mrs Hogan,' he said, 'you've really fixed it up.'

'Matt has been wonderful,' I said. Then, seeing Bridie bristling in the background, I added, 'And Bridie and Maureen, of course. We've all worked very hard.'

'I can see that,' he said.

He twisted the handle of the cup in its saucer and his face was set, as if he had something to say.

'Is everything all right,' I asked, 'with the house? No complications have arisen?'

The house had long since been mine, so I knew there wouldn't be, but he had never made a social call like this before. Aside from his tipping his hat at me as we passed in the street, I hadn't seen the man in months.

'Oh yes, yes, sure,' he said, 'no problems there at all.'

'Good,' I said, but he continued twirling the cup and I grew impatient with this way men had of not saying straight out what was on their minds.

'Is there something I can help you with?' I finally asked.

'Well, yes,' he answered, 'I have a favour to ask. Well, it is more than a favour, more a task – something of a mission? I don't know quite what I am asking of you . . .'

I had to coax it out of him. A few days previously he had had to evict a young pregnant girl from a room where she was living alone, in a tenement building in the North Bronx. The father had disappeared. 'I kept her there for as long as I could, even paid off the landlord myself for the first few weeks, but she is so young, and was living in such desperate circumstances . . . Well, to tell you the truth, Ellie, it played on me so bad that I have been letting her sleep in my office at night. During the day I have to put her out to walk the streets. If my wife finds out – well, I don't need to tell you how it looks.'

I knew at once what he was asking. Bridie, who had been stirring porridge on the stove behind him, listening to every word and sucking her teeth in disapproval, now widened her eyes in furious warning and shook her head wildly.

'She can stay here,' I said. 'Bring her up as soon as it suits.'

Bridie tackled me before I had closed the door on him.

'Another mouth to feed, Ellie, *two* soon enough – have you lost your mind? You can't go taking in every waif and stray in New York, woman! You don't know anything about this girl. She is clearly of ill repute – and *not* of wholesome character! If that man, who has surely seen the world, took her in, in that state, Lord knows how she repaid his kindness! You might be thinking you are acting with a kind heart, Ellie, but so help me, you haven't thought this through. You're a reckless fool!'

That much was true. It was neither a kind heart nor measured moral thinking that had made me jump at Mr Williams' request, but the hollow fear of standing still in the presence of my own heart.

I left Bridie to her complaints and went to prepare the empty bedroom in the attic of the house.

As I gathered clean sheets and blankets from the press on the first-floor landing, I felt the knot inside me loosen and knew I was running again.

# Chapter Nineteen

*Dear Ellie,*

*Thank you for your last letter. Although it was brief, I was glad to hear that you are well and glad to learn also that the sum of $3,000 was successfully transferred to your account there. I trust this finds you in good health and still enjoying your break. It seems you may have moved to a more domestic setting than The Plaza, but I have no wish to pry.*

*I have purposely left you alone until now, because I know you will be in touch when the time is right and, frankly, I have been so busy with the businesses that, with there being no great problems to speak of, I have been just been 'getting on with it'. However, as you will see from the enclosed accounts, an amount of cash has amassed that I am uncertain what to do with.*

*I have been placing all monies from the typing pool and school directly into the bank and drawing all salaries and everyday expenses from it, as per usual. The country shop is ticking along, with Veronica as shop-girl, and I have appointed her mother Mary to oversee its running, with a small wage. Mary has proven herself to be a competent manager and, while her literacy levels are basic, she is slowly getting the hang of the books and, despite the additional expense of her salary, it has turned a small profit every month since you have been gone! This may be down to the fact that she has started to sell her own freshly baked bread there, which has proven very popular. I have also taken the liberty of commissioning Mary to keep an eye on your home for as long as you are gone, feeding the poultry and taking as many eggs as she needs for herself. She was also most useful in finding a neighbour to take over the farm end of things. The Morans are paying a small rent for the land and cattle, but given that their taking it over was more suited to our needs than theirs, I could hardly charge them more. However, they pay cash – and are always on time – so there can be no complaint.*

*The salon is thriving due to Pauline's skills, but, as you already know, the girl is a flibbertigibbet and incapable of running the business end of things. I have employed another girl to manage the till – Assumpta Kelly, she was trained with us some two years ago, but has been unable to find a post elsewhere. She is a somewhat 'glamorous' type, but reliable and trustworthy, certainly more so than the other one. As instructed by you, a percentage of the shop takings are being kept as cash in the safe under my desk – and I am anxious about the amount, and wondering if there is anywhere else it can be safely kept, or perhaps you would like it sent over to you as bank drafts?*

*I should also let you know that the Fitzpatricks were very upset that you reneged on your offer for their drapery, which is still up for sale. They asked me to ask you to reconsider, and are willing to negotiate a better price for you. If you don't consider it presumptuous of me to say so, I would argue that the business as it stands is a good, solid proposition and, while I lack your flair for fashion, I would be more than happy to oversee its purchase and refurbishment for you. I attach a document proposing my ideas.*

*On a personal note, I have taken up your kind offer to move into the apartment, and am very comfortable and happy here. I have taken the liberty of packing away some of your things to make room for my own, and they are ready for me to forward, should that be your wish. You did not mention how long you would be away for, but I gathered from the tone of your letter that it might be for some time yet. I have also, on your advice, learned to drive, and am finding it to be an easy and most useful pastime!*

*As well you might imagine, everybody in the town is asking after you. I have told them that you are taking a holiday in America, and that I am holding the fort in your absence, and you may be assured of my discretion in giving news of your whereabouts or personal circumstances. I have reassured Maidy that you were asking after her and will doubtless be in touch soon. While she is still very sad after John, as we all are, I have called out to her a few times and taken up the habit of driving her to Mass each Sunday. She was in good spirits when I saw her last week and we took lunch in the hotel in Ballyhaunis afterwards, enjoying a most convivial afternoon. I feel sure that time will heal, as it always does, for dear Maidy and also for you, dearest Ellie.*

*I hope that you are well, and that New York is providing you with all that you hoped it would.*

*Your friend,*
*Katherine*

Nancy was six months gone when she arrived with us. She was a quiet, pretty girl, not yet twenty, and contributed to the running of the house as best as her age and condition allowed. However, the few days it took us to adjust to our new housemate were short-lived.

Two weeks after we had settled, Maureen arrived home with Anna Balducci, an Italian mother in her thirties with five-year-old twin boys. She had long black hair, slanting eyes and full ruby-red lips. The two tall boys' arms clung to either side of her curved hips.

'The house is full,' I argued, 'we can barely fit them in.'

'I'm sorry,' Maureen said, 'but she has nowhere else to go. They can all sleep in my room.'

We camped them in the dining room, bringing in our old mattresses from the shed. A few days later I was awoken from my sleep at 6 a.m. by the babble of Italian on the porch. I found Anna and the children outside with her husband, Mario, who had been sleeping rough. They were taking him out food. He looked desperate and they were all so apologetic at 'stealing' a few hunks of bread and some cheese that we found room for him, too.

It was Matt who first put into my head the idea of buying another house. Katherine's letter only compounded the idea. Firstly because she was managing so well, and secondly because she had reassured me about Maidy. Then there was all that cash that she wanted to get rid of.

'That house across the road is pure wrecked,' Matt said, 'and nobody has been to look at it in the time we've been here. I've half a mind to go in and tidy it up myself, just for the sake of it. Mario can turn a piece of wood, and there's precious little left to do in this place.'

There was no 'For Sale' sign outside, but I guessed that Mr Williams might know who to contact. The house had been repossessed and was now owned by a small lending institution, which was, in turn, in receivership to the bank with which I had my account. The bank was willing to sell the house for virtually any price I would offer them. I offered them two thousand dollars. They had another house in the area, and for an extra thousand dollars I could have that, too – they even offered me a mortgage to cover half the entire sum. I took them up on both.

Within a matter of months I had found myself in ownership of no fewer than three houses in the area. I had found there was no need for caution in wasting time thinking over business transactions here. In any case, I found that either because of the property owner's greed or the efficiency of the American legal system, all dealings were done at double the speed they were in Ireland. Under Katherine's care the typing school and salon were doing well, so raising money was not an issue. More importantly, the need for shelter was there, and the desire to help people had become all I needed to drive me forward. No mere practicality would be an obstacle to my plans to house the needy. I was on a mission, and I felt invincible.

Our new community now comprised more than thirty men, women and children – and we lived as one family. As the men, under Matt's supervision, worked to bring each house up to a reasonable living standard, the women cooked and cleaned and looked after the children. For the sake of both economy and ease, we ate all our meals together, ensuring that every man, woman and child had at least one full meal a day.

Bridie ran the kitchen in our house like a canteen, serving soup from two huge pots every day, spooning each serving into large tin mugs, and we mopped it up with hunks from the eight loaves of bread that she left rising overnight and put into the oven each morning. The two pans were then cleaned out and used to cook the dinner that evening.

Anna proved a worthy kitchen-mate to Bridie, and won her over with her matronly, frugal, traditional Italian cooking. Bridie called her the 'mama' and together the two women came up with ingenious ways of saving money, not just on ingredients, but on fuel and electricity. They cooked one vast batch of spaghetti, barely bringing the water to the boil before switching off the electricity to let the pasta cook in its own heat. That night they would serve it with a sauce made from tomatoes and cheap cuts of minced meat, then again the following evening as the main ingredient in 'Poor man's pasta' – frying it up with our own onions and eggs, with olive oil and cheese to bind it into a delicious, hearty cake.

Anna picked tomatoes from the bushes that had grown in Matt's glasshouse and also boiled them up into a sauce with olive oil and onions, then put them into empty jars that the children collected from the neighbours, and stacked them up in the store cupboard to keep for the winter. Piles of empty tins built up in the porch, and the children bored holes in the bottom of them, filled them with earth and planted seeds in them.

On Bridie's insistence, we fed the men first in the evenings, then sent them all out onto the porch to smoke before washing the plates and cutlery and letting the women and children sit down to their food. I objected initially – we all worked as hard as each other, I argued – but she won me around saying, 'Men are selfish creatures, they will always eat quickly. Women and children need time to take their nourishment. That child Nancy is as thin as a stick – the baby is sucking all the good out of her. If we eat late, I can make sure she gets what she needs and goes to bed with a full stomach.'

For all that she puffed and moaned about her work, Bridie was my greatest asset. It was on her advice that we kept a 'dry' house. She had caught two of the men 'helping themselves' to sugar and yeast from her store, and suspected, correctly, that they were making liquor. They confessed immediately and, apart from their kitchen foray, had both proved themselves to be good, hard-working men. I would have had no argument against a man's natural instinct for alcohol, and was ready to allocate them the ingredients to make it themselves. However, Bridie wasted no time in putting them in their place, before I had time to draw breath on my suggestion. 'Mark my words, you'll be out on the street if there is any more of that nonsense. Liquor! Is your time and energy not fully taken up, looking after your wives and children? You should be ashamed of yourselves!'

So the men washed down their meals with jugs of cheap, diluted lemonade poured into the same tin mugs that we took our soup in, making no complaint, and the house remained a sober, peaceful place of work – everybody knowing their place, everybody occupied with their chosen chores, and grateful for the opportunities we were creating for ourselves, and for each other. Although I was still paying for our basic welfare, I would not claim that the progress we made was all of my doing. I had my own reasons for getting involved in helping the needy, but everyone was eager to rebuild their lives, putting all of their work into the tasks in front of them and, when these were complete, finding more.

Matt and I met every morning to discuss the progress of each house, and to decide what materials he could salvage and what he needed to buy. He was creative in his thriftiness, disassembling a garden shed to replace floorboards, taking sidings from one house to complete another. In one of the sheds he found the carcass of an abandoned pickup truck. One of the lads was a young mechanic, and together they put new wheels on it and bought a second-hand engine. Using this, the men trawled the city dumps for bits of discarded pipe and other building materials.

In the evenings all families slept in makeshift bedrooms, made up in whatever houses they could, rising early and coming back to the communal comfort of our house for their breakfast and to plan the chores for the day. I placed myself at the centre of our routines, working alongside the women – washing out sheets in tin baths in the gardens, wringing them in a mangle that we had found abandoned, digging and planting vegetable gardens in whatever fresh piece of ground we could find, feeding and managing our poultry.

As time went on I came to rely on Matt as the man of the house. Aside from the fact that he took charge of all the building and renovation work on the houses, I sought his advice in most matters, and enjoyed his support in all things. In the evenings, after everyone had retired, Matt and I would sit on either side of the kitchen stove. Our hands warmed with tea or cocoa, we had already shared every detail of our day with each other and, there being nothing left to say, we would just sit and share the heat of the fire and the reward of a busy day being over. Sometimes we would be made awkward by the intimacy of our silence, and one or the other of us would break it with some trivial comment or movement: 'Those dishes won't wash themselves,' or 'I'll tackle that shed in the morning.' At other times I would relax into the closeness; listen for the fall of his breath as he stood to make his way to bed, and for a second I would imagine myself following him and crawling into the comfort of his strong body, as I did with John. But at the memory of my husband, any notion towards Matt would disappear with the speed of a falling stone.

# CHAPTER TWENTY

Nancy's labour came on suddenly while I was alone in the house with her. I moved her upstairs and sent Jake down to the village to call for Maureen immediately, praying that the girl would not get too far along, causing me to deliver the baby myself. Although I knew what to do, I was not capable of the emotional upheaval of bringing a new life into the world.

In Kilmoy I had aided Maidy, a midwife, with childbirth twice before. Once on a farmer's wife already seasoned with seven children, of whom five had survived, and another time on a young woman in a similar circumstance to Nancy. The new-born had been removed almost immediately by a nun who had sat in on the birth, then taken the baby away with her to a convent that organized adoptions. At that time I had lost one baby already, and the secret thought that I could have taken the infant myself from the girl had played on me for years afterwards. I was concerned that I would have to guard against those same instincts with young Nancy, and was relieved to find, as I struggled her tiny frame up the stairs, that I had no such feelings now. The powerful need for a child – the jealousy that had plagued me in seeing women heavy with child – had surely left me with John.

In any case, Maureen arrived before the pain took hold and

was as experienced a midwife as any doctor. Despite the fashion and facility that cities had for giving birth in hospital, Maureen had chosen to have both of hers at home and insisted that she would deliver Nancy's baby herself when the time came.

Bridie insisted on helping her. The old woman had no children of her own and, as far as I could gather from her initial flustering about, had never experienced childbirth before. However, her pride would not allow her to openly admit it, so she gathered water and clean towels, even sharpening and sterilizing her precious dressmaking shears to within an inch of their lives. Bridie involved herself at the centre of the drama, as she always did, gripping the young girl's hands throughout and, when nodded at by Maureen, encouraged Nancy to 'take a big deep breath and push hard now, like a good girl'. The courage Nancy showed in barely calling out during what turned out to be a mercifully short ordeal, less than three hours in all, had warmed the old woman considerably to the 'scrawny hussy' to whose tenancy with us she had so vociferously objected. And afterwards Bridie was finally given to concede that, in medical matters, Maureen was good for more than merely turning a nurse's sheet.

When Maureen pulled the infant and we heard its first urgent, squalling breath, Bridie blurted out, 'Merciful Mother in Heaven, the Lord Be Praised!' Her face was as red as a beet, not with exertion, but with emotion in response to the great miracle of birth. She openly swept her swollen, bloodied palms across her eyes to wipe away the tears, before cutting the cord with the same deftness with which I had seen her gut a turkey.

I smiled at the novelty and delight of seeing my gruff old friend so moved by the experience, and so caught up in her own achievement in being a part of it, but I did not feel moved myself. I let the others hold the baby and nurse the mother, quietly leaving the room before the miracle of this new life scorched longing into me, branding me barren, as had happened too many times before.

We all went to great trouble in decorating the attic room for our new addition. Anna had canvassed the church to get a bag of used baby clothes, which we had washed and pressed and laid in piles on the mahogany washstand. Matt had found an old iron bed discarded in an empty lot nearby, and he and the men had carried it up the narrow stairwell and restored it for the new mother. Even pregnant, Nancy was a sweet, pretty girl, not yet twenty, and because of that she inspired great patronage among the men. They welded the broken bed back together, and fixed it up until the brass bed knobs shone like gold. We women dressed the bed in brand-new linens, and Bridie presented Nancy with a bedspread made from multicoloured squares that she had crocheted using wool rescued from old sweaters. We softened and shrank woollen blankets by boiling them in soap for the baby, and placed them in a small cot that Matt had ingeniously fashioned from a dresser drawer. Bridie made a mattress from a small towel, and I caught her sewing a scapular of the Sacred Heart into the seams. On the wall above Nancy's bed she hung a picture of the Blessed Virgin that she had bought from a knick-knack shop on John's Avenue. We all knew she had gone to great expense, so Nancy could not object. When the old woman offered to bath the baby a few days after it was born, we knew she was performing a christening ritual, but said nothing. We all suffered Bridie's superstitious brand of Catholicism in the same way that we women, thrown together by a need to survive the realities of our lives, tolerated each other's foibles.

Bridie's sharp tongue, Maureen's faith in her own skills, Anna's reticence in her own and Nancy's childlike vulnerability were sources of irritation to all of us. For myself, I knew that I kept above much of the everyday bickering and, as such, was often seen as cold and aloof. However, each of us had a part to play in the successful running of each other's lives, so tolerance and endurance usually won out.

Kilmoy felt very far away. The businesses that had been so important to me for so long had receded in importance immediately John died. Almost two full seasons gone and they were of as little interest to me as if they belonged to somebody else. Katherine was my friend, my employee and therefore my responsibility, but if the businesses sank to the ground, I would feel no hardship beyond having let her down. In some part I blamed the businesses for John's death or, rather, my attachment to them. He was gone, and with him my need for independence and money had gone, too. I was independent now, but I was also alone. Finally, my false freedom had brought me back to the New York I had craved since my return to Ireland ten years before. Except that it wasn't my New York any more. This city belonged to the people I was helping. I was spending the money I had so urgently saved for my own future, creating a present for them. It seemed a small price to pay for the distraction and purpose that I was getting from helping them, and for the comfort of the company of people who knew little or nothing about me. Money itself – the acquisition of it – the luxuries I enjoyed and the freedom I had believed they would bring me had become meaningless. John was dead and, much as I would not give in to my own grief, I knew I wasn't free. In truth, I believed I might never be free again.

That being said, I kept up my correspondence with Katherine so that there was a letter going back and forth between us each week. We touched briefly on each other's personal projects, but kept the letters mostly about the businesses in Ireland. I gave her free rein, and signed off on documents and cheques as she needed them, offering advice only when it was asked for.

As I was sitting one day, composing a letter asking her to forward the sum of five hundred pounds, the irony of asking my employee for money in this way occurred to me. I thought about how much Katherine's life had changed since she had been in my employ. She had started as a trainee typist not eight years before, and now she was managing my entire life back home. With me on the other side of the world, the scale and breadth of my business interests in Kilmoy were to be expanded further with the opening of the Fitzpatricks' shop. It seemed impossible that all this could be happening without me being there, and yet I remained curiously detached from the whole thing. With an investment of five hundred pounds, surely I could start some sort of a business here? The Depression had robbed people of so much – their work, their homes – and yet surely the greatest thing it had robbed them of was their independence.

I dashed off my request for money to Katherine and cycled down into Yonkers, where I posted the letter, then called straight away to see Mr Williams in his office. Did he know of any empty business premises nearby for rental – in good condition? He did – any number. A bakery, an office space and a disused garage: take my pick. Would he organize a reasonable rent for me? For next to nothing, he confided.

I cycled back home and gathered Maureen, Bridie and Anna into the kitchen to tell them my idea. I was going to start a business, I explained. I would put up the initial investment, and the profits would be put into paying for the upkeep of our houses.

The three women bristled, mistrustful of my mentioning money. The bankrolling of their lives was too sensitive a subject. None of them outwardly acknowledged themselves as being the recipients of my charity, and it was certainly not a conversation

I had ever encouraged. It had been insensitive of me to barge in on the subject as I had. Maureen and Anna looked at the elder of the group, and she confronted me.

'So, what's going to happen to us?' Bridie asked. 'You were the one that dragged us all up here, and you're leaving? On to the next frippery? I can't run this house on my own, Ellie – and, anyway, what kind of a "business"? Sure, the whole country's in a Depression – or haven't you heard?'

'It's a partnership,' I explained, 'a cooperative, and you will all be a part of it. We are, each one of us, capable, healthy women – I have some money to put into starting something up, and I don't see any reason why we can't get a viable business off the ground! As for what kind of a business, I have no idea. I was rather hoping you would help me come up with something.'

The three women looked at me blank-faced and I became irritated with their mistrust and fear.

'I am not going to abandon you,' I said, 'but I'm not doing any of us justice with my charity. I want to start something so that we can make enough money to pay for all this.'

They were the wrong words. Anna stood looking at the floor, mortified at the mention of charity. Bridie looked fit to explode.

'Together,' I continued.

Maureen broke through the growing atmosphere, saying, 'I think that's a great idea, Ellie. Why don't I make some tea, and we can sit down and talk about it.'

She went to fill the kettle, but Bridie snatched it off her and set about making the tea herself. Anna sat down tentatively at the table, hands on her lap. I took a pen and paper from the sideboard.

Maureen started. 'I have an idea. Doctors' fees are so expensive – few people can afford to pay for medical treatment. If we were to start a small surgery, where people could come and have their ailments treated by a nurse? I am qualified, after all, I can treat smaller injuries and advise on nutrition and health matters generally? I could diagnose people for a small fee and tell them if it was worth going to a doctor?'

'I think that's an excellent idea, Maureen,' I said gratefully.

Bridie puffed cynically in the background and Anna shrank further into her seat. I needed the old woman's support, and she was annoying me.

'What, Bridie? Have you something to say?'

'Well,' she said, still faffing busily over the tea, '*she's* no doctor – you'd be as well off selling Anna's tomato sauce. People would pay for that quicker.'

Maureen went tight-lipped and blushed with shame or anger, or both. I got frustrated trying to figure out which. All this senseless emotion – and over what? Why were these women so reluctant to take up my offer to be self-sufficient? The men, I thought poisonously, would surely jump at the chance. I should have spoken to Matt about this first. All this awkwardness and dilly-dallying wouldn't do at all – I had half a mind to break the unpleasant atmosphere and let the whole thing go.

Anna coughed and quietly said, 'If you think it would help . . .'

Such reluctance! I held my patience.

'Go on, Anna,' I coaxed her.

'Well, if I had the time, and some help, and enough ingredients, I could probably bottle a hundred jars a day. My mother supplied all of our neighbours in Brooklyn with her *pomodoro* when I was growing up.'

It was Maureen's turn to butt in. 'And how much would people pay for a jar of ordinary sauce that they could make themselves?'

Bridie slammed the teapot down on the table.

'That sauce is far from plain, young woman, and you know it, from the way you and your greedy bairns guzzle it down each night. You'd pay good money to eat the way me and Mama feed you in this house, woman.'

With Bridie's back-up, Anna found her voice.

'I can bottle fruits, too – apples and apricots if we could get them. With Bridie's talent for pastry, we could bake tarts – and bread . . .'

'I could bake bread all day long,' Bridie said with a touch of wistfulness, then looked pointedly at Maureen, 'if I didn't have so many hungry mouths to feed.'

Maureen went to get up from the table, but I put my hand over hers to hold her there. Bridie's manner was appalling, her saving grace being that she was generally kept too busy to converse, but we were getting somewhere and I needed to keep all of us together.

'Maureen,' I said, 'is there anything you have a talent for – apart from the nursing?'

'Washing and ironing and general skivvying,' she said, looking directly at Bridie.

'She can iron a sheet all right,' Bridie said, 'I'll give her that.'

'She can do better than that,' Anna butted in. 'I've never slept on a crisper, cooler sheet.'

Maureen took her hand from under mine and gathered herself.

'Cornflour and water starch,' she said.

'I was wondering where all my cornflour was going,' Bridie said, sitting down, happy now that she had wound everyone up.

'. . . and a touch of peppermint oil.'

'Very fancy,' Bridie replied, with her reluctant, sarcastic smile.

'Well,' Maureen replied, 'I'm a very fancy woman.'

'As are we all,' I said.

We laughed, and our venture had begun.

We called our endeavour the 'Yonkers Women's Cooperative' and opened a disused bakery in the village, which our men, stopping work on the houses, remodelled to suit our needs.

I bought a typewriter and a small hand-printing machine, which Jake learned to operate, and we sent the older children around to the wealthy houses in the area to drop in leaflets advertising our services.

Our shop sold freshly baked bread, Italian sauces and conserves, and gave a drop-and-deliver laundry service. I invested all the money Katherine had sent in laundry machines, irons, ovens and as much equipment as the women needed to make the business run smoothly.

The local rich, of whom we discovered there were many, were happy to support an endeavour that advertised itself as being 'an opportunity to help the needy help themselves'. It eased their consciences to pay a few extra pence for their daily bread in a pleasant environment, rather than throw coins at the many vagrants who were littering their streets.

With the money we earned from the shop – even given a small premium that the women insisted I took each week, to pay off the 'loan' of five hundred that it had taken to set the shop up – gradually each of the families was becoming more self-sufficient. The men had started advertising their skills as handymen, electricians and builders, and the wealthier local community came to trust us as a respectable, valuable source of both commerce and labour.

As the houses were completed and the business acquired new ideas and volunteers, I still remained at the centre of the carousel, watching the people as it turned, paying attention to

165

the safety and welfare of each one of them – concentrating all my energy on keeping it turning and holding myself steady at its focal point as it gathered speed and grew.

My world was filled by other people's stories. Characters came and went, they entertained me, and sometimes I was touched by their plight, but mostly they kept me distracted and busy. Aside from our core group – Matt, Bridie, the Sweeneys and the Balduccis – some people got on, then off, and moved on with their lives. One young man was with us for only two weeks, before he was offered a live-in job as gardener with a wealthy family, who found him through the shop. They would never have employed him, had they seen the scraggy, homeless beggar who had turned up at our door not a month before, addled with drink and crawling with lice.

The Balduccis moved into one of the houses I had bought, and turned it into as close to a palace as one could imagine. With a taste for the ornate, Anna ruched oceans of fabric and covered every surface of the house in fripperies and ornaments. An enormous 'Child of Prague' statue, in his gold and crimson gown, stood on the mantelpiece flanked on either side by the Blessed Virgin, her blue ceramic robes hung with trinkets and cheap, glittering rosary beads. It was some sight for the older Jewish couple, Samuel Cohen and his wife Judith, who stayed with the Balduccis for two months. I had found them wandering down Riverdale, struggling with four large cases and bewildered with grief, having been forcefully evicted from their home of forty years. That they set foot inside Anna's Catholic sanctuary at all was testament to their own desperation, but also to the need that we all had to help and comfort one another. Each family was anxious to help others in the way they were helped, and so there was a steady flow of the needy and the grateful. So Catholic and

Jew lived in eccentric harmony. Samuel taught Angelo how to play bridge, Judith showed Anna how to make matzo balls.

The older couple moved on after I persuaded them to put aside their pride and contact their children to tell them what had happened. 'My son, he's a busy man – a solicitor – he has his own family.' Their wealthy son duly arrived in a big car and took his parents back to his house, apologetic for the trouble they had unnecessarily caused.

'Really, I don't know why they didn't contact me right away,' he said. 'You'd think I was a monster!'

'Pride,' I said.

'Is there anything I can do for you?' he asked.

He meant money, but I shook my head.

'Bring them back for a visit now and again,' I said, 'we have so enjoyed having them.'

We never saw the Cohens again.

The people I helped always expressed their gratitude to me, but that was never the point. I had changed their lives, but I remained a stranger to them – and to myself.

With each goodbye I felt ever more grateful to have found a place where my life was occupied only with the business of others. A place where I never had to look forward or back, but could just keep turning on the spot where I now found myself – forever.

# CHAPTER TWENTY-ONE

The third house I had bought turned out to be no bargain after all. It was in such a bad state that it was barely worth the land it stood on.

'The back of it is completely unsound,' Matt had warned me after the sale had gone through. Three weeks later, just as I was running out the door to the bank, he came into my hallway covered in plaster dust, breathing heavily with shock after an interior wall had collapsed.

'We need to secure the back of the house with iron columns – and we'll need scaffolding. It'll cost money, and I can't tackle this on my own with the men I've got, Ellie. I'll need to get some help in.'

He suggested a man he knew, called 'Chuck', whom he had met at the Labour Exchange. He was a dockworker who had lost his job, but he knew something about engineering and metal work. 'He's well connected, too, he'll be able to get us any materials we need.' I didn't care who he was or what he did, as long as he could help Matt fix the house and stop any of the men getting injured or killed.

'No problem,' I said with one hand on the door. The bank closed for lunch in twenty minutes and I'd have to run as it was, to catch it – but Matt was hovering.

'Is there something else, Matt?'

'Well . . .'

As Matt gathered himself for his pronouncement, my irritation must have shown.

'No, Ellie – it's not important.'

'Please,' I said, 'what is it?'

'Well, it's the men.'

'What about them?'

My voice sounded harsher that I would have liked. Matt's impassive face flinched. When did I become so irritable, so unintentionally angry?

'Is there a problem?'

I had run away from one life, and had now found myself entrenched in another – equally burdened with petty problems and personalities. How had this happened?

'Not a *problem exactly*,' he said.

I took my hand off the door.

'It's just that some of the men have been saying . . .'

Gossip – I was missing the bank because of idle gossip.

'. . . that you are paying more attention to the shop these days, and not enough to the work they do.'

I didn't have time for this stupidity. I had heard that some of the men had been quarrelling with their wives because they were earning more money than the men. The men worked on the houses in lieu of their rent, to make them habitable for themselves. They worked for the upkeep of their families. But men preferred to work, it seemed, to line their own pockets and pay for alcohol and cigarettes. The women liked things the way they were. They each took what they needed from the stores in the way of food and supplies, then drew a small salary each week, of which they were in full control. The men didn't like it – of course they didn't, because it meant their women were in charge. Well, that was too bad.

'What can I do, Matt?'

He looked at me blankly.

'What do you want me to do, Matt?'

Matt had never stood up to me. He had never questioned my judgement or asserted his better knowledge as a man over me. We had never fought, because there was never any question of a disagreement. Yet it sometimes angered me that he had cast me in the role of his employer to such an extent that he gave me, not just his unswerving, unthinking loyalty, but his manly spirit. He was my friend, I felt that – and at times, when I saw him looking at me in a certain way, I believed he was more than that. Then he would act like this gormless fool, and I would despair and wish that he would be more of a man and take control. I took a deep breath.

'Right. We'll have a dinner tomorrow night, for the men only. No women and children. We'll let them drink and smoke and let off steam. And your friend Chuck can come along and introduce himself to me, and to them. I'll cook. Is that agreed?'

Matt nodded, and I ran out the door to the bank.

I told Bridie I was entertaining the men exclusively the following night (she was 'scandalized!') and gave her money to keep everyone out of the house until at least nine o'clock. The women and children could have a meal in the small family diner down the road, and retire back to the Balduccis' house if they finished early, where I would have cakes, sweets and cigarettes ready for them to enjoy. I would get Jake to gather up all the children when they came in from school and deliver them down to her. She was to tell none of the women that there was any sign of discontent among their men. I did not want any of them feeling that the tenuous hold on the security of their families' lives was being threatened. This was in the manner of a 'thank you' from me alone, and their own evening out was to be presented as a sort of 'treat' or party.

I was not in the mood for cooking anything fancy. As I began to prepare the food itself I realized that, in actual fact, I was not in the mood for cooking at all. I felt, if the truth be told, discontented, and yet I was not entirely sure why. As I took my largest saucepan out from the cupboard, my mind flashed over the early days of my marriage, when John was a captain in the Irish Republican Army. My duty, as his loyal wife, was to cook and care for his men, harbouring them all in our small cottage as renegade fighters; cleaning their wounds; comforting them. When John came home half-dead with his leg hanging off, I nursed him then came to America to earn the money for his operation. Who was there to comfort me? In later years I fed his friends, and all but reared his farm-boys. Men – for all their bravado and physical strength – could be weak and stupid creatures without a woman to care for them. It seemed to me, as I pulled the pan of water over from the sink to the stove, that I had been looking after men all my life, and here I was again, keeping the men happy. Making sure they were fed and watered, and made to feel important. Who was going to do the same for me?

I did not care to answer the question because in my heart I knew that any number of my new friends would gladly have me sit back and be cared for. The truth was, I was never the kind who liked to be looked after; not even by my husband. I was happiest when I was taking charge. I would allow Maidy to cook and care for me, but never to offer me her comfort. I was too proud to take comfort from any person, be they man, mother or friend – I kept my own counsel.

I was looking after other people because I was unable to allow anyone else to look after me, but grief has no time for such logic. I was angry: with the world, with the men, with John, but mostly with myself. Angry at my own weakness, and for the feeling that, despite all my running and my money and my management, I still barely felt in control of my own life.

I prepared a simple, hearty meal that would keep them content, but at the same time would not cause me to go to much – if any – trouble. A large hunk of bacon, warm or cold as it came, could be sliced at the table and served with hot gravy, new potatoes and a loaf of Bridie's fresh bread. I also had her send up two apple pies from the shop, which I would serve with a large pan of custard. Again, hot or cold didn't matter. I set the table for eleven: the nine men, 'Chuck' and me.

I dressed for dinner and applied make-up. If I was to be the only woman among this gathering of men, I could at least make sure that I looked like a lady and not a skivvy.

My hair had grown longer, so I swept it back from my face and clipped it up in a hairslide. I wore a simple black dress, for authority's sake, and applied a little rouge and lipstick. It was as much armour as I needed.

The men started to arrive just before seven. In their usual manner they took off their hats at the door and wiped their feet. They were, without exception, dressed smartly, which was not always the case, as many of them ate in their work clothes. Cazper, a Polish lad, and Johnny, his Irish sidekick, were the first to arrive. Both in their early twenties, married and with five small children between, they were cocky, immature fellows who wound each other up. For all that, they were not bad lads, and my somewhat formal invitation had cowed their usual swagger somewhat. Mario, Anna's husband, was his usual charming self and brought a bottle of wine along with him, which he handed to me with a great sweeping gesture and an overly ebullient kiss on both cheeks. Matt was the last to arrive just after ten past, and I got the impression that his tardiness was because he had rounded them up and given them all something of a talking to beforehand, warning them not to misbehave. In all honesty, I was beginning to wonder if this evening had been such a great idea.

The food was all ready, with the huge hunk of ham and a pile of floury spuds warming in the oven. I invited Mario to help me pour everyone a glass of wine from the dozen bottles I had set aside on the sideboard.

'Bridie isn't here,' I assured him, 'so we can enjoy a civilized meal!'

He laughed, but did not add a clever comment, as I had come to expect from him.

As I took a place in the centre of the table, Matt stood up to give me his seat at the head – the other end being reserved for our newcomer guest.

'Chuck said he would be here just after seven,' Matt said to me, then an awkward silence fell. The room was ripe with expectation that I should say or do something, and it began to take on the atmosphere of a boardroom. I would have said, 'Lads, I'll head out and let you have the place to yourselves,' but the evening had been contrived now. I had cast myself as a sort of Lady Bountiful, feeding her troops. What had I been thinking of, and what had Matt been thinking of, letting me do this? He would have been better placed suggesting that I purchased them a barrel of beer and let them get on with it.

'Food,' I said, breaking the silence, 'let me get the food.'

'I'll help,' said Matt, and he followed me out saying, 'I'm sorry, Ellie, it's a bit odd, with you being the only woman. Chuck is a nice chap, civilized – he'll help the atmosphere.'

A civilized metal-working docker. Was I a snob? I felt I was looking and acting like one, in any case. I didn't need another guest – this evening or any evening. I needed to clear my head and get away from all these men, all these people. What was keeping me here – in America – after all? I could go back to Ireland; the pain was gone – not that it had ever come on me with the force I believed it would. Perhaps it was time to go home, to escape all these complications, all this work. I would think about it tomorrow.

There was a heavy knock on the door.

'That'll be Chuck,' said Matt, 'you get it – I'll carry in the food. It's in the oven, right?'

I nodded and straightened my dress before opening the door. One more stranger to deal with, one more night of hostessing, and taking responsibility for other people. I could return home as soon as I wanted to and carry on where I had left off. I was, after all, an expert in closing the door on one world and opening up another. If nothing else, this trip to New York had proved that.

As I opened the door a tall man in my porch was propping his bicycle against the wooden railings. He turned and took off his cap. He had a scruffy, reddish beard and blond hair that was too long for a gentleman, yet too short for a vagrant. He wore working men's boots, and his legs were tightened with bicycle clips.

'Ellie?' he said, then he smiled and said it again, in a tone shot through with something peculiar. Disbelief. *'Ellie?'*

I would not have recognized him, not if he had come with a gold-embossed invitation card announcing himself. But for his blue eyes and the soft, adoring way they were looking at me, I would not have known that it was my old beau, Charles Irvington.

# Chapter Twenty-Two

I got such a shock that for a moment I doubted it was really him.

'Charles? Charles Irvington?'

'I might have known – the way Matt talked about you. Ellie, this mysterious Irishwoman who picked him up off the street and gave him a new life.'

He was beaming at me with that wide, white, American smile that I had so teased him about all those years ago.

For a moment my dead heart fluttered and I was drawn back – a country girl charmed by his confidence, impressed by his erudition and good looks, seduced by the glamour and promise of his family wealth.

I shook it off. I wasn't that person any more – and, by the look of him, neither was he.

'What happened to you?' It just came out.

He laughed, more heartily still.

'God, Ellie, you haven't changed – always the charmer.'

'No, I mean . . .'

He looked down at his trousers and raised his arms to announce the change.

'The Depression, Ellie. I couldn't be part of the system any more, when so many people were – so many of my friends on the docks were – well . . .'

'Suffering?'

He nodded and kept smiling at his own joke.

'Plus, my family lost all of their money.'

'Really?' I said, and although I was immediately worried at sounding cheap, I stupidly added, 'They lost everything?'

The Irvingtons had been so wealthy – beyond measure, it had seemed to me, and it seemed impossible that they now had nothing.

'Yes!' he laughed heartily. 'Although my parents managed to hold on to their house upstate, oh and two cars – and my mother hid most of her jewellery – but my brother is living in "reduced circumstances", working for somebody else as a shipping clerk. Not as lowly as me, mind you . . .'

'Not that he ever was.'

'No – he was always the smart one.'

'So when did you become "Chuck"?'

'When I joined the union. It was kind of a teasing nickname, given my lofty background.'

'I bet Daddy wasn't pleased.'

'No, indeed – "Daddy" was most unimpressed – but then that was nothing new.'

None of this was any great surprise. Charles had eschewed his parents' money long before they lost it. When I had first met him, he had chosen to work at the docks as a labourer rather than take up his father's mantle as head of the company – working his way up through the office ranks, like his brother. His breeding, coupled with his affinity for the working man and their politics, meant that Charles had always been adept at straddling both worlds: enjoying the benefits and security of his family wealth and the camaraderie and respect of the men he worked with. It seemed he was still doing that. He had wanted to marry an ordinary Irish girl, but shortly after I returned to

John in Ireland, he had followed his family form and married a rich man's daughter. I had read about it in a society magazine.

We had not stayed in touch. Although it would have been neither appropriate nor possible for us to have corresponded after my return home, I had resented the distance that had suddenly come between us. It was me who had put it there, but nonetheless it had hurt me that he had married so quickly and so 'well'. Part of me secretly wished he had kept the cottage on his brother's estate where he had promised we could live together in peace whether we married or not, then sat there pining for my return for the rest of his life. It was an irrational and unreasonable idea, but surely that is the nature of dreams. They do not exist in reality, and Charles did not exist for me after my return to Ireland – other than as a selfish desire for what might have been.

Although Charles had slipped into my thoughts since I came back to America, I had not allowed myself to indulge my curiosity by looking him up in the phone books, or the society magazines. The very moment that the vaguest notion of him came into my head, I felt only a guilty deception in the backdraught of John's death. Now the culprit of my fantasies was standing in front of me in the flesh. Doubtless, as a younger woman, in the early years after my return to Ireland I had imagined this very scenario in my foolish fantasies: coming back to America and Charles finding me again, although not in this house and certainly not in this way. The truth was that whenever I was feeling disgruntled with my life, or angry with my husband, I was able to call Charles' face to mind as easily as one calls to mind the face of a film star. Yet earlier that very day I had found myself unable to call to mind the image of my own John. The inappropriate injustice of that fact unfurled inside me.

'Look at the two of us talking about money – God, Ellie, how *are* you? Are you still – you know?'

Married. That's what he meant.

'Anyway. You look great – tell me all about yourself. What are you doing here?'

This was neither the time nor the place for reminiscing. The mere idea of telling him about my life, of talking for one more second about what I was doing here or what had happened to bring me here, twisted my stomach. I did not want to say John's name, and I was angry with Charles for the invitation to do so, however vague.

I made myself remember why he was here.

'We'd better go in,' I said, 'the men are waiting for us.'

'Ah, "the men",' he said, smiling that knowing, nonchalant smile, as if nothing mattered, as if no great time or distance had passed between us. Charles, for all he had once been, was a stranger to me now – as I surely was to him – even if he didn't know it yet.

I allowed him to follow me into the house, feeling his smile boring into my back. He was so delighted with himself, and it annoyed me that he clearly wasn't as shaken up by our chance meeting as I was.

My irritation didn't abate when he entered the room, and the quiet, serious atmosphere that I had left immediately lifted. It seemed to do so with his presence, although in reality half the wine was drunk already, despite the short time I had been gone. The men had started eating without us and, true to form, many of them had half-empty plates. Matt stood up as we entered, almost knocking his chair backwards. He looked concerned, and it occurred to me that he suspected our tardiness was caused by me trying to negotiate with Charles outside.

I was tempted towards a Mother Superior sternness, to note their bad manners in starting their food and inviting them to say grace, but I knew I should never get away with such loftiness in front of Charles.

'I'm sorry, Ellie, we started without you – Chuck, won't you sit and eat?'

Matt was acting like the man of the house, as if he were in charge. Johnny and Cazper exchanged a smirk that suggested they had been gossiping about the handsome 'Chuck' charming their uptight benefactor outside. How infuriating men were, with their impertinent attitudes! How ungrateful for all I had done for them! How insensitive to the delicacies of a woman's needs! There was Charles, his swagger impressing itself upon their stupidity. Men were good for nothing except for asserting their own self-importance and hurting you. John – I had loved him, I had given my life to him. He swore daily that he would never leave me alone, and then he died. Without warning, suddenly and callously disappearing out of my life, leaving me alone in the world. Leaving me loveless. I would never – could never – love another man again. Charles was talking to Mario, yet looking over at me with a knowing twinkle in his eye – the low-down rotter. He could go to hell – they could all go to hell, for all I cared.

'So, comrades,' Charles raised his glass, 'to our beautiful hostess – Ellie, you are some cook, and this is some house.'

'Thanks to Matt's hard work,' the upstart Johnny butted in, before I had the chance to assert that opinion myself.

I wondered how the cheeky young fellow's head would look if I boiled it and put it alongside the lump of bacon on the table.

I stood up and said, 'Excuse me while I go to the kitchen – I'll leave you gentlemen to talk.'

I need not have worried about offending them by leaving.

'You're certainly a skilled carpenter, Matt – the panelling in here is magnificent. Mahogany?' Charles asked.

Matt was bristling with pride. Charles shot me an amused glance. He was teasing me!

Let them flatter each other, these stupid men. I'd make provision for the wives and the children, and let the men look after themselves – and we'd see how far they got before they were rotting by the side of the road, without me to stand up for them!

I went out to the kitchen. Matt, the stupid clot, had not brought out the bread or taken the gravy from the stove – it was almost burnt in the pan! I added water from the kettle and stirred it slowly back up to thickening point, then picked it up to siphon it into the gravy jug. Forgetting to use a cloth, I burned my hands.

'Damnation!'

I went over to the sink and turned the cold tap onto the red line that was rising across my palm, when an anger as hot as the burn came over me. *Here I was – the little woman – out in the kitchen preparing their meal, while the men – the useless, feckless ingrates – sat in my warm dining room. What in the name of God was I doing?*

I left the bread and the gravy where it was and marched back in again – taking my seat at the head of the table. I was the woman in charge of this house. This was my party, and I was going to take my place at the table – not run around in the background like a skivvy. I remembered why I was doing this: to appease a group of overgrown schoolboys and have a welcoming party for a man I knew to be as arrogant a blaggard as ever walked the Earth.

'Matt,' I said, 'would you please go out to the kitchen and bring in the bread and gravy – it is on the stove. Johnny? You might go and give him a hand. The apple pies are warming in the oven, and we'll need eleven bowls – you know where they are.'

Indeed they didn't, but let them look. They jumped up, recognizing my tone perhaps.

'Now,' I continued, 'I'd like to welcome Mr Irvington to our table,' and I raised my glass.

Charles flinched at my formal address. He leaned back in his chair in an attitude of false casualness and said, 'Well, it's wonderful to see the men doing the bidding of a strong woman, Hogan. As it should be, of course.'

Oh God, he was showing off – humiliating me, teasing me in front of his new gang. So childish! Cazper suppressed a laugh.

'Mr Irvington . . .'

'Please,' he said, 'call me Chuck.'

I ignored him and continued.

'. . . it might have passed your notice, but it's the case around here that the women earn the money. We have started a very successful business to serve the needs of the residents of Yonkers. Some of the men enjoy handymen work at good rates, but the majority of our work is done by the women. Perhaps you think we ladies shouldn't be working, or perhaps you think we should unionize?'

'Perhaps you should.'

He kept his face cold and straight, but his jaw was tight. I could see I was rattling him. Politics was a serious subject for Charles – the only type of conversation that could really get at him.

'Ah, but there is no need. We women work together in happy harmony and, in any case, the business itself is owned by no-one. There are no bosses, for we work as a cooperative, all of us doing our part and all of us earning equal share. Perhaps you are aware of the cooperative model of business – Mr Irvington? No need for silly unions or politics, just level-headed common sense and equality, where we women are concerned.'

'Unions are no matter for mockery, and as a woman, Ellie,

you should know more than to hold them in contempt. We are working for the rights of women such as yourselves.'

'Nobody has fought for me, or on my behalf!' I insisted, but he ignored me and continued with his rhetoric.

'As a national movement, the Workers' Union is increasing in strength all the time. If we stand firm against their oppression, we will win. After all,' he said, directly addressing me now, 'why should the fate of many be left to the greed, or indeed the conscience, of a few? Why should the bankers and the businessmen be in charge – certainly they have proven themselves unworthy of our respect. No, the future success of America rides on the shoulders of the ordinary man and his willingness to work. Why should good, hard-working men like these be driven to take charity? They should be paid for their work.'

I looked across at Matt and he shrugged. Had Matt confided about our business to this 'stranger'? I certainly hoped not! In any case I reacted as swiftly as if it had been a direct attack.

'So what does your socialite wife make of all this "union" business?'

Charles immediately reddened, and for a moment I feared I had gone too far. Then he put his glass down and lit a cigarette, saying, 'We're divorced.'

He paused for a moment, then added coolly, 'And what does your husband make of you moving over to the other side of the world – or has he come with you *this time*?'

I did not pause, but said quite suddenly, 'He's dead.'

The men were rapt, looking from one to the other of us at each end of the table, like tennis spectators.

It was only after it was out that I realized what I had said. I felt a choking in my throat as if the words were trying to force themselves back down.

'Excuse me,' I said, and ran from the room.

# Chapter Twenty-Three

I went straight out to the kitchen. I was shaking and tried to calm myself by leaning on the dresser. The tin mugs hanging from hooks on the shelf started to wobble, so I pushed my hands harder onto the tiled work surface and breathed deeply, in and out, in and out, until they steadied.

In the hallway I heard Matt usher the men out the front door. I hoped Charles was with them.

I was too raw for company. I had exposed myself in front of them all – especially Charles. I did not want to continue playing out the drama that had begun with our meeting on the porch. The spiked flirtation, the competition for the men's affections – all had turned sour. In leaving the room as I had, I hoped I had drawn the curtain down on my revelation. He could start his work here and we would say nothing more about it.

I could not fathom why the incident had shaken me as much as it had, except that I had barely spoken of John since his death. Nobody had asked about my marital status, and I had not volunteered. My wedding band was still sitting on the mantelpiece above the range in Kilmoy, where I had placed it when making my last batch of bread the day before John died. The woman from Ireland with the gold band, and the woman without it who lived here in Yonkers, were one and the same and yet oceans apart.

Admitting to the fact of John's death in front of all those men had felt like a confession. I was ashamed of never having mentioned him before, almost as if I had killed him myself. As if, in not remembering him, in not acknowledging his existence – in running away from his death in the way that I had – I had committed a kind of murder. Beyond the shame of that was the knowledge that I should have watched John more closely, loved him more thoroughly when he was alive. I might have, *could* have, kept him if I had cared enough, if I had not been so caught up with myself. There was no way of saying I loved John, no way of talking about our marriage, without acknowledging that he was dead, and that was too painful. Silence was my only route to peace and now I had broken it, and as good as told everybody my personal business. The only way to get the bit of stillness back was to keep myself busy. Too busy to think, too busy to speak. The kitchen was upside down, the women and children would be back in less than an hour. There was plenty for me to be getting on with. I picked up a pile of dishes from the table.

'I'm sorry, Ellie.'

I had not heard Charles come in behind me and nearly jumped out of my skin.

'I thought you'd left with the others.'

'I just wanted say "sorry" – for pushing you, Ellie. I had no idea.' He reached across and caught the crockery as I almost dropped it.

'No – no,' I said, 'I started it. I shouldn't have been so rude about your wife.'

'Ex-wife.'

'Well, I'm sorry anyway.'

I wasn't sorry. Charles was divorced from a woman he barely loved, while I had been widowed at thirty-four from the love of my life – it was hardly the same thing. I picked up more dishes and carried them over to the sink. Charles followed me with a tea-towel. I wished he'd leave. Leave me alone. What did he want? What was he still doing here? (Although I knew the answer to both questions.)

'When did he die?'

Oh Jesus, pretending to care when he didn't even know his—

'John – wasn't it?'

A flurry of rage spiralled around inside me, searching for a way out. I wanted to scream at him to get out of the kitchen, the house – the question hung in the air like a hungry dog, glaring at me: '*When did he die?*' It was not the question that offended me, but the answer.

It had been less than four months since John died, and I was ashamed to say it out loud. The distance I had travelled, and all the things I had done in the time since he had passed, made it seem as if I didn't care. Charles looked at me, querying and concerned; he was innocent in this. A character from a chapter in my past, asking me what had happened next. Wanting to know what I had done after I had left him and returned to Ireland some ten years ago. He could have no idea what I was going through.

'Some time ago,' I said.

'Well – I'm sorry, Ellie. Perhaps more than anyone, I know how much you loved your husband.'

That was true. I had walked away from all that Charles had offered me before – a life of independence and wealth and freedom in New York, a place that I had come to love – and returned instead to the simple life of a farmer's wife in Ireland. To a life with no electricity, no telephone, no radio – none of the luxuries, large and small, that I had become used to. John was the only reason I had stayed in Ireland. There could have been no other. Not to Charles' mind at least.

If he had been jealous then, he wasn't now. There was real compassion in his voice.

I looked at his face: the whiskers made him look older and

wiser than his years, and his expression somehow indeterminate, less easy to read.

I didn't know who Charles was any more. In truth, I felt I didn't really know who *I* was any more. Not the girl he fell in love with and yet, with the two of us here together, alone in the house, I felt not so far away from that girl as I would have imagined.

I had a sudden urge to cross the room and kiss him. Not for his pity or his kindness, but rather to silence him; to stop the talk of John and death. I wanted to turn his friendship to passion – to lose myself in the distraction of desire.

'I need a drink,' I said.

I took a bottle of whisky from the larder and two cups, then sat at the table and nodded for him to join me.

'John died of a heart attack,' I said. 'It was sudden, a shock. I came here to . . .'

I paused. It seemed suddenly ridiculous, me sitting here with Charles, drinking whisky in the shabby kitchen of this large house in a New York suburb. How strange life was! Stranger still that I had been propelled into this situation by John's death.

'To escape?' Charles suggested.

'Something like that.'

I knew he would continue to ask me about my marriage and John, if only out of politeness, so I sensed his next question and answered it for him.

'We didn't have any children.'

I drew a line under the conversation by drinking back a shot of whisky. Raising my cup, I invited him to join me, before immediately pouring us both another.

'So,' I said, 'when do you start work?'

'Now? Tomorrow?' he said, smiling. 'Whenever you want me.' He was flirting. I felt a flutter of desire – prettier, more casual, less wilful than before. Perhaps I had not simply been running away after all, but had come to New York in search of an adventure thrilling enough to make me forget. Perhaps the coincidence of meeting Charles again was that adventure. His sleeves were rolled up to the elbow, soft white cotton pressed in a tight line against the muscular arc of his arms. He played with a packet of cigarettes, his fingers square and strong as they deftly manoeuvred the pack back and forth across the back of his hands.

'Are you all right, Ellie?'

It was Maureen, followed by Bridie.

'She's fine – look at her. I'll put the kettle on. Matt said you had a "turn" and insisted that we rush back. I said there was no need . . . Who's this?'

Charles stood up and put out his hand. Bridie ignored it and looked him up and down, her eyes finally resting on his beard with open disapproval.

'Where are we going to put this one? He'll have a shave before he rests that head on any of the good linens in this house.'

'Charles, this is Bridie,' I said.

'Well, you must be the lady who runs things around here. I'm very pleased to meet you, I'm sure.'

Maureen was standing behind me rubbing my shoulder. She knew there was something up, and her touch was meant to be reassuring and loving. I felt it only as patronizing and infuriating.

I was at the centre of a warm, convivial, amusing scene, but I felt only anger and confusion.

In that moment, when everything should have seemed ordinary and comfortable, nothing felt right. Nothing – not Charles being there, or Bridie's familiar gruffness, or Matt's concern, or Maureen's warm friendship. It was all a contrivance, a construct. Inside me I could feel the pain brewing like an ulcer.

I slipped the whisky bottle in my apron pocket and took it to my room, then drank myself into a deep, impenetrable sleep.

# Chapter Twenty-Four

Charles put up the scaffolding on the houses and, as Matt had said, proved useful both in sourcing cheap materials and in making contacts with other skilled tradesmen who were willing to put in a few hours to help out a friend. Charles got along with everyone he met – that was his gift. He had been earning little or nothing since the break-up of his marriage. He didn't volunteer much information about his ex-wife and the life they led together, and I certainly didn't ask, but it seemed to me that for the last year or so Charles had been living like a happy vagrant, relying on the hospitality of friends and colleagues, much in the same way as he had always relied on the generosity of his parents. A bicycle and a bag of books and clothes were all the possessions he had in the world, and he slept on the floors and shared the meals of the families and individuals he met through his work.

A privileged upbringing meant that, unlike the people he mixed with, Charles had never known personally what it was to worry about money. While he paid lip service to the horrors of poverty, he had never experienced hunger or hardship himself. As a result he had a carefree attitude towards money that I found both curiously admirable and very irritating.

'Property is theft,' he joked – which basically meant that

we should all help ourselves to the communal pot of food and money and beds.

Charles differed from the people around him, including me, in one crucial way. We revered money because we had suffered the hardship of being without it. Charles had no interest in money *per se*. Despite having dedicated his life to the protection of the working man, and through his union work to the ideal of an honest wage, he felt no need of one himself.

His union principles and natural leadership meant that, as he worked alongside Matt, Charles began to share his responsibilities in managing the men. Matt still oversaw their everyday work, but it was Charles they turned to for counsel.

As his weeks with us went by, I learned that Charles had been more deeply embedded in union life than I had at first thought, often earning a small stipend from the unions for negotiating with the bosses on their behalf. For a long time, especially on the docks, the unions had been run by mob bosses, who charged the ordinary man a fee for getting and keeping them in work. Charles had been a member of the Communist Party and stood by their ideal of a ruling proletariat, but he became frustrated with the in-fighting and politics of unionism. He talked the talk in order to recruit men round to his way of thinking, and to strengthen their resolve in getting their dues, but Charles was more of a negotiator than a fighter. He was excited that Roosevelt had passed the second phase of his New Deal of reform programmes and seemed to be actively encouraging strong labour movements, but Charles was still sceptical as to how that was going to pan out with the bosses – both mob bosses and legitimate ones. Charles, for all his talk of 'men standing together', was a lone operator. He ploughed his own furrow as a freelance troubleshooter for the unions, who recognized his unique ability to play each side so that both thought they had won.

I got a taste of this when he negotiated a deal with some local landlords for me. Two more families had been sent to us, looking for our help. One of the women was very ill, having just lost a baby, and their need was so urgent that, despite already running three houses, I decided to try and lease another house nearby for them. Instead of paying a set rent, Charles suggested that I get Mr Williams to set up a meeting with two of the speculators who were leasing us their houses. His idea was that the men could do up the properties, thus increasing their value, in exchange for either a part-share in the property '. . . or whatever else I can drum out of them!'

'Gentlemen,' Charles said, walking into the small meeting room at the back of Mr Williams' office, 'such a pleasure to meet you both.' He shook their hands and greeted them with such natural and charming authority that they seemed happily engaged in anything he might say, before the meeting had even begun.

Despite his casual attire, Charles oozed money and privilege and class. I had learned that although America welcomed everyone, it was as snobbish as the next place. The American elite were newer, but they were nonetheless powerful, and the two landlords were smitten. I served them coffee and cake from our shop, and explained the nature of our cooperative.

'Of course, none of this would be possible without your generous patronage,' Charles said, as the landlords glowed. He then went on to explain Roosevelt's policy of labour reform, as if they would soon have to negotiate something of this nature by law anyway. The veiled threat was that if they left it much longer, they might find themselves dealing with angry sitting tenants over whom they would have no control, rather than a reasonable chap like himself. The landlords did not want to give away a share in their properties, so we left with an agreement that the men would be paid salaries for their work, which would be offset against a small monthly rent, requisite with the state of the properties. When they were fully refurbished, the rent could be negotiated again along the lines of a ten-year lease, and the men would be paid a smaller salary to maintain and caretake the properties on the landlord's behalf.

Charles would get one of his Communist Party comrades, a lawyer, to draw up watertight contracts that would secure homes for our six families for a good fifteen or twenty years to come.

'Are you impressed?' he asked, as soon as we were out of earshot.

'Should I be?' I said.

'Well, it's money you don't have to shell out from your pocket, and we came out of it with a wage for the men, which should keep them happy. For a while.'

'I suppose,' I shrugged. I didn't really pay much attention to what he was saying, because it had occurred to me, as we were walking side by side along the street, that Charles and I made something of a dynamic partnership. He had helped me out before in our past; he had secured me a first-class passage back to Ireland, all the more generous a gesture given that I was returning there without him.

'Where are you staying tonight?'

Matt had moved into one of the new houses (albeit temporarily, as he was working day and night to make it more habitable for the tenants) and so it seemed only natural that I would offer Charles his place in the small drawing room downstairs.

'I'm all out of favours with everyone else,' he said. 'Are you offering me a floor?'

And so that very evening Charles joined our family.

For the first five nights I lay awake in bed knowing that Charles was lying on a mattress in the room beneath me, staring up at the ceiling, willing me to come to him. Over and over again lying alone in my bed I euphorically recalled the first time we kissed. It was in the pink-rimmed dawn after a party on his brother's Hamptons estate, with me in my best party dress, Charles in a smart cream blazer. He had asked me to marry him before the party, despite the fact that I was already married to John. I had sharply refused, but later had been lured into the kiss by the glamour of my surroundings, the distance of home and the persistent friendship of my handsome pursuer.

My propriety, and his respect for my status as a married woman with good Catholic morals, had held us back from making love that night. I was young and beautiful and my love was a precious gift, and to grant or withhold it was my moral duty, however difficult it was at times. If I had not been forced to return to Ireland by the death of my father shortly after the incident, perhaps Charles and I would have consummated our affair. In the end I left him broken-hearted, with his failed dreams, and returned to my husband in Ireland with my morals shaken, but broadly intact.

No such quandary stood in the way of our needs now. He was below me, separated by a mere set of stairs. I could go to him any time I wanted. I was sure he would not turn me away. My stomach burned with excitement, my mind curled over a picture of his face, blocking out everything but his sharp blue eyes, the curve of his mouth, until it was all I could see when I closed my eyes. But I held myself back. If he wanted me, he could come and get me. I would wait and, in any case, I was enjoying the distraction. As long as I folded myself around thoughts of Charles, I was able to put John out of my mind. It was a familiar path – the quandary of choosing one over the other, except that now one of them was no longer here. I wanted Charles and knew, or sensed, that he wanted me. That was distraction enough for me.

I did not ask myself if I loved Charles, if I was being true to my heart, because I feared that any love I had within me had been buried with John. I loved Maidy, and if I had been cold-hearted enough to leave her behind weeping over her dead son, perhaps all love was gone from me.

What I felt for Charles was not love – the mental obsession, the burning physical sensation, the desire to be held by him; but it was the closest thing I had felt to it since John died, so I hung on to it.

On the sixth night the house was empty. Bridie and Maureen had taken Nancy and the baby to visit one of the new families.

The front hall door was not yet closed on the women when he grabbed me and we staggered backwards onto his bed. We made love with urgent, impassioned hunger – hard and hurried. I shut my eyes and strained my body against his, enjoying the intimate thrill of flesh on flesh, and when we were finished I closed myself confidently in and around his limbs, locking myself into the comfort of his strong body. John was the only man I had known in this way before. Just being with Charles made me feel alive and warm again – human.

We didn't speak for a while afterwards, but just lay there, breathing onto each other's skin. As the blue light of the evening started to turn dark grey I broke the silence and said, 'You'd better go, the women should be coming back soon.' My voice sounded hoarse and heavy, breaking through the stillness.

'Goodness, we can't upset the women.'

His words were light and teasing. But for a moment I felt hurt. Had he got what he came for? Then I remembered that I didn't, or at least shouldn't, care whether he loved me or not. I was a mature woman of the world – a widow, for God's sake, not a lovesick schoolgirl. I moved to get up, but his arm held me down for a second more.

'Ellie . . .'

As he paused over what to say next, Charles' arms loosened and I sat up and started to pull the dress over my head.

'. . . oh, it's nothing.'

I was convinced that Charles had been about to tell me he loved me, then realized, perhaps, that it was too soon. In that moment I wanted to be loved again. The loss of John's love had hardened my warm, womanly spirit. Perhaps, after all, Charles' love could open me up, make good on John's abandoning me with his untimely death. Perhaps life could return to how it had always been. With a man's love, I could feel whole again. That being said, I did not push him.

In truth, I was not ready for Charles to proclaim his love for me out loud and was relieved that he thought better of it.

# Chapter Twenty-Five

Bridie did not approve of Charles.

She did not approve of his union activities, and she did not approve of the amount of time Charles spent in our house, 'eating our food and contributing nothing but hot air'.

She pushed aside the fact that he was working alongside Matt. 'Matt is a *completely* different sort of man,' she insisted, but would not elaborate further. 'How long is he staying?' she asked, after Charles had been there for a week.

At the centre of the old woman's objection to Charles was his background as a 'gentleman'. Save for the past few difficult years since her husband's death, Mrs Flannery had been in service to the Boston-based industrialist James Adams all of her working life. She was proud of her position as his housekeeper. Even when she was posted out to his Manhattan apartment to keep an eye on his flighty young wife Isobel, she always spoke of him in hushed tones as a 'true gentleman'. 'Manners are bred into a man – and position, Ellie. It's important in this life to know your place.'

Bridie would have disapproved of me having moved from my 'place', in making money through business, but in reality she was more concerned that it was a masculine pursuit. I had never adopted the airs and graces that are the rich woman's entitlement, at least not so that Bridie had ever seen them; and in that sense, at least, she was able to accommodate the fact that her little parlour maid was now her patron.

However, for a gentleman to turn his back on his birthright and eschew the privileges and status that it was his responsibility to uphold – that was a travesty to the class structure that had been the backbone of Bridie's social system. It was a betrayal not just of his own class, but of hers, seeming to make a mockery of her servitude. The more Charles tried to woo Bridie by helping her around the kitchen and teasing her with schoolboyish pinches to the rump, the more I could see that he was offending her. Aside from those one or two early barbed remarks, Bridie made no comment to me about Charles one way or the other, which only made things worse. When she huffed and puffed and complained about people, she got everything out of her system and usually came round to them. I valued her friendship, and her dislike of Charles made me uncomfortable, although Charles was such a likeable chap that I knew what was really bothering Bridie was his relationship with me. Two unmarried people 'carrying on' with each other under the same roof – and, in his eyes, one of them still married.

'She's Catholic, Charles,' I told him.

'So are you,' he objected, as I pushed him out of bed and back downstairs to his own room to sleep.

'That's different,' I said, 'and you know it.' *It used not to be,* I thought. *I used to pray and go to Mass every week. I used to believe in it all.*

'A good – little – Catholic – girl.' He marked each word out with a small cross from my shoulder to my neck.

'Stop it,' I said, wrenching myself away, 'it's not right to mock religion.'

'I'm a Communist – it's what we do: we minister for the Devil.'

He pressed his lips to the nape of my neck, slipped his hands through my arms and around my breasts, until I collapsed back onto the bed.

We tried to be as discreet as we could, or rather I did, but as the weeks went past it became harder.

The dangerous thrill of passion passed into the comfort of being with somebody again. I still couldn't say if I had fallen in love with Charles, but I knew I liked the feeling of having him close. I slept better when he was in the bed next to me. At night, half-asleep, I would not know whether the warm mound of muscle lying next to me was Charles or John, but just to be sharing our breath in this small, closed space made the night feel safe.

Automatic acts of intimacy crept into our everyday lives. Standing up from the table, Charles would briefly rest his hand on my shoulder as he passed and I would reach for it. I would lay claim to him with a touch on his arm during conversations with him, and with others. These small signs of affection diluted the heaviness I felt pressing against my inside. His love lifted the rock that my soul had become. Although I did not think I was trapped, Charles somehow made me feel free.

'Is anyone else coming to Mass?'

Bridie was putting on her gloves. She wore gloves to Mass, even in summer, to hide the coarseness of her hands. She had on a brand-new coat that I had insisted on buying for her, and a beret that she had knitted herself, which was surprisingly smart.

'I'll come,' I said.

She raised her eyebrows at me and muttered, 'Makes a change.'

Not being able to express myself in my own home because I had to humour Bridie had started to wear thin. I needed to confront her, and this was my best opportunity to get her on her own.

'Well, you'd better hurry along – Matt will be here with the van in a minute.'

'We'll walk, Bridie,' I said. 'It's a fine day, and we've plenty of time.'

Bridie was no fool. She took the hint, and as we turned left down the hill towards the village she folded her handbag into her chest and walked in stern silence, waiting for my cue.

I was not nearly as afraid of confronting Bridie as I should have been. Her fierce, authoritarian manner was the matronly old woman's armour. It had seen her through a lifetime of servitude, and in the poverty and hardship of her senior years it had kept her pride intact. Bridie Flannery used her staunchness to protect herself, but also to control others. I was not going to be bullied by her.

'Why do you dislike Charles so much, Bridie?'

'I don't dislike him.'

'Oh, come on, Bridie – you're so frosty around him?'

'I can see he is very charming and, in his own way, a kind man . . .'

'But?'

'But?'

'But – well, I don't like what he is doing with you, nor you with him.'

So now it had been said. Much as I liked and respected Bridie, I wasn't going to have my life run by somebody else's moralizing. Religion was a personal choice, and my choice was to bypass the 'rules'. I had lived by them all my life, and where had placing my trust in God got me? Widowed, childless – so confused and unhappy that I had run away from my own life and started another. When I had begged God to give me a child, He had simply used my womanly need to torture me, snatching two babies from my warm womb to keep their souls for Himself, in His cold, eternal Limbo. Perhaps Charles was right and it was all nonsense. In any case I was going to play by my own rules from now on. I wasn't going to turn away pleasure and happiness for the sake of some outdated moral code. Especially not when it was simply for the benefit of not offending somebody else. No matter how much I liked and respected Bridie, she wasn't going to dictate to me how I should live my life.

I told her as much, in no uncertain terms.

By the time I had finished admonishing her, her religion and her God, we had both come to a natural halt at a low suburban wall some yards away from the church. Church-goers were quickly nipping in through the tall creamy doors, mothers poking their dawdling children in the back, waving angrily at their husbands to hurry along, indicating that the Mass service had started. Bridie did not rush to join them, although she was never late for Mass. Instead she looked at me carefully and said, 'You can't hide from yourself, Ellie.'

'What do you mean?'

Immediately I had said it, I wanted to take it back. I didn't want to know what she meant. I didn't want to hear it.

'You think that by being with him, you can either bury John for good or bring John back, Ellie. You can't run from grief, Ellie – it'll find you. Believe me, I know.'

With that she grabbed my arm in her gloved hand and gave it a tight squeeze and, shaking it gently, said, 'I'll light a candle for you,' then walked off into Mass.

Bridie knew I wouldn't follow her; she knew that a part of me was lost to God and to the world.

# Chapter Twenty-Six

The shop in Yonkers was completely different from my small country shop at home. There you could sew or read from one end of the day to the other, greeting customers from your chair until they sat down and joined you for a chat, more often than not forgetting what they came in for.

Everyone here was in a hurry, although it made little sense. The wealthy clients were ladies at leisure, and the poorer customers had no jobs to keep them busy, but rushing about was the New York way and it suited me just fine. The shop itself, thanks to Matt and the boys, was beautifully laid out. At the back was the bakery and kitchen, where Bridie and Anna worked; a refrigerated countertop separated the work area from the front of the shop, whose walls were lined with shelves full of storable produce, and the floor taken up with a hotchpotch of tables and chairs where we had set up a cafe. Put simply, our prices were low and Bridie's bread was the best in town. When she added cakes and biscuits to her repertoire, we bought a coffee machine, dug out a few side tables and chairs from our own houses, and the cafe was born.

We had two contrasting types of clientele. The first was the middle-class women of Yonkers. Many of them had had to tighten their belts and let housekeepers go, and shopping for

Bridie's and Anna's produce was the next best thing to having somebody in your house cook for you. The business had built up at an extraordinary rate, developing different services in a matter of weeks on a supply-and-demand basis. One day a woman came in and lunched on a plate of lasagne that Anna had tried out on the customers, and asked if she could buy a tray of it for her family. It went down so well that her friends started coming in looking for home-made takeaway Italian meals.

The opportunity to make money meant that we never refused a customer. Maureen ran the sales and cafe, the front of house, and never said that we couldn't do something. One day a man came in looking for a sandwich, and she went out back panicking to Anna, who scooped a ladle of bolognese sauce into the husk of one of Bridie's loaves, and he declared it the best sandwich he had ever eaten. That night Bridie roasted a huge ham, and the sandwich bar was open. Scandalized at the price of smoked fish, Anna sent Mario down to the docks to negotiate with the fishermen, then built a small smoking shed in their garden. Before long she had added a smoked-fish counter at the front of the shop, and while Mario was doing that, he might as well try and get a better price on wholesale pork and start curing ham, just the way his mama did.

Another day a woman came to the back kitchen door of the shop with three children, looking for food. Young Nancy opened the door and, seeing her own well-fed infant strapped into a chair, chewing on a lump of bread, she took her life in her hands and gave the woman a loaf and a hunk of good ham that Bridie was keeping to feed the house that evening.

When the old woman found out, Bridie roared at her. 'You can't feed every hungry person that comes looking for food, child!' Then, realizing how bad that sounded, she added, 'There were more ordinary cuts you could have given her.'

'She was a really nice lady – not a beggar or anything – and she was so embarrassed. She gave me a dime,' Nancy said, taking the coin out of her pocket and, rather sweetly, handing it over to me. 'She just said she couldn't afford the food in the cafe, and the children were hungry and—'

'A dime!' Bridie said. 'Sure, what good is that to anyone?'

I knew Bridie. Her particularly hardline huffing meant that she was flustered with guilt. She'd have fed every homeless waif in the city from her own kitchen.

So I took her aside and we came up with a plan. Away from ears that might be offended, Bridie and I were able to agree that if we started giving away food, we would become a charity serving everybody but ourselves. We could give away leftovers from the back kitchen door at the end of the day, but we agreed it was humiliating for people to take the scraps from another man's table, like common dogs. I had truly learned that people always prefer not to take charity when they can prove their independence in some way. For that reason we decided to run a 'five-cent' counter in the shop and cafe.

Bridie and Anna came up with ingenious ways to make delicious food for almost nothing. Using ends of meat and crusts, they made up piles of sandwiches. They sold corners of lasagne, and slices of 'poor man's spaghetti omelettes'. Slightly burnt cookies and cakes and day-old loaves were all sold for five cents. We opened the five-cent counter between three and six every day. It was first come, first served. When the food was gone, it was gone, and nobody's money was turned away. We were not a soup line or a charity – and there was no dress code. You could eat your food in the cafe or you could take it away; it made no odds to us.

The fancy, upmarket housewives often queued for bargains alongside the homeless, and sat side by side on crowded tables eating their sandwiches and spending their money. Some of our regular customers were so taken with the atmosphere of our shop that they offered their services to us as volunteers. We explained that we were a business cooperative, not a charity.

Bridie reckoned that the five-cent line was paying for itself. I asked her to put the money from it aside, so that we could account for it separately. We were taking money from the poor, after all, and if we got the opportunity it would be nice to give some of it back some day. Maybe start up a new charitable venture with it.

All these things were possible because we worked together. There were so many of us, and because we lived and worked as a community there was always somebody there to help – always an extra pair of hands to make a new project happen. There was bickering from time to time: Anna wanted the walls of the cafe painted yellow, and was offended when Maureen replaced her red gingham tablecloths with new blue ones. Johnny was angry because he had helped Mario build the smoking shed, and felt that entitled him to a cut of the food business. There was always somebody who felt they should be earning more, or that somebody else should be earning less than the next person. But in reality everything was divided equally.

Charles delighted in pointing out to me that we were living in a Communist utopia. In those early months, however, there were still so many mouths to feed, so many houses to finish, that it was hard to keep a track of everything. Charles turned out to be a godsend, able to arbitrate disagreements, as he had a way of making everything seem fair. Where Matt was afraid of confrontation, and I was too fond of it – always pushing back the compulsion to remind people to be grateful for the roof over their heads and food in their stomachs – Charles was able to charm everybody and keep them all on the path of working towards helping each other.

I believed, cynically perhaps, that it was only a matter of time before the petty sniping developed into a full-scale war. Sooner or later people would tire of helping each other and would want to help themselves. I didn't know how that would happen, or when. I knew that the labour and money would have to be divided more equally, but for the time being I just ran the show as best I could.

I worked in the shop myself most days. Giving myself no set task meant that I could set about doing whatever needed to be done, from hour to hour, day to day: waiting on tables, sweeping up, wiping around the kitchen and, when things were running smoothly, simply sitting at a table out front, pottering through the paperwork, listening to the ping of the new till and soaking up the convivial atmosphere of flying trade and friendly chat.

When I had no desire for company, I sat at the same corner table for one.

It was early one morning and, while the door was unlocked, the 'Closed' sign was clearly up. I had been in there since six with Bridie, helping her in the kitchen, as Nancy's baby was unsettled with her teeth, so the old woman's scullery maid (as she insisted on calling Nancy!) was off. With the first batch in the ovens, and two more ready to go, I was enjoying a break by reading the morning edition and drinking a strong black coffee at my favourite table, when a sleazy-looking man came to the door. He briefly studied the sign, then gave it a little flick of his hand and marched right in, bold as brass.

'We're not open for another hour, if you'd like to come back then?'

He was in his mid-thirties with a badly shaped, thin moustache and a cheap suit. The kind of undesirable character you'd

see peddling their wares outside speakeasies and nightclubs. It
was early for the likes of him to be out.

He pulled over a chair and sat down at the table opposite me,
spreading his lanky legs out on either side of the narrow table.

'You're the boss?'

Operators like this were two-a-penny, petty criminals making
money on the black market from other people's misfortunes. He
was probably trying to sell me something. But even as I raised
a disapproving eyebrow at him, I knew he wasn't. There was a
nasty slant in his eyes.

'What do you want – as you can see, we're closed for—'

'Coffee would be nice, black and strong, with plenty of sugar.'

He lit a cigarette and leaned back in the thin chair, crossing
his long, spindly legs over each other at the ankles, settling in as
if he owned the place.

I knew what this was.

I went behind the counter and poured him out a cup of coffee
from the pot, then I put it in front of him and nodded at the
sugar bowl. 'You can sweeten it yourself.' I held out my hand
and said firmly, 'That will be five cents, please.'

He smiled at me and shook his head in amusement. Patronizing me. He put the cigarette between his curled lips and reached
into his pocket, pulled out a dime and left it on the table. Then
he held the lit stick between his forefinger and thumb and, pointing it at me, said, 'You're a clever lady, I can tell – but you're not
from the Bronx.'

He stubbed the cigarette out in the saucer of his coffee cup
and took a noisy slug.

'Where you from?'

'Ireland,' I said, curtly. I knew exactly what was coming. I
walked back over to the counter and started to go about my
business.

'The Bronx is a rough place, lady. Even up here, in this nice area, you got some nasty characters running around. It's a dangerous world, lady – bad people running about with guns and such like, niggers riding up on the train looking for trouble, you get my drift. All sorts of bad things happening about the place, which nice ladies like you don't wanna worry your pretty little heads about.'

He stood up and walked towards the counter, giving me a thoroughly charmless, grimy grin. There was only Bridie and me in the shop. The street outside was quiet. My hand was resting on the long-handled sandwich knife.

'Now me and my friends, we run a little business . . .'

'I see,' I said. I wouldn't be threatened like this, not in my own shop. 'And this little business of yours,' I asked, 'does it require you to carry a gun yourself?'

'Sometimes,' he said, slightly wrong-footed, but rather pleased at the same time.

'Do you have one on you now?'

He pulled back his jacket to reveal his skinny torso in its striped shirt. Then he slithered towards the counter hatch and leaned on the gate towards me, saying, 'What would I need a gun for, visiting a pretty thing like you? '

He drummed his fingers quickly along the counter as I chopped a tomato for no reason. As I pretended to work, my eyes glanced quickly over at the flimsy latch, the only thing that stood between him and me. He saw me looking. The drumming speeded up along the white-painted wood, his filthy nails running up and down like cockroaches.

'No gun today, lady – at least not one that's made of metal.' He put his hand to the latch.

'Good,' I said, pointing the long, sharp blade of the bread knife at him, 'then you'll be interested to know that we don't need protection in this shop, from you or any of your friends.'

He raised his hands, still smiling that dirty, sleazy smile.

'Whoa – hey, pretty lady, careful now who you point that knife at.'

'I'll do a lot more than point it, mark my words, if you don't get out of my shop this instant.'

I walked towards him and put the tip of the knife as close to his face as I dared. He leaned back, laughing nervously.

'Okay, okay.' He skipped backwards out of the shop, waving his hands and still laughing at me. He seemed not so much frightened as a little deranged – drugged perhaps? When he was gone, I ran and locked the door after him.

Bridie called out from the kitchen and I told her I'd be with her shortly.

I decided that if he had been a genuine mobster looking for protection, he would surely have come armed. He was just some cowardly fool, chancing his arm.

In either case my heart was pumping with fear or rage, I was not sure which. I felt something drip from my hand and realized that I was holding the handle of the knife so tightly that the blade had dug into my thumb without me having noticed.

'Mother of Christ, Ellie, you're bleeding all over the clean floor!'

'I was . . . chopping tomatoes.'

'Well, that's a fine cut, you silly girl – run it under the tap and I'll get a bandage. Why is the door locked? There are deliveries due . . .'

I didn't tell her. I didn't want to worry her. I could handle this myself – in any case, Charles would surely know what to do for the best.

When I arrived back home later that afternoon I was relieved to see Charles' bicycle parked on the porch. I guessed that everyone else was working and that we would have the house to ourselves for a few hours. He was the only person I could talk to about the mobster's visit; the only person who would be able to tell me what to do.

I found him sitting in the dining room with his head in his hands. On the polished table in front of him was a torn envelope and an opened letter. It looked like bad news.

'What is it?' I asked straight away.

'It's my wife,' he said, 'she's going to remarry.'

'Oh,' I said. I had not asked Charles about his marriage because I had not wanted to answer questions about my own.

'She wants me to take Leo.' He blurted it out suddenly.

'Leo?' I said.

'Our son.'

I didn't know Charles had a son – a child. My knees buckled slightly with shock, but I did not sit down. I did not want to commit to this conversation. I did not want to think about what it might mean.

He did not look at me, just put his hand to his mouth in a gentle fist and then, leaning on his elbow, stared thoughtfully out of the window. Perhaps he was waiting for me to respond; to say that I would take his son in, that I would welcome them both and create an instant family for them. Seeing how I was taking in all and sundry, feeding and housing the poor and hungry, he could surely rely on me to step in and take responsibility for his child.

'I didn't know you had a son,' I said.

'There never seemed the right time to tell you.'

Perhaps he was right, but it felt like a deception. Children changed everything.

It was up to me now to respond. But it was too huge a thing either to take the child or refuse him. If I refused, I would be rejecting them both. But to take him?

'Oh dear,' I said, 'well, I'm not staying – I'm only running an errand for Bridie.' And I quickly left the room.

I never ran errands, and I had left the house as suddenly as I had come in and was empty-handed. Charles knew I was lying; he knew what I was avoiding and certainly would have intuited why – he was a clever man.

Over the coming days we carried on, both of us, as if the letter had never come, and I didn't mention the mobster's visit. Life was an exchange of favours and kindnesses. In not offering to help him with his family predicament, there was no way I could now ask for his help.

That night, after we made love, I lay with my head on Charles' chest and thought: '*Charles has a child. I have no child.*'

'I love you,' he said, murmuring it into my hair. It was the first time he had actually said it out loud, although I felt I had heard it many times before.

I pretended I had already fallen asleep.

# Chapter Twenty-Seven

Matt had barely come near me since he had moved out of the house. With building work starting, and new living arrangements being made because of the new houses we had leased, it was easy to tell myself this was because we had both been busy. In reality I knew that Charles' presence had changed things between us. As my right-hand man, Matt seemed to have laid some claim to me before Charles had come back, and in truth there had been a warm friendship developing between us, although never anything that I might have described as love, as I understood it. I know he regretted bringing Charles into our lives, and although it was never spoken of, his dislike of Charles was obvious to everyone, and I assumed that jealousy lay at its root.

For this reason Matt had been avoiding me, taking his meals with the Balduccis rather than with us. So when he arrived mid-morning and called me into the dining room to talk, I knew there was something wrong.

He was holding his cap in his hand and nervously rolling the edge of it round and round with his coarse, square fingers. 'The men have gone on strike,' he said.

'What?' I squealed.

He moved his large hands up to his face and stroked his chin.

'They are refusing to work today. They say they want to be paid.'

How had this happened? Where was Charles? Then I remembered that he had said he was going to see his wife, to make arrangements for their son. He must have left already.

'But do they not understand that they are working on the houses instead of paying rent? Perhaps that hasn't been explained to some of the newer—'

'Oh, I've explained all right.'

He turned his face to look out the window, afraid to hold my eye. There was a fresh gash under his ear, a drip of dried blood gathered in his neat sideburns.

'Have you been fighting, Matt?'

He instinctively moved his hand up to cover it, saying, 'It's nothing.' I saw that his knuckles were bruised.

His jaw was set in fury. I had never seen him like this before. Was he furious with the men, or with me? I could not quite tell.

'It's like I said before: they are complaining that the women aren't looking after them, because they are working for you in the shop – and meanwhile they are working as hard, for no pay . . .'

'But they are being paid,' I was getting angry, 'with food in their stomachs and roofs over their heads!'

'They say that you're creaming off a profit from the shop and—'

'What! And you put them straight, I hope – defended me?'

He indicated his bloody ear. It wasn't the first time, I suspected, that Matt had bloodied himself, and I was certain it wouldn't be the last.

'I'm sorry,' I said, rather more curtly than he deserved, but it seemed to soften him.

'They are all roused up into a rabble, Ellie. I can't talk sense into them.'

I was incandescent: with the men, with Matt for being so weak as to let this happen and so stupid as to fight. Charles would have all this sorted out in an instant. I cursed him for going away, then cursed myself for having chased him off as I did.

'I am going over to see them and sort this out.'

'No, Ellie, really. They are all roused up, I just wanted to let you know so that—'

I turned on him, 'So that what? I would start paying them from the money the women are earning in the shop, to pay for the food to put in their bellies? For the upkeep of the children? So that they can spend the money – *my* money – on liquor and cigarettes and hats to make them look like big, clever gentlemen?'

He followed me out, saying, 'No, Ellie, please . . .' as I marched into the hall, threw aside my apron and straightened my hair.

'I'll not have it, Matt – and I'll not have you scrapping like a *fool* in my defence. I can look after myself.'

'Wait – let me talk to them again this afternoon.'

But it was too late. My blood was up.

Mario was sitting on the wall of his house, smoking and talking with Cazper and Johnny.

'Morning, gentlemen,' I said.

'Morning, Ellie,' Mario replied. He seemed normal enough, as if he were simply on a work break.

'Matt, would you please go and gather the rest of the men?'

I stood there, my arms folded. Johnny casually lit a cigarette, smiled at me and doffed his cap, saying, 'Morning – *Ma'am.*'

He was surely the ringleader, cheeky little upstart. I marked his card.

'Follow me inside,' I said, moving towards the Balduccis'

front door. 'We've business to discuss, and I'll not do it out on the street.'

'Hadn't you better wait to be *invited* into Mario's house?' Johnny said. Cazper laughed, his cheeky, sneering sidekick. I turned, and as Johnny raised the cigarette to his lips I saw the cuts on his knuckles.

'Mario,' I addressed him directly, 'please may I conduct a meeting in your house?'

'Of course,' he said brightly, 'no problem!'

He wasn't on their side. Thank God. In all likelihood he didn't even know what was going on. These two upstarts were the problem. Punching Matt? A good man – an older man they'd do well to respect! I'd fling them out on the street in a heartbeat, although their wives were both lovely girls and hard workers. Shame on them, the ingrates! Taking advantage of my generosity and my kind heart. They'd soon see what I was made of – they all would!

Mario offered to make coffee for the nine or so men who were gathered in his cosy sitting room, but I said, 'No, Mario, let's get this over and done with. Matt has brought it my attention . . .'

Nine big, heavy men all stood with their arms folded, looking at me: defensive, expectant, ready. All except Mario, who sat re-laxed in his favourite armchair, signalling at one or two of them to do the same, like a good host. Matt stood 'guard' at the door behind me. Those who remained standing – among them Johnny and Cazper – I assumed to be the discontents, so I aimed my firmly delivered words directly at them. How I wished Charles were here, but I could do this.

'Matt has brought it to my attention that some of you are unhappy with the arrangement we have.'

Johnny raised his top lip and looked at Cazper, who shrugged. I couldn't read them. From his place in the armchair Mario spoke.

'Is like this, Ellie. We know the men in the new houses is getting paid by the landlords to do the work. We just want the same as them.'

'But those men are paying rent,' I said. 'It's a different set-up entirely.'

'So we've formed a union,' said Johnny.

Mario put his head in his hands. 'What you go tell her that for?'

I was completely flummoxed. I thought Mario was my friend.

'You've done what?' I truly was as angry as hell. I looked at Matt and he shrugged. He seemed as angry as I was.

'All above board, like,' said Cazper.

'Is this true?' I asked Matt.

'Don't look at me, Ellie – this is nothing to do with *me*.'

'We've all signed up with the Socialist Workers' Union.'

'Chuck arranged it,' Johnny said.

'Clever guy,' Cazper added. 'He reckons if we working men stick together, we can just about get anything we want.'

'It's men like us that are going to rebuild this country,' somebody said from behind Mario.

'If we stand together and fight, the poor man will win out.'

'We've got to stand up for our rights as US citizens.'

I stood, dumbfounded. Charles had arranged all this. Behind my back. This was his doing.

I looked at Matt, half-expecting a triumphant sneer, but he was looking at the ground and would not catch my eye. He, too, was embarrassed for me.

Mario moved over and placed his hand reassuringly on my arm. 'Chuck's one of the good guys, Ellie. He's just looking out for us.'

'Like you,' Cazper said.

'We're grateful for all you've done for us, Ellie,' said Johnny. 'We just want the chance to make things more even. Pay you back properly.'

I didn't care about any of that. Charles had betrayed me.

'Chuck said he was going to sort things out with you – then, when he went away and hadn't said anything, Mario said—'

'Well, Charles didn't say anything at all about it to me,' I said. 'Mario? Matt? I'll sit down with you both tomorrow and come to an arrangement we're both happy with. As to whether you work or not, I really don't care. It's your families who have to live in the houses, not mine.'

Brave words, but my insides were shaking. How could I have been so naive, so blind? I had given Charles the part of my heart that still belonged to my husband, and he had thrown it back in my face.

# Chapter Twenty-Eight

I went straight back to the house and calmed myself down. I was shaken by Charles' betrayal, but there was also a creeping fear that I was into something that was over my head.

All the other women, aside from Nancy who was upstairs nursing the baby, were down in the shop working, so I started to prepare the evening meal to keep myself busy.

Matt came into the kitchen as I was cooking. I ignored him as he sat down at the table and waited for me to join him.

Doubtless he was here to gloat about Charles.

'I'll not talk about it now, Matt,' I said, continuing about my work, 'we'll talk about it all together later – I have a meal to prepare.'

'They're not bad men, Ellie.'

I huffed. 'Surely you mean "we"?'

'Ellie . . .'

'No, no, Matt – no need to explain. I get it. You and your "comrades" must stick together.'

I hated the way my comment sounded – sarcastic and clipped. I made tea and resigned myself to talking to him. He looked contrite enough, although made no attempt to apologize.

'What was all that about, getting into a fight on my behalf?'

He put his head down and mumbled awkwardly.

'That was something else entirely.'

'Drink?'

God! – I had turned into Bridie.

He shook his head gravely.

'You don't need defending against *the men*, Ellie – *most* of us are very grateful to you for what you've done.'

He didn't need to spell it out any further. The set jaw, the tight lips – he had fought with Charles. Both his manner and the gash above his ear told me that Charles had won.

'Why, Matt – why didn't you come and warn me that this was happening? Why didn't you come straight to tell me, when this union business became a problem?'

'Because . . . I don't believe it is a problem.' He was facing me fully now. 'Much as I,' he closed his eyes to find the right word, '*disagree* with Charles on some things, I agree with him on this.' The contrite schoolboy was gone, as he added assertively, and with all the intelligence I knew him to have in him, 'The only problem with a fair, happy arrangement for all of us is you.'

So he was betraying me, too.

'I'm not listening to this nonsense. I have work to do.' I was confused and hurt. I'd deal with this another time – later, not now.

'Listen, Ellie . . .'

He reached across for my arm and held me at the table. His grip was firm; I shrugged it off, but stayed sitting, putting my hand to my forehead and holding my face down. I could feel tears stinging the back of my eyes. I tensed my mouth and held them at bay.

'We are all grateful for the help you have given us: you have changed our lives. But no man likes to take charity – not from anybody – especially not from a woman.'

I wanted to argue back, 'Why not from a woman?', but I was

afraid that if I spoke I would have to face him, and he would hear a tremor in my voice and see the vulnerability of emotion that I knew was spreading softly across my face. I was losing control. I had been the one spinning the carousel: deciding who got on and who got off – where and when, and how they were a part of my new world. This hurriedly thrown-together universe that I had created was spinning faster than I could manage. What would happen if I let go? I had tried to pass the baton on to somebody else, and Charles had sent me spinning off in another, unfamiliar direction. What mire would I be flung into next? What would become of me, if I let somebody else take charge?

He continued.

'Men are proud, Ellie – maybe it's a false pride, that's what I thought at first; but then I realized that what they – Charles – was saying made some sense. Not the way they planned to go about it; and, in fairness, the strike was never Charles' idea.'

Matt didn't call him Chuck any more. He called him Charles, as I did.

The two of us worked out an agreement, based on the numbers and principles of the contracts that Charles had drawn up with the landlords of the new house. Matt was delighted at the opportunity to steal his rival's thunder.

I gave him the address of my own lawyer to draw up some papers. The men could join or not join a union, as they pleased, I assured him.

If it made them feel more important, more power to them. I had had my fill of them all.

After Matt left I struggled to get up from the table. I was exhausted with the strain of it all, and so I sat for a while, thinking. About what I was doing here, what murky political and complicated personal situation I had got myself into. I did not feel angry any more, I was just tired. Tired of working, and of being in charge and of running. I wanted to go home: back to John. How long had it been since I had been away? 'One short year,' I had promised him. 'I'll be back in one year, as soon as your operation is paid for – you'll be walking again, and we'll have the money to start a new life.'

But no, it wasn't 1920 now; it was 1934. John was not waiting for me back in Ireland, not any longer. Those ten years in Ireland that I seemed to have forgotten had passed in a haze of happiness and small domestic struggles. I had given myself over to some trick in time; grief's clock had turned time back, and my world upside down. *'John is dead.'* I said it to myself aloud: 'John is dead.' The same three words I had said to Maidy the night he died. They were as meaningless to me now as they had been then, but the panic was gone. I could say the words and know they were true – but when I closed my eyes I could not bring John's face into my mind. It was as if he had disappeared, was buried somewhere beneath the mountain of worries and daily duties and chores with which I had filled my life. In my head I had not forgotten him, but John had always lived in my heart. It was where he had resided since we were children. He had stepped into the cold, hollow cave that my strict parents had created, lit a fire and brought me to life. He was dead now, and so was the fire. If John was still in there, he was a cadaver wasting in a dark corner. I didn't want to look on him with my heart, or my mind, any more than my eyes had wanted to look on his body back in Kilmoy.

# CHAPTER TWENTY-NINE

Two days later I was alone in the house. The children had left for school. Congregating on our porch at 8.30 a.m., they followed each other single-file for the half-mile walk down to the village, with the older children at either end of the younger ones. All of the women had gone to the shop.

Katherine had been writing every fortnight, keeping me updated on the businesses back home. Her letters were so reliable in both their frequency and content that I had taken to merely skimming through them, while reaching for the envelope in which I would send her enclosed cheque to the bank.

On three occasions now she had enclosed short, warm letters from Maidy. Despite her sharp intelligence, Maidy was not a greatly literate person; her husband Paud had done all of the reading, and most of the writing, during their sixty years of marriage. That she had put pen to paper herself in her shaky, spidery hand and not merely dictated something, as an appendage to Katherine's missive, was the greatest indication to me that all had been forgiven.

*I miss John every day since, but he is in heaven now alongside Paud, God rest them both, and I have comfort in that I will meet them there when my time is come. I miss you as well, but*

*I was as glad as any woman could be to get your last letter and news of how you are helping the poor of America. You were surely the kindest of girls and for all your beauty and good humour I know that was why in his heart John loved you as he did.*

I could not read Maidy's letters without the jagged pain of tears welling up in me, so I made sure that I did so when I had no time to indulge in emotions: a few snatched moments before we all sat down to dinner, or just after my morning coffee when I was due in the shop. I had taken the cheque out already, put the rest of the letter in my apron pocket to read another time, and gone straight to the bureau in the dining room. I heard the front door open again and presumed the postman must have come back. Although it was unusual for him to let himself in, I assumed he was just leaving some overlooked post in the hall and didn't want to trouble me by knocking again. In any case I wanted to catch him, so that he might deliver the cheque to the bank for me and save me the journey.

'Pat,' I said, running out into the hall, stuffing the cheque into the envelope.

But it wasn't Pat.

I recognized the man instantly; his thin, angular face and malevolent features were seared into my brain. The mobster was there, in my hall, in my home, his presence as intrusive and un-wanted as that of a common rat, except that I understood – with a rising sense of fear – that he could not be simply chased back out the door with a kitchen broom.

'What do you want?' I said. 'How dare you walk into my house without knocking – get out at once.'

My voice was shaking, and so were my legs, although I could only hope that he sensed neither. His eyes were wide and staring, with the pupils dilated, and his tongue was protruding, moistening his thin, dry lips. He was probably high, and looked more like a dog than a rat. I must not let him smell my fear. I knew what he wanted – the worst thing: worse than robbery or murder. In instinctively knowing his intentions, I already felt dirty and afraid and, worst of all, somehow complicit.

'Did you not hear me?' I said. 'Get out of my house.'

He took a step closer to me.

'Hey, pretty lady, what's the big fuss?'

His arms were hanging nonchalantly by his sides, his hands flicking out at the wrists as he spoke, his palms curling and uncurling themselves into loose fists – soft fists, not fighter's ones. He wouldn't need much of a fist to overpower a woman. He was simply releasing tension from the fingers. His nails were dirty and unnaturally long.

I had nothing to hand. No knife, no walking stick, not even an umbrella. In a hallway – why were there no umbrellas in the hallway! Why did I never lock the front door? Leaving it on the latch, so that anyone might walk in and out! What kind of a fool lives like that in a big city?

I took a step back. One step. I did not want him to see that I was afraid, and I could not turn my back on him.

'Take one step closer and I shall call out. There are people upstairs . . .'

He widened his eyes and raised his brows quizzically – was he having second thoughts? He was clearly a little crazy, so his face was hard to read. I began to convince myself.

'. . . and I don't want any fuss, or to have to call the cops, so if you would just kindly leave now, we'll say no more about it.'

'Ooooh,' he said, half-turning towards the door – then, just as quickly, he spun on his heel and jerked his whole body towards me, flashed his palms quickly in my face and shouted, 'POW!'

I jumped a full foot in the air and called out with shock.

He threw his head back, laughing.

'You shoulda seen your face, lady! Oh, man!' He was weeping with hilarity. I thought of making a run for the kitchen and a knife, while he was distracted, when he suddenly stepped forward and said, 'There ain't nobody in this house, pretty lady, 'cept you and me. I watched them go: one, two, three, four, five . . .' He scattered the last number into stardust with his fidgety fingers and whispered almost silently, pushing his mouth into an extended pout: 'Po-owww . . .'

I took a step back, but my foot hit the wall next to the dining-room door. There was nobody there. He had been watching the house. He had thought this through. His face turned nasty and he spat in my face as he spoke.

'You owe me an apology, lady. How d'you expect you gonna pay me back, huh? I got some ideas about that. I got some real good ideas.'

Oh God, this was it. If I fought, he'd kill me. Maybe he'd kill me anyway. This was worse, smelling his acrid breath, feeling the filthy warmth of it so close to my skin, his hand reaching out to touch my breast. I closed my eyes in horror, and as I raised my hand to try and push him away or plead with him, I realized that it was still holding the fountain pen with which I was going to address the envelope to the bank. Grabbing at idiotic ideas to try and stay calm, I thought: *'The pen is mightier than the sword.'*

In an act of pure instinct, I pulled my hand up and plunged the sharp end of the pen as hard as I could into the side of his neck.

He staggered backwards and fell down onto his knees, cursing and swearing. I stood for a split second, wondering how badly he was hurt, but then he looked up at me, his face contorted into a furious grin, and although his hand was pressing against his bloody neck, the pen had fallen to the floor and I could see he wasn't badly hurt. He seemed mad with a mixture of lust and rage; his blood was up, and I had certainly made things worse. As he started to stand up, I stepped to one side, hoping to negotiate a route past him, when the front door was flung open and three men – Matt, Mario and Charles – came crashing into the hall, shouting. My would-be assailant fell immediately to his knees again and covered his head with his arms, saying, 'Don't shoot! Don't shoot me! I ain't armed!'

The three men stood around this pitiful figure, and for a moment I felt like laughing at the ludicrousness of the situation. Could this quivering wreck really have put the fear of God into me, just seconds before?

'She stabbed me! The bitch stabbed my neck!'

Matt, the biggest and most physically threatening of the three men, grabbed the mobster by the collar, hauled him to his feet and gave him a backhanded slap across the jaw, which cracked so loudly it made me jump.

'Wash your mouth, scum!'

'Matt!' I shouted.

'Please, please, don't hurt me,' he snivelled, splashing blood onto the floor with each word. Then he addressed Charles: 'Mr Irvington, tell him to let go. Tell him I'm harmless, I didn't mean no harm.'

Charles waved at Matt. The big man hesitated, uncertain that he wanted to take instructions from Charles, then violently shook the man free from his grip, throwing him back down onto his knees. There was blood pouring from his nose, which was possibly broken, and on the side of his neck where I had stabbed him. He made such pitiful sight that I almost felt sorry for him.

'What are you doing here, Dingus?'

'I was just talking to the lady. Me and the Irish lady was just talking about . . . I didn't know she was a friend of yours, Mr Irvington. I never knew, I swear . . .'

I was surprised to hear him use Charles' name, but then no man could be involved in the mob and not know who was running the unions – the ones within and outside their control. Charles knew everyone; he had to. Life in the Bronx during the Depression was, I had discovered, all about survival, and if you wanted to survive you had to negotiate. We women made our money go further by bartering, swapping our eggs and cakes and skills with various suppliers – charming landlords and fellow tradesmen with flirtations and good home cooking. Aside from cash, the men too had their own brand of currency: the threat of physical violence and humiliation. Charles did not have a gun (to the best of my knowledge, in any case), but he could throw a punch and he could lead men. He knew everyone and he commanded respect.

I could see from Dingus' face that he understood Charles could crush him there and then like a flea.

'You go back to Frank Delaney and you tell him this lady is running a charitable organization, that she is under my protection and he's not to trouble her again.'

Dingus got to his feet and started towards the door.

'And, Dingus?'

'Yes, Mr Irvington.'

'If I ever see you again, not just in this house, but in this neighbourhood – and I mean just *see* you – across the street, travelling on a passing tram – I will come after you with six men like Matt here. And we won't shoot you, Dingus, you know that, don't you?'

'Yes, yes . . .'

He was shaking, terrified. I looked at Charles, and his face was impervious; his voice was calm and cold.

'We will slice you open like a pizza pocket. Do you understand?'

'Yes sir, Mr Irvington.' And he scuttled out like the cockroach he was. Matt slammed the door at his back.

The whole scenario had been shocking – the attack, of course, but also the rescue; Matt's violent reaction, and Charles' cold, terrible threats. I had not seen Charles since the union business, and had not even known he was back. As my lover crossed the room and took me in his arms, I was aware that I should be pushing him away, yet I did not. My heart was pounding and my breathing short, but despite that I collapsed gratefully into Charles' chest and was surprised to realize that I felt neither shocked nor afraid. In actual fact I felt a thrill run through me. In the backdraught of this violent madness, I imagined that I felt truly alive. The feeling wasn't real, and it wasn't to last.

# CHAPTER THIRTY

Charles left Yonkers four days later. He was the hero of the hour (a role to which he was well suited) and deftly avoided any reference to how he knew Dingus or had managed to strike such fear into him. The gangsters, the unions and the cops were all tied up with one another. The reins changed hands so often that it was impossible to keep up with who was in power on any given day. Charles' weapons were his charm and intelligence and his manly bravado; doubtless his union ties and rough docker links had afforded him some legendary status in the underworld. He had saved me from Dingus, and I knew that questioning him beyond that would be pointless and would ultimately cause me more worry than I would be able to manage.

In addition to denying his mob links, Charles also made light of my accusations of betrayal. The union business was politics, he said, and nothing to do with his feelings for me. He assured me that he had been going to talk to me about it, when he had heard from his wife and had to rush off to sort things out with his son.

On the trip he had made the decision to move upstate and live near his wife, until such time as they could decide what was to be done about Leo. Now he paused to allow me to respond. He was still hoping I would invite them both to live with me.

We had made love over an hour beforehand, and Charles was sitting on the edge of the bed as I lay on my side. He was addressing me, but was looking away, and I was hiding – my eyes staring at an empty corner, the bedcovers draped over my shoulders. I was no longer hurt or angry with Charles, but neither could I engage in what he was saying. I felt numb, apart from everything else. I had never felt this way before, as if I wanted to fall into a deep sleep that lasted forever. It felt strangely comforting.

As I stayed silent, Charles continued talking. He loved me, he said, and wanted to marry me, as he had intended to do before I had returned to Ireland. He knew I was still getting over John, but still hoped that we would be together one day. I was the great love of his life, he said. I listened, but although he was saying things to me that I might have dreamed a man as fine as him would feel, his words felt meaningless; they did not reach me, but crept instead towards the open window and were carried off into the enormity of the outside world. He continued: he understood that it was too much to ask me to take on his child. Perhaps one day in the future I could meet Leo and things might be different. He was going now, but I was to be reassured that he would return soon. He would never give up on our being together one day. He would always love me.

I curled my legs up to my chest and closed my eyes. I wanted him to leave.

Charles came over and kissed me. I stayed curled up in my tight ball and didn't respond to him.

He gathered his things from around the room and left. I did not move from my position or speak. He paused at the door and looked back at me – confused, perhaps, at my not responding – then left, walked down the stairs and out of my life.

As I heard the front door close behind him downstairs, the black clouds of grief gathered in my head.

I had kept this storm at bay for almost five months. Now it was coming.

Thick, black puffs crowded all light out of my head, and tendrils of spidery smoke drew themselves in a deadly circle around my heart.

'John is dead. He's dead and he is never coming back.'

The whisper grew louder and louder until it thundered through me, then with a sharp clap the rains came, and I started to cry.

Charles had opened the door of my heart, only a few inches, but as he went I had carelessly left it ajar.

For days there was nothing but the pain. 'John, John . . .' His name repeated itself over and over and over again – the only word I could say, could think. There were no 'what ifs', no regrets, no memories, only the four letters of his name – 'John, John . . .' – speaking them out loud, murmuring them through my breath, calling him back, bringing him into the room. My John, not some other. 'John is dead, dead, dead and he is never coming back.'

Noisy, painful tears hammered through me, burning my eyes and salting my skin to a mottled red; shuddering sobs that made the bedhead clatter against the wall. The whole house heard me, but I did not care. There was nothing else – nobody else but him. Nothing but the raw, untethered hugeness of this terrible emotion.

Bridie ran in shortly after it started:

'What's this racket?'

'It's John,' I said. I wanted her to know I was not crying over Charles.

She came and sat next to me on the bed and stroked my head as I put my face to her bosom.

'There there, girleen,' she said, 'let it all out now there, like a good girl.'

I did not move from the bed that day, or the day after, or the day after that, until I lost count.

Bridie brought me up meals and kept everyone away from me. She did not judge me, or chide me for not eating her food, or nag me to pull myself together. In that sense she helped reassure me that what I was going through was the natural route of a widow's grief. Although it felt anything but natural.

I could see, feel, hear and taste nothing but the sharp bitterness of my loss. My eyes would well up, my jaw tingle and my mouth fill with water. As the days went on, my tears lost their jagged edge and became automatic, inevitable, commonplace. With that familiarity the pain changed shape and became a dull ache.

I emerged from my cave of crying and came back downstairs, but the colour of the world looked different. The carousel had stopped spinning and its bright, whirring colours had dulled to a still monochrome. Everything looked ordinary and grey: the faces of my friends, new exoticisms they had introduced into the shop, the garish autumn leaves that littered the porch – all were reduced to a dull, joyless symptom by my depressed mood. Everything was an effort. Getting dressed, washing myself, putting on the water to boil for my tea – even the smallest, most everyday actions were weighed down with my all-but-crippling sadness. The crying had stopped, and I was coping. But that was all I was doing.

It seemed that, while to all the world I looked alive, something vital inside me had died. Not my love for John; that ember still burned gently at the base of my soul. It was my love for this life that was gone – my interest in being where I was, or anywhere that was not with him. *I could die tomorrow and join him,* I thought. *If I were to die, what would it matter?* Some days this bleak thought was the very thing that got me out of bed and down the stairs: the ludicrous idea that I might get run over by a tram or be

murdered in an alley – that I might die, and see my darling John
again.

Everyone was glad to have me back. The women cautiously re-
involved me in the shop and the running of the house, anxious
that I should neither feel left out, nor under pressure that they
could not cope without me. Bridie managed their concerns,
presiding over my recovery with her matronly assertiveness. For
once I was happy to let somebody else manage me, and was glad
of her bossiness.

'You might bring some dinner home from the store tonight,
Maureen? Save us cooking. Anna – I'd be grateful if you would
get in early tomorrow and start the ovens. I want to stay here
and help Ellie get the washing started.'

I couldn't take charge of anything, and Bridie took over,
while still giving the impression that I was holding the reins. She
knew I'd want them back. She made sure all the other women
were in the shop all day, and she stayed at home with me on
some pretence of helping get back into the swing of my work.
In reality I wasn't doing the washing, nor did I have any interest
in the house, the shop or anything beyond simply getting myself
from one end of the day to the other without losing my mind.
Everybody knew that I had had a kind of emotional breakdown
after Charles left, but Bridie made sure they were all put straight
that it had been a bona-fide illness brought on by exhaustion
and overwork: 'Thanks to taking it upon herself to offer charity
to a bunch of feckless, ungrateful vagrants,' was how I think I
heard her describe it to one of the men, who had the temerity to
ask after me one evening as I lay upstairs in my bed, 'who saw fit
to thank her by starting up a union!'

The old woman made sure that I got up every day, and craft-
ily kept me busy with small tasks so that I did not draw to a

complete halt. She treated me with the careful patience reserved for a child, and I followed her around the house like a clueless acolyte. Bridie would give me a pile of three pillowcases to iron, instruct me to set milk and sugar on the table for tea, to roll the pastry out for a pie, to fold the tea towels into a neat pile and to clear out a cutlery drawer for sorting.

'Why don't you sit down there and read the paper for a few minutes while I make us a sandwich,' she said. 'Read out the crossword clues to me, why don't you?'

Bridie had never done a crossword in her life, but I was afraid to offend her by pointing this out. I read out two clues, one of which came to me as I was asking. The following day I read two items from the news section, and the day after that I took an unopened letter from Katherine and placed it on my desk upstairs.

Day by day, bit by bit, Bridie introduced me back into my own life. I started running the shop again. I coloured my hair a deep brown and had it cut back into my old bobbed style. I bought myself a smart new coat, and instructed Matt in various small improvements to the house: a dowelling rail under the sink, presses to be painted in the scullery, and installing a washing line on a pulley system for the bathroom upstairs.

Matt's relief that I had emerged from my 'illness' was palpable. Those first few weeks after Charles left, Matt irritated me so much that I could not bear to be in his company. He was, I knew, worried for my welfare, but I found his concern fawning, his affection stifling. He fussed about, pulling my chair back out before I sat down to dinner, fixing a cardigan about my neck, jumping up and down to fetch me salt or to fill my glass with water, and all but lifting it to my lips for me. In those few days I understood that Matt was in love with me. He treated me like a precious, delicate orchid – yet he only made me feel like a cripple.

*

As the weeks passed, life returned to normal. Bridie snapped back to her gruff self, and I gathered back my poise and assertiveness, although happiness remained a distant relative that I could not imagine seeing again.

Then one afternoon I found myself alone with Nancy's baby, Tom.

Nancy had turned out to be a natural mother and, mindful of my own losses, I had been careful not to get over-involved with the infant.

For all that, he was no stranger to me and I easily agreed to watch the charming, bubbly, fat baby while she ran down to the shop to collect some groceries for our evening meal.

As soon as Nancy left, the baby began to cry. Tom was less than three months old and still nursing. I wrapped him up in his blanket and bundled him downstairs and out onto the porch, thinking the cool autumn air would settle him. But he continued to cry, his mewling giving way to an almighty screech as I stepped outside. I walked him around, jogging him and shaking him gently, trying to find a motion to comfort him, but his cries just rose into a continuous siren of objection – 'Mwaah, mwaah, mwaaaah . . . ha, ha, ha, ha' – until it seemed he had lost his breath in all the sobbing and might choke. I started to panic.

The baby's screaming was so persistent and ear-piercing that I worried the neighbours might think he was being killed. So I went back into the house and up to Nancy's room. Perhaps if I put him back down into his cot, he would settle. But he thrashed wildly, his fat legs pumping at the side of the cot that he had almost outgrown, until I thought it would topple over.

I was desperate. I knew I could not feed him, so I picked him up firmly and held him to my beating chest. He howled out as he felt the rough wool of my working shirt, so I quickly unbuttoned it. He grunted and squawked, his tiny hands thrashing at my breasts, searching out milk.

'Ssshh,' I hushed, pushing air through my teeth so that it sounded like waves on a pebbled beach, 'sssssssshh.' I rocked from side to side and held him close to me, asserting my calm strength over his petulance. After a few seconds his wail went down to a whimper. Still holding him, I lay down on my side on Nancy's unmade bed.

I could smell the bitter tang of mother's milk from the sheets as I held my lips to his silky scalp and whispered, 'Ssssh – ssshhh, little baby.'

After a while his limbs loosened in mine and his face softened into sleep. I continued to lie there, letting his short breath warm my neck, his wet mouth pressed open against my bare skin, vaguely sucking, and I drank in the exclusive baby scent of his velvety head.

This baby is alive, I realized, and so am I. I am still here to comfort him in this moment, to smell his skin – a fleeting joy, a borrowed pleasure, a temporary taste of the sweetness of existence – but for all that, I am still here, in this moment. John is elsewhere, not here with me, not now, not in this world. He is in my heart and my head, but we occupy different worlds. I am alive, and I am here – holding a child. This still moment of breath-on-breath is all I have, all that matters. This is not John's breath, nor the breath of the child we longed for, but nonetheless it is a beautiful taste of humanity – a dream so small it is barely worth dreaming. A moment worth being alive for.

When Nancy came back, she said she found Tom and I entwined, fast asleep on the bed.

She put a blanket over us both and went downstairs to make a start on the dinner with Bridie.

# CHAPTER THIRTY-ONE

'Surprise!'

I had thought I would never see her again, but there she was. Sheila, standing on my porch.

'Aren't you going to invite me in?'

I opened the door fully and walked through it myself onto the porch, turning my back to her. I was still mad. No, that wasn't true. So much had happened since our falling-out that I had all but forgotten about it, but as soon as I saw Sheila – glamorous as ever in a matching day-suit, hair coiffed, make-up perfectly applied – I felt like slamming the door in her face.

The shallow-minded, vain little madam had abandoned me in my time of need. I had real friends now: good, warm people. I had moved on. I should kick her as she had kicked me – tell her to march back to wherever she came from and leave me alone. Anyway, what in the hell was she doing here?

And therein lay Sheila's power. What *was* she doing here? Much as I was furious with her, I was also desperately curious to hear what adventure had brought her to my door.

'What the hell are you doing here?' I asked, without turning around.

'It's a long story,' she said, 'will you give me time to tell it?'

She had interpreted my frosty greeting correctly and was at

least pretending to be contrite. I took a packet of cigarettes out
of my pocket and lit one for us both.

'Sit down,' I said, nodding towards the bench.

She fussily cleared it of leaves, flicking her gloves across it
before sitting down. Adopting the affectations of a lady, when
she was no such thing. God, she was infuriating!

'Ellie, you were right. Eric and Geoff were complete cads.
How I wish I had listened to you.'

She looked over, her eyes wide and coy, anxious to appease
me. I gave her no response, so she continued with her story.

'As you know, Eric and I hit it off – but it turned out he was a
fly-by-night, and Geoff was the gentleman of the two.'

I huffed sarcastically.

'All right – Geoff was the one with the money.'

That was more like it.

'What can I say – he took me on, but I quickly discovered he
was married. Can you imagine?' She spread her hands in shock.

'No, I can't imagine – but I'm sure you can.' Despite everything,
I was enjoying myself. 'So you milked him for as long as you could,
then went looking for more money and he dumped you?'

She puffed hard on the cigarette like a navvy.

'He had me on an *allowance*. Can you imagine the humiliation of that, for a woman like me who is used to spending as she
pleases?'

'Indeed,' I said, 'it must have been dreadful for you.'

'Oh, and *not* a generous one at that – barely enough to keep
me in stockings and suits, and in the apartment he set me up
in. Downtown, Ellie, and you're not going to believe what I am
going to tell you next . . .'

She put her cigarette out and I lit us both another.

'It had a *shared* bathroom. I had to share a bathroom. Ellie, it
will tell you how desperate I was that I stayed there for six full

weeks before I could stand it no longer. I went back to Boston –
to Alex, of course.'

'Of course.'

'He wasn't there. The snivelling coward left his mother to
deal with me. She gave me a 'payoff' – a piffling amount, an
insult. She said it was pointless going after him for a big divorce
settlement because they hadn't a penny to their name. They'd
moved out of the big house already, and it seems Alex had gone
over to Canada, or somewhere desperate like that, looking for
work. I said I was just there to collect my things, and she said
not to bother, they had sold anything of worth – meaning my
jewellery, of course. It took me years to amass that collection,
Ellie: my pearls, they had no right, it was stealing . . .'

'Terrible.'

'Well, exactly, I shall sue them, of course. Anyway I suddenly
realized that the only person I really wanted to be with, to tell all
of this to, to share my misfortune with, was you – my dearest,
oldest friend . . .'

She gave me a smile that was so fake I almost laughed out
loud. Sheila was such a terrible liar. She had spent our entire
school days failing to charm her way out of trouble with the
nuns. She was stealing the biscuits from the larder for some
dear, sweet, crippled man whom she had met on the grounds
and who had mysteriously disappeared. The raunchy novel was
not hers – she was minding it for a friend of her mother, whose
husband would beat her if he found it. She did *not* pinch Sinead
O'Toole – the girl was a fantasist! Then she would invite the
nun to look into her eyes: are these the eyes of a pincher? A liar?
The answer was, of course, yes, but Sheila was so inherently
bold that lying was simply a necessary part of life.

'So I went back to The Plaza, expecting to find you still
there . . .'

'After all that time?'

'Why not? Where else would you be living, if you had the money?' She thought better of it. 'Except here, of course – this is lovely.'

She looked around unconvinced, then remembered herself and fixed a smile onto her face.

'Anyway, I stayed there for a full week in all style, then ran out of money and started my proper search for you. The door-man still had a forwarding address, and a nice man in an office in the village dropped me up here himself – can't remember his name – and here I am!'

Mr Williams. Delivering me another homeless, penniless desperate – albeit in the most unlikely of packages.

I would keep her in suspense, worry her into thinking I would not take her in, for a few moments more at least. That I was still angry enough at the way she had treated me. I stubbed the cigarette under my heel and noticed then the large trunk and two smart suitcases standing at the base of my front steps.

'Darling Ellie,' she said, flinging her arms around my neck, 'let's never fight again. I've been *devastated* since we fell out, my darling, oldest, dearest friend.'

I could have argued it out with her and tried to make her understand that it was, of course, all her own fault. But I knew Sheila better than that. Stubbornness and pride would drive her away and, if she was as down on her luck as I believed she was, then she would not be able to cope for one night without a roof over her head. Especially with all that baggage! Doubtless that was why she had brought it with her and, in any case, I knew this was as close to a contrite apology as I was ever going to get.

I walked across the road and called for one of the lads to

carry her cases in, then stepped aside and opened the door of my home for her.

I brought Sheila straight into the kitchen and told her to help herself to tea. I had to get down to the shop, I said.

'Stay and talk,' she said. 'Don't leave me here all on my own!'

'Sheila, don't be petty. I have to go and let the other women know there is somebody else in the house.'

I had to warn Bridie she was here. I knew the old woman would not be impressed, and if she came home and found Sheila here without warning, Lord knows what she would do or say.

When I told her, Bridie lost it, 'I'll not step one foot inside the house, I'll move in with Anna and Mario. I'll not stick her bossing me about!'

She was genuinely upset, her face blowing up bright puce, her portly frame puffing out until I thought she might explode. Perhaps it was as important to her as it was to me that the past was left where it was. Perhaps she too had drawn a line under her comfortable life as the Adams' housekeeper after her husband had died, and did not want to be reminded of those days. She had been uncertain about seeing me again, but then I had brought her into fresh new circumstances, better than the ones that her husband's unfortunate investments had led her to. It was a betrayal of sorts, bringing Sheila back into Bridie's life after all she had done for me, and I was anxious to reassure her.

'You're in charge of the house, Bridie, you know that. Sheila being there won't change things, I promise. You're as much the boss of her now as ever you were, and I'll be on hand to make sure she doesn't give you any lip.'

Anna and Maureen, anxious to continue the drama, closed up the shop and we all walked quickly back up to the house. Bridie told them stories of Sheila's cheek and insubordination as the spoiled Isobel Adams' personal maid: 'She thought she was a lady herself! Pfft. Mind you, she learned her manners from the worst of them. Our "mistress" – not that she deserved such a title – she was all lipstick and lounging, and no care for the house, no class of any kind!'

As we reached the door I warned Bridie, 'Remember, however it appears, she is desperate. That's why I have taken her in. Sheila has found herself in very reduced circumstances and has nowhere else to go.'

When I opened the front door, we were greeted by the sound of loud jazz and uproarious laughter. We walked unnoticed into the kitchen, and found Mario and Sheila dancing the jitterbug, and Matt standing on a chair by the radio shelf, turning the volume dial with one hand and clapping the other to his thigh like a disabled seal. There were two upturned chairs on the floor and an opened bottle of wine on the table.

'Now!' Bridie said and turned on her heels. Utterly vindicated, she was thoroughly delighted with herself. Maureen did not know what to make of it and gave me a half-smile, but Anna – mild, pretty, maternal Anna – started screaming in Italian.

'*Porca puttana!*'

She leapt over the chair and across the room in one move, then grabbed Sheila around the throat and pushed her up against the wall.

Mario tried to placate her: 'Anna, *cucciola mia,*' but his words came out in a kind of amused pleading and he made no attempt to remove her grip from Sheila.

Matt didn't know what to do. So I went over and wrenched Anna off.

'Jesus!' Sheila cried, her hands holding her neck. 'The woman's a lunatic!'

Anna growled at her, 'Bitch! *Puttana!*'

'. . . she broke my necklace!' Sheila wailed.

And that was how it was for the next few weeks. Sheila came into our happy, well-managed lives and brought her uniquely destructive manner of mayhem with her. She flirted with Matt until he became convinced that he could make me jealous by pretending to be slightly in love with her. She took advantage of Maureen's kind nature, until she was treating her fellow Irishwoman like her personal maid. She struck up the role of an older sister to the pretty, but easily led Nancy, encouraging the young mother to go about in garish make-up and neglect her young child in favour of finding a lover. 'Ellie doesn't have any children – you could give the baby to her until you find a rich husband, then come and take him back? If you still want him,' I overheard her say. On a number of occasions she went out of her way to upset Anna so that, at least twice, Anna came at her with a knife. Sheila always did it in company so that she knew no harm could come to her, and only ever to make Anna look bad. And Sheila offended Bridie on such a regular basis that the old woman quickly tired of getting upset and actually became so stoic in dealing with her that one might almost have imagined them friends.

As for me, not a day went past when I wondered how this crazy woman and I had ever become friends? Yet I loved her and, in her own strange, deluded way, I knew that Sheila loved me, too. It was an old love, fuelled by the familiarity of time. I had realized that such a love – good or bad, from whichever corner it came – was too precious ever to let go of.

# Chapter Thirty-Two

Winter came unexpectedly early, before the leaves had fully fallen from the trees. I woke with the sharp tang of cold on my skin and, rubbing my arms, jumped from the bed and instinctively went to the window. The street was covered with a light dusting of frost.

I checked my watch and it was nine. I had slept through, but the shop was closed today. Mario and the men would have been down there from dawn, laying new floors and making some adjustments to the kitchen. If they made an early start, Matt assured me we would only have to close the business for one day. Matt himself was up on the roof of the house opposite. We had arranged for someone to come in and fix the broken slates, so that Matt could go down and oversee the work on the shop.

We wanted to make sure that all of the houses were at least protected properly from the elements before the ice and snow came. The snow in New York was ferocious. Not the mild, occasional event we had back in Ireland. In Kilmoy snow arrived for just a few days, a week at most, and only every third year or so. The novelty of it generally outweighed the temporary hardship of the additional cold and having to take the animals indoors. Like an annoying relation come to visit, by the time you remembered that you didn't like snow very much, it was gone.

New York snow, I remembered from my time here, was inevitable and relentless.

I caught myself wondering at its imminent arrival, and realized that two full seasons had passed since I came here. It seemed like a long time to have been away, and yet a short time given all that had happened. So much since John had died and yet, somehow, it was not enough. Not enough for me to feel ready to go back; not enough for me to fully realize he was gone, to be ready to say 'goodbye'. How many snows would come and go before I was ready? I was on the other side of the world, embedded in a fresh life with new people, and yet if I looked into my core, I was still standing, shocked, in my cottage kitchen looking at the corpse of my dead husband. I had cried, and said out loud that he was dead, and had ranted against the injustice of it. I had seen glimpses of hope, had experienced brushes of realization that life goes on, moments when I felt alive – happy even. Yet still these small steps amounted to nothing against the yawning, heart-wrenching knowledge that John was not in my life any more. My relationship with Charles, my personal and financial investment in the community – no matter how much work, romance, adventure, achievement I stuffed into each day – each experience amounted to a mere drop in the ocean compared to John's passing.

I quickly dressed, throwing on an old dress, cardigan and boots.

'The frost makes the world as pretty as a cake,' Maureen said as I passed her in the hallway.

'Not us, though, it seems,' I said, looking down at my working boots poking out from under the plain dress. 'Any drama this morning?'

In other words, what had Sheila been up to? Maureen smiled broadly. Sheila may have been our only topic of conversation these days, but much as she was a source of stress, her shenanigans had a strangely unifying effect on the rest of us. She gave us all something to talk about, and when I was worrying about what Sheila might say or do next, I was not worrying about myself.

'There's a strange man in the kitchen – she's been entertaining him.'

It must be Matt's roofer.

'Trust Sheila to keep him hanging around the kitchen. I'd better get down and make sure he's fed and out the door. Matt will be waiting for him, and we need to get that roof sealed before the weather turns any worse.'

I found Sheila alone in the kitchen, in a silk robe drinking coffee. There were coffee grains all over the table and a splash of milk dribbling down onto the floor. I took a cloth from the sink and dabbed it, tutting like an old nun.

'Maureen said the roofer was here?'

She didn't look up.

'A man was here all right – he's gone.'

'Did you tell Matt?'

'Which one is Matt?'

'Jesus, Sheila!'

She looked up and laughed.

'I'm only joking, it's just that you have so many men wandering around the place here, it's hard to keep track.'

'I don't suppose you fed him?'

She went back to her magazine.

'No, but he feasted his eyes all right – seedy type.'

'Perhaps if you didn't walk around the house half-naked?'

'Perhaps if you kept a civilized house where a lady might enjoy a bit of privacy?'

Bridie came in.

'You're no lady, and you don't know the meaning of the word "civilized".'

'There's plenty of privacy up in your room,' Maureen snapped from behind her. 'Where's the man that was here?'

'How the hell should I know?'

'Well, you seemed to be entertaining him happily enough.'

'I can't help it if I'm attractive to men.'

'Lord knows you make enough of an effort at it.'

'Says the woman who couldn't even hold on to the father of her brats.'

Maureen's husband Patrick still had not returned, and Maureen was worried that if he did come back to look for her, it would be to Central Park and he would not be able to find any trace of her. So as soon as Maureen was settled, we had returned to the area where I had found her and approached a vagrant who seemed as though he was more or less resident there, although Maureen had not seen him there before. We showed him a photograph of Patrick, which he studied with great care, then we gave him cigarettes and money and two pieces of cardboard (in case he should lose one) with our address clearly written on them. He told us that he would watch out for Patrick most carefully, and perhaps if we were to come to him again with more cigarettes – and whisky in a week or so?

When we hadn't returned with more money ten days later, he rode the train up to Yonkers and arrived at our door, demanding his 'rightfully earned fees', saying that we had hired him as a 'private investigator'. He had even acquired a trilby hat to drive home his point (I imagined him stealing it, amid great fuss, from a businessman on the train), which he wore on top of his filthy matted hair.

'Have you found this woman's husband?' I asked, knowing full well the honest answer.

'Well . . .' he said, 'not exactly.'

I sensed somebody behind me, turned and saw Maureen – her eyebrows raised, her eyes full of pitiful hope.

'But if you can give me some more time,' he said, trying his very best to sound sober. The effort caused him to stagger and almost fall in the door.

'Jesus – come on then,' I said.

I fed him, and after Bridie had scolded him roundly and instructed me to remove him wholesale from her kitchen, I assured Maureen that I would gladly give the old scoundrel more money to keep his eyes open for her husband.

'Perhaps he will find him,' I said, 'you never know.' Miracles might happen – but Maureen had already told me that her miracle had happened when I had found her and taken her and her family under my wing. She wasn't due another miracle, she had said – so she was adamant that we send the old vagrant packing.

'False hope is worse than no hope,' she said.

Maureen had already written and heard back from the cousins in California with whom she had been to stay, and they had not heard from Patrick, either. She gave them her details nonetheless and, if he did call, they said they would surely pass the message on.

Matt and the men had registered Patrick Sweeney, along with a description of him, in every cop station around Central Manhattan and in Yonkers, in case he had the foresight to come back to their old home. They did not tell Maureen, but his details were also in every hospital and city morgue.

'Dead bodies turn up quicker than live ones,' a cop friend of Matt's had told me. Matt had brought the cop up to the house when Maureen was out. 'People can hide,' he said, 'but corpses – they don't have a choice. They gonna wash up, whether they want to or not.' If Patrick had been murdered, buried in concrete or dismembered by some brutal gang, he told us, he might never be found, 'But suicides are never dead more than twenty-four hours before we get our hands on them,' the cop said, 'under trains, off bridges – the bodies are warm when we get to them, most of the time. No, if he's missing, and he weren't a criminal, aye, well . . .'

He didn't want to say it in front of me, but then shrugged and went ahead anyway.

'Sometimes people just don't want to be found – do you know what I mean?'

I knew exactly what he meant, and it was the same assumption that Sheila had made. That Maureen's husband was living a new life somewhere else. I hoped, especially for the children's sake, that it wasn't true, and the least I could do was defend her against cruel taunts. Why did Sheila always have to take things a step too far?

'Stop it!' I shouted. 'Maureen, would you tell Jake to run across the road and tell Matt to send that roofer over for a bit of breakfast before he starts. Bridie, have we some of that cured bacon left from last night?'

'Surely.'

'Well then, you might put it in the pan for him – I'll go and get some eggs, and for God's sake, Sheila, go upstairs and put some proper clothes on.'

Bridie was always happy when I scolded Sheila. It made a change from her doing it. Not, indeed, that Sheila made any attempt to move from her chair.

I took a man's coat that was hanging on a hook by the back door and stepped out onto the wooden back porch. I was stopped in my tracks as surely as if I had hit a wall.

Dingus was down in our garden talking to Nancy. She was sitting on the swing with baby Tom in her arms, and he was standing behind her, pushing gently. He looked up at me and grinned. He had been waiting. Everything inside me loosened. I didn't know what to do. I could not turn my back on him, neither could I just stand here looking. I could move neither forward nor back. I was paralysed.

I tried to call out.

'Bridie?'

I said it in such a whisper it was as if to myself. I could not shout for her properly. I dared not make a move, in case Dingus followed it with one of his own. Bridie knew about the incident with the gangster by now – everyone did. After that afternoon, Charles' bravery in seeing him off had been the talk of our household for weeks. The horrible reality of it, and my initial silence about my encounter with him, was dwarfed by the men's bravery. They had solved everything with their chest-beating threats, and made sure everyone knew about it. It never occurred to them that Dingus would come back; not after they had 'seen him off', although I had never quite let go of the idea that he was not finished with me – I had injured him, and a dog like that does not forget a beating, especially not at the hands of a woman. The men had seen a snivelling, frightened wreck who had been bullying a lady. They had not seen the crazed look in his eye. The hatred.

If Dingus was here now, he meant business. He was either unhinged enough not to be afraid of the men any more, or smart enough to know that they were all down at the shop. Either way, he had succeeded in terrifying me. It was me he wanted to punish, yet he was flirting with Nancy. This was some game he was playing, and I had no choice but to play along. He had me trapped in the cold sneer of his gaze as surely as if there was a steel wire connecting me to him. The women in the kitchen directly behind me might as well have been on the other side of the world, for all that I could reach them.

'Matt's not there, Ellie.' It was Jake. I breathed out with relief, but did not turn round. 'There was a man over there looking for him too, to see him about the roof. I sent him down to the shop.'

I held Dingus' eye and said, really quietly and calmly, 'Go inside, Jake, and send your mother and Bridie out to me now.'

'Who's that guy?'

'Immediately, Jake.'

He paused – teenage insubordination or his male instincts smelling danger made him dither.

'Now, Jake!'

A few seconds later I felt Maureen and Bridie at my back.

'It's him,' I said.

The two women knew whom I meant from my stance alone.

'The man that was in the kitchen this morning . . . ?' Maureen said.

'. . . was not the roofer,' I replied. 'Where's Sheila?'

'I sent her down to the basement to collect some laundry,' Bridie said. 'Will I get her? If there's a gang of us, we might be able to overpower him?'

He was smarter than that. Twice I'd got the better of him – but he had the better of me now, and his face said that he knew it.

Nancy waved over at us, smiling, delighted with her new beau. Sweet, dear, stupid Nancy, although it was her very innocence that was keeping her safe at that moment. Dingus was playing with me through her. If she were to run or I was to confront him, I could only imagine what his next move might be. He would not have come here unarmed. Not after the last time.

'No,' I said, 'leave Sheila and stay where you are.'

I smiled over at Nancy and lifted my hand in a shallow greeting. Dingus kept his eye on me as he pushed her higher in the swing, and as she came back down he whispered something pretty in her ear that made her hunch her shoulders coyly and blush. We all just stood there looking and let him play this teasing game of torture with us – Nancy his unwitting partner. His hands stayed close to the top of her back, flicking against her shoulder, and his fingers lingered around the sinew of her slim neck as he gently pushed. It was important for us not to move, not to say anything as long as he was within reach of Nancy and Tom. How far would he need to move away from them for us three women to run down and drag them to safety? We none of us said it, but were all thinking the same thing.

I couldn't take it any more and chanced taking one step forward. As I did so, Dingus grabbed the rope of the swing and pulled Nancy in to him. I stopped and raised my hands, letting him see I knew what I had done and wasn't moving any further. Nancy looked up at him and smiled, as if she was hoping for a kiss. I felt sick. The big baby was heavy against her chest, asleep from all the rocking motion.

He leaned down to her and, as he did, I saw something flash in his palm. A knife! He was going to slash her anyway as we were watching!

I flew down the steps towards them, but before I reached the bottom there was a sharp clap near my ear. I tripped over the last step and looked up, just in time to see Dingus fall to his knees. Then, in one heavy, reckless motion, his face hit the ground in front of him, twisting his neck to one side with an audible crack. Nancy stood up from the swing and her chest heaved with shock as she gathered her breath to scream.

In that second of silence Maureen came thundering down the steps behind me, pushing me aside as she leapt towards Nancy and grabbed Tom, just before his mother's arms loosened and she started to wail. Bridie, who was immediately behind her, pulled Nancy firmly into her chest to ground her hysterics.

I walked over to them in a daze, unclear what had happened, but holding on to the idea that I still needed to take the knife from Dingus' hand. I stood over him for a moment and put my foot to his leg. His body was lifeless. I leaned down and found his hand splayed out to one side. It was wrapped around the blade of the knife, and the blood seeping through the closed fingers was already congealing into black worms. My eyes were drawn to his face. He was dead.

I shivered as the memory of finding John's body visited me. This was the same thing – the shock, the sudden vacuum; here one minute, gone the next.

*His mouth half-open as if waiting for a kiss. 'John, John – wake up, John.'*

Yet the menace was gone, the slick appearance, the sleazy threat of Dingus' expression, the evil intent – all snatched away in an instant. Dingus had gone from being a terrible threat to a lifeless, life-sized doll dressed as a gangster; a mere and meaningless corpse.

As I stood up I noticed a black pillow of blood spreading in a pool underneath his chest, creeping around the soles of my boots.

I quickly stepped to one side. What had happened here?

'Is he dead?'

I turned and saw Sheila, standing at the door of the basement, just under the porch steps, still in her silk robe. Her right hand hung loosely by her side, and hanging from the crook of her forefinger was the jewelled handle of a small lady's pistol.

# CHAPTER THIRTY-THREE

My heart started to bang in my chest. Panic! A man was dead. What to do? What should I do? Would we call the police? My first instinct was 'No'. We had shot a man: how would we explain it all to them? Dingus' previous visits, his threats to me, my stabbing him, Charles and the men seeing him off – it was too complicated, and they might not believe us. In any case, I knew that some New York cops were in cahoots with the gangsters. Supposing we got one of those? No. Dingus would be missed only by his criminal friends – and after all, the way he carried on, anyone might have shot him. My mind was racing. We had to act fast, now: what to do, what to do?

Bridie told Maureen to take Nancy and the baby inside. Nancy was heaving and Tom started to cry, a crisp, loud wail that would draw attention.

As they were leaving, Bridie knelt down by the body of the dead gangster and began saying the Last Rites in an automatic, hurried murmur: '*O Lord Jesus Christ, most merciful, Lord of the Earth, we ask that you receive this child into your arms . . . As thou hast told us with infinite compassion . . .*'

My blood was fizzing with fear. As she was praying, Sheila came over and stood by my side. She handed me a lit cigarette.

'Calm down, Ellie, you're pure shaking.'

I drew deeply on the cigarette and filled myself with its white, calming smoke. Sheila was right. I needed to calm down. The garden was not overlooked – there was no sense in panicking.

It felt wrong to be standing there smoking over the body while Bridie was performing a religious ritual. We took a few steps backwards.

'I've never seen a dead body before,' Sheila said.

I found I couldn't answer her. I was still too shocked to speak. Had anyone heard the gunshot? The neighbours? Were they at work or at home today? What day was it?

'I've been to funerals, of course,' Sheila went on, 'but never actually seen the body. I've always avoided them, to be honest. The very idea of it made me feel a bit sick. A corpse – all laid out in a chapel surrounded by flowers, like some kind of ornament? No, thank you.'

My mind paused from its racing. That was how I had felt about John.

'Actually, I don't know what the fuss was about really. It's not nearly as bad as I thought. Anyway, don't expect this chap will get much of a send-off. What are we going to do with him?'

How could Sheila be so flippant? She had killed a man. Shot him! Still I couldn't speak.

Bridie was praying away, doing her duty. God! – how much longer would she take? What *were* we going to do? Sheila flicked her cigarette butt across the garden towards the vegetable patch, and my voice came back.

'A man is dead, Sheila, show some respect.'

'Ellie, he was a murdering maniac. He had a knife.'

'Nonetheless,' I said. I was not about to congratulate my friend for committing a murder. She had surely, probably, maybe, saved two lives in the process – but I was confused. Murder was always wrong. John had killed for his country, but

253

he had almost been killed himself. So now he was dead anyway
– what difference did it make? Was this man's life worth less
than my husband's? Was his murder at Sheila's hands more justified than the sudden heart attack that John had suffered?

'You're glad I shot him, admit it.'

I could tell from Sheila's tone that she was hurt. She had shot
Dingus because she had sensed his menace, and seen the knife.
In her impulsive way, she had simply grabbed the gun from her
purse, pointed it at his heart and fired. Perhaps she had been
trained to use the gun, or perhaps it was a lucky shot – either
way, I did not want to dwell on it. Nor did I want to think about
the fact that I had been standing on the steps like a fool, engaging in Dingus' dangerous manipulation, and that if Sheila had
not acted as she did, it would be Nancy lying in a bloody heap
on the floor, and possibly me beside her. Yet much as Sheila
wanted my approval, I couldn't give it to her.

Bridie drew a cross on the dead man's face, closed his ghoulish, staring eyes, then put her hand out for me to help her up.
She groaned as her knees creaked.

'What are we going to do with him?' she asked as she
stretched her body upright again.

I took off my coat and laid it over him, then the three of us
stood over the corpse all thinking the same, dreadful thing. For
all Bridie's prayers and my propriety, Dingus' dead body was no
more to any of us than a rather messy pile of garbage that we
had to dispose of. I spoke before Sheila had the chance to say as
much in front of Bridie.

'We should bury him. Jake and Matt dug up the last of the
potatoes last week before the frost came. We can put him in
there.'

'Oh yes – the spuds will do a treat next year!'

'Sheila, that's enough!' I said.

'You are such a hypocrite, Ellie,' she retorted, then nodded at Bridie, 'and you – you old baggage! I kill a savage – save that little slut's life – and you're still looking down your nose at me. Well, screw you – the pair of you!'

'How dare—' I was about to reprimand her again when Bridie took my arm and held me back.

'Leave her,' she said. 'She just killed a man, she needs some time.'

Maureen had put Nancy to bed in her room with the baby and given her enough whisky to calm her down and let her sleep for the afternoon. Jake had come out when he heard the clap of the gunshot, so we had little choice but to enlist his help.

Not yet fifteen, yet as tall and almost as broad as a man, he dug out a deep hole and measured it the length and breadth of the body, then went across to the sheds at the back of Mario's house to fetch the workers' wheelbarrow, and hoisted the covered body onto it with only a little help from me and Maureen. His face was full of a fake sternness, covering the fact that he was enjoying this responsibility, being the only man helping out the women in this terrible misadventure. Maureen was heartbroken to see her son playing out such a role, as was I. Disposing of a body was the worst type of criminal activity, and one that both his mother and I had hoped this new life would protect him from.

Jake wheeled the barrow with the body to the edge of the hole, then Bridie insisted that I take the boy inside.

'You take Jake in, Ellie. Maureen and I will finish off here.'

She made it sound like laundry. I wanted to insist that I stay, and let Maureen take her son inside, but Maureen said, 'I'll help Bridie, Ellie – you take Jake in and make some tea. We'll be in shortly.'

At that point Jake lost any semblance of adult decorum and started to complain like a child.

'Let me stay. I'll tip him in – the dirty pig – let me finish the job.'

'Come on,' I said, 'you've been a great help, but come inside with me now and we'll have some cookies.'

He looked pleadingly at his mother, whose face was shot through with such disappointment and pain that I felt this was truly the greatest tragedy of the morning. Nancy and her baby had been spared, but Jake had not. The rest of us were adults and must deal with whatever life threw at us, with God's good grace, and put it down to experience – to learn from, or not, in whatever way we could.

By lunchtime we were sitting around the kitchen, eating as if nothing had happened. Anna had missed the whole incident – having the day off meant that she had spent the morning cleaning her own house and had come over just after midday, having prepared us a spaghetti dish, which she carried in a large pan.

'Where is Nancy?' she asked.

'Upstairs,' Maureen said, 'she's feeling a little under the weather.'

'But she loves my spaghetti!'

'She'll be down later,' Bridie reassured her.

Bridie, Maureen and I looked at each other. Anna sensed the awkward atmosphere and knew she was missing something, but assumed that, as usual, it was probably something to do with Sheila having acted out of turn. Sheila had not come downstairs since storming off, but Anna didn't push for our anecdote, knowing that we'd tell her in our own good time.

The truth was that none of us who were involved could find words to put on what had happened that morning. Immediately after Maureen and Bridie came back into the house (having done what they had done), they both bathed and changed their clothes. We then all sat in the kitchen and drank tea in an exhausted silence. There was nothing to be said. Sheila was upstairs, Nancy asleep. There was no reason for us not to discuss what had happened, except that the words – gun, dead, body, corpse, shot, blood, gangster – felt unseemly somehow. What we had done was classified as a crime, even though it was self-defence. Had we acted like criminals in dumping the body? Should we have called the cops?

These questions were too complicated, too crass to put into words. What had happened was ugly – and none of us wanted to repeat the experience by talking about it. In any case, there was little to be said. We were all safe (bar the dead man) and there was nothing more that needed to be done. So an unspoken agreement to keep silent immediately developed between us. If Jake talked – to his school friends, the men of the house – it was unlikely anyone would believe him. After all, the whole thing felt like an illusion, the wild boastings of a schoolboy fantasy. Before he was cold in the ground, Dingus had disappeared from my conscience like a rat down a sewer pipe.

After lunch Maureen went with Anna to meet the children from school, and Bridie went down the basement to do some laundry. I went upstairs to check on Nancy and Sheila. Nancy was fast asleep, with Tom stirring quietly in the cot beside her. I left them both.

# CHAPTER THIRTY-FOUR

The snow came and took over our lives.

Some of the houses were centrally heated, the radiators being fed from coal-fired furnaces in the basements, but coal was expensive and problems in the systems only emerged when they were put under the pressure of constant use. Water and air banged through the pipes as if some mad percussionist was living behind our walls. Plus fuel was expensive, so most of us chose to burn cheaper wood in whatever open fireplaces we had, and that had to be hulked about on roads too icy to walk or drive on. Some of the chimneys started to crumble when they were cleaned, and two chimney fires were caused by overenthusiastic lightings in the first week after the snow came.

The children had to be bought boots and heavy coats, and it was a challenge to get many of them to go to school at all, instead of playing out in the snow. One of the younger boys broke his arm falling off a sledge, so that our first hospital bill had to be paid, and three other children caught bad chills and had to be nursed at home by Maureen. The weather seemed to be causing us to lurch from one drama to the next.

Water pipes in the house and the shop would freeze and have to be coaxed back to life with kettles and warm towels. The path in front of the shop had to be cleared of snow and ice to make it reachable, then fires had to be lit and grates cleared of the ashes twice and sometimes three times a day. All this work meant that just getting out of bed in the morning and getting ourselves to work was a challenge.

At this time the homeless began to emerge from the corners of the city. They had survived in small shacks like the one where I had found Maureen, hiding and coping – but the severe snow had driven in not just the desperate, but those too proud to look for help. They came to the shop in their droves, begging for warmth and comfort. Bridie's small soup kitchen could barely feed the hordes who were turning up there each day. We were all despairing as to what we could do, when Maureen was approached by a group of our wealthy customers to ask if they could help in any way. It seemed they were anxious to volunteer, but the charity rotas at their churches were already full up. The freezing temperatures had not only brought the needy into sharp view, but had pinched the good hearts and consciences of the affluent, too.

'They're bored!' Bridie had puffed cynically when Maureen told us. 'Sure, those spoiled biddies would be no use to anybody.'

'Their money would be useful enough,' Maureen added.

'Don't be so unkind,' I said, although in truth I was thinking the same thing. The last thing I needed was to be appeasing a group of rich ladies – finding something for them to 'do' might only create more work for myself, and make the women in the shop feel uncomfortable.

I need not have worried because shortly afterwards I was approached in the shop by Lavinia French, the wife of a property prospector (and one of our landlords). She was a tall, slim woman with an angular, intelligent face, and a demeanour more suited to the army than the nursery. I had served her in the shop a few times and always found her rather aloof and snooty. She told me that she intended to open up one of her husband's empty buildings that very day as an emergency hostel, and could we supply enough soup and bread to feed up to one hundred people? She would pay us, of course. On no account was there any need to pay us, I assured her. It would be our pleasure to *continue* to help feeding the poor of the village. I lifted my chin to let her know that I was every bit as capable of giving charity as she was, and had plenty of means by which to do so. I was mad that I was wearing my apron, no make-up and had my hair tied back like a scullery maid. As she shook my hand and bustled her beautiful cream wool coat out the door, Sheila emerged from the back, where she had been listening.

'You'd better get your halo polished,' she said, sucking on a sweet that she had stolen from the counter jar. 'I'd say there'll be a bit of competition with that one, Ellie.'

'Don't be ridiculous,' I snapped. Although I knew exactly what she was talking about, I was not about to admit it to her or to myself. 'And I've told you before not to steal that candy.'

Lavinia enlisted the help of the middle-class women of Yonkers to run her soup kitchen, which took over from our service, and a badly needed men's hostel. We prepared all the food for her, and I swallowed my pride and gave way to good sense by allowing her to source and provide ingredients donated by wholesalers as old stock that they could not sell. The same woman canvassed for money from local businessmen, gathering clothes and blankets from all around the neighbourhood. Every night they put down mattresses on the linoleum floor of the now-empty offices on the first floor of the building and opened the hostel. Heartbreaking numbers of homeless men would queue up for a place. The next day they would be given a blanket to take away, and a hot cup of tea with a slice of yesterday's bread, before they wandered back out into the cold, to look for enough work to keep a home for their families in some softer, smaller American town.

It being an unsuitable environment for a woman at night, the homeless men policed and ran the night hostel themselves as volunteers on a rota, making sure that there was no drink and no trouble, and that everyone left the building in the morning, clearing away their bedding and emptying and swilling out their chamber pots. There were street vagrants as well as respectable family men fallen on hard times, but there was seldom any trouble. It was too cold, and their relationship with survival too tenuous to accommodate petty fights or unreasonable emotions.

'It's a slick operation,' Matt told us after he volunteered to stay there one night. 'I was impressed.'

'She's some flier,' Sheila said from behind her book. We were all sitting around the fire, reading and relaxing.

Matt added, 'Lavinia? She's some woman all right.'

I smarted. Sheila was setting me up and, as usual, it was working.

'She surely is,' Bridie added. 'I'll take my words back, but she's a good person – a better one than I gave her credit for, I'll say that. I'm not too proud to admit when I'm wrong.'

'A heart of gold, and not afraid of hard work, either,' added Maureen, looking up from her knitting. 'I saw her there at ten o'clock the other night, bringing in food.'

Sheila shielded her face with her paperback, but I could see from her eyes that she was laughing.

'I admired her silk scarf the other day, and she took it clean off and gave it to me, there and then!' Nancy said.

I flew at the girl.

'Don't go taking charity off those women,' I said. 'Do you

hear me, Nancy? You're well cared for here! You've no need of it.'

'There's no crime in wanting to look well,' the young girl snapped, 'you should try it sometime!'

Nancy ran from the room.

'I don't know what's wrong with that girl,' I said, 'ever since . . .'

Although I stopped myself saying it out loud, I knew that the incident with Dingus must have had a traumatic effect on her, for Nancy had become petulant lately. She had been tardy and lazy at work and, more worrying, seemed to have lost interest in her baby, Tom. For the first three months of his life she had treated him like a precious doll, wary of other people even holding him. Recently, however, she appeared less enthralled by him. She left him for hours sitting in his cot, and often it would take us to tell her that he was crying upstairs. On one occasion she left him in the house without telling us, and closed the door to his room so that we could not hear his cries. I was passing her room on the way to my own before I heard him. I opened the door and found the poor mite purple with bawling from hunger. Immediately I felt sick, realizing that he had been there on his own, crying for somebody to come for him. I picked him up and he clung to my neck, his tiny hands grabbing gratefully at the loose strings of hair around my face as his cries gradually reduced to relieved, breathy sobs. He had been sitting in his own dirt for a long time, so I carried him downstairs and called for Maureen to help me clean up the sore, sorry mess of him, as I mashed potatoes and butter into some warm milk.

He was still too small to sit up unaided, so I put him on my lap, balancing the bowl on the edge of the table. His mouth stretched opened comically as he strained forward for the spoon.

I laughed, and just as Bridie, Maureen and I were all gathered round him, Nancy walked in.

'What are you all doing with my baby?' she said.

Automatically jumping up, I stood and handed him to her.

'You should not have left him with us, without asking first. He was starving.'

She pouted and said, somewhat defensively, 'I don't know what the fuss is about. I fed him this morning before I went out.'

I gasped. He had been there all day.

'It's after three in the afternoon,' I said. 'He's your child, Nancy, you have to take responsibility for him.'

Suddenly she shouted back, 'I don't have to do anything you tell me to do. You're not my mother! I have my own life!'

Now that he had got over the novelty of his mother being back, Tom started crying loudly again and straining towards the food on the table. Maureen took him and started feeding him again, as Nancy stormed off to her room like a spoiled, angry child.

'That young woman's not fit for motherhood,' Bridie said when Maureen and I were telling her later. 'She's simple. Sure, she's barely able to look after herself.'

I felt horrified by her language, but couldn't disagree.

'But she was so wonderful when he was born,' I said. 'Why the change?'

'It's easy to love them when they're completely dependent on you,' Maureen said. 'It's harder when they start growing up.'

'But he's only a few months old,' I said.

'Bridie's right,' Maureen added, 'the novelty has worn off. It happens. I saw it as a nurse. That's how half these babies end up in orphanages – the mothers are barely more than children themselves. We'll just have to keep an eye on him.'

Maureen was such a warm-hearted woman, never judging

people, a calm and capable mother. Although rarely a day went past when she did not thank me for my kindness to her, I knew that the thing she really wanted was not to be living here with us, but with her husband. Perhaps she envied me my dead husband. I knew where he was. I could move on with my life. Or at least pretend to.

With the hostel now open, many of the women and children in the area were taken in by the churches and convents. To the cynic in me it seemed that the church organizations had suddenly galvanized themselves to help in the run-up to Thanksgiving and Christmas. In reality they had been helping people all along, but I had only recently come to their attention, as they had to mine. Through our local priest I was recommended to various charity groups who would send me people that they could not accommodate, sometimes for one or two nights until places came free with them, sometimes for longer.

However, it was becoming harder for us to take people in. Partly because we had no more space to spare, but partly also, I had to be honest, due to lack of will. Most of the families under our care were now living independently, earning a wage from the shop, with the men earning a stipend for me from their labour on the houses as well as any other casual work they could pick up. They were paying their way now, and not all of them were keen on the idea of taking strangers into their homes. 'Eating bread is soon forgot!' was one of Bridie's favourite wisdoms and, I had to admit, it appeared to be true. Once people moved beyond their own needs, the needs of others, while not entirely forgotten, were certainly demoted. The community in general remained sympathetic to the needs of others, but while they were happy to share their meals and labour with homeless unfortunates, they were less and less willing to have somebody else's child share a bed with their own, or to meet the figure of a lonely widow on their stairs in the middle of the night. There were enough of us now that they could always tell themselves it was somebody else's problem, somebody else's turn.

For me, that was never the case. I was happy to open our house to anyone who needed it, and Maureen and Bridie went along with what I wanted, believing me to be a generous and warm-hearted person. However, I knew that wasn't the whole truth. I never believed myself a better person for helping others out in their time of need, nor did I think those who did not want to were in the wrong. I knew I was no saint. I felt as much anger, spite and pride as the next person, and it was that, I sometimes believed, that drove me to do all that I did. It was not charity, but guilt that fuelled my good deeds – the need to prove myself, to let others (but mostly myself) know that I could somehow redeem myself from the tragedy of my husband's sudden death. It was as if this trip to America was making up for the last one: the time when I came here to pay for John's operation and almost stayed because I was falling in love with another man; the time when John had begged me to stay in Ireland with him, but I had gone anyway. Like the last day of his life, when he had asked me to walk the fields with him and I had gone to work instead.

How many needy would I have to feed, to house, to help before I had paid myself back for losing John? One more family, one more time – I had told him I would be away for one short year and had stayed for three. I regretted those years I might have spent with him, and that one last afternoon when he asked me to walk his fields. Every needy person, every new task helped hold at bay all that I had lost.

A week before Christmas our house was packed with people. We had two extra mothers and five additional children in the house. Their husbands were sleeping nights at the hostel and, it being so close to Christmas, we accommodated them too. One mother and her infant were sleeping on mattresses in Nancy's room, and the other mother and her four children in the dining room. The men slept in the living room next to the kitchen. During the day I, Bridie, Nancy and Maureen went straight down to the shop as early as 6 a.m. to get ready for the seasonal rush that had overtaken us. The husbands walked over to Matt, who gave them odd jobs – clearing snow, tidying sheds, sorting sticks for kindling – and a few dollars to get them through the holiday. Sheila stayed behind with our women guests to look after the children, clean the house and prepare our evening meal.

Not a domestic being, Sheila turned out to be a godsend in entertaining the older children. The schools had closed early for Christmas due to the cold weather, and as soon as breakfast was eaten she would bring them all upstairs to her room, where she would have a fire lit and would keep them there for almost the whole day. She read them stories and put on plays, making their faces up with rouge and lipstick. She drew with them, and taught them to play cards. The children idolized her: the girls for her glamour and style, and the boys for her adventurous imagination and bawdy tongue.

'It's like they love me, Ellie,' she said one night when she was tipsy enough for me to question her about it.

'And do you love them?' I asked.

'Don't be ridiculous!' she snapped, then we laughed at the unlikeliness of it all. Although I could see that, in the children, Sheila had acquired an audience of admirers, it was not as ridiculous an idea as it seemed that she should be gifted with children. Sheila had been bright at school – with a vivid imagination, she had been a talented young artist, as well as an avid reader and writer. Her schooling had ended when her family moved to America when she was sixteen, and she had found herself in service when she fell out with them. If Sheila's education had continued, she could easily have become a teacher, or a writer and artist – she certainly had the temperament for the last!

Perhaps, I thought, Sheila had found a vocation in life beyond money and men.


The day before Christmas Eve the shop was hopping. It seemed as if everyone in Yonkers had ordered one of Bridie's Christmas puddings or cakes, as our customers rushed in and out doing their last-minute chores. The cafe tables were jammed with rest-ing shoppers; Lavinia's soup kitchen needed more soup, more bread – it was mayhem.

'Nancy!' Bridie was shouting every few minutes. 'Nancy! Nancy! Where is that wretched girl – I need more potatoes peeled. So help me God, Ellie, roll your sleeves up and give me a hand – I'll skin that lazy strap when I find her.'

Nancy did not come in all day. Despite being dressed early, she had been dawdling at the door that morning and told me to go on without her and that she would follow. I had assumed she must have stayed at home with Tom. Perhaps the baby had taken ill.

We closed the shop at six sharp, even though there were a few people still milling about outside. I put a notice up saying, 'Closed until 29th December'. God knows, we deserved a break. The women had worked so hard, and I had taken a big lump of cash out of that day's register to give them all a bonus.

When we got back to the house, Sara – one of the temporary mothers we had taken in – was walking a bawling Tom around the kitchen.

'He won't settle,' she said.

One of the infant's cheeks glowed an angry red. 'I think he's teething.'

'Typical!' Bridie was red with rage herself. 'NANCY!' she hollered up the stairs.

Sara looked confused.

'She's not here,' she said. 'A car came to collect her at about nine this morning. I thought she was down in the shop with you?'

I ran up to Nancy's room and on her bed was a note in her large, childlike hand.

> *You killed my last beau so I found another*
> *Ellie, you can look after Tom.*

# Chapter Thirty-Five

Even though it had been hours since the mysterious car had been to collect her, I ran out onto the porch and looked up and down the road for Nancy and her 'beau'.

She had left her child behind. How could she have done that?

Aside from Tom, Nancy was little more than a child herself – she had been fooled into trusting Dingus in a matter of an hour. Goodness knows what kind of a man she had run off with, and what his intentions were?

'We have to find her,' I said to the women after I had shown them the note, 'we can't just let her disappear like that.'

'How?' said Sheila. 'We have no idea who she has gone off with. Where would we start?'

'We could send Matt and the men out in the van?' I said.

'In what direction? The city is huge – they were in a car and they might have gone out of the state,' she went on.

I looked over at Maureen. Her lips were tight and angry. She was being reminded of the search for another missing man, her husband. She attacked before the thought entered Sheila's head.

'This is all *your* fault – putting vain ideas into that simple child's head.'

Sheila drew a breath, but Bridie intervened.

'It's nobody's fault, and there is no point in looking for her,' the old woman butted in. Tom had started whingeing, and Bridie lifted him from Sara's lap and started to bump him up and down on her hip, which made him cry even harder. 'The girl was in trouble when she got here, and she'll surely be in trouble again after too long. When that happens, we can only pray she has enough sense to find her way back here. In the meantime we have to look after this little chap – he's the innocent one.'

Tom was screaming up a storm. Bridie, for all her matronly manners, had no way with children. I put my arms out to her and she handed him over willingly. He calmed down and rested his head into the curve of my neck.

From then on, apart from when he was crawling into corners and causing mischief, baby Tom was barely out of my arms. While I had not taken to heart Nancy's words that it was I who should look after her child, it seemed that the other women had. Each stepped to one side of Tom and cleared a path for me to be with him. Bridie instructed Matt to move the heavy cot from the attic down into my room the very night that Nancy left. Maureen took over the early shifts at the shop, so that I could sleep through with him in the mornings. They made a show of saying how they had enough to do, without minding an extra child, and how selfish Nancy had been in leaving us all to manage a baby, but in reality they could see how important being with this child was for me.

Nancy's leaving, and the other women's approval, had given me permission to love baby Tom. Good sense told me that I should be more cautious about allowing myself to indulge my maternal instincts. That Nancy could come back any day, and that it would be wise to hold onto some of the distance I had maintained around him up till then. However, I could not help but throw myself into the role of motherhood with absolute abandon. My attachment to Tom was as instant and as natural as if he had been my own, and it seemed to me that it was the same for him. He craved love, and much as I knew in those early few days that he was crying for his natural mother's smell, her warmth, the comfort of her milk, I made myself believe that he would grow used to love from whatever quarter it came. That my love would be enough for him. More than enough.

Perhaps it was because he had been in a house with so many of us women looking out for him that he took to me easily. I found he sat comfortably in the groove of my hips and that I could fill the kettle and butter a slice of bread with one hand. I drew my fingers gently down over his chubby face, to comfort him and draw his eyes to sleep. When I bathed him in the sink, he would scream with delight as I splashed water into the ridges of fat on his belly and legs. When he laughed I laughed – and the laughter came from a child inside me that I had thought had long since left; the child who had chased rabbits and run through fields with her skirts flying. When I was changing Tom and placed my worn, working hands against his smooth, creamy skin, I would stop for a moment and marvel at the privilege of being with him. I held him up to the mirror in my room and we would look at our joint reflection. His small, round face made mine look angular and old, even though I was far off forty. I never failed to be surprised at my own face when I was holding him.

On the dullest, plainest of days, when Tom was in my arms, I looked – even to my own critical eye – calm and relaxed and beautiful. My eyes shone with joy. Sometimes, mesmerized by his reflection, he would give me a curious smile. It was the look of an old sage rather than that of an infant, and I would think that perhaps he knew something of the truth that I was barely able to admit to myself: that he was the antidote for much of what had been missing from my life; that my loving him could change everything.

\*

We had a full house that Christmas. Bridie had asked Matt to spend Christmas Day with us. 'The Balduccis deserve a bit of time on their own. Besides, they do things different in Italy, and it's only right that we should be feeding the Irishman.'

He came over at dawn on Christmas Day. The rest of the house was still asleep and I was sitting in the kitchen giving baby Tom a bottle. After a fretful night's teething, he was finally falling asleep. Sucking on the milky teat, he opened one lazy eye to Matt and closed it again.

'I thought I'd get over before Mario and Anna woke up – otherwise I might get dragged in for the day.'

'The kids will all be running around here soon enough,' I said.

'Grand so,' he said, pulling the coffee pot down from its shelf, 'they'll be dying to see what Santa got them. Times have changed from our day, surely.'

'Just a few sweets and daft little trinkets, that's all, Matt,' I replied. 'These kids deserve as much as we can give them, after all they've been through.'

'Coffee?'

'Of course.'

Tom stirred and, as I adjusted myself in my seat, my cardigan fell from my shoulders. Matt set the coffee cup down in front of me and then, my hands being full, leaned across me to put a spoon of sugar in it. As he did so, he let out a long yawn.

'Oh God – excuse me,' he said.

I chided him gently.

'I heard "the men" were out celebrating the Lord's birth last night all right. Did you go to bed at all?'

As he stood up, he stopped and looked me in the face, quite deliberately. His expression was querying, his eyes burning with intent. He paused as if to say something, then moved around my chair and gently adjusted the cardigan back up onto my shoulders.

Although I knew that he was full of longing for me, Matt's hands never lingered over these small gestures. When our arms brushed as he laid a cup in front of me, or patted the top of my hand to comfort me over some failing, or helped me on with a coat, or pulled a falling cardigan up over my shoulders – these automatic, meaningless gestures of friendliness were a facade of paternal affection that I was happy to go along with. I had always been flattered that Matt loved me, while remaining comfortably confident that he would never act. But that morning, with my body warm from sleep, the intimacy of our shared domesticity and the ordinariness of our words, coupled with the impropriety of me being in flimsy night-attire, sent a shot of hunger through me.

With Tom still feeding, I reached up to my shoulder and put my hand over Matt's hand to hold it to my neck. He hesitated, unsure what this meant, but before he could move away I turned towards him and, reaching my hand up to his face, pulled him firmly towards me for a kiss.

He fell on me like a hungry wolf, and as he reached for my breast, I shuddered so hard that I feared I would drop the dozing child.

'Morning – we're up early?'

Matt leapt back and knocked over two chairs as Bridie marched past us both. I grabbed the baby in both hands and stood up so suddenly that he let out a yelp.

'Hope I'm not disturbing anything?' she said, without looking at either of us.

'No, no,' I said.

'I'll get the fires started,' Matt replied, tripping over both fallen chairs in his hurry to get out onto the porch.

'I'd better go upstairs and get dressed,' I said. Careful not to meet her eye, I hoisted Tom up to my chest and flicked my hair back from my face.

'Yes, indeed,' the old woman replied as I passed her on my way through the kitchen door, 'you better had.'

Matt and I markedly avoided each other for the rest of the day. We passed each other in the kitchen after lunch. Tom was napping, and I was taking some dishes into the kitchen as he was coming in from the garden with an armload of wood. His arms were bare where he had rolled up the sleeves of his clean shirt to protect them, and the hairs curled up in the cold along the muscles. As he brushed past me I could smell the musky scent of the wet wood mingling with his pipe smoke. He walked straight ahead, deliberately not meeting my eye, and it was all I could do not to pull him out onto the porch and kiss him again. If Maureen and Anna had not been in the kitchen with us, I might well have done so.

As it was, I retired to my room early, settled Tom and waited for Matt to come to me, as I knew he would.

My mind was alive with objections: What am I doing? This is ridiculous – only a short time ago you shared this bed with Charles, and now another? You're a widow: sleeping with two men in less than a lifetime is bad enough – but two in as many months? And no thought of marriage in your head? Or even what could be understood as true love in your heart?

Yet the more I tried to reason with myself, and the more 'wrong' I told myself my behaviour was, the greater my desire became. I was breaking my own moral code; merely to think of consummating such a thing was against God and all religious convictions; Matt was a completely unsuitable match for my passions – more brother than lover. But the more reasons I put forward not to act, the greater my intention to do so became. I knew that he would surely be thinking all the same things about me, and that he would be considering the obstacles that had stopped him making a move before: my respectability, my reputation my mourning for my dead husband. In Matt's eyes, Charles' public seduction of me would have been a thoughtless act of disrespect and would have angered him. My reciprocation may have hurt, but it would also have shown Matt that I was not untouchable. If he had had any doubt about that, then my behaviour earlier that day would have clarified things for him.

Tom was curled up fast asleep in his cot when Matt quietly opened the door and entered my room. We tore at each other with no introduction or apology, making love semi-clothed and in rapid desperation. He held his hand to my mouth to muffle my passionate shouts, as I bit and buckled against his strong, certain touch.

Immediately afterwards I fell asleep, on my back, my body a flat, wet cross. When I woke some hours later Matt was still in the bed beside me – half-sitting up, with the baby nestled into the bend of his chest. He put his finger to his mouth to indicate that Tom was about to drop off again, then put his arm back down to form the child's cradle. I curled back under the sheets and half-closed my eyes as if to sleep. Although it was the middle of the night, the snow outside reflected a shaft of blue light through a gap in the curtains. It threw the soft features of Matt's face into chiselled contrast and made him look stronger and more sophisticated than I knew him to be. With Tom lying across his chest, they both looked like a marble statue: man and baby, their naked skin creamy and smooth, shadows falling across their still bodies.

Here was a man – no more than a friend – whom I had known for less than a year, and a child who belonged to somebody else; yet, in that moment, in some part of my heart, I laid claim to them both.

We felt like a family.

# Chapter Thirty-Six

The secret, illicit nature of our love affair did not last beyond that night.

I was past worrying what people thought of me, particularly those in our close circle. There had been times, in the earlier days of our friendship, when I had thought Maureen had her eye on Matt herself, even just as a father figure for her son. However, Maureen could not open herself to any such possibility as long as there was a chance that Patrick Sweeney was still alive, and she could not consider getting intimate with another man. My own husband was dead less than a year, and already I had been with two other men. Strangely, Bridie showed no signs of disapproval. I could not say that she actively encouraged the union, but then she was not given to commenting if she liked things – only if she disliked them, and she liked Matt.

'He's honest,' she said one night when I asked what she thought about him, as she was peeling some spuds by the sink, 'and strong. Men are weak, stupid creatures at heart – that's as much as you can hope for in any of them.'

'Do you think I'm terrible, Bridie – carrying on with him in the way I am?'

'There's worse things than *that*, Ellie. In any case, who am I to judge? Only the good Lord can judge any of us in the end.'

Then, as she gathered the peelings up for the hens, she muttered, 'And I wonder about that too sometimes.'

Had God deserted Bridie, I wondered? If that Catholic stalwart's faith was floundering, what hope was there for me that mine would ever come back? The safety net for all hardship – the certainty that, no matter what happened in this life, you would be rewarded in the next; the ability to put the responsibility for one's fate, one's happiness in the hands of an all-powerful God – I missed it. The worries of the world were on my shoulders now, not His. He wasn't going to look after the poor and the hungry, so I had to do it – and He certainly wasn't going to look after me. God had proven that, by taking John from me and refusing to give me a child. Was this petulance on my part? Was He simply punishing me for my lack of faith? Or perhaps there was no lack of faith in me, because perhaps there was no God.

In any case I decided that after all the passionate ups and downs I had experienced in my marriage to John, and then the complex confusion of my affair with Charles, Bridie was right. Perhaps strength and honesty were the best, simplest foundations on which to base love.

I could not say that I loved Matt – certainly not in the same way that I loved John, or even Charles. What I could say for certain was that I felt satisfied in his bed and safe in his company. Life fell into a settled routine after I decided to be with Matt. It felt like the right thing to do at the right time.

Baby Tom woke me every morning with a gurgle, the burgeoning curls above his ears sticking out in milk-gelled spikes, banging the empty bottle on the bars of his cot until I picked him up and took him downstairs.

Tom inched his way to physical independence: sitting up on his own, rolling around the floor, grabbing his own bottle and lumps of bread. Once he discovered that he could hoist himself high enough onto his short limbs to crawl, he was away – into every dark corner, seeking out mischief – and at all times I was not far behind him. I was not his real mother, but I did not give Tom the chance to question the difference between young Nancy and this other woman, who was familiar, but didn't share his blood. When he found a dead spider, I was the one who leaned over him and grimaced it away. If he fell, I scooped him and comforted him before he barely had the chance to draw breath on his cries. The other women graciously stepped aside, taking up the slack in the household chores and shops, so that I could dedicate my time to this abandoned child.

As quickly as I adopted the role of Tom's mother, Matt took on that of an attentive husband to me – even though neither of these roles was grounded in fact, we gave each other what we needed. We formed a family unit in the house and, with Nancy gone, moved to the top floor, where we created a living space independent of the others.

There was a small conservatory area on the landing, which we furnished with two low cane armchairs and a table, turning it into a comfortable day-room. Matt built a wooden playpen in the corner; he painted the slats a bright blue and I filled it with a nest of blankets. After a hectic morning, Tom would nuzzle his head into the milky softness and doze as I sat and did my paperwork. We opened up the fireplace in Nancy's bedroom and covered the bed in broad cushions, turning it into a small drawing room, where we spent our evenings quietly sitting in each other's company, reading and listening to the radio. Matt wore glasses to read, and smoked a pipe; I took up knitting and began embroidering a small tapestry with Tom's name on it. On evenings like that, lost in a comfortable domestic silence, it was easy to imagine that we were married, and that the small child asleep in the next room was our own.

Matt pre-empted my every whim. He carried baby Tom into the bed and placed him in my arms each morning, before bringing me up coffee and toast in bed. He ran a bath for me when I seemed tired; he even noted the rose-scented bath salts that I used, replacing them from the drugstore before they ran out. He came and stood behind me as I was brushing my hair or applying my make-up, told me I was beautiful and kissed my neck. At another time Matt's attention might have felt cloying; I might have interpreted his constant affection as the desperate ingratiation of a man too much in love, but I was exhausted from the cycle of grieving and giving in which I had been caught up, so his attentions brought me grateful relief – a sense that perhaps things were coming together for me at last. Matt was happy to shower me with love, and I was happy to receive it now; I was ready for the love of a good, honest man again. I took his love and banked it away in the grey hollow where my heart once lived. It seemed to help.

In early March 1935 Matt bought a brand-new forward-facing 'buggy' for Tom, with polished chrome on the handles, a smart navy body and wide wheels. It would only be used for a few months, but Matt was pleased as punch with his new purchase and had bought and tied a balloon to its handlebars, which Tom grabbed at busily, then chased around the room as if it were an elusive fly.

'A waste of good money,' Bridie puffed, when Matt manoeuvred it into the kitchen to show off.

'I'll not have Ellie out walking the neighbourhood with that shabby, second-hand perambulator, Bridie – and the child hanging out the side of it, like a ruffian. Not a lady of her standing, it wouldn't look right.'

I waited for Bridie's sarcastic rebuff – Matt's comment was

certainly begging for one – but she simply shrugged and said, 'I suppose you're right,' and carried on slicing yesterday's ham.

'We can take him up to Mass in it this Sunday,' Matt went on, 'it's about time we got him started in church. I don't even know that he's even been christened yet?'

'He most certainly has not,' said Bridie, 'unfortunate godless mite.'

'Perhaps we should talk to Father Michael about it this Sunday?'

'Excellent idea,' she said.

Matt had seemed to grow in stature in the few months since we had been together. While I would never had described him as being weak in character, the unfortunate circumstances in which I had found him had caused him to be a somewhat reluctant person, almost deferential both in his manner and in the way he carried himself physically. It was only after we had been together a few weeks that I realized how very tall he was. He had been compensating for his great height with a slight stoop, but since we got together he had started to walk with a straighter back, and the sleeves of his jackets actually seemed to shrink.

Being with me had increased Matt's confidence to such an extent that he began to take much greater pride in his appearance, too. He started to shave every morning, sometimes in the evening as well – and his way of dressing and carrying himself took on a more respectable, gentlemanly demeanour. I was pleased that he had decided to smarten himself up, although I insisted that it was entirely unnecessary to make such efforts for my benefit. If I had any reservations at all about being with Matt, it was that he tended to change the person he was to please me.

When the question of religion came up, I was irritated at

how eagerly Matt embraced Bridie's engrained conventional attitudes, especially after flying so thoroughly in the face of them
by sleeping with me. However, there was something comforting
about the idea of falling back in with the old habits of church
and religion. After all, and God aside, the familiarity and routine of prayers and priests had formed the solid moral backdrop
of my childhood and most of my adult life, and there would be
surely no harm in allowing myself to be drawn back into the
Catholic world of good coats and respectability.

The following Sunday Matt and Tom and I made our 'debut'
as a threesome at Mass. I wore a mid-calf-length navy-and-white
houndstooth coat with a hat trimmed in the same fabric, navy
gloves, bag and silk scarf. I stuffed Tom into a new sailor suit I
had bought him, alarmed to note how big he was getting, as it
was already slightly too small for his chubby frame. I knew the
little peaked cap would not stay on his head past the porch, but
put it into my bag anyway, along with a big pile of dollars for
the contribution plate and a lipstick for retouching just before
we went in. Matt wore a new brown suit with draped trousers,
and a jacket that hung loose almost down to his knees. He was
all style, cocking the trilby on sideways over his freshly shaven
short back and sides.

Matt insisted on pushing the buggy, even though his enormous frame made it look like a small toy in his hands. Tom's
head moved from left to right, silenced with awe at this new,
fascinating view of the world, and he pulled on his dummy with
the excited ferocity of an old film gangster pulling on a cigar.
A man walking to Mass with his woman and child on a sunny
Sunday morning: Matt looked fit to explode with joy, and for a
moment I too felt impossibly grateful for this slice of ordinary
life in what had been an extraordinary year.

'I didn't know you'd bought a new suit?' I said.

'There's a lot you don't know about me,' he answered. I raised my eyebrows in reply to the implication, although it was far from the truth. Matt was not the mysterious type – that was one of the things I had come to like about him. The fact that he was an open book, and I knew everything there was to know, made me feel safe. I had seen the menswear bag hanging in the hall two days beforehand and had accurately guessed what it contained, and why.

'What a smart pair you are!'

Lavinia French pulled her car up alongside us. Lavinia had been courting my friendship of late, and I had surprised myself by finding that I liked this older, rather strident, confident woman. She was wealthy, but no silly socialite – and I had come to admire the straightforward, to-the-point manner that had so offended me when we first met. I was also, in honesty, flattered by the attention of this doyenne of the Yonkers establishment. She had doubtless thoroughly investigated my background through Mr Williams before befriending me, and discovered that I owned several properties in the area and had not only independent means, but the business acumen of a man, as well as a woman's charitable nature. In her desiring my friendship, I saw myself briefly through her eyes and felt some pride in my own achievements.

'Good morning, Mrs French,' Matt said, touching his hat like a servant boy. His deferential attitude embarrassed me, but seemed to delight her.

'Good morning, Matt – and so handsome in a new suit? Off somewhere special?'

'Church,' I said.

'How terribly worthy.'

'Somebody has to pray for the saving of our souls, Lavinia, and I'm afraid that today that somebody is me!'

'Well, good for you – why don't you call by our house on your way back? Jack is having some rather rich friends over for luncheon, and I could use a hand squeezing some more cash out of them for the hostel.'

'I don't know,' I said. Although I knew where Lavinia lived, I had never been to her house before – and for a meal? I wasn't dressed for it, and my nails needed a manicure if I was going to sit down and eat with strangers. 'We have the baby with us, Lavinia, and he's so much trouble . . .'

'Oh, nonsense, Ellie – one of the maids will take him: we can put him out back with the dogs if he gets too rowdy.'

'If you don't mind – another time.'

'Matt, talk to her! I'm only joking about putting the precious child out . . .'

'Of course we'll be there: about one?'

'Perfect, see you then!' And she drove off, waving cheerily.

'Matt!' I was furious. 'How dare you make arrangements over me like that.'

He was undeterred.

'What?' he said. 'You like the Frenches – you were just being polite.'

'I was not! I am not in the mood.'

'Of course you are,' he said. 'You're all dressed up anyway – we all are. You just say "No" to everything because you are still afraid.'

I was furious because I knew he was right.

'I am not afraid! Afraid of what exactly?'

'Afraid of life, Ellie – afraid of settling down and making a proper life for yourself. It's always about other people, for you. You need to make something for yourself, Ellie. Make friends of your own standing, and don't always be helping those less fortunate.'

Like him – that was what he was thinking. Yet how had I been fortunate enough to find him? A sensitive friend who wanted to put me back together again.

'You build people up, Ellie – that's what you do. You need to build yourself up now. Take a break from helping others, and help yourself. Show yourself off to the Frenches – you're as good as them . . .'

'So are you.'

'You said it, lady! Anyway, you're dying to get a look inside their house. I know I am. Sure, what else would we be doing today?'

He was right. This was what I wanted, what I needed. To socialize with nice people, to settle and feel safe and happy again in my own life. If I wasn't sure exactly how that was going to happen, if I was ever uncertain or wavered in what I wanted, then I had found a sensible man who loved me and could fill in the gaps.

I made a mental note to say 'Yes' when Matt asked me to marry him.

I knew it was only a matter of time before he would.

# Chapter Thirty-Seven

Over the next couple of months Matt took my hand and I slowly stepped off my spinning carousel and onto solid ground. He had a way of making things steady and it seemed that my world was easier, and the ground beneath me more stable, with him around. I felt as if my life was falling into place, and I allowed myself to be persuaded to pass the responsibility for the businesses and houses more thoroughly onto others' shoulders, so that I could enjoy some of the rewards of my hard work and charity. 'Let us look after you for a change' was the message from everyone, and it felt like progress to be able to take a step back.

Maureen and Bridie took over the everyday running of the shop, and Matt had the building end of the houses running like clockwork, with Mario now managing the men so that Matt could take more time off to spend with me and Tom. On top of that, the money kept rolling in from Ireland, with letters that contained neither questions nor complaints from Katherine. She assured me that Maidy continued to cope with both John's death and my absence. In short, there was nothing to worry me, and nothing to run from any more.

So Matt and I built a life for ourselves.

\*

In May we took a day trip out to New Jersey. Matt sat Tom up on the railings of the ferry and he stretched down, reaching frantically for the separating lines of foaming sea. Matt put him up on our shoulders as we walked along the beach; I tasted the salt on my lips – watched the swell and crash of the spring waves until they crumbled into simpering gold sniggers of sand – and I felt alive.

I became interested in fashion again. Finding that I could not face the grandiosity and bustle of the city stores, I discovered a competent dressmaker in Yonkers and bought fabric and Vogue patterns, which she made up for me, adding quirks and tailoring details of my own – a ruff across one shoulder, a ribbon detail to the collar of a jacket.

I had both the opportunity and the inclination to dress up after I became something of a figurehead for charitable causes. It started when the Yonkers newspaper, *Home News & Times*, came to interview me at the shop. I insisted that they interview and photograph all of us women together as a group, but they took me aside afterwards. The photographer stood me under the sign saying 'Yonkers Women's Cooperative' and urged me to smile a broad, proud smile – that was the picture they used alongside my words alone, in a two-page article entitled 'Irish Woman in Successful Endeavour for the Homeless'.

Matt's brown suit was quickly added to, with full black dinner dress, as we dined with judges and councillors and, with Lavinia's social patronage, entered the elite world of philanthropists and power-mongers.

Any sense of self-doubt or insecurity that I may once have felt at moving in such lofty circles was gone. John's death had changed me; so perhaps had my other brush with death – that of Dingus. I could no longer judge other people, or myself, as harshly as I had once done. Life and death were not opposites after all, but close allies; prince or pauper, beggar or banker – we were all made of nothing more than bone and sinew, flesh and blood. We lived at the mercy of the delicate operation of our bodily functions; the heart could stop beating in an instant, by whim of God or gun. *'Pow!'* – as Dingus himself had so aptly put it – and life was gone.

What, then, was the sense in worrying about etiquette or what other people thought of you? I found that now, when I was faced with the trivialities of social etiquette that used to concern me – the tidy appearance of my nails, the cut of my dress, the positioning of my hair, the manners and status of my gentleman companion – the very moment such concerns entered my head they were banished just as quickly, for the insults to humanity that they were.

I dressed well and observed good manners, as I had always done; it was just that I worried less about how I would be perceived, and was therefore better able to present myself properly as an intelligent and opinionated person. Matt proved to be a sociable companion. Unfazed by other men's wealth or erudition, he found that being by my side gave him all the confidence he needed in any company.

'They have money and education, Ellie, but I've got you!' he once said, as I was fussing over his collar on our way into a fundraising dinner in the Waldorf.

As I moved around the tables, gathering donations with Lavinia, I looked across the vast, glittering ballroom and saw Matt flirting with two judges' wives. He looked right at home, and as I saw his broad Irish face laughing heartily, a punch of reality thudded through me. I got a picture of how I had found him: down on his luck – broken. I may have plucked Matt from the Labour Exchange line, I thought, but that was where his luck had ended. Everything he was now he had earned, through hard work, respect for the dollar and his love and loyalty to me.

That's how things are in America, I remembered. You can go from pauper to president – reinvention was not only encouraged, but admired. Change, progress, the shedding of one life and stepping into another were what America was built on.

In Ireland you could never shake off your history; the sins of your forefathers clung to your coat, leeching you of your achievements, constantly reminding you where you came from. You were kept so busy seeking atonement that there was never the opportunity to move on, never the room to breathe freely. No matter what success I achieved in Kilmoy, I was always the daughter of a crown-loving, traitorous father and a stand-offish, unpopular mother. The best I ever was – despite my achievements in business, my efforts to ingratiate myself with the local people – was John Hogan's wife, now widow.

In America, nobody knew John Hogan, and they liked me anyway.

Matt and I even appeared once in a tiny picture in *Vanity Fair* magazine. All dressed up and smiling, we grinned out of the pages with all the swanks and socialites as if we were part of them. For a split second I allowed myself to wonder if Charles had seen it. I was mixing in the world that he had been born into. He had rejected that world, and so would certainly not have seen my picture. Perhaps he had heard I was with Matt now? Charles had not come back, but, in any case, I could barely recall him without being carried back to the tremendous black pit into which I had fallen after he left. He was the lover who had plunged me into the terrifying chasm of grief, while Matt was the one who had lifted me out of it.

'Are we,' I said to him one night, 'like them?'

'Like who?' he asked.

We were still living on the top floor of the shared house. Perhaps we should move, get a house nearer the city together, get married, I thought.

'Never mind,' I said.

Life seemed settled, as if I was being invited to move on, yet in the core of me I was still uncertain.

Sheila was sceptical about my relationship with Matt.

'You're just with him because you can walk all over the poor man,' she said. 'You've always longed to be respectable, and you can make him do as you please. You don't love Matt, not really. You're still longing to be with that cad Charles – tell the truth!'

Sheila could say things like that to me without me taking any notice.

'The red or the blue?' I asked, holding up two new silk scarves just to annoy her.

We were having coffee in the shop.

'They are both ghastly!' Sheila was envious of my money, but I had decided I wasn't going to support her beyond her food and board. She borrowed my clothes, ate well out of the shop and could drink her fill with the men (who thought she was hilarious), but she was constantly frustrated with not having 'her own' money to spend. Sheila had tried working in the shop, but always ended up causing mayhem by bossing everyone about, while not dirtying her hands by so much as lifting a cup.

'Flirting with the male customers and letting them off paying!' Bridie complained.

'She's trying to find another rich fool to look after her,' Maureen added.

Much as I hated to admit it, I had come to think that perhaps finding a rich man to look after her was the best – or rather only – option for Sheila. She pestered me to take her to charity functions, but after she made a holy show of herself, getting blind drunk and sitting on the knee of another woman's husband, I drew the line. I was excusing her behaviour to Lavinia, when she shocked me by informing me that Sheila's reputation as a money-grabbing flibbertigibbet had spread from Boston to New York, with word out that she had single-handedly brought down Alex Ward and his family's successful glazing firm. It was an exaggeration, but it certainly didn't help her cause, and neither did her increasingly cheap manners. Without the enforced social boundaries of being married to a 'good' family, Sheila had taken to smoking and drinking like a navvy and 'dressing like a whore' – Bridie's words, not mine.

'She won't find a rich man in here,' Anna said about Sheila's flirtations in the cafe.

'Certainly not dressed like a floozy,' Maureen added.

It turned out they were both wrong.

On this particular morning Sheila had barely bothered getting dressed at all. She had been out all night – I did not dare ask where – and had wandered into the shop mid-morning as I was taking my elevenses, making the most of Tom being asleep in his buggy.

Last night's kohl and mascara rimmed her eyes in a smoky black, and her panstick was flaky in the stark morning light.

'You're a mess, Sheila,' I said.

She snapped open her compact and reapplied some lipstick over the pale stain.

'There,' she said, 'good as new. All I need now is a cure – Anna? Coffee!'

'Jesus, Sheila, don't talk to Anna like that.'

'What? She works here, doesn't she?'

Anna came over and placed a cup of coffee in front of me, before giving Sheila a look of pure Italian poison.

I pushed the cup towards her and she took a flask from her purse and poured in a drop of whisky.

'Where did you get that?'

'Somebody gave it to me.'

'Who?'

'Urgh! I've always had it. Why must you treat me like a wayward child?'

'Why must you behave like one?'

We were busy bickering when Sheila's eyes rotated towards the door. A man had come in. He was middle-aged, his peppery hair slicked back, his square frame wearing an impeccable three-piece dove-grey pinstripe suit with a pink kerchief in the pocket. Money!

He came straight over to our table and said, 'Ladies.'

Sheila's face lit up, but he more or less ignored her and addressed me directly.

'Mrs Hogan, isn't it? Excuse me for being so forward, but I know you from your face in the paper, and I believe you know an associate of mine?'

'Lavinia French?' I asked.

'No,' he said, 'I don't know that lady. I am looking for a man called Dingus McGonigle.'

It took a second for it to sink in. Dressed like that, he wasn't a cop, which meant he could only be from the mob. The cafe was empty. I looked over to signal for Anna to get help, but she had scuttled out back to the kitchen.

'My name is Frank Delaney,' he said, 'and I believe that Mr McGonigle was seen in these premises trying to do some business some months ago.'

I stuttered something like, 'I don't recall.' A big black car had pulled up outside the door and two slick-looking gangsters had got out and were standing by it. I looked over at Sheila: her face was calm, but her hands shook slightly as she lit a cigarette.

Her eyes were thoughtful slits – I knew that look, and goodness knows what scheme she was thinking up. Whatever it was, I hoped it was better than what I had, which was nothing.

'Come now, Mrs Hogan – perhaps it will jog your memory if I tell you that he had a run-in with a man I believe you are well acquainted with: a Mr Charles Irvington – "Chuck" I believe his friends call him?'

'What do you know of Charles Irvington?' I asked. My voice sounded defensive, shaky.

'Well, I believe he was residing in your house for a time?'

I could feel my face tighten, my lips pursed, my jaw stuck. Tom was still asleep in his chair. The shadow of that morning with Dingus fell over me. It was happening again. Sheila looked over towards the kitchen; she was panicking too – what did he want?

He pulled a chair over from the table next to us and settled himself in between us both, at the round table.

'This Chuck is a dangerous character, Mrs Hogan – involved in the unions, he was running roughnecks out of the docks and had many dealings with some of my friends in the police department. You may not be aware of this, but my associate Mr McGonigle disappeared soon after a run-in with him at your residence.'

'I don't know where Charles is,' I said. My voice sounded high, as if I was guilty of something. Where were all the cursed men when you needed them? Where was Matt? Mario? These men had guns – our men would be no use to us anyway. And curse Charles! He was more trouble when he wasn't here than when he was.

'Is this what you're looking for?'

I looked up. Bridie had suddenly appeared behind me, flanked by Maureen and a rather shocked-looking Anna.

She flung what appeared to be half a pound of sausages down on the table in front of the man. He flinched, and as he did so, one of the men outside opened the door. The man raised his arm and waved them away, his eyes transfixed on Bridie's package, resting on the gingham tablecloth in front of him.

I looked closer. It wasn't a pound of sausages, it was a human hand.

'That's what's left of your "friend",' Bridie said. 'We took the liberty of leaving on his signet ring, so you could identify him – although I'm sure that your "friends" in the police department would be happy to fingerprint him for you.'

I was speechless. Bridie had cut off Dingus' hand. Why? (I chose not to think about how – although I had seen her easily butcher half a pig, so I had some idea of what she could do with a knife. I later discovered that Maureen and she had tried to remove his signet ring, failed, and Bridie decided it would be simpler to cut off his whole hand than a single finger!)

Our guest was completely taken aback.

'Who are you?'

'Don't you mind who I am,' Bridie said – she was thoroughly enjoying herself – and actually reached up to adjust her grey bun as she was talking. 'Let's just say I'm the person who knows that your toughest lackey was brought to justice by a handful of women. How do you think your protection racket would survive a rumour like that?'

As Bridie was talking, a small smile played across his lips. He wasn't a cruel-looking man. Not like the unfortunate employee whose hand he lifted carefully between his thumb and forefinger.

'So Charles Irvington butchered Dingus, huh?'

'For your information, around here we don't get the men to do our dirty work for us – we do it ourselves,' I said, suddenly infuriated by the implication that we women were helpless.

'Your business runs on fear, Mr Delaney, and we're not afraid of you,' Maureen piped up.

'. . . and neither will anyone else be, when they find out a bunch of charity ladies have Dingus' hand in their freezer.'

'I shot him,' Sheila suddenly blurted out, anxious for attention and afraid she was getting left out of the party. 'I didn't like the look of him, so I shot him.' Then she did the dumbest thing she had ever done (and she had done some pretty dumb things) – she took the small pistol out of her purse and waved it about, saying, 'With this . . .'

The two men outside came thundering through the door. Tom woke up and started crying.

'See now, you woke the baby!' Frank said. 'I love kids.'

My whole body tightened as he leaned over to see Tom in the buggy, and on his way coolly leaned across Sheila, snatched the gun from her hand, then in one quick flick flipped it open, took out two bullets the size of small earrings and gave it back to her.

'Pretty ladies like you shouldn't play around with guns – even cute little ones like this.'

He leaned back, took a deep breath, then pushed air through his mouth as if he were exhausted.

'Ladies – I don't know what to say? Except that Chuck Irvington sure is lucky to have you ladies on his side.'

'We're on nobody's side, Mr Delaney – except our own and the poor of this parish.'

I meant it. Charles and I were finished. I had a child in my care now and needed a responsible man to look after us both. If I ever needed evidence that Matt was the man for me over Charles, this was it.

'Perhaps I should be paying *you* protection?' Frank looked up at his men and they all laughed at the great joke.

'Perhaps you should.' I held his eye, deadly serious. 'And you can be assured that any money you do give us will go to a good cause.'

He looked at me, sharp and cold, then scraped his chair back from the table. His two lackeys were silenced and stony-faced. As Frank stood up he reached into his inside pocket, and for a split second I rattled with fear and automatically checked that I was in front of Tom's buggy. He took out his wallet and counted eight ten dollar bills onto the table.

On his way out he turned to Bridie.

'You do soda farls here?'

'The best,' she said.

'Like my mammy used to make?'

'If you had a mammy, which I doubt, you can be sure mine are better.'

Then Bridie picked Dingus' hand up from the table and put it into her apron pocket.

Frank flinched, either at her comment or the sight of a dead man's hand going into the cook's apron, then sucked his teeth and said, 'I'll be back, so.'

# CHAPTER THIRTY-EIGHT

Frank came back the following morning, and most days after that. He had a full cooked Irish breakfast featuring Bridie's soda farls and a pot of strong builder's tea. He sat alone at the same corner table – he always paid, and he always left a ten-dollar bill in the homeless box. This regular, generous cash donation served to bankroll a mother and children's refuge for Lavinia, although we never told him what happened to his money, and he never asked.

Despite being married, Frank fell head over heels for 'the crazy red-headed broad with the gun'. He set Sheila up in an apartment, a world away from his wife and family in Yonkers, and gave her a good time.

'You can't go, Sheila,' I said, 'I don't want you to go.'

'Yes, you do, Ellie,' she replied. She was at the door and her bags were packed and in the car. I was being sentimental. We both knew it was time for her to move on. I had hoped for a while that it might have been somewhere else, with someone else, but there was something inevitable about Sheila becoming a gangster's moll.

'I know you think I'm crazy, Ellie – maybe I am?'

'There's no maybe about it.'

'But I love him . . .'

'No, you don't.'

'Okay, you're right – I love what he can give me: I love the parties, and the dresses, and the *excitement*, Ellie. It makes me feel *alive* – you know? I know you think I'm stupid, reckless . . .'

'I don't, Sheila, I don't think you're stupid at all.'

As I said it, I realized it was true. Everyone had their own furrow to plough, and this was Sheila's. Yes, my oldest friend was a selfish, reckless fool who, I believed, could do more with her life – but wishing for people to change was as pointless as wishing them alive when they were dead. I wasn't worried about Sheila any more. I knew she could look after herself, and that she always would. I loved her, and that meant I no longer had to be her keeper; it meant I had to let her go.

'Stay in touch,' I said, 'and you know where I am, if you need me.'

'Me, too,' she said, then touched my arm and kissed me tenderly on the cheek before walking to the car. As she was opening the door she turned and hesitated before saying, 'You know, Ellie – I *do* worry about you.'

I smiled and waved. I was surprised to find I felt brave at waving her off and realized that, for all her chaotic madness, I had needed her this past while, more than she had ever needed me. She had picked me up and pulled me out of the pit of my despair; provided entertainment and distraction when I had been in need of it; had even shot a man on my behalf. You can never know how life's chapters will unfold, or how even those closest to you will react.

I watched the black sedan car drive off, and when it had disappeared down the hill, I stood for a moment on the porch and breathed in spring.

Anna was out sweeping her porch opposite, and waved across at me before going back inside. Jake was out with another boy, collecting bottles and cans from our neighbours. The two cloth

bags hooked to the handlebars of his bicycle swung precari-
ously, his bravado reserved for how high he could fill them and
still wheel it home.

This was my neighbourhood. Most of these houses had been
empty when I moved here, but now they were full of life and
people; people I had helped get on their feet, people who were
my friends. I had left one life and, within a year, used the money
from it to build another from the ground up. In a sudden flash I
realized what I had done: I had created not just a life for myself,
but virtually a whole neighbourhood in which to live it.

'Is she gone?' Bridie called out of the window.

'Just left,' I called back.

'She'll be back – there's breakfast here, if you're interested,
and Tom is out back at the coals again.'

I ran around to the side of the house and grabbed him up from
the porch, where he had just woken and was crawling off his rug
towards the steps. He tumbled and I seized him, then pulled him
down onto the grass and rolled around on the ground, nuzzling
his face. He let out a delighted squeal as I lay on the warm grass
and lifted him up in the air above me, and his head glowed with
the sun behind him, a globe of light and laughter. As I brought
him down to hug him, he wriggled to be lifted up again. 'Again –
again, do it again!' Over and over, up and down, up and down
– he never tired of this game, never tired of seeing the world from
two different angles: up close, far away, up close, far away –
his view changing in the whim of another person's arms.

Bridie stuck her head out the back window this time. 'For the
love of God, Ellie, the breakfast will be stone-cold, and look at
the state of you. Come in here and get washed and feed that child
– we only just got rid of one fool, and you're behaving as bad!'

I struggled to my feet, Tom tucked under one arm, objecting
wildly that our game had stopped so suddenly. As I steadied

myself and began to walk towards the back door, I suddenly saw the rest of my life pan out ahead of me. I would be tending the vegetable patch, season after season, year after year; the wire on the chicken coop would rust and be replaced; Matt would paint the back of the house every five years and be up on a ladder cleaning the guttering every six months; I'd sweep leaves from the porch each autumn and never tire of the red and gold, the crispy crunch of them underfoot; Tom would grow up here, and Bridie would die here – both under my tender care. Maureen was all but running the shop now. She was drawing a good salary and was already looking for somewhere of her own with the children. There was a reason I had found her, and it was so that she could bring me to this place; this place where I created a new life.

Yonkers was my safe haven. I would marry Matt, and this would be our home.

But first I had to go and lay my old life to rest.

'One month,' I said to Matt, 'I'll be gone a month.'

'Will that be enough time?' he asked. 'Are you sure you wouldn't like me to come with you?'

'A month is plenty of time, Matt, I just need to wrap a few things up. I'll bring Tom along with me. You stay and look after the house, and *Bridie* . . .' I called out to the next room.

'I can look after *myself*!' she hollered back.

'. . . I'll be back before you know it.'

The night before I left I lay awake in Matt's arms, unable to sleep. I listened to the stirrings and murmurings of my sleeping charge, and felt Matt's breath rise and fall under my face.

As early dawn made a blue canvas of the sky, the tree outside our window turned to a silhouette and Matt woke up and said, 'Don't go, Ellie.'

I knew he didn't want to let me out of his sight. He was afraid I wouldn't come back; he was afraid he would lose me to Ireland – to John.

'I'll be back, Matt – I have to go and sort things out in person.'

He sat up and faced me; his face was heavy with shadows, his eyes glinting with fear.

'Will you marry me, Ellie?'

This was the last thing I needed to hear!

'For goodness' sake, Matt, this is hardly the right—'

'Will you marry me, Ellie? Before you take off halfway around the world – I need to know.'

'Probably, maybe . . .'

He looked away.

'Matt – don't be like this. I need to sort things out first. I need to go home and—'

'I thought this was your home, Ellie: here with me and Tom – and Bridie.'

'Of course it is, Matt, but . . .'

He looked me square in the face again. His lip was quivering. If I didn't know and trust him as well as I did, I might have read it as anger.

'Will you marry me, Ellie? Tell me now.'

This was what I wanted. I knew that. This life, with him and the baby. This was where I felt safe, in this life that I had created; this was the man I was going to settle with, spend the rest of my life with in comfortable, harmonious peace. So now I just had to choose, to make it real.

'Yes, Matt,' I said. 'I will marry you.'

He wrapped his arms around me, and kissed and kissed the top of my head and said, 'Thank you, thank you,' over and over again. I turned around and clambered across his wide torso to kiss him. As I touched his lips with mine I tasted the salt of his grateful tears.

# IRELAND, MAY 1935

# Chapter Thirty-Nine

This was my fourth time journeying across the Atlantic Ocean. Normally it was a leisurely experience, there was time to think and reflect – too much time – when I had taken this trip. Travelling with Tom was a completely different experience, and it was also the first time I had been entirely on my own with him for any length of time. Matt, Bridie or Maureen was always on hand. Now it was just me and this child, in each other's company.

Tom was crawling now, an unstoppable tank of a child, full of energy and adventure. The speed with which he could topple a glass, or grab the corner of an opening door, or locate and stick a sharp object into his mouth frightened, amazed and amused me all at the same time. He put my heart sideways in me ten times a day, sliding along the deck until I became inured to the drama of his accidents. When he got his hand caught in a railing, or banged his head on a corner, I would simply pick him up, hold him until he stopped crying, then put him back down into his favourite position: sitting square in the middle of whatever floor we happened to be on so that he could survey his domain. His big blue eyes would blink excitedly and his head turn from side to side as he decided which direction to go in next. At nine months old, Tom commanded the centre of attention and, being an engaging and attractive child, he got it. I was, to anyone looking at us, his mother now and took compliments on his rosy cheeks, and good looks and charm, as if I were his natural mother.

I barely had time to think or eat myself during the day, I was so caught up with caring for Tom, and I missed the help that Matt, Bridie and the others gave me with him. I bedded down in my cabin each night, smiling to myself at the thought that soon I would be seeing my beloved Maidy and be able to introduce her to baby Tom.

On the last day of our journey I sat at the bureau in our cabin and thought about all of the things that had happened, all of the things I had done. John dying, Charles, Matt – the women, the shop, the houses, Sheila. I started to make the list of things I had to do when I got to Ireland, and when I got back to America. Planning ways to persuade Maidy to come with us, planning my wedding to Matt: a small or large affair? My mind was intent, always working towards some end, some goal. Perhaps I was returning to my old self, the Ellie that had been with John – always plugging the gaps, putting bricks in the wall of our life to make us more secure. Plastering the cracks in our finances, our crumbling house, our unconventional lifestyle. I was doing the same now: solving problems, working out ways to have a better future while the present slipped away.

Tom had somehow hoisted himself up and was standing, holding onto the wall. He turned his head to me, slowly, so as not to unbalance himself, and grinned at me. His eyes were sparkling as if enraptured with the mere fact of being alive. He looked in that moment like – freedom. In the past year I had craved freedom more than anything, yet life had seemed to close in around me – I had, despite myself, sought out pressures and responsibilities. Fear of my own grief had led me off in a direction that I was no longer certain of. Tom, I could see, was so full of possibility – the fearless innocence of adventure. I must have felt like that once?

The baby's legs buckled and he crumbled back down onto his knees. Just as quickly again he plonked himself onto his backside, and crawled towards the door of our cabin. I opened it and let him off up the corridor for a while; his toes like grey pebbles already, his knees like leather, his wet nappy wobbling its way down his chubby thighs.

He looked totally alive. I thought sadly that perhaps my adventure was over while Tom's was only beginning.

I was fine until I got onto the train from Cobh to Ballyhaunis. Tom, who had been demented with the excitement of getting off the boat, fell asleep in my arms the moment we pulled out of the station. As he slept and I looked out the window, I felt myself being sucked back in time. It was as if I had never been away, as if the past year had been nothing but a dream, and I had been jolted awake and was back in my real life. The life where I had gone out to feed the hens and come back to find John having a heart attack; where I had gone to get help and come back to find his dead body. The life where I had been unable to face my neighbours, my friends at his funeral; the life I had fled and to which I was now returning as if the intervening years had never happened. The years before, the year after, did not exist – all I felt now was the grief I had run from. America, Charles, Matt, the baby, Bridie – the people I had helped, the business I had set up, the houses I had renovated, the adventures with gangsters and socialites: what had been the point of it all?

John was dead. I was crying again. There was no escape. Was this to be my life now? Running from these tears?

As the train sped towards the place I didn't want to be, the

place I was not ready to return to, my regret turned to resigna-
tion. I would do what had to be done, and leave. The only thing
here for me, the only person I really needed to see, was Maidy.
I would bring her back to America with me! She would be re-
sistant, of course, but I would persuade her. I concentrated my
mind on making a plan. I would have to rearrange everything
to suit my scheme. Bridie and Maidy would not be able to work
and live in the same house; the very thought of how disastrous it
would be to have the two women under the same roof made me
smile. Perhaps Bridie would move in with Maureen for a while,
just while Maidy settled and found her feet? How she would
love baby Tom! And Matt? That was too complicated to think
of. I put him aside – out of my mind.

I would invite Maidy to return with me on a holiday. That
would be the best thing. A couple of months – once her creaking bones had experienced the heat of a New York summer she
would not want to return to Ireland. Katherine could send the
rest of her belongings over in a trunk; along with the rest of
mine, in time for the winter.

By the time I reached Ballyhaunis everything was settled in
my mind. The future was decided and everything was back
under my charge. There was so much to do before our return
that there was no time for tears or regrets; no room for painful
memories to poison my plans.

Katherine met me at the station with my car. How worn and
muddy it looked; I was glad to see that something had changed,
even for the worse. Katherine, in contrast, was still wearing the
dirndl skirt and sensible expression. We embraced awkwardly,
put Tom into the back, then I drove. I tried to persuade myself
that I felt uncomfortable now driving along these narrow country
roads with their hedgerows scratching our sides and small birds
flitting across the windscreen. In reality it took me just a few

seconds to get used to it; my year of change fled from me once again. Tom crawled around the back seat and tried to clamber into the front once or twice, but eventually, with the jogging motion, he settled down to sleep on the car floor. He was the thing I had there to remind me that I had been away, but even his presence couldn't bring me solace from the twisting truth.

In the car I told Katherine my plans for the business. I didn't want to wait. I wanted to get everything done as quickly as possible. She could have everything, buying me out at a price that we would agree between us, then paying me off on a monthly basis, transferring the money directly to my bank account in America. The money could be paid off on a short-term basis with no interest or long-term for a low-interest fee, whichever she preferred. Once the money was paid, everything would be transferred into her name. We both agreed quickly that short-term would be best. I wanted no business interests back here in Ireland, and she wanted outright ownership, as I knew she would. The bank would, we were sure, gladly lend her the money to purchase the typing business, salon and Fitzpatricks' Drapery as going concerns.

When the finality of our arrangement had been agreed there was a lull when we both sat in contentment, me driving and Katherine looking out the window at the ordinary, still Irish day. After a few moments I tried into put words how I was feeling and simply said, 'Thank you, Katherine.'

'It's me that should be thanking you, Ellie, for this extraordinary opportunity you've given me.'

'If it wasn't for you taking the reins this past year, Katherine, I don't know that I could have survived.'

'It was as much for me as for you – you trusted it to me and that was so important.'

'I was able to trust you, Katherine: you were so capable, and you never questioned me.'

307

'Yes, but you let me—'

'Stop – take your due.'

We both laughed, realizing we could go on complimenting and praising each other like that all day.

'Sometimes,' she said, 'things happen for a reason, Ellie.' Then, realizing how I might take it, she quickly added, 'I'm sorry, I didn't mean it like that . . .'

'No, no,' I reassured her, 'I understand what you mean.'

'It just makes you realize that God has a plan for us after all, the way life works out sometimes. Don't you think?'

I didn't like to think about God or His plan for me. I had been paddling my own canoe for the past year, and wasn't planning to hand the reins back to Him any time soon. This fortuitous arrangement that had come about was down to me and Katherine, and the strength of our professional capacities and personal will power. In any case, none of this would have been necessary if He hadn't taken John away from me. If God had snatched my husband from my arms just to give this young woman a business and me a future in America, then He was more callous and cold-hearted than the Devil himself!

'God works in mysterious ways surely,' was as much as I could say, but it was certainly true, and Katherine seemed happy with that.

# CHAPTER FORTY

Maidy was standing at the door as we pulled in through her gate, her arms already open to greet me. I pulled up and, without even switching off the engine, scrambled out of the car and ran to her.

'Maidy, oh, Maidy . . .'

I said it over and over again, my face buried in her bosom, and she stroked my head and said, 'There, there, sweetest Ellie – you'll be all right.'

This was the moment we should have had a year ago. The tears I should have cried at John's funeral, the comfort I should have garnered from my dearest, oldest ally before running away to America. Perhaps if I had done this, I might not have gone to America at all. Or perhaps, when somebody you love dies, there are no answers, only questions.

I went to the car and gathered Tom up, half-asleep, into a blanket and carried him over. I had not told her I was bringing him.

'This is Tom,' I said, 'the baby I adopted from the young girl who couldn't manage?'

Maidy put her hands up to her face and let out a squeal, her emotions switching from pain to joy. As she took him, Tom began to bawl, but Maidy gathered him firmly to her bosom and kissed him on the head and said over and over again, 'Come here to me, my precious, precious boy,' with as much voracious love as if she had been his own true grandmother.

We went inside and Maidy had prepared all of my favourite food. Boxty pancakes sat warming on a tin plate by the fire; there was an apple tart on the table and the very best of her crockery all laid out. Tom sat at my feet, and Maidy handed him morsels, which he chewed sporadically between going on explorations. 'Maidy, you went to so much trouble . . .'

'And my girl home from America? And with such a precious gift you've brought me in this little ladabuck?'

She ruffled Tom's hair and he looked up at her like a suckling lamb. I felt a momentary shot of gratitude.

Katherine had followed us in and sat at the table with me as Maidy served us both, then Maidy stood and watched us eat, as she had done John and I when we were children. She never sat down with us, but watched smiling as we glugged down our milky tea – replacing each hunk of bread, each slice of tart with another, until all of the food was gone and we felt like exploding.

I had noticed at the station that Katherine had put on weight, and as she shared Maidy's table with me (the only other person ever to have done so, other than John), I had to brush aside my childish petulance as I realized that she was the new recipient of Maidy's unique hospitality.

When we had eaten, Katherine took the car back into town.

'Would you like me to send a taxi for you?' she asked. 'Jack Flanagan has a new car – will I get him to come out and collect you? You're welcome to stay in the apartment?'

Katherine had my business, my car, my apartment and my Maidy. I had given them all to her, and yet now I felt I wanted

310

them back. This was my life, after all. My history, my heritage – everything I had worked for, barring this past terrible, peculiar year.

'They'll stay here!' Maidy exclaimed.

Neither of them suggested that I go back to my own house.

When Katherine had gone I didn't waste time, but just blurted straight out, 'Maidy, I want you to come back to America with us. You're on your own here, with John and Paud gone – we only have each other left and, I promise, you will love it. I could use your help with Tom here. I have a big house, and you'll have everything: electricity, a beautiful room, the weather is wonderful – the heat will warm your very bones, Maidy – you won't know yourself . . .'

I trailed off because, as I spoke I realized how pointless each of my words were. The very idea of Maidy coming to America was ridiculous; there was no argument that could make it otherwise. She loved me like a daughter, but she had dozens of friends and old neighbours around Kilmoy, and if she missed me, Maidy would always find someone like Katherine to satisfy her mothering instincts. Everything she needed was right here – she had no interest in pretty things or grand furniture; she was terrified of electricity; and her creaking bones would be just as well off where they were, rather than taking her across the world when, in her eighty-odd years, she had never been as far as Galway!

Maidy laughed – her eyes were bright, but not with the possibility of adventure. They were filled with the good-hearted love she had always shown me when I came up with one of my schemes. Her laughter was for the way she knew I was: her ambitious daughter-in-law Ellie – always wanting more, always trying to persuade people round to my way of doing things. It had not worked with her when I was a child and wanted to leave my parents' cold, grey house and move into her cottage. Nor when I had tried to drag her up to the Dublin on the train simply to buy a new hat.

'You pick one out for me,' she had said.

'I'll need you for size,' I had insisted, determined to take her on a great adventure.

'Here's my old bonnet – I trust you to find one that'll suit me.'

Maidy didn't like what she didn't know: trains, cars, cities – they weren't for her.

She wore that hat on every special occasion after that. On Christmas Day she tied a red ribbon around its navy felt base, to give it a seasonal trim. Each time she wore it, she inflated with a pride that was unusual in someone with such a humble demeanour. She would stand in front of people in that hat, smiling until they commented upon it.

'I like your hat, Maidy,' the same people would say year after year, as if they were seeing it for the first time.

Her voice would rise with the slightest affectation and she'd say, 'Ellie bought it for me – in the millinery department of Clerys of Dublin.' And that was her boasting over for another year.

That somebody had shopped for fashion on her behalf was as much adventure as Maidy wanted, or needed. She had no need to chase after life; she was content to sit and let it come to where she was. John had been the same. All he had ever wanted was already under our roof in Kilmoy, including me. His adventure was in his fields, in the miracle of a good crop of potatoes, a breeched calf, grey clouds chasing him home as he scrambled across streams and ditches to get back before the rain came.

'I'll stay then,' I said, 'I won't go back – I'll stay here with you. We'll raise young Tom a proper Irishman.'

Maidy laughed again, but I leaned over and took her hands.

She was a substantial woman, but her hands were wiry and

worn with work, mottled with age. I looked up into her face and she stopped smiling for a moment. She was certainly an old woman now, her eyes sinking behind her skin, her hair thin and pure white.

'I want to look after you, Maidy.'

'I know you do, Ellie,' she said and squeezed my hands. 'You're a good girl, but you're to go back America. Both of you.'

I flinched, for I felt as if she was turning me away.

'You don't want me to stay?'

'Of course I do, Ellie. I miss you every day.' And she nodded towards the mantelpiece. There was a photograph of me that I had sent home to John from America during my first trip there. I was posing in a photographer's studio in 1922 wearing a tight-fitting cloche hat; my eyes were heavily made-up and burned out at the camera from under the tight brim; my lips were dark and pencil-thin with lipstick. The picture was in a new frame.

'I hope you don't mind,' she said. 'I took that from the house, and Katherine had it framed in Archer's for me. I light a candle for you every day, Ellie.'

'And John?' I said.

She patted her heart, then reached into the top apron of her pocket and pulled out a photograph, which she handed to me. I recognized it as a picture taken of John just after he'd left Kilmoy as a young man of fifteen. He was wearing a woollen waistcoat and cap standing in front of the General Post Office building in Dublin, grinning. It was his first year away from home – the big man working in the capital on his apprenticeship as a carpenter. He was so happy then. Maidy and Paud were so proud of him, but I was miserable that I was still a schoolgirl and that he had left me behind. Five years later I pressured him and we ran away and got married against our parents' wishes. I knew I could not live without him and, as with all things in my life, I could not wait.

The picture was so worn you could barely see the image. Neither of us needed to, for the familiarity of John's face in that photograph was etched into our memories. Maidy didn't need to light candles for her son because his light was still alive inside her.

'Don't you want me to stay?'

'You need to go and live your life, Ellie, you're a young woman. You don't want to be wasting your time minding an old soul like me.'

'Suppose that's what I want to do, Maidy?'

She stood up, moved the steaming kettle from the stove, and reached up into the tin on the shelf above the fire for more tea.

'Things happen for a reason, Ellie. It's time to move on – things can't always stay the same.'

It felt like something of a rejection; she must surely have been injured when I ran away on her after the funeral, although it was not like Maidy to hold a grudge.

'If you ask me to stay, Maidy, I will. It's what John would have wanted, for me to be here with you. I'm sorry I went away – I realize now I was wrong.'

'No, no, Ellie,' she shook her head, 'you were not wrong to go – look at all the wonderful things you did there? Of course I want you to stay in Kilmoy, Ellie, and to see you every day, of course I do; but I won't ask you to, and neither would John if he was here . . .'

'That's not true . . .'

'Perhaps not,' she said, laughing. 'God, he was an awful stick-in-the-mud!'

I was shocked.

'How do you mean?'

'I tried to persuade him to join you in America all those years ago – you didn't know that, now did you?'

I didn't.

'Oh yes – even Paud tried to give him the push . . .'

'Why didn't he come?'

'Too stubborn, I thought at the time. He wanted you to come back – wanted to prove his point.'

'That's what I thought – God, I was mad with him!'

'But now, Ellie, I think differently. I think he was afraid.'

'Afraid of what?'

'Afraid of you, Ellie – of all you could do without him. He loved you so much, you see: he wanted to be your hero.'

'And he was!'

'Ah, but you could look after yourself too – always, even as a young one – and he didn't like that. John wanted to keep you on home turf where he could keep an eye on you, where he knew where he was – I told him that if he didn't give you your bit of freedom, Ellie, you'd stray.'

'I would *never* had done that . . .'

'Well, indeed, and you might have, Ellie, and I wouldn't have blamed you. You were great to come back to him at all, and that's the truth of it.'

This was all a complete revelation to me. I didn't know what to make of it.

'We're too stuck in our ways, this family – you're different, Ellie, you're a breath of fresh air . . .'

And with that she started to cry, pulled a tea-towel out of her pocket and wiped her face, before the tears troubled themselves on her skin.

'So come to America with me, Maidy . . .'

'That's what I miss more than John himself, more than Paud,

more than the men themselves: it's the way things were – with all four of us together.'

'. . . or I'll stay. I'll stay. One or the other, Maidy, but I'll not leave you again.'

She pulled herself together.

'You'll go – and you'll go without me, Ellie, and I'll not have it any other way. You came back this once and you'll come again, and sure if you don't, we'll write.' Then, before I had time to object again, she turned her back to me and started picking potatoes out of a tin bucket by the back door. 'Make yourself useful and fetch me over the peeler and basin from the press, then get yourself out of the house, like a good girl – you have me distracted.' She leaned down and picked up Tom just as he was about to pull a saucepan down from the fire. 'And you can leave this little fella here with me while we become acquainted . . .'

I conceded not least because, after two weeks in his constant company, I was glad to get a break from Tom.

I found my boots on the wooden stool John had made for that specific purpose, under a rack jumbled up with a curtain of long coats and rugs in Maidy's porch. They sat there alone – John and Paud's boots were both gone, while Maidy wore the same shoes inside and out.

I pulled them on over my stockinged feet, leaving my shoes behind – smart green leather on the gnarled, muddy wood; they were out of place, didn't belong here.

I climbed over the stile to the right of the yard and walked towards my husband's land.

I walked for an hour or more. My boots carried me across the familiar terrain, dodging the bog holes, negotiating the small valleys and streams that John and I had walked so often that our legs were all the maps we needed. I stopped at every tree we climbed, knelt and touched the ground on the hills we had tumbled down, grabbed a handful of fresh new mint from the corner of the field where we had first made love and rubbed it into a spicy, sticky paste in my hands. I stopped and drank water from the stream where we used to wash ourselves in summer and picked a palmful of sheep's coat from a barbed bush. I held the fleece to my face and smelt John coming home in the early morning, his hands rough with the blood of his animals, touching my face.

He was the earth and the grass and the breath of a newborn lamb. All those things were still here, as they had always been, but he was gone.

I cried, seamless automatic tears; tears of freedom; tears of love without the desperate, jabbing regret.

Our own house came into view, but I did not feel ready to go in. Instead I walked towards John's smoking tree. The ground around it was strewn with leaves and shreds of bark, such a dry surround that I did not think of placing anything down before sitting with my back against its mossy hollow, as he had always done. For a moment I felt glad for the comfort of just sitting in such a soft, dry spot; a contented feeling, as he must have felt every day when he came to his special place.

I reached up and found John's tobacco pouch; the cigarette inside it was dry as the day I had left it, the day he had died. In my imagination I wondered if John had come in the meantime and replaced it, and I smiled at the thought of it. Perhaps it was true; or perhaps all I had to do was believe it was true to make it so. Like God.

I fumbled in my pocket for matches and drew out the sheep's wool and held it to my nose again before lighting the cigarette.

I drew deeply and, as the smoke bit through my lungs, I closed my eyes. Two birds on either side of the tree were calling to each other – *pwheet, pwheet – pwheet.* I loved listening to birdsong. As a child I had always wished I was a bird, and had been so envious of their ability to fly. I had never lost my sense of awe at these tiny creatures, with their brassy, loud voices and their cheeky ability to flit and escape on a whim. Even now I wondered what they might be saying to each other; alerting each other to my presence perhaps, musing on the likelihood or quality of worms in the vicinity? I was amusing myself listening to them, when suddenly their tweeting stopped and a silence descended on the oak. I opened my eyes and looked across the fields. The landscape was as still as a picture – blue skies, green fields, purple bogs on the horizon – like a postcard, as if it wasn't real.

I heard a wind push its way through the bushes that separated me from the house, then fill the branches of the oak above me, whispering through the leaves like an almighty sigh. The strong breeze descended down over me in a warm, shimmering wave, then was drawn off across the fields in front of me. As it travelled through me I felt as if it were taking some of my pain with it, and leaving in its wake something that I needed. Not freedom – I had that already. Despite the emotional imprisonment of my grief, it had been the first thing I embraced after John died.

What I needed now was greater than freedom, or the reasonable purpose of the good life I had built in New York.

I needed to find a new a reason to live – and now I knew what it was.

# New York, June 1935

# CHAPTER FORTY-ONE

I took a taxi straight from the docks to Mr Williams' office in Yonkers, where I met him and Lavinia and conducted all the business that needed to be done.

I had telegrammed Matt from the ship to tell him about my plans, but had not given him a specific date or time for my arrival. I had told him that I did not want a welcoming party and hoped he would respect my request.

I said I needed time, and that I could not marry him. I still wasn't over John, and he deserved better than merely some of a grieving widow's love. He was too good for that. I knew he would be heartbroken, angry, humiliated, and was not looking forward to facing him, so it was with some relief then that I found the house in Yonkers empty. It gave me the chance to gather myself, and my things, before the others got back. I went straight upstairs and, containing Tom in his cot, started to pack my bags.

I opened each cupboard and drawer and laid out all the things I had acquired in the past year. It wasn't much; most of the new clothes I had bought in my first few weeks here with Sheila and had taken with me to Ireland, so they were already packed and left in the front hall. Aside from them, there was the baby blanket of Tom's that Maidy had knitted; a handkerchief embroidered with my initials by Maureen, which she had given me as a token of her friendship shortly after I 'saved' her; a blue bead necklace that Sheila had given me after I said I liked it, and insisted I took it, saying, 'You've such an eye for cheap rubbish, Ellie.' 'Perhaps that's why I like you!' I replied. I missed her.

Matt's good shirt and trousers were laid out neatly on the bed. I flinched. He would be changing into them for dinner. I didn't plan even to stay that long.

On my way back downstairs I reached up to unpin my hat, but stopped myself. I had better keep it and my jacket on, or I might be tempted to change my mind. It would be so easy to take them both off, hang them in the hallway and stay.

I could walk straight back into where I had left off, settle for a while, perhaps even marry Matt.

Except that now I knew this was not the life I was meant to live. All this had been a stopgap, a symptom of my grief. Rescuing families, setting up this house and the others, the shop – all of it had been a distraction, and when the novelty ran out, I would have to go in search of who I was again. Without John, I did not know who I was. Not really. Oh, others would say I was this extraordinary woman who helped people – had said it about me already, in the papers and to my face. I demurred, for I knew it wasn't true. It was what I did – what I had done – but it wasn't who I was. I wasn't a particularly 'good' person. I was just human. A mixture of circumstance and good fortune, and the need to escape my own grief, had led me to do what I had done. I saved Maureen because she had one set of needs – shelter, food – and I had another – distraction, guilt. My friends had given back to me as much as, if not more than, I had given them; they had given me a family when I needed one, and they had carried me through my depression and out the other side. They had amused and occupied my thoughts and my heart – as I had theirs. That was all.

The past year had taught me one thing: with a few notable exceptions, people were essentially good. There was nothing outstanding about what I had done – anyone would have done the same, had they been in my shoes.

Now I was going to leave them to do just that.

I had signed each of the houses over to the individual families who lived in them, and taken my own name off the shop cooperative so that it could be shared out equally among the other women. Lavinia French now had my power of attorney and could complete all of the legal paperwork on my behalf.

I went through the kitchen and out onto the back porch to look round the garden. The hedging was trimmed, the chicken coop cleaned, the vegetable patch dug with ridges for the potatoes. Matt had painted the back porch and put in a new swing.

Was I mad to be leaving this walk-in life; this secure, domestic paradise that was, after all, largely of my own making?

From childhood I had been terrified of being alone. John had taught me how to love, he had been everything to me, and as such I had altered the course of my life by coming back from America to be with him. When he died I had filled the gap he left with people and things to do: fixing problems, engaging in dramas, and friendship and romance. I could continue like that, but in a few weeks, months, a year – perhaps even two years, if the weakness of being too comfortable, the fear of change took hold of me – I would have to move on. Sooner or later I would have to go and fulfil a destiny of my own, instead of riding on the back of other people's.

I went back into the house just as Bridie, Maureen and Matt were all coming in. There was another man with them whom I didn't know, and their bustling friendliness stopped when they saw me. I had been dreading this moment. Had Matt told them I was leaving for good? Or had he stuck with the 'holiday' story, as I had asked him to? That I had been invited upstate to visit long-lost relatives and would be gone for another month?

Maureen came straight over and embraced me, then signalled to the stranger.

'Ellie, this is my husband Patrick.'

'Goodness!' I was surprised, but my happiness for her was muted by Matt's dark expression.

'The old tramp came through,' she said, glowing. 'Can you believe it? Two miracles in one year, Ellie – you, and now my Patrick is back.'

I gave her a huge hug and shook his hand warmly. 'I'm delighted for you both. You must tell me the whole story.'

Patrick's reappearance was the answer to Maureen's prayers – and it was wonderful for the children to be reunited with their father.

'Oh, but I can't believe you are going off from us again – you've just got back! Still, we'll tell you all about it over dinner: you're staying the night, of course.'

'No,' I said, and my eyes flicked across to Matt. He looked away, cold and angry. Tom called from upstairs.

'Ma, ma, ma!' he cried.

I ran upstairs, glad to get away from Matt's coldness, picked up the baby and went back downstairs. I held him tightly to my chest, hoping neither Tom nor the others could sense the urgency of need in my grip.

This was what I had missed, what I had been missing all my life, the thing that even John had been unable to give me – a child. Tom was the gift this last year had given me, the link with life, my reason to carry on. I would cherish him and give him all my love and then, when I had to, I would let him go; just as I had been forced to do with John.

Nobody belongs to anyone. Everyone dies or grows up and leaves. It amounts to the same thing: you are on your own, so you had better know who you are and what you want. I didn't, but I knew that I had been given the job of being this child's mother and, beyond that, I had to move on from this life and start on my journey to find out who I really was.

'I'm sorry I can't stay, Maureen. I'm afraid I'm expected tonight. Matt has to take me straight down to the station.'

'But we've hardly said hello . . . and baby Tom!'

'I'll be back soon,' I lied. I would write, I would visit – if I didn't go now, I would never leave. Already Maureen's kind pleading was knitting my feet to the floor.

'But Anna will be so cross I let you go! There's no rush surely – your relatives will understand. Bridie, tell her to stay, for a night at least.'

Bridie had her apron on and was already standing with her back to me at the sink. She did not turn round.

'If you're going,' she said crossly, 'then just *be on your way.*'

She knew.

Matt and I exchanged a look outside Maureen's range of vision. He raised his eyebrows – he hadn't told her. Bridie just knew. She could feel it in her bones, for the old battleaxe could intuit everything, and there would be no persuading or placating her. I loved the old woman, but I was as weak in her presence as I was with Maidy. One word, one look from her and I would be powerless to do anything but stay.

I backed out of the kitchen and picked up the small leather bag I had packed with Tom's things. Matt carried my large case out and put it in the pickup along with Tom's new buggy.

Maureen followed us out, but Bridie stayed resolutely where

she was. Maureen raised her eyes to heaven and shook her head at the old woman's rudeness, but knew better than to confront her. I felt sick leaving her like that. I was so fond of her – she had been and still was, to all intents and purposes, like my mother in America. She felt my going as a betrayal, and I felt it too, but I knew I could not stay.

Matt opened the door and I clambered up into the seat of his truck and gave Tom a bottle so that he would settle in my lap for the short journey to Ludlow.

As we were pulling away, Tom flapped at the window, squealing, and I turned round to see Bridie coming towards the car.

I could not help smiling, a broad, grateful smile that I could feel reaching to my ears. Entirely inappropriate, given my abandonment of her.

I opened the window and she shoved in a brown paper bag.

'Soda cake for the journey, for the boy. He likes it.'

'I'm sorry, Bridie,' I said.

She picked up the corner of her apron and wiped it across her face, exactly as Maidy had done with the tea-towel. When the apron came down, her face was still contorted and she lifted it again to hide her pain.

Matt turned off the engine and I went to open the door and get out.

Bridie shouted in at Matt, 'Turn it back on, you fool,' then bashed the door shut on me and said, 'If you don't write soon, Ellie, so help me God I will find you and flatten you. You'll not abandon us that easy.'

'Am I doing the right thing, Bridie, going off like this with the child?'

'You have to do whatever you have to do, Ellie. I learned that after Mr Flannery died. There's no right nor wrong in it, only whatever has to be done next.'

Then she stuck a hand in the window and patted Tom awkwardly on the head.

'Be on your way now,' she said and lightly tapped the door.

At the station Matt got out of the truck and walked to the train platform with me and Tom.

'Are you sure you don't need me to take you as far as Grand Central?' he asked. 'This bag is awful heavy.'

'Here is fine,' I said, 'we'll manage.'

I didn't know what to say. *'Thank you.' 'I'm sorry.' 'I love you.' 'Goodbye.'* They all seemed so trite and meaningless and inadequate. I had promised him so much and wouldn't – couldn't – now deliver.

Should we hug, or kiss, or have some grand farewell? That, too, seemed like a lie now. We were friends, then lovers: now what? Friends again – maybe some day – but not today.

Matt kissed Tom on the head and then, as he opened the door of his pickup, he turned and said, 'Is there any point in my waiting for you, Ellie?'

I closed my eyes and thought carefully, then replied, 'No, Matt, there isn't.'

So that chapter of my life ended with another truth, except that it was one of my own making, and with it I felt free to start the beginning of the rest of my life.

# ACKNOWLEDGEMENTS

I would like to thank the following people for their emotional and practical help and their personal and professional contribution to the researching and writing of this novel: Johnny Ferguson, Peter Quinn, Dan O'Connor, Jimmy Kelly and Lisa Ferguson, Helen Falconer, Marianne Gunn O'Connor, Pat Lynch, Vicki Satlow, Trish Jackson and Thalia Suzuma.

To my husband Niall Kerrigan for putting up with being married to a writer and lastly to my mother Moira for letting me read aloud my work to her every day and providing me with a constant supply of love and encouragement.